12018

By Terry Brooks

STREET FREAKS

TERRY BROOKS

GRIM OAK PRESS
SEATTLE, WA

Cover design by Shawn King.
Interior illustrations by Marc Simonetti.
Book design and composition by Rachelle Longé McGhee.
Proofread by Michelle Hope Anderson.

Trade Edition ISBN: 978-1-944145-20-0
Limited Edition ISBN: 978-1-944145-19-4
Lettered Edition ISBN: 978-1-944145-18-7
E-book ISBN: 978-1-944145-21-7

First Edition, October 2018
2 4 6 8 9 7 5 3 1

Grim Oak Press
Battle Ground, WA 98604
www.grimoakpress.com

For Judine

- 1 -

When the soft beep of his vidview sounds and the chip implanted in his retina flashes red in the corner of his eye, Ash Collins thinks nothing of it. It has been two years since his father's warning, and nothing has come of it. There is no reason for this message to be anything special. Ash never took any of that BioGen stuff seriously in the first place. He still doesn't.

So he almost ignores the vidview. He is right in the middle of taking notes on robo-prof Faulkner's lecture about matter transmission. But he is bored by the lesson, so he uses the vidview as an excuse to tune out. He touches the tiny node imbedded behind his left ear to activate it, and the message projects onto an air screen.

And there is his father's face, darkly intense and clearly frantic, his words stumbling over each other as he speaks.

ASH! GET OUT NOW! GO INTO THE RED ZONE. GO TO STREET FREAKS. DON'T WAIT . . .

The connection terminates. His father's face disappears, wiped off the screen. He is gone, taking the rest of whatever he was going to say with him.

Ash thinks his father was messaging from BioGen, but he

can't be certain. He was in a stairwell, moving quickly, climbing if Ash isn't mistaken, maybe fleeing.

For a moment, Ash doesn't move. He replays the message— sees his father's face and hears his voice anew. The strain of whatever threatens him is reflected in both. Which is not at all like his father, who is always so completely in control. Brantlin Collins, cool nerd guy. He reveals almost nothing of how he feels. He never seems stressed out. A cocked eyebrow is as much as Ash has ever seen in the way of a reaction.

Except when his wife died. Ash saw him cry then. For one day, his father was a real person.

So what is going on here? Is it happening? Actually happening? The warning his father gave him two years ago? The instructions? His father's fears realized?

His father must think so. What he told Ash that night was so out of character it was laughable. He said he was in danger. He said he had crossed a line he shouldn't have, but he didn't regret it. He warned Ash that if the truth of what he was doing were discovered, they would come for him. When that happened, he would get word to Ash and tell him what to do. Because they would be coming for Ash too.

Faulkner is still talking, unaware that Ash has stopped listening. The bot is a rental, a tutor his father secured for him about the same time he gave Ash the warning, claiming he was far enough advanced in his studies that he needed private instruction. But what if that wasn't the real reason? What if it was something else altogether? Maybe his father didn't bring him home from boarding school to improve his education but to better protect him by keeping him?

Ash blinks. He is suddenly afraid. What if his father wasn't crazy? What if he was right about being in danger? If so, Ash can't waste time questioning what he was told. He can't ponder the pros and cons. Either he does what his father told him to do or he ignores the warning.

"Excuse me, Faulkner," Ash says, getting to his feet.

Faulkner is like family. He lives with them. He frequently sits at the dinner table, even though he doesn't require food. Ash knows Faulkner is just a bot, but his intelligence quotient is much higher than his own. His father once said that if Faulkner had a sense of humor he would be human.

Ash slips past him without slowing, saying something about being right back.

I have to get out of here, he thinks, the decision made. But where should he go? He is supposed to go to Street Freaks, which is in the Red Zone. But his father has told him for years to never, ever go into the Red Zone.

He passes Willis4, the robo-cook, wheeling down the hall with a collection of dishes and linen piled in his arms.

Master Ashton, the machine intones.

Always calls Ash that. Master Ashton, not Ash. Can't seem to program it out of him.

"Willis4." Ash tries to sound nonchalant.

Do you need anything to eat?

"Not just now."

There are three of them working the suite—Willis4, Faulkner, and the robo-maid Beattie. Willis4 and Beattie are not rentals. Both came with the penthouse when his father took the lease on it after returning to L.A. following Ash's mother's death. Ash was bounced around a lot during his early years because his parents traveled extensively and were reluctant to leave him behind. At least, his mother was reluctant. Not so sure about his dad. Probably didn't matter that much to him. His father has never admitted it and probably never will. But he once said the research was all that really mattered to him.

He's aware that he's moving without a destination in mind. Just moving to be moving. But he has to get out, doesn't he?

Think, damn it! Choose a door, a window, but get out!

No, wait! The backpack!

It has gathered dust in a laundry room cupboard for all this time, waiting for the day it would be needed. Which was the day Ash had thought would never come. But he had packed it anyway. Still not sure why. Maybe because his father had suggested it, and it hadn't cost him anything to do so. Maybe because he was thorough about things, and at some point had decided that being prepared couldn't hurt. His K-Bar knife, some clothing, some packets of prefab food . . . what else? Is his ProLx in there? Did he remember to pack any? He hadn't paid close enough attention to remember. And he can't leave without his medication . . .

He reverses course, rushing now, heading back down the hallway and up the stairs. He can't do anything without his medication. He has to retrieve his ProLx, then go back down to the laundry for his backpack and—

The front door explodes in a shower of wood and metal shards that take out half the entry wall. The sound is deafening, a concussive force that blows through the entire penthouse. Smoke and dust boil out of the hole left behind, and figures in crimson jumpsuits rush through.

He freezes. *Hazmats.* Scrubbers. Cleaners. Scorched-earth guys.

The Hazmats are carrying weapons. Big, heavy automatics and lasers. Sparz 200s and Gronklins. From high on the staircase, Ash recognizes them at once. They blow up Faulkner in mid-sentence. Metal parts and wires erupt in a shower of sparks, springing out of the bot's midsection as he crumples to the floor. They charge after Willis4 and Beattie without slowing, down the hall toward the back of the house. Ash doesn't wait to see how that turns out. He bounds up the remaining stairs, gaining the next floor in a rush, tearing down the hallway toward the back rooms. He is screaming inside, terrified.

How could this be happening?

Weapons discharge below in electric *spizzes* and hollow *crumps*. Willis4 and Beattie are gone too. Ash grits his teeth in anger and frustration and pain. Why are they doing this? The bots never hurt anyone. They don't even know what is going on! What is the point of destroying them?

What do they have planned for me?

Whatever it is, he doesn't want to find out.

Even though he has had two years to think about this, he hasn't done so more than a couple of times. How could he? It's so bizarre. As such, he is unprepared. Choices flash through his mind. Using an elevator to get to the lobby is not a safe option. He can't jump out a window; his home is at the top of the building, eighty-two stories up. He could chance using the exterior delivery door. But there is every likelihood the Hazmats will have someone out there on the loading platform, waiting for him.

He rushes into his bathroom, grabs what remains of his supply of ProLx, and rushes back out again.

He hears footsteps pounding up the stairs. *Hazmats, coming to find me. Hazmats, between me and the backpack.*

The laundry chute is just down the hallway. Without stopping to think about it, he runs to it, flings open the door, and dives in headfirst. He is slender, so he goes through the opening easily. Because it operates on spring-loaded hinges, the chute door closes behind him. Maybe they won't know where he's gone, he thinks, as he tumbles away. The drop is twenty feet, so maybe he'll just break his neck and his problems will be over.

But he lands in a pile of dirty linen instead, shaken and a bit banged up but otherwise with everything still working. Now he is seriously panicked. He scrambles from the bin, finds the backpack, and fumbles it open. It contains clothes and food but no ProLx. Good thing he grabbed what he found upstairs. He digs deeper and at the bottom finds the vintage K-Bar army knife he bought as a souvenir when they lived in Africa many years back. Not much of a weapon against a Gronklin, but at least something.

He cracks the door and peers out. Smoke roils down the hallway. His heart is pounding like a jackhammer and his composure is out the window. What remains of Willis4 lies in a heap several yards away. More explosions sound. He searches the smoke for phantom movement, hearing most of the noise coming now from the floor just above.

Just get out, you idiot!

He closes the door to the laundry, locks it, and hurries over to the window that opens onto the service ledge used by the maintenance staff. The ledge is two feet wide and ten feet long—just big enough to stand on. But it is almost a thousand feet to the street below if he falls. Or a little bit closer if he should happen to land on one of the many public transport vehicles moving through the elevated traffic lanes.

He finds himself wishing he had thought this through earlier, but it is too late for regrets.

He opens the window and steps outside.

It is three floors down to the hive level where his father keeps a jumper. Jumpers are supposed to be reliable; everyone says so. You just have to be careful to harness yourself in nice and tight and stay in the traffic lanes. Ash has flown a jumper two or three times and survived to tell the tale. But he has heard plenty of stories about people who didn't.

Not that it matters if he falls while trying to get down there and breaks every bone in his body. But getting down there is exactly what he has to do.

He tamps down his instinctive fear of being outside in the open air of L.A., reputed to be among the five worst in all of the United Territories. You can breathe the air in some places. He's done it in other countries. But not here. Not in L.A. If you venture outside the sanctity of the buildings with their connecting corridors and tubes and filtered air without wearing a mask, you better hope your immune system is sufficiently bolstered by all the vaccines they inject into you growing up.

The prospect of what he faces terrifies him. But what is he supposed to do? He can't go back inside. He has to get out of there.

The rungs cut into the side of the vertical cornice are there to accommodate maintenance workers. They are supposed to be used in conjunction with safety lines. They are not intended for climbing up and down untethered. Anyone doing so could only be a fool.

Ash hesitates. The Hazmats will be inside the laundry in moments. He edges his way over to the cornice and steps onto the narrow rungs, not stopping to think further. He descends quickly and does not look down. The rungs hold his weight; he does not fall. Once at the hive level, he works his way over to the platform fronting unit 82C, punches in the locking code on the exterior pad, and when the door swings up, he slips inside. By now, he just wants to get this over with. Maybe using the jumper won't be as bad as he thinks. Maybe he can escape without anyone even seeing him.

Maybe pigs can fly.

He is almost to the jumper when the lock on the interior door to the storage garage disengages. A second later, it nudges open and an arm reaches through.

With no time to ponder choices, Ash does the first thing that comes to mind. He rushes the door, slamming into it. The door is constructed of a weather-resistant composite metal that seals the unit against the outside atmosphere. Its programmed function, if pressed sufficiently hard from inside the hive, is to close. So when Ash throws himself against it, that's what it does. Forcibly. The Hazmat tries to push ahead anyway, his arm struggling to find the release. But the door's mechanics are much stronger than he is; it keeps closing, drawing in on itself, the pumps and sealing devices grinding away.

Ash realizes suddenly that the man is not going to quit.

"Pull your arm out!" he yells in spite of himself.

But the Hazmat has waited too long. His arm is trapped now. He continues to struggle, but it is futile. The door closes on his arm, severing it.

Ash looks away, horrified, waiting for the screams. But there are none. The severed arm rolls past him on the floor, and he sees pieces of machinery and wiring hanging out one end.

It's a bot!

He loses it momentarily, laughing and shouting in a mix of relief and anger. He'd never thought that maybe the Hazmat wasn't a man! He'd fought to save a man, and it was only a bot!

Then he catches himself. *Only a bot. Like Faulkner. Like Willis4 and Beattie.*

He brushes aside the surge of relief that floods through him. No time for that. Quickly, he leaps into the jumper—an efficient little two-man blue-on-blue Neo—slamming the hatch shut. He does it without thinking, reacting instinctively, scared to death. No time for donning protective gear; no time for caution. He needs to get out of there.

For one terrible moment he can't remember what to do. His mind screams: *Do something! Anything!* He finds the starter that ignites the solar-powered engine and listens to the whine of its drive as it engages. A surge of relief rushes through him. Seizing the handles to the lifters, he hauls back. The jumper lurches forward and drops away from the platform.

And immediately goes into a spin that threatens to turn into something worse.

He gasps in dismay, fighting to bring the Neo back up. A few frantic seconds of working the controls steadies the little craft, and he maneuvers into the designated traffic lane. He points for a nearby cluster of residential sky towers, intent on gaining one of their public landing platforms and getting down to the street and into foot traffic as fast as possible. Jumpers have limited range and are not intended for anything but short hops, so he doesn't bother struggling with the thought of trying to pilot this one all the way to the Red Zone. Another mode of transportation will be necessary.

Which is not an inviting prospect. He can take a robo-taxi or a substem, neither of which requires anything beyond showing up and boarding. But they are both public transport, which means being out in the open air again. And they aren't always there when you need them. So, although it makes him nervous even to think about it, Ash might spend the credits needed to use a matter transporter. But how desperate is *that*? He doesn't trust jumpers, but he *really* doesn't trust transmats; there are stories about people who transport to one place and arrive somewhere else—sometimes with their limbs missing or body pieces rearranged in hideous fashion.

Still, a transmat will slow anyone looking to find him. Transmats are untraceable. Tracers are embedded in all jumpers and robotaxis, but there is no way to track someone using a transmat without contacting a coding station and tracking the source.

He is only marginally less panicked than earlier. He no longer doubts that his father was right to warn him. But it would help if he knew exactly who was chasing him. Hazmats, sure. But someone had to send them. Was it BioGen? There is too much he doesn't know and no time to sort it out now. He pilots the jumper toward the public landing platform that services the residential sky towers he has been pointing toward. Fighting to hold the little craft steady, he sets her down on one of the empty landing pads, coasts toward the storage bays until an air lock opens, continues inside, and waits for the air lock to close again. Disengaging the drive, he grabs his backpack, releases the hatch lock, and steps out.

He half expects to find Hazmats waiting to intercept him. But except for the attendant, the bay is empty. He hurries toward the elevators that will take him down to transportation services. At least the worst is behind him.

Except it isn't.

It is waiting up ahead.

- 2 -

Ash Collins does not think of himself as anything but ordinary. Sure, he's gotten into trouble a few times. Well, more than a few. Got thrown out of boarding school once when he was eight. Got dressed down by a warden when he went out tracking lions in Africa inside the fences of a game reserve on a dare. Got in a few fights. Skated a whole bunch of other times because his parents never found out what he was up to or they might have grounded him for life.

But none of this was real trouble. He didn't go to jail or anything. He doesn't smoke or drink. He doesn't do drugs—excluding his daily dosage of ProLx, and that is on his father anyway because he was the one who had prescribed it in the first place. And besides, it's medicine, isn't it? He does his chores, completes his homework, performs the tasks assigned him, helps without being asked, and generally makes himself useful when he sees it's needed.

But he is woefully out of practice with being on his own. He was more self-assured when he was younger and they were living in Africa, but since coming back to Calzonia he has lost his edge. He is no longer confident he knows enough to be self-sufficient. He has experienced a lot during his teen years—traveling constantly, living in Africa, being exposed to different cultures and peoples.

But since his mother's death and his diagnosis, his father has been very protective of him. In L.A., he is not allowed to venture anywhere without an escort, and then only by private transport. He has seen little of the city beyond the view from his home. He has never been much of anywhere in greater Calzonia besides going twice to the BioGen Corporation offices with his father and to a few museums with Faulkner.

Alone in the descending elevator of the sky tower, trying to decide how to proceed, wondering how much time he has before he is found by the Hazmats, Ash realizes he is poorly prepared for what lies ahead. A swift cataloging of strengths and skills reveals how inadequate he is for the task that faces him.

He has only one advantage: his memory. He sees something once and remembers it. In preparation for a mythical time when he would be allowed out on his own, he has memorized the transit routes crisscrossing the city. He has studied the online manuals to discover how to navigate them. He has traveled them over and over in his imagination. So any lack of actual experience or practical usage should not be a problem; all he needs to do is follow the signs to the transport devices and stations, engage or board whichever one he chooses, and be on his way.

At least, that's what he tells himself as he leaves the sky tower elevator and heads for the building's transportation center.

Of course, things don't always work out the way you plan. Especially when you need them to. Which explains why both transmat chambers are shut down with warnings taped to their windows that read in big red letters: OUT OF ORDER.

He looks around for signs that might direct him elsewhere but doesn't see any. His fears surface anew, but he beats them back. Being afraid won't help. He asks a few people here and there for the location of a more complete transportation center, but they shrug or shake their heads, barely slowing to acknowledge him. Everyone seems to be in a hurry, anxious to get where they're going; no one seems to have any interest in trying to help.

Finally, he goes back out to the lobby and finds a bot doorman working the tower entrance and asks him. The bot says to go two blocks farther on to the Elysian Residences. A transmat in working order can be found there. The catch is, Ash will have to go outside to reach it. He cannot use the tunnels. To enter the Elysian through the tunnels, he is told, he will need to be in possession of a security card.

Ash doesn't want to waste any more time. So he takes a deep breath and goes out into the poisonous L.A. air. Immediately he encounters people wearing protective masks. Some are fed from portable oxygen cylinders, and some consist of nothing more than a cloth filter fitted over the mouth and nose. Ash glances at the windows of the buildings as he passes and sees himself looking back—a little ragged and windblown, a bit worse for wear, blondish hair sticking out all over the place. An average sort of kid with little to mark him as distinctive. In his opinion, anyway. Ashton Arthur Collins. He doesn't mind most of what he is looking at, which admittedly is not all that much. There isn't anything special about him. Has a nice smile, he thinks. He's neither big nor strong. He works out and lifts weights and studies tae kwon do, so he is reasonably buff. Well, sort of. He's maybe a little bit buff. But he doesn't care about such stuff. He has never participated in organized sports. Not in Africa, because there weren't any, and not in Calzonia since his return, because you don't get to do that when you are homeschooled in a sky tower.

He enters the building to which he has been directed, still safely in one piece, still free of any apparent effects from the poisonous air. Miracle of miracles. Crossing the lobby to the green booth that houses the transmat, he stands looking at the controls. They are completely unfamiliar. They look nothing like the controls he studied in the manuals. Apparently, while he was busy memorizing old transmat systems, new ones were installed. Is it possible he could figure out how these replacements work? Thing is, when you're transporting yourself from one place to another in a screed of particles, you don't want to make a mistake. You would think something like operating a transmat would be more intuitive. But few people use the machines; they are too expensive, and the rumored danger if something goes wrong is off-putting.

Ash leaves the booth and the building and goes back outside. The transmat idea isn't working. Maybe taking a robo-taxi is best after all. At least the taxis are reliable in terms of getting you where you want to go. His parents refused to take them, however, and he understands why. He rode in one with Faulkner over to the Calzonia Museum of Natural History when he was somewhere around twelve and public transport was still permitted. It was a ride he has still not forgotten. Kind of fun then, but with age comes wisdom.

Nevertheless, it is probably the best he can do.

A thought occurs. Perhaps he doesn't need to taxi all the way to the Red Zone, which is a considerable distance. He calls up his memories of the substem system. If he takes a robo-taxi to substem #23, he can catch a train directly into the center of the Zone. Even on brief reflection, this seems an infinitely better choice.

He walks to a hotel several doors down and asks the doorman to call him a taxi. He does not use his vidview because he believes messages can be sourced and tracked. Taking a seat in the air-filtered hotel lobby, he waits. People going in and out of the hotel ignore him. Passersby barely give him a glance. He is invisible, which is fine with him.

Within a few minutes, the summoned robo-taxi descends from the allotted airspace to which all public transportation is assigned and settles into the loading zone in front of the hotel. Ash rushes over, climbs into the back seat, buckles up, and mentally prepares himself for what he knows is coming.

Please fasten your restraining straps, the bot driver advises.

"Already done," Ash mutters, his uneasiness skyrocketing as memories of his last ride in a robo-taxi recall themselves in brilliant detail. He tests the straps, lengths of padded mesh that crisscross his body and wrap his waist, pinning him to the seat.

Destination, please.

"Substem #23."

Substem #23 recorded and entered. Thank you for your cooperation.

The robo-taxi rises slowly into public transportation airspace and then shoots off like a rocket. No warning, no hesitation, it just catapults out of there, accelerating into a maze of traffic where it proceeds to weave through the vehicles like a scalded cat. Objectively, Ash knows the taxi is equipped with all sorts of protective equipment, including sensors linked to automatic thrusters and brakes to prevent collisions. But such preventatives have been known to fail, and trusting in fate and the odds with this form of transportation feels decidedly like gambling. Regulation is a good thing, but it can only do so much.

He endures the seemingly endless ride to substem #23 with clenched teeth, tensed muscles, and the uncomfortable realization that he has surrendered any personal control over his fate. The taxi lurches and jumps, twists and turns, and generally travels at impossible speeds through the obstacle course that comprises the airspace thirty feet above the much calmer city streets and walkways of L.A.

When the robo-taxi finally disengages from the traffic flow and casually lowers to the curb in front of substem #23, Ash is already vowing never to ride in one of these insane machines again, no matter what the extent of his desperation.

Substem #23, the bot driver announces needlessly. **Please deposit twenty-five credits.**

Ash does so, unable to voice what he is thinking, even to a bot. Accordingly, the harness locks release, the door opens, and he is set free.

Thank you for your patronage.

Right, Ash thinks. *The last patronage you maniacs will ever get from me!*

He gets out of the robo-taxi and hurries toward the station entrance. *No more robo-taxis*, he tells himself one final time. *No way.*

Inside, he slows to look around, keenly aware that he can't assume any place he goes will be safe. It seems unlikely the Hazmats could have tracked him here, but he cannot be sure what resources they have at their disposal. If they are desperate enough to blow open the door to his home and turn harmless robot servants to junk metal, they are probably capable of anything.

He walks the length of the cavernous lobby, passing beneath the scrolling lights of the scheduling signs, navigating clusters of ticket scanners and rows of waiting benches, trying his best to be inconspicuous. The latter is a problem. He is wearing a high-end, single-piece sheath, a much sought-after item of clothing that is incredibly comfortable but so unusual that it stands out in a public transportation station like a neon sign. At least it is a nondescript gray and doesn't draw the attention a brighter color would. But even so, it is entirely too noticeable.

Which immediately becomes a problem when he sees his face staring back at him from the giant News Reader overhead.

Ash stops and reads the caption beneath.

HAVE YOU SEEN THIS FACE?
IF SIGHTED, PLEASE CONTACT L.A. PREVENTATIVES IMMEDIATELY.

That was fast. He has barely escaped the Hazmats, and already they have him posted on News Readers. Except that Hazmats don't have the authority to put you up on a national reader board. That has to come from much higher up.

Ash watches the words crawl across the giant screen beneath his picture, a very public indictment. There is no reason given for why he is being sought. Why has he suddenly become so important?

He hurries to the closest washroom, brushing past people with his head down and his backpack held open in front of him as if he is looking for something. Once inside, he locks himself in a cubicle and sits down heavily on the sani-seat.

What am I going to do? Panic tightens his chest like a vise. *I am in so much trouble, and I don't even know the reason!*

After a few horrific moments he collects himself sufficiently to realize something odd. The authorities do not seem to be looking for his father. It isn't Brantlin Collins's picture up there on the reader board; it's his. Which means he is the priority for them. Which means . . . what? That his father is already in custody? That something worse has happened to him, something that makes finding him unnecessary?

Now Ash is really afraid. He squeezes his eyes shut against a wave of nausea. He is barely seventeen years old and the police are hunting him like a criminal and his father has disappeared and he has no place to go and whatever he does . . .

He stops himself just short of losing control.

What is the time? He starts to engage his vidview to find out and then stops. He keeps forgetting. They can track you that way if they are keyed into your signal. He takes a moment to remember the time on the clock in the lobby of the substem station. Almost midday. He needs to take his ProLx. Purpose provides him with a way of calming down. He rummages through his backpack until he finds the container, shakes out a pill, and swallows it dry.

The pills are his lifeblood. He has a rare immune deficiency that requires he take ProLx once a day, every day, without exception. He was diagnosed a little over two years ago. Taking his medication is all that prevents a complete collapse of his auto-immune system. His father, who gave him the news after reading the results from a routine physical, has been very specific about this. No matter where Ash is or what he is doing, he has to take his daily dosage. No exceptions, no excuses. Not if he wants to stay alive.

He repeats the words silently. *Not if I want to stay alive.*

He stays where he is, sitting on the sani-seat in the toilet stall, until he calms down again. He needs to move. His father might still be waiting for him, no matter what the absence of his face on the reader board suggests. He has to stop assuming things; he has to stick to the plan.

He considers what he should do next. It would help if he could assume a different, less obvious look. But when he opens his backpack, he finds nothing but sheaths, all packed two years ago, all now too small for his larger frame.

He closes the backpack in disgust. Sufficiently recovered from his panic attack, he stands up and leaves the stall. He walks over to one of the sinks, triggers a flow of reasonable-looking water, and splashes some of it on his face before leaning into an automatic air-dry. He starts for the door and is almost on his way out when he spies the recycler. He glances around. No one else is there. Impulsively, he rummages through the recycler, chooses a discarded shirt, and tries it on. Ripped in one shoulder and way too big. But with the shirt covering it, his sheath doesn't stand out quite so much.

He wishes he could do something about his face too, but that isn't going to happen. He further messes up his already-tousled hair to change it completely from how it looks on the reader board. Then, with his pack slung over one shoulder, he goes back out into the main lobby and sits down next to an elderly couple and a teen girl with lots of face metal. His picture is still staring out at him from the overhead screen, and the admonition to the public about reporting him if spotted is still scrolling across underneath. It disappears long enough to allow a short report of continued unrest in the Dixie Confederacy, where the separatist movement continues to gain followers and demonstrations and general unrest suggests things are building to a crisis point. Then his picture reappears, almost as if the problems of the Deep South are his fault.

He turns up the collar of the overshirt and studies the digital readout on the scheduling board.

There is a train leaving for the Red Zone in ten minutes.

This is his chance. He has to catch it. If he doesn't, it could be an hour before another comes through. If he waits, he is risking everything. Sooner or later someone is going to recognize him. They might not decide to alert the authorities—involvement in what doesn't concern you has never been a priority for the average L.A. citizen—but there is nothing to say they won't either. He can't afford to leave this to chance.

His determination is reinforced when he sees a flood of black-clad police enter the cavernous lobby and slowly begin to fan out.

His blood goes cold and his fear returns.

These aren't freelancers or Hazmats or even L.A. Preventatives. Not in those outfits. Each bears a silver patch with a wolf's head, an insignia resurrected out of another age and country long since gone but still vividly remembered.

Ash takes a deep, steadying breath, gets to his feet, and moves away quickly.

The black-clads are members of Achilles Pod.

- 3 -

Everyone who lives anywhere in Calzonia, largest of the semi-autonomous regions carved out of what used to be called the United States of America but is now known as the United Territories, knows about Achilles Pod.

Mostly, they know that whatever else happens in your life, you want to do everything possible to avoid coming into contact with it.

It works like this. The Global Reach Government oversees and manages the entire civilized world: all seven continents and within those boundaries all territories, provinces, colonies, regions, and the like, including the U.T. ORACLE is the G.R.G.'s law enforcement and investigative arm. It consists of thousands of active divisions established throughout the world's population centers—each with its own particular central command and tactical units (and in the cases of the larger territories, its armies). ORACLE is the primary police force for the entire region.

In Calzonia, and most particularly in L.A., the most feared tactical unit serving under ORACLE is Achilles Pod.

The stories about the Calzonia arm of Achilles Pod are legion, and all of them are pretty much the same. A situation arises, one in which lives are at stake and ordinary police are swiftly determined to be inadequate. A call goes out, an order is given, and members of Achilles Pod are dispatched. In short order the dangerous situation is diffused, hostages and innocents are rescued, and those in the wrong come to a bad end.

Those who serve in Achilles Pod are not governed by ordinary rules of propriety and fair play. They are not particularly concerned about human rights or bloodless resolutions. Their mandate has always been the same—put an end to the problem with minimal loss of life on the side of the innocent. If you are on the wrong side of that equation, it's just too bad for you. Justice and rights run a poor second to keeping the peace. The common perception is that when you bring Achilles Pod down on your head, your life span is likely to be dramatically shortened.

This isn't always the case, of course; it is an exaggeration of the actual facts. These are the United Territories, after all, and even if they aren't the dominant superpower they were when still called the United States of America (that distinction belongs to China now), they still maintain their core values. A respect for law and order and justice for all is central to their culture. Still, it isn't an exaggeration to suggest that avoiding an encounter of any sort with Achilles Pod is a good idea.

And now an entire squad of these men (and possibly women too—who knows?) has arrived at substem #23 searching for Ash.

At least, he has to assume so. Maybe it's coincidence, but likely not. Probably someone recognized him from the reader board and called it in. What he can't figure out is why an Achilles Pod unit has been dispatched. He's a seventeen-year-old boy. Why not just send in the L.A. Preventatives to handle things? Why this level of firepower?

Ash walks quickly down the ramp leading to the boarding platforms, intent on catching the #41. Waiting around any longer is exceedingly dangerous. Maybe Achilles Pod is here for another reason, but he can't afford to find out the hard way he is wrong. Better to catch a substem and get out of there. Even though he doesn't want to go into the Red Zone no matter what his father has told him to do. No one in his right mind does. The very idea of going there is absurd. If his father is protective about Ash when it comes to public places in civilized Calzonia, he should be ten times more so when it comes to the Red Zone.

He should never have asked Ash to go there.

Yet that is exactly what he has done.

Which brings something else to mind—something that in the rush of things Ash has forgotten to consider. His father's brother is Cyrus Collins, director of the Calzonia branch of ORACLE. No one in his right mind would mess with Uncle Cyrus. While they are not close, Brantlin and Cyrus Collins are still blood. If his father was in trouble, why didn't he go to his brother for help? And why not send Ash to him?

But there isn't time to consider this or anything else. Not with members of Achilles Pod breathing down his neck. There is no time to think; there is barely time to act. At the bottom of the ramp, he buys passage from a ticket dispenser before hurrying on. Hunched down in his overshirt, his backpack slung across his shoulder, Ash tries to blend in with other passengers, staying close to large groups, just one of the crowd.

Only once does he glance back. There is no sign of the black-clads. Maybe he is mistaken. Maybe they are there for someone else.

He melts into the crowd waiting for the #41 to arrive. Standing at the rear of the platform, he keeps an eye on the connecting walkway. He doesn't see anyone from Achilles Pod. A small measure of relief rushes through him. Even if they come after him, there are more than fifty platforms. They can never search all of them in time. Without knowing which one he is on, they won't be able to find him before his train departs.

But in the next instant he notices a woman standing off to one side, glancing at him as she whispers in a furtive way while using her vidview. When she sees Ash looking at her, she turns away. But there is no mistaking what she has done.

A good citizen, doing her civic duty, she has given him up. What are the odds of that happening in this city? Better than he thought, obviously. He despairs. This is all so unfair. He has done nothing, and everyone in L.A. is involved in trying to have him arrested and imprisoned. Or maybe worse, since now Achilles Pod is involved.

The woman is moving away. Ash doesn't try to stop her. What would be the point? The damage is done. He waits until she is out of sight and then quickly walks the other way. Others have prob-ably noticed him as well and made similar reports. It is a foolish to think they wouldn't. In any case, he can't take the underground now. They will know which train he is on and set up reception committees at every stop along the way until they find him. He will have to find a different way.

As the #41 pulls in, the first of the black-clads appear and make the turn onto the platform. People are stepping aside hur-riedly, shrinking back. Ash holds his ground, waiting as passen-gers begin disembarking from the train through the doors on the opposite side. But the instant the doors open on his side, he shoves his way to the front of the crowd, rushes into the car, and immediately exits onto the platform on the other side. Without slowing, he races to catch up to the departing passengers and disappears into their midst. It is a desperate act, but the only chance he sees to escape.

Halfway up the stairs leading to the street, he turns down a connecting corridor, runs at full speed to the next set of stairs, and continues up. A small deviation from the shortest route, but it might help throw off his pursuers, and he doesn't have time to think up anything more creative.

He is filled with rage and despair.

This is all so stupid! Why is this happening to me?

He emerges from the tunnel exit onto the sidewalk, frantic and disoriented, sweating hard. He races to the curb and is almost squashed by a robo-taxi dropping into the landing zone right in front of him to disgorge its passenger. Without a thought for his earlier vow, he jumps into the rear seat as soon as its former occupant departs.

Please fasten your—

"Red Zone!" he shouts, overriding the mechanical admonition. "Take me to Street Freaks!"

—restraining straps. The voice ignores him. A maddening pause. **Destination, please.**

"Red Zone! Red Zone! I already said!"

Red Zone is a prohibited destination for this vehicle. Choose another destination, please.

Prohibited. Ash glances out the window, scans the streets, the substem exits, the faces passing by. "The *perimeter* of the Red Zone, then!"

Red Zone perimeter recorded and entered. Thank you for your cooperation.

"No, wait!" he screams. "Get me close to Street Freaks! Can you take me close to . . .?"

But the robo-taxi is already lifting away into public transportation airspace, revving up its engines. Then they rocket away into the overhead traffic, just another robo-taxi joining the swarm, all of them looking the same.

Ash leans back and closes his eyes. At least he has escaped Achilles Pod—for the moment, although they'll discover quickly enough where he has gone. But the Red Zone is a big district, and he will be a needle in a haystack with any luck. All he has to do is find Street Freaks. He still doesn't know what it is, but he assumes it is some sort of business, though he can't imagine what sort. He doesn't know if his father will be waiting for him or what to do if he isn't, but he can't worry about that now. Maybe he will be able to find out what's happening from someone who works there if his father fails to show. Maybe someone will let him use a non-embedded vidview so he can call his father without being traced.

Maybe, maybe, maybe. It makes him want to scream.

The robo-taxi ride is traumatic, stomach lurching, and seemingly endless. But finally the driver descends to street level, demands payment, releases the restraining straps, and boots Ash out. He watches as the taxi lifts away, grateful to be back on solid ground.

Then he turns around and is not quite so happy.

He is standing at the edge of what looks like Armageddon. Blocks of buildings that are either already collapsed or seemingly on the verge stretch away into the distance. Some are burned out, some merely missing pieces of walls and roofs, some lacking doors and windows. All of them look derelict. The dull, paint-faded surfaces stand in sharp contrast to clusters of brightly colored wildflowers that grow in tiny patches along sidewalks that are cracked and buckled.

No one is in sight. All of the buildings appear to be abandoned. The streets are empty. A dog wanders into view, gives Ash a cursory look, and passes on. He waits a bit to see if any people will appear. None do. He wonders where he is supposed to go from here. But he already knows the answer. Ordinarily, he would use the map function on his vidview. But his vidview might be compromised, so that's out. Vidviews are supposed to provide help if you are in trouble, but somehow he doesn't think it will work that way here.

He wishes momentarily that he had a mask to protect himself against the L.A. air. He takes a deep breath, testing for taste and smell, and there is a little of each, but neither is intense enough to cause him to cough or gag. Maybe it will be all right.

So he begins walking into the Zone, searching for a street sign. If he can find one, maybe he can use that fabulous memory of his to figure out where he is. He remembers a little of how the Zone is laid out, a geometrical grid-work of streets forming even-sided blocks. But when he looks at the devastation around him, he despairs. These derelict buildings can't be all there is. There are businesses in the Red Zone. There are people living here. Somewhere.

But he also knows what sorts of businesses and people occupy the Red Zone, and he knows that if you don't have a firm idea of where to go and how to get there, this isn't a good place to be wandering about. Even the L.A. Preventatives stay out of the Zone as much as possible. Even members of Achilles Pod probably think twice.

Or maybe this is where they come from.

Once again he wonders what on earth his father was thinking when he decided to send him here. Of all the places he shouldn't have sent him, the Red Zone should be at the top of the list.

And what the heck is Street Freaks?

He walks for a long time. He pushes on through acres of devastation with rats scurrying in and out of weed patches before things start to change. The collapsed buildings and abandoned warehouses give way to clusters of residences evidencing better upkeep with fences and yards. Aged and worn, they are nevertheless inhabited. He passes a playground that has been stripped of everything that isn't made of iron and set in concrete. He hears the voices of children playing. Two little girls frolic on the sidewalk. They move out of his way quickly and watch him carefully until he is well past them before resuming whatever game they were playing.

The quality of the air remains unchanged, and he continues to breathe it without difficulty. It makes him wonder about all the warnings, although not every danger to your health is visible.

Ash sees no robo-taxis, so he guesses the prohibition against their entry into the Zone is real. He sees men and women sitting on porches and in lawn chairs, staring out at the world while drinking beer and smoking. A few of them acknowledge his presence with a nod. Most ignore him. No one speaks. No one wears a breathing mask. Faces appear at the windows of some of the houses before disappearing again. The midday sun beats down, and the heat rises off concrete streets badly eroded and weed-cracked.

His attention is drawn to the vehicles parked in the driveways and against the curbs of the houses he is passing. They are repli-cas of machines from a much earlier time, cars that were actually driven on streets, cars with rubber tires and no crash-protective devices. Some are behemoths—what they once called muscle cars—with rear tires larger than the front ones, the chassis raked steeply forward and the canopy cut down low and tight to limit the amount of exposed glass and wind resistance. Some are small and compact, scrunched down and closed in. Their bod-ies are wide and low slung, and they have a tight turning radius and spoilers arched across nonexistent trunks. Many are dented and scratched, their paint jobs worn and their heavy use evident. Some are pristine and alarmed in ways that suggest you should keep your distance. All are tricked out with wicked paint jobs and speed enhancements. Almost every house has one.

It is an odd sight. In the Red Zone, most people ride the streets the way they used to before the U.T. was formed. Not along elevated sky lanes but on pavement. Ash smiles, thinking of what it must feel like to travel on streets that could tear the underpinnings from a vehicle if you hit a rut or struck an obstacle. It explains why most of these vehicles have been installed with various forms of lifts to keep them sitting up higher than usual. Not all are like that, though; some hunker so close to the ground it is as if they do so in deliberate defiance of the damage risk.

And these vehicles use drivers—real people, not bots or oper-ating systems. When you climb into one of these cars, your fate is in your own hands and not in the hands of a robotics engineer you will never meet. You are master of the vehicle, and the choices made are yours.

He is reminded of his time in Africa, when he had access to old vehicles like these and could race them across the plains at ridiculous speeds, ignoring the danger, heady and exhilarated by the speed and the power. His parents never knew about any of this. If they had, they would have shut him down in a minute.

Losing patience with his apparent lack of progress, Ash

approaches an old man sitting on the steps of his porch. The old-
ster is grizzled and sour-faced and drinks an unknown liquid from
a large plastic container.

"Can you tell me where to find Street Freaks?" Ash asks.

The old man turns his head to one side and spits. He is chewing
something rigorously. "You're not one of them 'tweeners, are you?"

Ash hesitates, having no idea what he is talking about. "No. I
just have to meet someone."

"At Street Freaks? Bad choice for a meeting place, boy. Your
funeral, though, not mine." He nods his head left. "Six, seven
blocks to the intersection with the building that says 'Heads &
Tails' on it. You can't miss it. Then you go left about a mile. You'll
see it, though you'd be better off if you didn't."

Ash is unsettled by the old man's words. He thinks momentarily about asking what exactly he is being warned against but
decides it doesn't matter. He is going there regardless.

He continues walking toward a range of mountains that he
knows lies some fifty miles farther east. Eventually he passes
beyond residential territory and enters a district of strip malls and
specialty shops. When he reaches Heads & Tails, an establishment that offers up garish neon silhouettes of women in seductive poses, he turns left down a street that seems light-years away
from the ones he has just traveled.

Like all the other streets, it carries no identifying sign. But he
is pretty sure that those who live in the Zone know this one. It is
broad and flat without a single crack, indentation, or other irregu-
larity to mar its smooth surface. The composite is matte black and
heavily layered and ends in a smooth curve along its edges. Ash
follows the walkway paralleling its length, intrigued. He can think
of only one purpose for a street like this.

Street racing.

Not in vehicles like the ones he's been seeing parked in driveways and along curbs since entering the Red Zone, but high-tech
machines designed and built specifically for preformed tracks,

machines costing hundreds of thousands of credits and driven by drivers whose skills are extraordinary and sanity questionable. Some are even said to be bots.

He has watched dozens of officially sanctioned races on the entertainment vids, and the street he is walking down is an exact duplicate of the racetracks these vids. But those racetracks are dedicated to the sport and set far out in the countryside. Why would this street—if it were a racetrack—be situated here, in the heart of a Red Zone business district?

He walks on. Vehicles roll down the sculpted surface of the street and occasional walkers pass him by, but overall traffic is light. He passes strip malls, specialty shops, distribution centers, and personal service offices, all of them enclosed by chain-link fencing topped with concertina wire, gated against uninvited entry. At each gate, there is a call box where customers can announce their business and either be admitted or turned away. While there are no cameras anywhere on the street—a condition you would never find in the rest of L.A.—hundreds top the buildings and entries that line it, all of them focused on the businesses they protect. Some of those businesses provide additional incentives for staying out if you are not expected. Some are memorably persuasive.

PREMISES ARE MINED.
UNWARRANTED ENTRY WILL DETONATE.

VALUE YOUR LEGS?
BETTER USE THEM TO WALK AWAY.

BEWARE OF ROBO-DOGS.
LOTS OF TEETH.

WEREN'T INVITED? THEN KEEP OUT!

Ash is slightly unnerved by the fact that while the buildings and grounds inside the fences are protected, anything outside apparently is not. It doesn't seem like a very friendly neighborhood.

He has traveled a little more than half the distance to his destination when he hears the roar of a vehicle coming up from behind him, engine howling like a crazed banshee, sound system blaring out the latest metalhead music. He keeps walking without looking around, hoping that whatever is back there will just keep going. But his luck hasn't been very good so far, and it doesn't get any better now.

The front end of a brutish vehicle draws even, engine racing, the music a wall of sound that threatens to flatten him.

"Hey, pissant!" a voice growls over the competing sounds. "Hey, you little piece of dog shit! Look at me!"

Ash stops and turns. When he sees who is doing the talking, he wishes he had just kept going.

- 4 -

Neither the speaker nor the machine in which he is riding is like anything Ash has ever seen. They remind him of the covers of old science fiction books he used to secretly pull up on his vidview during some of Faulkner's more boring lectures.

The machine is huge, a massive iron monster covered with layers of armor. It has the appearance of a weapon, stripped of everything decorative and reduced to a carapace on wheels that looks as if it could break through walls. Huge tires, ladders to doors that open into a cockpit wrapped by an cage with serrated edges and wicked-looking spikes that jut menacingly, crimson flames painted along its slate-gray body from the front wheel wells back—it is a rolling nightmare.

The speaker, who is also the driver, is a perfect match for the machine. A man-boy just on the cusp of changing over, maybe Ash's age or a little older. Big and leather-clad with metal studs and rings fastened to both his clothing and his face. Head capped slantwise with shiny metal that suggests either some portion of his cranial bone was replaced after an accident or that a metal-head affectation inexplicably captured his fancy and persuaded him to undergo major cosmetic surgery.

Riding in the vehicle with him are three other boys, one of

them barely a teen, all of them apparently seeking to emulate the appearance of the speaker. There is a girl as well, Goth and cool as she stares out the other side of the vehicle, ignoring everyone.

"Hey, pussy boy," the speaker demands, "where do you think you're going?"

Ash stands his ground. You don't run in these situations; he knows that much about how the world works. He points up the street. The big kid's three male companions imitate this gesture and break out in fits of derisive laughter. The girl keeps looking elsewhere.

The big kid shakes his head in dismay. "What, you can't talk? You a retard? A chemoid? Answer me!"

"I'm meeting someone."

"Oh, you're *meeting* someone," the big kid repeats, mocking him, showing off for his friends. "That explains everything."

"Ask him for his hall pass, Ponce," one of them suggests.

The youngest boy has climbed out on the hood of the machine and is dancing, keeping time to the music in a frenetic kind of shimmy. Ponce takes a swipe at him with one huge arm, and the boy vaults back inside again. The girl elbows the boy sharply as he plops down next to her, and he shrinks away.

"Which club you with?" Ponce snaps. "Tigers? Sheeners? Vapor Hearts? Which? Speak up, pig slop. Let's hear it. What kind of club uses those crap colors you're wearing?" He points at Ash's sheath. "Butt-fuckin' ugly, you know?" He pauses. "Say something, shit-for-brains. Why am I doing all the talking?"

"I don't belong to any club," Ash answers, wondering how he is going to get out of this. "I don't live here. I'm just looking for someone."

"Yeah? Who?"

"My father."

"Your *faaather*," he sneers. "Sweet. You lose him or something?"

Big joke. Everyone laughs. "No, I'm meeting him."

"Yeah? Where?"

"Street Freaks."

"Street Freaks!" Ponce is suddenly enraged. His companions start yelling and screaming like madmen. "I thought you said you didn't belong to a club, you lying little bastard!"

"I don't!" Ash shouts, trying to back him off. "Look, I don't know anything about this place. I live in the Metro. I just . . . just have this . . ."

He loses his train of thought and his voice along with it as Ponce kicks open the driver's door, jumps down, and stalks toward him. He would have run if he thought it would do any good, but he knows it won't. Ponce is not only big; he is cat-quick. He is on top of Ash in seconds, one big hand clutching the front of his sheath and yanking him close enough that he can smell the reek of his breath.

"We don't like Street Freaks," he hisses. "We *hate* fuckin' Street Freaks. We hate people who have *anything* to *do* with Street Freaks. Which means we got a problem with you."

Ash doesn't know what to say. So he just stares.

Ponce shakes him like a toy. "Speak up!"

"I don't know anything . . . about them!" He tries to loosen the other's grip. "I was just doing what I was told!"

"Big mistake," Ponce snaps. "This is our part of the strip, not theirs. All the way from Heads & Tails to the beginning of the Scrounge. Ours, twit! You think you can come down here and walk right through our space and not even ask our permission? You think you're something special? Is that what you think? Hey, I'm talking . . ."

Ash is struggling hard to break free when a voice says, "Let him go, Ponce."

Everyone turns. A tall raven-haired girl is standing near the rear of the big machine. Not doing anything, just watching. She looks to be about the same age as Ash, but the resemblance ends there. She is much bigger than he is and does not look the least bit intimidated by Ponce. Her sleeveless leather one-piece reveals a sculpted body. Her short-cropped hair frames a face so chiseled and otherworldly it is arresting.

Ponce and his companions go still, their raucous talk reduced to mutterings and whispers. Ash catches a few of their words— "bird" or "bitch" maybe, "freak" and "robo-slut"—but he is not sure. The only one who seems unbothered by her appearance is the girl sitting in the machine—although, even she has turned around to watch.

"Let him go," the newcomer repeats.

Ponce shakes his head. "This isn't your mix, Holly."

Holly saunters forward, glancing up into the cab of the vehicle. "You reach for that chopdown, Penny-Bird," she says to the other girl, "and you won't be celebrating turning sixteen."

Penny-Bird finally glances over and holds up both hands, showing they are empty. For an instant, they lock gazes. Then Holly's eyes shift back to Ponce. "He says he is meeting someone at Street Freaks. Happens to be me. That makes it my business. Tell him, Jack."

She says this last to Ash. Recognizing an escape hatch when he sees one, he immediately nods. "That's right."

"He said he was meeting his father!" Ponce snaps.

Holly shrugs. "Not your business, is it? Let him go."

"He's in our space," Ponce insists, tightening his grip further. His face is dangerous, angry. A flush creeps up his neck, and the studs and rings glitter. "He don't have an invite; he can't just walk in."

Holly looks at him like he is an idiot. "He's a *civilian*, dodo. He doesn't *need* an invite. We don't mess with civilians—remember? That's a major-type rule in the Zone. You're so big on rules, try obeying a few once in a while!"

Ponce shakes his head stubbornly, the sunlight glinting off his metal plate in quick flashes. "No, you can't just . . . He didn't say nothing about . . ."

Holly comes right up against him now. As quick as Ponce

is, she's even quicker. "You want to let him go, please? If I have to ask again, I might decide to take your ride apart and sell off the pieces for scrap." She pauses, her eyes suddenly as hard as stones. "Ponce? You hear me?"

The big guy releases Ash with a hard shove that sends him careening into Holly's arms. She barely moves as she catches him, straightens him up, and moves him aside like a cardboard cutout.

Immensely strong.

Ponce starts back toward his machine and then turns. "I ain't afraid of you," he hisses at Holly. "Don't think for a minute I am. One day soon, you'll find out."

Holly watches him climb back into his machine, standing motionless as the engines roar and the music cranks.

"Penny-Bird!" she calls out. "Why don't you ditch these losers?"

The other girl looks away, staring off into the distance. Ponce engages the engine on his machine, and the group tears down the strip a short distance, swings around sharply, and roars back again. As they pass, Ponce thrusts his arm skyward in a universally recognizable gesture. Holly waves genially in response.

But when they are out of sight, she wheels on Ash. "What do you think you're doing, coming into the Zone without protection? Who are you, anyway?"

"Ash Collins," he answers her at once. "This wasn't my choice. I had to come . . ."

"You had to show some common sense, is what you had to do!" she interrupts. "What happened to that? They would have dismantled you if I hadn't come along. Those are Razor Boys! Cripes sake, you idiot! This is the Red Zone!"

Ash is thoroughly chastened. But he is also tired of being treated like a child. "Look. If I made a mistake, I'm sorry. But this hasn't been a very good day for me. It's taken everything I have just to get this far."

She snorts. "Everything, huh? Which is what exactly, big guy?"

Big guy? Ash can't help himself; he leans right into her. "Which is escaping a gang of Hazmats that broke into my home and tried to kill me! Which is watching them deliberately blow up the entire bot staff! Which is *then* only barely avoiding Achilles Pod by hopping a robo-taxi to get here, and now *this*!"

She stares. "Bullshit. You're making this stuff up. Achilles is after your skinny ass?"

"I just said so, didn't I?"

"Well, you're lying. What would they want with you?"

"Long story." He is only barely holding it together. Even though she has rescued him, he doesn't feel saved. But he takes a chance. "Can you help me?"

"Already have, in case you missed it." She sticks out her hand. "I'm Holly Priest."

"Ash Collins."

They shake, and he is acutely aware of how careful she is to let him do the squeezing. It's like gripping a piece of smooth steel. She studies him. "Why are you here? Civilians don't come to Street Freaks unless they get a special invitation or want to do business. Which is it with you?"

"Neither. The people I'm running from are after my father. He sent me here. To find Street Freaks."

She nods slowly. "Huh. Okay, let's walk while we discuss this some more."

She sets off down the sidewalk at a pace that forces Ash to work hard at keeping up. After a hundred yards, she notices this and slows. "How did you get away from Achilles Pod?"

She keeps looking straight ahead, waiting on his answer. "I was trying to catch a train out of substem #23. Then my face flashed up on the reader board like I was a criminal or something, and the next thing I know Achilles Pod comes in. I ran down into the tunnels, then back up to the street and caught a robo-taxi to the Zone's perimeter."

He looks down, watching the progress of his feet. "It all happened pretty quick. I really don't know how I got away."

Holly laughs, a huge guffaw. "Sounds like balls and brass to me, baby boy!" She shouts it out as if he were maybe half a mile ahead. "I love it!"

"Well, I don't. I just want to find my father."

"So you don't know how he's connected with Street Freaks?"

"I don't even know what Street Freaks is."

"Well, I can help you with that. It's a specialty shop. Puts cars together in new and exciting ways. Makes them into street machines. Big powerful engines, stripped-down chassis, racing tires, turbo thrusters, the whole lot."

"Really?" He frowns, confused. "I thought cars like that were gone except for professional racers, and those are all regulated. You can't do anything that doesn't conform to the racetrack rules."

Holly bursts into a fresh gale of laughter. "That's funny!" She stops, grabs his arm, and turns him toward her. "We don't build our machines for racetracks, dodo. That's racing for candy-asses! We build cars for street racing and sometimes for people who just want to go faster than whatever kind of law enforcement is chasing them. You get it? All legal on our end, not always so legal on theirs."

They start walking again, Holly still chuckling to herself, past buildings fenced off by chain-link topped with razor wire, down sidewalks mostly empty of people. Ash thinks through what she has told him. "So they race right here? Right on this street? That's why it looks like a legal racetrack?"

"Now you're getting the picture. It's called the Straightaway. It's where we race the way racing should be done. In the streets."

"But don't the Preventatives try to stop you? If it's illegal, don't they come in and . . . ?"

"Why would they do that? Think about it. Street racing is pretty far down the list of things the public worries about. Just the opposite, in fact. They support it. Besides, we don't take our machines outside the Zone. We keep them in our backyard. You think the Preventatives want to come in here and mess around with that? In the Red Zone? Not a chance. They're content to leave us alone as long as we leave them alone. No trouble from us, no trouble from them. You see?"

"I guess."

"Keep working on it." She pauses. "You know where Street Freaks gets its name? From the machines. That's what they call our racers—*Street Freaks*."

The boy nods. "*Street Freaks*, huh?"

"You think your father was buying himself a street machine? You think that's his connection with the shop? Is he that kind of guy—an outlaw? What does he do for a living?"

Ash hesitates before shrugging away caution. "He's a bio-genetics researcher."

Holly laughs. "Not much of an outlaw, then." She looks off into the distance, a thousand-yard stare. "Biogenetics. I know a little about that stuff. Yeah, I know some things." She pauses. "Wait a minute. What's your father's name?"

"Brantlin Collins."

"The Sparx guy?"

Sparx. The energy supplement invented by his father. Ubiquitous in the United Territories, they were everywhere.

"Yeah, that's him."

She goes silent again. Ash waits for something more, but it doesn't come. He senses she knows something about his father, but he hesitates to ask what. He feels dwarfed by her. Not quite insignificant, but close. She just seems like such a large presence. She dominates his space.

"Maybe he's thinking about buying you a racer," she says finally. "Maybe it was going to be a surprise."

Ash grins at the idea of his father giving him a street machine. Or even letting him drive on the streets. "You don't know my father."

"Wouldn't do that, huh?"

"I'm barely allowed out of our home. We used to travel a lot, but not anymore. Now there's always someone with me, wherever

I go. I've never been to the Zone—alone or with anyone else—in my whole life."

"Your life must be boring."

Ash nods, thinking maybe it used to be but not so much now. Where before, the Straightaway and flanking walkways were relatively empty, they are now busy. He glances up and down the street and at the storefronts and parking lots. People are coming and going from vehicles to stores and back again, busy shopping here just like in the Metro. Only these people are driving their cars through razor wire and chain-link fencing. These people are driving machines that look like they have been built to withstand a collision with a brick wall. These people, even in the momentary glimpses he catches of them, look tough and capable.

"How did you find your way this far into the Zone?" Holly asks after a minute or two.

He shrugs. "I walked. Then I asked this old guy, who wanted to know if I was a 'tweener. He told me . . ."

"Wait a minute," she interrupts. "Back up. What did he ask you?"

"If I was a 'tweener. But I didn't know what he . . ."

"Okay, stop right there and listen to me. You don't use that word." She speaks quietly, but her face is suddenly dark and dangerous. "Don't *ever* use that word. It's an ugly word. We don't call anybody that down here."

Ash stares at her in surprise. "Okay, I won't. I didn't mean anything. I never heard it before."

"Yeah, I get it. I'm just letting you know."

Ash doesn't say anything after that, and neither does she. They walk along in silence, glancing at the vehicles that pass them (he out of genuine interest, she in a more watchful way). Some of the cars are exotic and colorful, some only a little tricked out, and some so customized they scream for attention. These are all in addition to the ones that are layered in armor. Ash has never seen so many strange and different types. You almost never saw machines like this in the Metro, where all transportation was homogenized and almost entirely public transport. Even the racing machines he's seen on the entertainment monitors aren't as exciting and imaginative as what he is seeing here.

"'Tweeners are what they call people who aren't considered human," she says suddenly. "It's meant to indicate you're defective. Mostly, it refers to people who have been genetically altered. That old man was using it like that. He's one of those who think you're either all of one thing or you're nothing much of any. A lot of those kinds of people out in the world." She glances over. "I wouldn't like it if I thought you were one of them."

She says it calmly enough, but Ash can sense the underlying tension. "I'm not," he replies.

She nods. "I didn't think so." She points. "We're here."

Ahead, the mirrored surfaces of a blocky two-story steel and glass building glitter in the sunlight. The lower floor is a garage with half a dozen work bays, but the interior of the upper floor is concealed behind heavily tinted windows. The building occupies a fraction of its huge lot, the space much larger than required for its size. Vehicles are parked all over the back portion of the lot, most of them in various stages of cannibalization. A scattering are parked directly out front, utilitarian in appearance and showing nothing of the exotic look of so many of the machines Ash saw on his way coming up the strip. A couple of the doors to the bays are open, and he can see figures moving around inside.

The building itself is set well back from the street, as if to discourage passersby from trying to peer inside. The fence surrounding the building is ordinary—chain-link topped with razor wire just like almost every other building on the Straightaway. But the entrance is a different story. A mesh steel gate has been rolled aside, and a cluster of huge spikes juts out of the driveway in its place, looking as if they will not only shred your tires if you try to drive through but will likely take out the underside of your chassis and maybe your legs in the bargain. Rows of laser beams crisscross the entrance in case the spikes aren't warning enough.

Holly takes him right up to the opening and stops. A vidcom is set atop a metal stalk to one side of the concrete apron where drivers looking to shop must check in. Holly ignores it, her eyes on the building inside the fence.

"Doesn't look like much, does it?" she says.

"I don't know. You can't tell much from out here."

"Yeah, you shouldn't prejudge, should you?"

He glances at the call box, but she says, "We don't need to bother with that."

She puts her fingers to her lips and gives a shrill whistle. All work in the open bays stops, and an instant later the laser beams go off and the spikes retract into the ground.

Ash stares at her. "They must know you pretty well here."

She grins. "They ought to. It's where I live."

- 5 -

Everything about this day has been beyond weird for Ash Collins—right from the moment he received his father's vidview and started running. But going inside Street Freaks takes things to a whole new level.

Holly Priest walks him into the first open bay, shouting out greetings and calling for everyone to come over and meet "the new fish." That's what she calls him—"the new fish." He winces inwardly, wondering what that means, uncomfortable with the designation. He almost says something but decides to keep his mouth shut.

He catches a glimpse of the machines being worked on in bays 2 and 5—both of them sleek and sculpted with lots of polished metal surfaces—before Holly's summons is answered and his expectations get turned on their head.

A boy balancing atop a catwalk that is fastened by heavy cables to pulleys and tracks attached to the ceiling of Bay 2 shouts down in response. "New fish, huh?" His blue eyes check Ash out before shifting away dismissively. "Throw him back."

"Be nice," Holly says sternly.

The boy gathers himself and vaults twenty feet onto the composite floor. He lands effortlessly, as if he does this sort of thing all the time. Even through his clothing it is apparent that he is ridged with muscle.

He walks over and plants himself right in front of Ash, looking him up and down. "I don't know. Kinda small, Holly."

"Hey, give him a chance. He's got a good vibe."

The boy shrugs, looking doubtful. Then he offers his hand. "Tommy Jeffers." Ash shakes reluctantly. Tommy laughs. "Hey, not so hard. You didn't try that with Holly, did you?" He glances over at her, winks. A joke. Holly looks irritated. "Didn't think so. What's your name?"

"Ash Collins."

"What's your thing, Ash?" Tommy is white-blond and deeply tanned. He would have been the prototypical all-American boy a couple centuries earlier, but he looks curiously out of date in what is now a predominately multiracial culture. He gives Ash another quick up-and-down. "You don't look particularly athletic. Must be an intelligence factor. How are you tweaked?"

"Don't get ahead of yourself, T.J.," Holly interrupts quickly. "He's not looking for a home. He's a civilian. Just a fish I offered to help out. He's looking for his dad."

Tommy bounces on his toes. "You lost your dad? How'd that happen? Did you misplace him or something?"

Ha-ha, Ash wants to say. "He sent me a vidview telling me to meet him here. I think he's in trouble."

Tommy frowns. "What sort of trouble?"

"Let it alone, T.J." Holly takes Ash by the shoulders in a curiously protective gesture. "He's a guest. He'll tell us what's wrong when he's ready."

"I'm just trying to be helpful," T.J. protests. But he doesn't sound it.

"Well, stop it. You've said hello. Go back to work."

She pivots Ash away, and a dark-skinned girl with fine black hair and narrow features walks up. The girl is wearing a sheath ribbed with parallel lines of flexible tubing buried in the fabric, and because they are darker in color than the sheath, they look like stripes. At least that is the image that pops into Ash's head. The tubes are connected to each other and to a pair of narrow cylinders strapped to her back.

"Ash," Holly says, "This is Jenny Cruz."

The girl nods wordlessly. Her gaze is steady and the expression on her oval face is serious and introspective. Ash sees that several of the tubes sprouting from the tanks are inserted into ports embedded in the back of her neck.

"Nice to meet you," Jenny Cruz says finally. "What brings you to Street Freaks?"

"I just . . ."

"He's looking for his dad," Holly repeats. "I found him on the streets."

"Who's your dad?" Jenny asks.

"Brantlin Collins. Do you know him?"

She hesitates. "The biogenetics engineer? *That* Brantlin Collins?"

He nods. At least she didn't call him "the Sparx guy." Even if she doesn't know his father personally, she's heard of him. "Do you have any idea why my dad would tell me to come here? Does he have something to do with Street Freaks?"

She shakes her head. "I don't think so."

"Why do you think we would know anything about him?" T.J. is back. "You sure he told you to come here?"

The question distracts Ash from asking Jenny Cruz anything more. It's only been a few minutes since they met, but he is already growing irritated with T.J.

"Ignore him," Holly says, giving T.J. a strong push.

But Tommy Jeffers holds his ground. "You don't run things around here," he tells her.

"For which you should be eternally grateful." Holly glances past him dismissively. "Hey, Woodrow! Come here! Don't be shy. This fish doesn't bite."

Ash turns and has to work very hard to keep from gaping in astonishment. A five-foot-tall bot approaches. It lacks legs and its cylindrical upper torso is fastened atop a rectangular metal container that houses whatever computers and power sources enable it to function. The container, in turn, is attached to a complex platform of treads that allow it to move easily over any surface. A smoked-glass panel set into its chest reveals switches and digital readouts. Colored lights blink from behind the panel. Hinged at the wrists, elbows, and shoulders, its flexible arms can move in any direction and are comprised entirely of interlocking metal parts—fingers, hands, forearms, upper arms, and shoulders.

Everything says it is a bot except for its head.

Which is the head of a mixed-race, dark-skinned boy, one younger than Ash but unmistakably human—kinky hair cut short, round face flushed, and wearing an expression of mixed uncertainty and discomfort.

"Hey," he mutters, rolling up.

He has a boy's voice, a real boy's voice, a human voice, not a mechanical one.

"Hey," Ash replies. Woodrow does not offer to shake, so he doesn't either. "I'm Ash."

Woodrow can't seem to meet his eyes. He keeps his own downcast, almost as if he is afraid of what looking up might cost him. Ash finds himself studying the way the boy's neck disappears down inside a metal collar where it is somehow attached to his robot body. He has never seen anything like it; he didn't know a bot like Woodrow could even exist.

"I was an experiment," Woodrow says suddenly, eyes lifting all at once to meet Ash's.

Jenny Cruz makes a dismissive gesture. "He doesn't need to know that," she says quickly. "Do you, Ash?"

Ash shakes his head in agreement, although he really does want to know. Instead, he asks, "Why is Holly calling me a 'fish'? What does that mean?"

"Oh, it's just an expression." Holly gives him a broad grin. "It means you're a newbie, a first-time visitor to the Zone."

"An outsider," T.J. adds pointedly. "Not one of us."

"You've been thrown into the pond with the rest of us, so now you need to learn how to swim," Holly continues.

"So, Ash." Jenny takes hold of his arm and turns him away from the others. He can hear the soft humming of pumps in the cylinders she wears. "You're looking for your dad? Why is that?"

"Yeah, he was coming here to find him when—" Holly starts to say.

"Don't interrupt, Holly." Jenny cuts her short. "Let Ash speak for himself."

Holly Priest flushes, but in spite of her dominating physical presence, she backs off with a shrug. It's apparent that Jenny Cruz is in charge—at least in this situation.

Ash hesitates. How much should he tell these four? All of them are waiting. He can feel their inquisitive eyes watching him. This is some sort of test. They want to know the specifics of what brought him here, and he senses that hedging or lying would be a mistake. Jenny Cruz, at least, is making up her mind about whether or not to trust him. At the moment, she is undecided.

"I got a vidview from my father this morning. He told me to leave and come into the Red Zone. To come here, specifically. Then Hazmats came through the door, just blew it down, and started shooting the bots. I climbed out a window, took a jumper to another building, and got down to street level. I thought about taking a transmat, but I wasn't sure how it worked. So I took a robo-taxi to a substem, thinking I could catch a train into the Zone. The next thing I know, I see my face on the reader board with a warning to report me to the L.A. Preventatives if I'm seen. Then Achilles Pod shows up, and I start running. I go down into the tunnels and out to the departure platforms. But someone in the crowd recognizes me and calls it in, and Achilles Pod comes after me. I know I can't take the train because they'll be waiting for me down the line. So I run back up to the street and hop another robo-taxi. But they can't go into the Red Zone, so I get dropped on the perimeter and have to walk in. I tried to find Street Freaks, but Holly found me first, and here I am."

He runs out of breath and story at about the same time. His listeners just stare at him.

"You see!" Holly exclaims. "Not your average fish. I found him on the strip about to be eaten for lunch by Ponce and his crew. You think maybe his dad's a customer?"

"Achilles Pod is after you?" T.J. interrupts. He purses his lips. "Really? What's so important about you?"

"That's none of your business," Holly snaps, glaring at him.

"Maybe it is, now that you've brought him here," T.J. replies.

"Where do you live, Ash?" Jenny Cruz asks. "Somewhere in the Metro, right? Did you say you took a jumper to get away from the Hazmats?"

I nod. "I live in a sky tower."

"But he says he's not usually allowed to go anywhere alone," Holly interjects. "Isn't that right, Ash?"

"My father travels a lot. So I'm homeschooled and I don't go to regular . . ." He trails off. He is talking too much. "Like I said, this is the first time I've been out alone for a while. So far, it's not much fun."

"Kind of exciting, though, huh?" T.J. declares with a grin. "Damn! Achilles Pod!" He looks out the open bay door. "Maybe we shouldn't be standing around like this where anyone looking in can see us."

"So your dad didn't tell you why you were supposed to come here?" Jenny presses, ignoring T.J. "You never heard him say anything about Street Freaks before?"

Ash shakes his head. "Not a word. I didn't even know what Street Freaks was before today."

"You still don't," T.J. adds.

"Shut up, T.J.," Jenny says quietly. She keeps her eyes fixed on

Ash. "We have to be careful about who we let in here. The Shoe doesn't like strangers. And this is his shop, not ours. We just work for him. Our customers insist on a high degree of privacy. They depend on us to keep everything we do for them a secret. The Shoe gives them that guarantee. Letting strangers into the shop doesn't help with that."

Ash gets what she's saying, but it makes him angry. "The only reason I came to Street Freaks was because that was what I was told to do. I just want to find my dad. I don't want to know any secrets. I don't care what goes on here."

"Hey, calm down." Holly makes a soothing gesture. She puts a hand on his shoulder, and it feels oddly reassuring. "I brought you here to help you because you asked me to. Remember? The point is, you don't know why your dad sent you here, but he must have had a reason for doing so. He didn't just pull our name out of a hat. We need to find out what the connection is. But you have to help us."

"Because your dad's not here," Jenny Cruz finishes. "There's no one here but us."

"So maybe this is turning into a search and rescue," Holly adds. "Maybe finding your dad is going to require more from you than just standing around waiting for him to show up."

"Now might be a good time to ask him how he's tweaked," T.J. says. He flashes his disarming beach-boy grin at Holly. "Hey, don't look at me like that. If he's tweaked, it might explain why Street Freaks was chosen as a meeting place."

"Do you know what T.J. means?" Jenny asks him. "About being tweaked? Have you heard the word?"

"He's heard the other 'T' word," Holly grumbles. "The bad one. He didn't know what it meant."

"I don't know what 'tweaked' means either," Ash answers.

"If he was tweaked, he would know it," Woodrow says. He's been mostly quiet all this time. The buttons on his metal chest are flashing.

"It means you have special abilities as a result of the way you are put together." Jenny considers her choice of words. "It means you can do things other people can't because of the way you are enhanced or reengineered."

"Not because of how you are born or because of the genes you inherited," Woodrow adds, sounding put out. "You can do things because your physical makeup has been significantly altered through science."

Tubes feeding into your body, strength that would crush a regular human, an athleticism that lets you drop twenty feet from a ceiling, and a boy's head improbably mounted on a robot's body. Ash nods. "Like all of you?"

Jenny nods back. "Like all of us. We're tweaked, each of us in a different way. The Shoe found us and brought us together to help him work the shop. He doesn't judge us like some people do. He accepts us for who we are."

"Remember when I told you what Street Freaks meant?" Holly jumps back into the conversation. "How I told you it referred to the street machines we build for our special customers? Well, it means something else too. It's street slang for people like us—me and Jenny and T.J. and Woodrow. It's what we're called. Street Freaks. It's not meant in a nice way, but we've turned it back on those people who use it by adopting it as our own."

"It's what we call *ourselves*," T.J. adds. "Openly, not in secret. Street Freaks. That's our identity. It's who we are and what we build. We construct the machines, and we own the name."

"Like a club," Ash says. "Like Ponce and his friends are called Razor Boys."

"Not exactly." T.J. looks irritated. "We're not a club and we're not dumbass thugs looking for trouble. We're a family."

"Bet you've never met anyone like us before, have you?" Holly cocks her head at him. "Being homeschooled, never going into places like the Red Zone, pretty much keeping to yourself? Or am I wrong? Maybe you know more than you're saying."

"How about it, Ash?" Jenny gives him a questioning look. "You think you might be like us? Are you tweaked in any way? Your dad is a biogenetics engineer."

Ash shakes his head. "Yeah, he's a biogenetics engineer, but I don't think he's ever done anything to me. I can't do anything special. I'm just average." He pauses, considering. "Except that I'm good at remembering stuff. I can see something once and remember it for weeks afterward. Sometimes for months."

"Like you see people you don't know, and you can remember their faces?" T.J. asks.

"Well, yeah. That too. But mostly I'm good at remembering things that are written down." Ash looks around, suddenly eager to feel like a part of the group, to belong in some way. "You show me the specs on a machine, I can draw out copies that look just like the originals. Well, you know. Not stylistically, maybe. But the details would be accurate. I keep it all in my memory, and I can bring it out or recognize it again without hardly thinking about it."

The other kids exchange glances. "That sounds like a pretty useful skill," T.J. observes. Ash can practically see the wheels turning. "Does it mess with your head to be able to remember so much?"

Ash grins in spite of myself. "I can see how you might think it would. But it doesn't. It's there if I need it or if something triggers my memory of it. It isn't like my brain's about to explode because there's too much stuff crammed inside."

T.J. laughs. "Well, there's some good news! Now we don't have to worry about asking you to step outside if you feel a major thought coming on."

"Which is why we feel so safe about you, T.J.," Holly says.

Even Jenny Cruz smiles.

Ash begins to feel comfortable with these kids, to get beyond his first impressions, to see past their strangeness to what makes them seem as ordinary as he is. In spite of the unexpectedness of the situation and the unusual circumstances that brought them together, he finds himself liking them.

"You think I might be tweaked like you are?" he asks, genuinely curious.

"Maybe." Jenny preempts the others. "Tweaked, that is. But not like us. Look, you can wait here for your dad, if you want. Maybe he'll show up later. Meanwhile, I'll check our business records and see if there's any mention of him. Maybe he's been here and hasn't told you about it. I'll have a look."

She turns away. "The rest of you better get back to work on Starfire. The Shoe wants her ready for pickup tomorrow morning first thing. Ash, you can watch if you promise to stay out of the way."

She walks back through the door from which she entered and closes it behind her.

"Who died and made her special?" Holly mutters.

Ash doesn't have the answer to that question, but he is pretty sure he has the answer to another. She isn't going off to see if there is any mention of his father in the shop's business records. She knows there is, and she is trying to decide what to do with the information. She is trying to decide whether to give it to him.

T.J. claps him on the shoulder. "Come on, fish. Let's you and me go have a look at the world's most beautiful street machine."

- 6 -

Ash follows T.J. down the line of bays to the most beautiful car he has ever seen. It is cobalt blue with narrow silver pinstripes, and it gleams so brightly that it mirrors every detail of his face. It is clearly a racing machine, its big muscular body supported by four wide-tread tires tucked under wheel wells that hunch above them like powerful shoulders. It is deeply raked, and its rear tires are massive. The body is smoothed out and aerodynamic; no protuberances or sharp edges blemish its alloyed skin. The cockpit is small, space for two seats only, and the passenger side is nothing more than a flat surface. Deep padding surrounds the cockpit area on all sides. The wheel is small and heavily wrapped in dark leather. There are levers and knobs and buttons everywhere; Ash cannot begin to know what they do.

"Is she something or what?" T.J. asks.

Ash nods. "She's beautiful."

"Two thousand pounds of RBH thrust from an 850 Watson modified with turbo-eights and dual intakes. Runs on rocket fuel. The real deal. Goes from zero to 150 in—get this—3.5 seconds. Almost faster than your brain can think to control it. It's been tested at three hundred miles per hour top end, though in the kind of racing we do, top-end speed is less important than acceleration and control. It's quick, smooth, and faster than anything on four wheels." He grins. "Come here."

They walk over to the rear end, and he triggers a release. The engine cover lifts noiselessly. Inside the housing, the component pieces gleam as brightly as the exterior surface. The engine is recognizable, but the rest is a mystery. Components of various shapes and sizes display digital readouts and blinking lights. They give the vehicle more the look of a computer than a racing machine.

T.J. takes it all in reverently. "Ever see anything like this? Computers everywhere. Woodrow builds them. Fourteen years old, and he builds engine computers! He's a certifiable genius. You might guess he knows something about computers from looking at him. A strong sense of self-preservation gives him good reason to keep learning."

Ash nods, but it is Starfire that has his attention. "Who owns her?"

"Oh, fish, I can't tell you that!" T.J. says at once. "We don't give information like that out to just anyone. Besides, I don't know myself." He laughs. "Hey, want to take a ride?"

"In this?"

"No, not in this! Look inside!" T.J. points to the empty platform next to the driver's seat. "That's where you would have to sit. This is a racing machine. One driver, no passengers."

He slaps Ash alongside the head chidingly, not holding back. "Over here."

He leads the way to the office space where Jenny Cruz is hunched over piles of documents, sifting through them with studied care. She looks up quickly when she senses his presence.

"What is it, T.J.?" She sounds annoyed

Ash hangs back, wishing he hadn't followed T.J. in, sensing he is an unwanted distraction. He doesn't even want to go for a ride; he wants to stay and wait for his father. Intrigued as he is by Street Freaks, this isn't where he belongs.

T.J. gives Jenny Cruz a shrug. "I thought I might take the fish out for a ride in the Flick. Can you spare us? I've done all I can with Starfire. She's ready."

Jenny stares at him. "You can go if you promise not to do anything reckless. Don't get him hurt. I mean it. You're responsible for him while you're out of my sight, T.J."

"Got it." T.J. wheels away. A flicker of anger crosses his face as he grabs Ash's arm. "What a pain in the ass she is."

"I don't think . . ." Ash begins and then trails off. Doesn't think what? That he should go with T.J.? That he should do anything with someone who doesn't seem to like him all that much in the first place? That maybe it's not safe?

But he's not going to admit it. Not to T.J. He trudges along in silence, through the garage and out a back door into a storage lot full of damaged street machines, all sizes and shapes and in all sorts of condition.

He gestures. "You work on these? Rebuild them?"

T.J. laughs. "Naw. This stuff is junk. It's just for show. We want people who don't know us to think we work on junkers. But you saw Starfire. That's what we really do. High-end street machines built for racing. And a few other things," he adds.

Ash glances over. "What other things?"

"Oh, this and that. Over here, fish."

He steers Ash toward a low-slung two-door power ride tucked back behind the wrecks and uses a handheld pulse key to open its doors, and they both climb in.

"This is the Flick," T.J. announces, depositing the pulse key in a compartment in the center console. "She's mine. Built her myself." He pauses, glances at Ash, and shrugs. "Well, the others helped too. A little. I couldn't do the computers without Woodrow, couldn't pay for it without the Shoe's credits, and couldn't design it without Jenny. Couldn't do some of the heavy lifting, either, without cyber-girl."

"You mean Holly?"

"Yeah, Holly. Let's go. Buckle up. Here, put on this helmet. If I let something happen to you, hard telling what Jenny might do to me. So you do what I say, all right? Power up, Flick!"

The engine starts immediately, voice activated. Once T.J. has her running the way he wants, he puts her in gear and ushers her through the lot to the front gate at a speed that doesn't quite break the sound barrier but causes Ash to jam his hands against the dash to brace himself.

"What a wussy little fish!" T.J. crows. "You haven't seen anything yet."

Ahead of them, the spikes begin to retract. T.J. revs the engine until it is howling. As soon as the spikes are all the way down, he puts the vehicle in gear, floors the power thruster, and they rocket through the gate as if shot out of a cannon. Down the raceway fronting Street Freaks they fly, tearing ahead so fast they catch and pass other vehicles almost before they know what's happening. T.J. never once lets up on the thruster. The Straightaway only goes in one direction, but this doesn't lessen the feeling of insanity that marks the experience. If Ash thought the taxi driver bots were crazed, then T.J. is insane. He howls and whoops and bounces around in his seat as he drives. Ash is certain they are going to crash. His heart is in his throat and his hands are glued to the padded dash as Ash waits for it to happen.

Finally, at the far end of the straightaway, T.J. rips past checkered signage that marks what appears to be a finish line.

"There you go!" he exclaims jubilantly and reaches over to give Ash a friendly shove. He slows the Flick to a crawl. "Whoo! That's what real racing is like! That's what real driving is all about!"

Ash exhales slowly. "Real racing, huh?"

"Oh, come off it. You loved it!"

Truth is, now that it's over, he has to admit it was sort of fun. All that power vibrating through the car, all that speed reducing the landscape to flashes of color and stretched-out images—it was exhilarating. It reminds him of racing in Africa. He had forgotten how much he loved it.

But that was when *he* was driving. What he doesn't find so easy is the idea of putting his life so completely into someone else's hands. Or entrusting it to several thousand pounds of composite materials not directly under his control, if you preferred to look at it that way.

"I used to do some driving," he says quietly.

"Sure you did." T.J. is dismissive. He barely spares him a look. "But this is different."

T.J. turns the Flick into a parking lot that is virtually empty and parks it facing a river. He pulls out a pack of cigarettes and offers it. When Ash shakes his head, T.J. takes one and lights it with a tiny torchpin.

"I wouldn't go swimming in there, if I were you," he advises, gesturing toward the river.

"How can you breathe the air in the Zone?" Ash asks, brushing at clouds of exhaled cigarette smoke. "Doesn't it bother you? Or are you immune?"

T.J. gives him a look. "I'm immune to everything. I never get sick. If I get injured, I heal overnight. I'm Superman."

"What does that mean?"

"It means, *fish*," the other says, putting added emphasis on the last word as he leans close and blows smoke in Ash's face, "that I am *perfect*. That's how I'm tweaked. I was genetically altered while still in utero to be a superior male specimen. Ta-da! Tommy Terrific! I was created to be the perfect athlete and trained to be the perfect soldier. I was one of the first of a new generation of protectors genetically manufactured to serve the greater needs of the United Territories. I was the prototype for what was to be a new army."

He leans back in his seat, lip curling. "Of course, I wasn't given a choice about this, was I? No one stood up for me. I didn't live in a highrise in the *Metro*." Again, a deliberate taunt. "I had a surrogate who carried me to birth, and then I was given over to the tender, loving care of the scientists who had manufactured me and the military establishment that had requisitioned me.

Along with some other flesh-and-blood puppets created for the same purpose. Funny, thinking back on it. I never knew the names of my brothers-in-arms. We were given numbers. I was twenty-five. Number twenty-five. I never found out what happened to the other thirty-nine after the grand experiment failed. Classic, huh? Never found out."

His voice drifts off. Ash waits a moment and then says, "So what part of this grand plan didn't work out?"

"*I* didn't work out, fish! That's what didn't work out. Me, myself, and I. A frickin' failure! Told you I was tweaked. Well, it's *how* I'm tweaked that's the problem. Not that the geniuses that made me would accept any responsibility for it. Not that they would ever admit it. The others at Street Freaks, they don't think it matters. They're different too. But not different like me. No metal parts in me. No artificial pieces. Just a stew of steroids and additives and toxic potions and scientific swill! All flesh, blood, bones, and iron determination, and all of it a frickin' mess!"

He shakes his head. "Now, Holly? Holly's another story. Born to real parents, raised by real parents. An ordinary girl who suffered an unfortunate accident and an even more unfortunate recovery—one that required she become slightly reimagined by her helpful neighborhood mad scientists so she could break iron and bend steel!"

He slams the dash with his fist, causing the entire vehicle to lurch. "Did you look at her closely, fish? Do you know what she is? Well, you know she's not like anyone else, right? A whole lot not like anyone else! She's a frickin' cyborg! You know what a cyborg is? She's human—flesh and blood and bone—but she's had some replacement work done with metal and plastic components. A lot of work, actually. She's been rebuilt from the ground up to be what she is—as much a creature of inanimate material as of human tissue. The accident tore her up. She was still alive, but there wasn't much left to save. So her parents gave up on her. Gave her over to science."

His eyes fix on Ash. "Can you imagine that? Her parents abandoned her! What sort of parent does that? They listened to the doctors who said she was going to die, and they let her go. They listened to all that bullshit, the jerks! Then the doctors gave her to the mad scientists who wanted to experiment on her. And they did too. Boy, did they ever! New arm and leg, part of her body, piece of her head, a few new organs—all replaced with composite materials. They recreated her, and when they were done, they had something of what those other wackos had envisioned for me. They had the perfect fighting machine. They also had one angry girl."

"She's awfully strong," Ash agrees.

T.J. looks away. "You don't know the half of it." He sighs wearily. "Okay, I'm done talking. I just think a fish like you ought to know a little about what being 'tweaked' means. You come into the Zone, you ought to know. Put your helmet back on. Flick, power up!"

The engine springs to life, growling ominously in the stillness of the afternoon.

"Hey, I wasn't making it up about the driving," Ash says suddenly. "The kind you do. Racing."

T.J. glances over. "Yeah, so?"

"I just wanted be sure you heard me."

"Just don't talk to me, okay?"

They return to Street Freaks in silence, T.J. driving a different street now at a much slower speed and not looking at him. Ash has questions, but he doesn't think this is the time to ask them. T.J.'s demeanor suggests he shouldn't. Besides, he will probably be out of there by day's end, so he doesn't see much point in asking anything more about any of these kids. His father is probably waiting by now, or there might be news of his whereabouts.

His thoughts return to the events that led to his flight into the Red Zone, and he is immediately depressed anew. He sees Faulkner being blown apart. He recalls the sound of weapons fire and explosions, the smell of smoke and ashes and scorched metal, and the sense of fear he experienced on looking at the long drop to the street below as he stood on the ledge outside his sky tower home.

Why didn't his father prepare him better for what might happen? But he realizes almost immediately that his father couldn't be sure how to do that. He was probably hoping all along that none of this would ever come to pass, believing that if he were careful enough . . .

But he hadn't been careful enough, had he? They'd found him out. Whoever *they* were.

At the gates, as the spikes lower back into the composite, T.J. says, "Look, fish. I said too much back there. I usually don't do that. My life is good. I don't have room to complain."

Ash shrugs. "I think maybe you do." He pauses. "But could you stop calling me *fish*?"

T.J. laughs. "I'll think about it."

They park the Flick where they'd found it and walk back inside the building. As they pass the office where they'd left Jenny, they find everyone crowded around her desk looking up at a wall-mounted vidview. A live report is being broadcast. A picture of the BioGen building is being shown, and a newscaster is standing in front of it, speaking into a vidcam.

". . . investigation continues into the terrible incident that took place earlier today at the offices of BioGen, where prominent scientist and biogenetics engineer Brantlin Collins . . ."

The stricken faces of those gathered turn toward Ash, and he doesn't need to hear the rest of what the newscaster says to know what has happened.

". . . apparently Collins fell or jumped from the roof of the building in front of which we are standing. Although the authorities are offering no official comment on the cause of death at this time . . ."

He tries to shut out the image that immediately comes to mind, tries to make what he is hearing not be so. He feels himself go cold all over.

". . . the prevailing opinion of those investigating the incident suggests that the most likely cause of death was suicide . . ."

"No!" he shouts, unexpectedly furious at the suggestion. "My father would never kill himself!"

". . . shocking loss of a man whose contributions through research on genetic deficiencies in the human body resulted in the development of supplements to and replacements for damaged organs. Perhaps his most recognizable achievement was in the development of genetic tracking, which led to the production of mood enhancers, commonly known as Sparx, which are now used almost universally . . ."

"This is wrong. It's a lie! He wouldn't do that!" Ash spits out the words as if they were poison, impassioned beyond reason. He never believed his father was at risk, and now that he is gone, Ash just flat-out refuses to believe it was suicide.

". . . while an investigation continues into this tragic event, one thing remains clear. The world, and the United Territories in particular, have lost a talented biogenetics pioneer whose research into the nature of the human species has changed our lives for the better. Brantlin Collins, dead at the age of forty-two. Allen?"

Jenny Cruz points at the vidview, and the screen goes blank. "I'm sorry, Ash."

Murmured condolences immediately issue from the rest. Holly moves over and wraps one arm around him in a brief hug, and in an incongruous and surreal moment, Ash finds himself trying to decide if her metal-and-composite arm feels different than his own.

"This isn't right," he says. "He wouldn't do that. Not my father. He wouldn't." He cannot leave it there, refuses to permit it to take on the trappings of truth. "If he's dead, he was killed."

"That's a big jump you just made," T.J. says, the doubt in his voice unmistakable.

"No, it isn't. My father said he was at risk, and this proves it. He said there were people who wouldn't like it if they found out what he was doing. Why couldn't it be BioGen he was talking about? That vidview he sent me this morning? I saw the look on his face. I heard how he sounded. He was really scared."

T.J. shakes his head. "What could he have done that would get him killed? That's pretty extreme, even for corporate greed-heads. You sure he wasn't just depressed about something?"

"Maybe he just fell," Holly says. "Accidentally, I mean. People fall accidentally all the time. Off bridges and porches and ladders and everything."

"Off the tops of buildings they work in?" Ash asks. He rubs his eyes. "I have to figure out what to do."

T.J. shrugs. "Well, you can stop waiting for your father."

Holly wheels on him. "Shut up, T.J. Do you have to be such a dick all the time?"

"Ash stays here," Jenny Cruz declares. "With us. At least until the Shoe gets back and can tell us what he thinks. That okay with you, Ash?"

It is not okay, but at this point nothing is. Every hope he had of sorting this out depended on his father meeting him. Even in the darker moments when it occurred to him that his father might not be coming, he kept telling himself he would. But now there is no doubt remaining, and he must accept that his father is gone. He must begin looking for another solution.

"It's okay," he says.

They begin to file out of the office, but Jenny calls him back. "Wait a minute, Ash. Don't leave just yet. Close the door."

He does, and she motions for him to sit across the desk from her. "What?" he asks. "Did you find something out?"

She shakes her head. "Not yet. But I'm not finished looking. I need to try a different approach. After listening to you, I think I'm going to shift my search to BioGen. I want to take a peek at their corporate records."

He starts to ask how she can do this, but she holds up a hand in warning. "Don't. What we do here requires that we know more about those we do business with than they know about us. It's my job to find a way to make that happen, but

I can't tell you how I do it. So let it be. Understand?"

He nods. *Those we do business with? Street Freaks does business with BioGen?* But he leaves these questions unasked for now. "Whatever you can find . . ."

"I know," she interrupts. "I'll pass it on to you. Just so you know, I don't think it was suicide either. From everything you've told us, it doesn't sound to me like that's what happened. But what do these people want with you?"

Her narrow face is stern but encouraging too. It is her eyes that trouble him. They seem veiled, fixed on him with the kind of look that suggests she already knows the answer to that question but wants to find out if he does.

"I don't know," he says finally. "Everything my father told me, I've told you. I don't know anything else."

"Then we have to find out another way." She leans back in her chair and studies him. "The Shoe is gone until tomorrow; the others don't know this because I haven't told them. It helps to keep T.J. and Holly in line if they think he might return at any moment."

Not for the first time, Ash is struck by the fact that she sounds so much older than she looks. He pauses before answering, thinking about what she has just said. "Okay, so why are you telling this to me?"

"Because I think maybe you belong here with us. Don't ask me to explain. Not just yet, anyway. Just accept it for now. But whether I'm right or not, you have to find a way to fit in. So I want you to take these next few days to get to know the others better. Spend time with them, work with them, and then see how you feel about being here. Or do you have somewhere else you can go?"

Ash considers telling her about Uncle Cyrus but decides not to. He knows his uncle only slightly. His father hardly ever even talked about his brother. Even if Cyrus agreed to take him in, he couldn't be certain where he would end up. An old phrase occurs to him: *Better the devil you know than the one you don't.*

"I'd rather stay," he says.

She nods. "So let's talk a little about what you can do while you're here."

But then the door flies open and T.J. rushes in. "Trouble, Jen."

She stands at once. "What sort?"

"We have visitors coming up on the gate. They're all over the Straightaway, working up and down both sides. Looking for something." He glances at Ash. "Or someone."

"Who is it?" Jenny asks.

T.J. flashes his trademark smirk. "Achilles Pod."

- 7 -

"Go into lockdown," Jenny orders. "Make sure all the places we don't want them going into are sealed. I want everyone to look like they're doing what they normally do. Everything out in the open and visible, just like always. Except for Ash. Put him in the loft. Give him a com unit so he can listen in."

She begins shoving the files off her desktop and into drawers. As Ash follows T.J. out of the room, he sees the computer she has been working on recede into the top of her desk and then the entire desk disappear into the floor. A final glance back shows the office is bare save for Jenny and her chair, log books shelved against the walls and a few flat work surfaces.

T.J. shouts to the others, relaying Jenny's instructions, then quickly ushers Ash to a stairway at the back of the building and up the steps to the second floor. There is an open space with assorted equipment and furniture at the top of the stairs, but he takes Ash down a short hall that dead-ends at an empty wall. He touches the heads of several nails that secure the wallboard, and the entire wall swings open to reveal a small room beyond.

"Clever, huh?" T.J. says. "Look over here."

He leads Ash inside and over to one of several windows with darkened glass that overlooks the front gates and the Straightaway.

"From the outside, you can't tell these are windows. You probably noticed coming in. But from here you can see everything that's happening out there. So pay attention, okay? You might learn something. Take this."

He hands Ash a small device with a speaker grid and a pulse knob. "You can listen in with this. The knob controls the sound level. Don't put it up too high; this room isn't soundproof. And don't move around either."

He starts to leave, but just before closing the door, he turns and grins. "Don't look so worried, fish. You'll be fine. We'll take care of you."

The door closes.

Achilles Pod. Ash escaped them once, but what are the odds he can do it again? He peers out the window cautiously, unable to stop worrying he might be seen. The black-clads are all over the Straightaway, silver wolves' heads glittering in the sunlight as they conduct their search. There are dozens of them, far more than there were at substem #23. Closer in, the gates to Street Freaks stand open, as if inviting entry. But entry is impossible because horizontal lasers shimmer in narrow bands across the opening.

Ash spies Jenny Cruz as she walks out of the building. There is an Achilles Pod unit standing on the other side of the lasers waiting for her. Ash remembers the listening device and turns it on, keeping the sound low.

One of the black-clads is speaking.

"I'm ordering you to remove the force field. We need to search every building on this street." His voice takes on a decided edge. "Right now!"

"I can't do that." Jenny's voice is calm but firm. "These premises are exempt from any form of entry by police or military units. You'll have to move along."

"What a load of crap!" The speaker is enraged. "We're Achilles Pod, lady. We have authority to search anywhere we choose, no exceptions."

"I have it in writing that your authority doesn't extend to these premises," Jenny interrupts. "You may read it for yourself."

She does something with a control box she holds in her hand and passes a document through a narrow opening in the force field. The black-clads crowd forward to look over the speaker's shoulder. To Ash, peering down from his hiding place in the loft, Jenny Cruz seems awfully small standing in front of them, force field or no. She is a slender tiger facing much bigger black panthers. Where are the others?

The leader of the Achilles Pod unit shakes his head. "This doesn't countermand our orders. It doesn't even apply. We have the right to enter any and all businesses and dwellings . . ."

"You don't," she interrupts. "Not here. It says quite clearly in paragraph six—and I quote, in case you missed it—'any and all situations.' That's what this is, isn't it? An 'any and all situation'? Look again. See it, right there near the top of the second page? In bold letters, for the sight challenged."

She is not quite mocking him, but she is definitely in his face. He reads and tries once more. "I don't know who you think you are, you 'tweener garbage, but no one shuts out an Achilles Pod unit when it . . ."

"It doesn't matter who I am," she says sharply, stopping him once again midsentence. "What matters is the signature at the bottom of the page. Did you bother to take a close look at it?"

He pauses, looks down, reads carefully, and mutters something. The others in his squad glance at each other. A few step back at once.

"How did you get this?" the speaker demands. "You must have stolen it! No one has this sort of exemption! We're coming in! How about I just use this on you?" He holds up his weapon for her to see. "How about I just blow you to pieces and then we come in? Think that might do the job?"

Jenny Cruz shrugs. "That's your choice. I can't stop you. In fact, you don't need to bother with weapons."

She holds up the control, and the air between them shimmers and the laser bars disappear. The way in is open. Ash can hardly believe Jenny has done this. She is allowing them inside!

They start to crowd forward when she holds up her hand.

"Not so fast. I am denying you the right to enter. If you ignore me, you do so in defiance of the written order of exemption you hold in your hand. I have noted your badge and unit number on my vidview, Unit Commander Cray. In sixty seconds a message will be dispatched automatically to the gentleman who approved and signed this order, to tell him you have willfully disobeyed it. Whether or not I am dead. I suggest you have your excuses for whatever you choose to do fully prepared."

Long moments follow in which no one moves. *They will enter now*, Ash thinks. *They have to. They will lose face if they don't. Besides, who could these men be so afraid of that they would back off?*

But back off they do. The unit leader draws himself up, gives Jenny a smirk. "There's no reason for us to force our way in. There are other ways. I can promise you, though, you little freak, I will be back, and I'll tear up your little piece of paper and feed it to you."

Jenny steps forward again. "You do whatever you feel you have to. It won't change anything. Good day."

She turns and begins walking back toward the building. She leaves the laser bars down, an indication of her confidence. The black-clads hesitate, and Ash clearly hears a few of them use "freak" and "'tweener" among other, less pleasant words before the entire bunch begins moving down the street to the next set of buildings, muttering among themselves.

Jenny Cruz lets them go. She never looks around. She never flinches at the words they speak; there is no change in her expression. Her courage in the face of such threats is astonishing. Ash doesn't know if he has ever seen its like.

T.J. reappears. "Did you see that?" he asks, grinning from ear to ear. "Was she not wonderful? She's never afraid, that girl. Not our Jenny. She'll stand up to anyone. She never backs down."

Ash is impressed; there's no denying it. He finds himself smiling along with T.J. They leave the safe room and descend into the bays where the others are grouped around Jenny, congratulating her on the way she handled herself.

"Are you all right?" she asks Ash at once.

"I should be asking you," he responds with a grin.

She pulls a face. "We've had this happen before. The Shoe saw it coming years ago when he first started Street Freaks. So he got the exemption. I don't know how he managed it, but he did." She looks past him to the others. "Let's get back to work. T.J., find something for Ash to do. Teach him a skill."

She moves off. Ash follows T.J. over to a panel with a digital readout and a bank of response nodes and watches him maneuver his way through a set of stations and commands until he reaches one marked FRONT GATES. It takes him seconds to do this, his movements so fast that Ash can barely follow them. Although follow them he does.

"You stick around long enough, one day I'll teach you to operate it," T.J. says in what seems to be an attempt at suggesting Ash might have a future at Street Freaks.

But Ash is not sure he wants a future with these people. He's not sure this is where he should be. He is still conflicted about what to do now that his father is dead. Just thinking about it causes him to cringe.

"Let's go," T.J. says.

He leads Ash into Bay 2, where a snow-white racer with fins and massive air scoops sits up on the lift. The racer is the opposite of Starfire. It has protrusions and add-ons everywhere, a muscular, dangerous-looking vehicle with little regard for sleekness.

Ash walks around it, taking a closer look, as T.J. lowers it onto the composite. "What are the air scoops for? Does the engine need cooling?"

T.J. smirks. "Naw. This one's for some rich guy who thinks he knows what a racer should look like but hopes never to have to prove it. He just wants something to show off. Fancies himself a stud, thinks the car will prove it." He shrugs. "A weekend warrior. Took him out for a drive in the Flick a while back. Begged me to let him find out what racing was like. He crapped himself. Literally. Worse wuss than you, fish."

Ash says nothing, just stares at him. T.J. shrugs. "She's ready for pickup after a final polish. That's your job for today. But it isn't as easy as you might think. A proper polish requires some skill. I'm here to teach you how it's done."

He does so, introducing Ash to a series of small handheld polishing and buffing machines with attachments, each suited for use on certain parts of a car—body, tires, chrome, leather, carpet. After a few experimental tries and a few corrective comments from T.J., Ash is left to complete his task.

The best he can say, when he is finally done, is that it has helped pass the time. But T.J. seems happy with his efforts, and that provides a much-needed sense of satisfaction. By then it is nightfall, and the others are closing up shop for the day. No one has come by for Starfire, even though Jenny said the racer needed to be ready.

But Ash has other more pressing concerns. Jenny Cruz has decided he needs a makeover.

"You can't leave the building looking the way you do," she says. "Reader boards all over the city are still showing your face. You can still be found on vidviews too. 'Has anybody seen this person? Where, exactly?' You look entirely too much like yourself to go anywhere. We have to give you a different look."

She and Holly take Ash into one of the bathrooms and make some changes to his appearance. They dye his hair brown and give him tinted contact lenses. The lenses aren't magnified and his vision remains unaffected, but the feeling of something in his eyes is uncomfortable. Holly laughs when he complains, telling him he can't begin to know about real discomfort.

They take away his clothes too, replacing them with a gray work uniform bearing the Street Freaks logo. The clothes are loose fitting and well worn from previous use. More will be provided later when they can scrounge them up. They take away his expensive shoes and give him a pair of work boots, the leather scuffed and cracked. They pierce his ears and fill the holes with rings and studs—seven of them in all. They shave portions of his newly dyed hair along the sides with parallel lines above each ear. Racing stripes, they tell him.

When they are done, they let Ash have a look in the mirror. What stares back at him is a metalhead wannabe caricature that makes him cringe but is at least different enough to suggest he won't be recognized.

He sits down afterward on a bench in the bays, watching T.J. and Woodrow install a voice-sentient navigator in a new vehicle that has mysteriously appeared during the time of his makeover, and tries to get used to his new look. Holly is working on placing the steel exoskeleton of a Viper 80 over in Bay 1. She does this by simply lifting it up and adjusting it in midair before setting it down on the lift. He stares in disbelief, not quite believing what he has just witnessed. He has never known anyone with such strength.

A few minutes later, she comes over to sit down beside him.

"Cool look, fish," she says, giving him an approving nod.

He shrugs. "If you say so."

"How you holding up?"

"Okay."

"I'm sorry about your father. I need to say it again. Losing a parent is the worst."

"Guess you would know. T.J. told me how you lost yours."

"Does require some adjustments. Especially when they chose not to want me anymore. Just gave up and let me go." She makes a face. "But I've had time to get past it. You haven't. You're still in the middle of it. You have to stay strong."

"I'm working on it. Being here helps."

He says this because he thinks it will make her feel good, and he wants that. After all, she saved him from Ponce and the Razor Boys, and she's been looking out for him ever since.

"Is T.J. still giving you a hard time?" she asks.

"Not really. At first, yeah, but he pretty much let it go after we took that drive. He talked about how he was made, how he was a genetic experiment. He's pretty bitter. But he says it was harder for you."

"Yeah, he likes to think so. It gives him some sort of emotional uplift thinking someone has it worse than he does. But he's not fooling anyone. He's emotionally crippled by what was done to him. He hates it that he wasn't made like most kids. Even Woodrow had parents. T.J. was a test-tube baby. His parents don't exist. That's why he leaned on you about your father. He's just unhappy about not having one himself."

"He was good about showing me how to do stuff with the racers."

"Well, he's a good guy when he wants to be. Very talented. Physically, he can do anything. He's got all the skills."

"He doesn't think so."

"That what he told you?"

"In so many words."

"He would. Didn't explain, I bet?"

"Not really. Just stopped talking."

"Okay, then." She leans close. "He talks about me, I can talk about him. Genetic engineers conceived him and his fellow test-tube babies to be perfect soldiers, the first of a new army for the U.T. It all worked out just as everyone expected except for one thing. Almost all of them lacked the sort of killer instinct their makers were looking for. T.J. was one of those who never found it. They threw him out once they knew. Threw all of them out in the end, I guess. The Shoe found T.J. on the street and brought him here. He was good enough for Street Freaks."

"But he drives like he's not afraid of anything."

"Oh, sure. But wars aren't won by driving fast. You have to kill people. The scientists who made him and the other test-tube soldiers were told to produce killers; that didn't happen."

"So why is he bitter about that? Seems like he should be happy. Does he want to be a killer?"

Holly smiles sadly. "What he wants is to be needed. What he wants is not to be a discard. He can't get past the fact that this is how things are. Doesn't matter that we're all in the same boat. Doesn't matter we don't think of him that way. It's enough that he does." She shakes her head. "He's always trying to prove himself. Always trying to make up for some imagined failing."

Ash doesn't quite understand, but he doesn't know T.J. well enough to press the matter.

"There's probably something more to all this," Holly allows after a moment. "But if there is, T.J. isn't talking about it."

They are quiet after that, sitting together companionably, watching T.J. and Woodrow. Ash tries to imagine what it would be like to be either T.J. or Holly—the one with no parents, the other with parents who gave up on her. Both living in engineered bodies, both living with enhancements to their physiques and suffering emotional problems as a result. Holly hasn't said this is true of her, but he senses it is. There's anger that lurks just below the surface of her confident, snarky self. He remembers T.J.'s reply when he said that Holly seemed very strong.

You don't know the half of it.

He probably doesn't. There's probably a lot he doesn't know about all these kids.

Which is reinforced when Holly says, "Jen, T.J., and I have to go out later. We're leaving you with Woodrow."

"Okay," he agrees. What else is he going to say?

"You'll bunk in with Woodrow and T.J. while you're here. We'll show you your bed before we leave. We might be back late, so don't wait up."

She waits a moment for his response, and when he doesn't provide it, she nudges him hard.

"Sure," he answers quickly.

"That's what I thought you said." She rises, gives him a look, and walks off.

Ash stays where he is until dinnertime, thinking over his decision to take up temporary residence at Street Freaks. There aren't that many choices to begin with, of course. He can stay put and wait for the mysterious Shoe to appear. He can leave and go to his uncle Cyrus. Or he can grab onto some nebulous third choice that maybe, possibly, improbably might miraculously prove superior to the other two.

But staying put is the only thing that makes sense at the moment. He wants to feel secure, and while finding his way to Uncle Cyrus might seem a more logical choice, he can't quite convince himself it makes sense. Maybe it's the distance that exists between his uncle and himself, a distance of more than miles and years. If there had been shared holidays and vacations, vidmails exchanged, vidchats initiated, regular visits of some sort, it might be different. But his uncle hasn't seen or even spoken to him since he was maybe ten. He doesn't remember the last time his uncle or father visited each other. Wouldn't you expect brothers to try to get together more often than once a decade?

But it's also about wanting to see what Jenny Cruz can come up with. She seems to believe she can gain access to protected BioGen files, an impossibility on the face of things. But he would have said that about standing up to Achilles Pod too, and she managed that quite handily. So why not give her a chance?

He eats dinner with the others, but he doesn't talk much and they choose to leave him alone. Even T.J. lets him be. After dinner, everyone but Woodrow disappears through a door that opens underneath the second-floor stairway, locks clicking into place as the door closes again. The bot with a real boy's head, this strange combination of flesh and metal, pays no attention. Instead, he invites Ash to sit down and talk while he begins putting together a new computer, the parts laid out all around him in meticulous order.

"We build our own at Street Freaks," he says. "Well, mostly me. I do the actual construction. I have a talent for it. Jenny does programming. Hand me that bit of wire, please. No, the larger one next to it. The red one with the yellow band. Yes, that one. Uh-huh."

He is focused and intense. His head bends close to his work, his flexible limbs twisting this way and that as he maneuvers various pieces into place and fastens them. Circuit boards, chips, and tiny bits of metal and composite materials that have no meaning to Ash are obviously no mystery to the bot boy. Ash watches silently, fascinated at his dexterity and sure-handedness. Woodrow pauses now and then to glance over and smirks when he sees the look on Ash's face.

"You're wondering how I can do all this without a real body, aren't you?" Woodrow shrugs. "You get used to it. I have artificial limbs, but sometimes it seems like I can still feel things. Like I'm still flesh and blood."

"How does your brain communicate with your body?" Ash asks. "If you want something done, how do you . . . ?"

Woodrow smiles. "It just sort of does. I think about what I want to do, and my body does it. I suppose it's pretty much how it works for you—only my body doesn't feel anything." He shrugs. "It's weird, I know."

He goes quiet again, his mechanical digits moving dexterously to fit parts in place, tiny wires and screws.

"I had parents once," he offers finally. "A mom and a dad. I remember them. They died in an accident. Right after I turned eight. I lived with an aunt after that, but I didn't like her much."

"Were you always like this?" Ash asks. "You know." He makes a gesture in the general direction of the boy's torso and appendages.

"Uh-huh, I was born like this. Metal body and all. First of a kind." He pulls a face. "No, I wasn't always like this! Don't be stupid."

"No, I meant, do you remember how it was before?"

Woodrow shakes his head. "Not really. My body started to wither when I was ten. A wasting disease, the doctors called it. They had a more scientific name for it, but I forget what it's called. My body just started to shrink. It just gave up. Everyone thought I was going to die. My aunt even said I should prepare myself. How do you do that, I wonder? Prepare to die. Is there a way to do that? I sure couldn't find it."

"But you didn't die."

"Obviously."

"But you didn't get better."

"No, I got worse. The only reason I'm still alive is because my IQ is off the charts. I had something of a reputation by then in certain scientific and medical circles. I was tested early and often, and some of those who tested me thought I was worth saving. In the end, they could only manage it by making me like this. Half of one thing and half of another."

"They saved you, but they let you work at Street Freaks?"

Woodrow laughs. "No, they saved me, and I ran away. Well, wheeled away, actually. My running days were all done by then. I just waited for the right moment, and off I went."

He seems so cheerful about it that for a moment Ash doesn't know what to say. A preteen boy dying of some unnamed wasting disease gets turned into a bot with only his human head salvaged. And then he decides to run away from the very people who helped him?

"I know what you're thinking," Woodrow says. "But being saved doesn't always turn out to be as beneficial as you might think. Once I was turned into this, I was looked at differently. All of a sudden, I was considered valuable property. The specialists who turned me into a bot boy did so to save my brain. The rest of me was just a necessary add-on. Anyway, they intended to benefit from their efforts. It became apparent early on what they had in mind. They wanted me to behave like a regular bot would—to do what I was told and not argue. They didn't think of me as a boy anymore. Guess that was because I was more bot than boy by then. I didn't feel that way inside, but they never cared much about my feelings."

Ash leans back and exhales sharply. "You must have been scared out of your wits. And really angry."

"That would be true. But as the old saying goes: All's well that ends well. It all worked out."

Ash finds Woodrow's equanimity astounding. He knows he would not be so forgiving. But listening to the boy speak of it makes him feel a little embarrassed that he is spending so much time worrying about his own situation. Woodrow has had a tougher time of it than he has.

"So how did you end up here?" he asks.

"The same way I escaped all those doctors and scientists that wanted to make use of me. The Shoe."

"He brought you here?"

"He did. I'm still not sure how he managed it, but I've been with him ever since. He found a way to keep me, to stop all those mad scientists from taking me back. Except for not being able to go out much in public, my life is pretty good. I like what I do, and I like my friends. We're a family."

It is the second time the word "family" has been mentioned by someone at Street Freaks, and once again Ash feels it is the right word. One way or another, all of them have been recruited by the Shoe, brought to Street Freaks, and given a place in a world that doesn't like or trust differences as extreme as what Woodrow and the others represent. It reminds him a little of what he shared with Faulkner, Beattie, and Willis4. They had been a family too. Not a normal family but a family nevertheless. Not as advanced as the boys and girls of Street Freaks, but they had shared his home and given him someone to hold on to after his mother died and his father retreated into his work. They had provided him with a sense of security, and he had never thought of them as anything less than family.

"What's the Shoe like?" he asks, wanting to stop thinking about what was lost.

Woodrow cocks an eyebrow. "Hard to describe."

"Like a father?"

Woodrow goes back to work on his project. "Once you've met him, you can decide for yourself."

Moments later, a side door unlocks and a girl walks into the garage. For just a moment, as she passes through the beam of light cast by a streetlamp shining through the building's windows, her face is visible. Ash catches a glimpse of short-cropped blond hair, exquisitely perfect features, and bright cerulean-blue eyes. She glances over but does not speak as she continues on and disappears up the stairs.

"Hi, Cay," Woodrow calls after her without looking up.

There is no reply. Ash stares after her, thinking, *Holy crap!*

"Who was that?" he asks, his throat tightening as he tries to keep his voice steady.

"Oh, that's Cay Dumont. She lives here too." Woodrow tinkers with the computer parts. "Don't worry. You'll meet her tomorrow. She'll be here at breakfast."

Ash looks up the stairs into the dark emptiness left in the wake of her passing. He saw her for perhaps two seconds, but it is enough.

Whatever else she might be, Cay Dumont is heartbreakingly beautiful.

- 8 -

Ash wakes early the next morning. His sleep was sound enough that he didn't hear T.J. come to bed, but the other boy is there when he looks over. Woodrow, it turns out, doesn't use a bed; he sleeps standing up. He is parked in a corner of the room with his head supported by a neck pillow and his eyes closed. That portion of the early-morning sky visible through the windows is still dark, moon and stars hidden behind a screen of clouds.

After taking a minute to register where he is—because at first he is uncertain, at least until he sees T.J. and Woodrow— Ash climbs out of bed and dresses in the clothes he was given yesterday during his makeover. He uses the bathroom down the hall, looking at the stranger in the mirror for long moments as he applies soniclean rays to his teeth, trying to get used to his new look. He decides quickly enough it will take some time and effort.

Still only half awake, he goes downstairs into the kitchen and prowls around until he finds some orange juice in the refrigerator and some bread in the pantry and makes this his breakfast. He thinks it will be enough, but he is hungrier than expected and wolfs down everything.

After finishing, he sits there for a time, waiting to see if anyone else will appear. No one does. So he gets up and walks out into the bays, looking around in a darkened space lit only by a bank of dim lights that run the length of the back wall and barely penetrate the gloom. He starts thinking about the girl from last night—Cay—even though he is fully aware he should be thinking of other things. He is pondering the quixotic nature of his instant attraction to her when he notices a pale light coming from the office Jenny Cruz occupies. Through the interior windows, he sees her sitting in the dark at her desk, studying a computer screen filled with images of documents.

When Ash knocks on the door, she looks up and beckons. He enters and stands there for a moment, looking around. Everything that disappeared during the confrontation with Achilles Pod is back in place, restored as if by magic.

"We've had some practice dealing with unexpected visits," she offers, noting his surprise.

"Weren't you afraid out there? Telling Achilles Pod they couldn't come in?"

"Once, I would have been terrified. But I've had some practice with being scared, and I know from experience how to deal with it." She paused. "Did you sleep well?"

He sits in the chair across from her. "I slept okay. It was weird waking and not knowing at first where I was. How long have you been up?"

She shrugs. "I don't sleep much. I don't seem to need it. Maybe it's because of my condition. I have to sleep on my side because of the tanks. I have to be careful of the exterior ports. When I was little, I used to sleep like a normal person. But after the operation, I never slept well again. It's all right, though. It was a fair trade."

"What sort of operation did you have? Do you mind my asking?"

"I don't mind. I'm used to it. When I was six, I developed a blood disorder. My blood was so bad it required constant cleaning. I was confined to bed twenty-four hours a day, every day, while a machine constantly washed my blood to keep me alive.

This went on for more than a year. But then one day the doctors told me of a new procedure that would allow me to leave the bed and return to the world outside my room. If I survived."

"They told you that? If you *survived*?"

"By then, we were beyond mincing words. My parents were desperate to find something to help me. They could see what was happening. I was growing more and more depressed. I couldn't see the point of my life anymore. So I said yes. Any gamble was worth taking. The operation took ten hours. They installed ports in my body to circulate my blood—to pump it out and then in again. The tanks on my back clean it for me. My own portable blood washer. Everything is connected to my body sheath. I remove it only to wash myself. I have a spare if anything should go wrong with this one."

"It must have taken some getting used to."

"What took getting used to was moving around again after a year in bed. I couldn't even walk without help at first. It took months of rehab. I learned how to move around in my new skin. I learned how to do everything in it. This was going to be my new life, so I had to make it work."

"They couldn't just replace your blood?"

"Sure. But my body would just turn it bad again. I know because they tried that too. They tried everything before they went to the blood washer." She pauses. "Do you want to talk about your father?"

Ash nods. "Did you find anything out?"

"A few things. Your father was working on a special project when he died, something sensitive enough that BioGen locked out virtually everyone. Since I don't know which people aren't locked out and can only guess at their identities, I have to work my way into the records through the back door. But for something to be kept this quiet, it must be toxic."

"I told you he said it was dangerous for him if they found out he was trying to do anything about it."

"Well, I can't tell if he was actually doing something or not since I don't know what it is. But I think we can assume that there was some sort of involvement. BioGen works on all sorts of genetics-related projects. You know that, don't you? Your father must have told you."

"He did."

"So it's like hunting for a needle in a haystack. Your father helped developed Sparx, didn't he—those energy supplements everyone takes? Supposed to help keep you positive and focused, help you work better? They've been offering something like that for decades, but Sparx are the first that actually work, and they don't appear to have any negative side effects. Do you take them?"

Ash shakes his head. "I don't like medications."

He says nothing about ProLx, still unwilling to talk about it. It occurs to him suddenly that he hasn't taken a dosage since yesterday after fleeing the high-rise, and he needs to take one again by midday. He still has a small supply, but he will need to find a pharmacy before it runs out.

"I was just wondering if your father ever said anything that might suggest what this secret project was. Did he talk to you about it?"

Ash shrugs. "He never talked about much of anything work related."

"Did he ever suggest he might be talking to someone else? You know, to the media? Do you think he might have been a whistle-blower?"

"He never said anything to suggest that."

"Well, anyway, here's something else I found out. Since your father's death, BioGen has gone into lockdown. They've closed their home office and central lab and restricted admittance to staff. Your sky tower home has been sealed off too. No one is being allowed in. L.A. Preventatives have closed off the unit to everyone, the building management included."

He stares at her. "Why would they do that?"

She cocks an eyebrow. "Good question. What are they investigating that requires your home be sealed? There's been no public report on what happened there. Everything has been about your father's death and BioGen. So that's what I'm looking into. The Shoe will be back later today. He might have information about your father that I don't. I'll make it a point to talk to him about it." She glances past him. "I see that the others are up and about. Why don't you go out and join them?"

He immediately thinks of Cay and feels a rush of anticipation. He tries to appear casual as he departs, even though every fiber of his body screams at him to hurry. He doesn't know what it is about this girl, but the feeling is intoxicating.

It is also ridiculous. He is not so far gone that he can't realize this. He hasn't even met her. He knows nothing about her. Why should he feel like this just because she's pretty?

Well, for one thing, she's not just pretty—she's beautiful.

He leaves Jenny and goes into the dining room. Cay is sitting alone at one end of a long table. If possible, she is even more beautiful in the daylight. She has an ethereal quality that is mesmerizing. As if she might be too perfect to be real. As if she were otherworldly.

Holly and T.J. are engaged in an intense conversation at the other end. Woodrow is nowhere to be seen. Without pausing, Ash walks directly over to Cay and holds out his hand. "I'm Ash," he tells her. "I just got here yesterday."

"Good for you," she says, barely glancing up.

He hesitates and then withdraws his hand. Not exactly the response he was expecting. "I wanted to say hello . . ."

"And now you have. Go sit with the others, why don't you?"

Anger surfaces. "I just thought it would be polite to introduce myself . . ."

Suddenly she is looking directly at him, her eyes so intense he cannot finish what he started to say. She regards him with such a flat and openly hostile stare he finds himself wishing he could sink right into the floor.

"Look, Jesse or whatever your name is, you don't have to explain yourself. What you need to do is notice that I am sitting here and *they*"—she gestures toward the other end of the table—"are sitting there. There's a reason for this. Can you guess what it is?"

Ash turns without a word and walks away, thoroughly humiliated.

Moving over to the serving table, he fixes himself a bowl of cereal while trying to recover his composure and then walks over to sit with T.J. and Holly. He tries hard not to look down at the other end of the table, but he can't help himself.

"Feeling a little hot until the collar?" T.J. presses, exchanging a look with Holly.

"Let him alone," she says quietly. "Give it a few minutes."

The cereal has no taste to it. The other two sit with him, sipping coffee and saying nothing. The world seems to have come to a stop; Ash can't even be sure he is breathing. He thinks he should walk back over and defend himself. But when at one point he starts to rise, Holly pulls him firmly down again and shakes her head no.

Eventually, Cay leaves the room. No words are exchanged when she does. Once she has departed, Holly speaks.

"Sorry about that. She's just in one of her moods."

"Should have told you what she's like when that happens," T.J. adds quickly.

Ash looks from one to the other. "What's wrong with her?"

"Where to start?" T.J. sneers. "Lots of attitude, for one thing."

"No kidding. She could give you lessons."

"And she's not real, for another."

Ash is not sure what T.J. is saying. "What do you mean by that? Not real how?"

"Don't talk about her like that, T.J.!" Holly snaps angrily. "How would you like it if we said that about you?" She turns to Ash.

"What he's trying to say in his irritating T.J. way is that Cay Dumont is a synth. She's manufactured. Worse for her, she's a pleasure synth. She was made to satisfy men's sexual needs. She was built specifically for that purpose and that purpose alone; it's her function in life. To attract men and provide them with sexual pleasure. She doesn't do it because she's hot for the idea. She does it because that's how she's made."

"She's always got her mojo working," T.J. chimes in, which earns him a solid punch on the shoulder from Holly. "What? Am I wrong?"

Ash sits back, digesting this new information. Ash has heard of pleasure synths, of course. He doesn't live in a cave. He knows about their function. He knows they are made to look impossibly beautiful and to be irresistible. Still, his attraction to her feels natural, even knowing what she is. But does it matter how he feels? Doesn't it only matter that it was induced?

"Oh, don't look so hangdog." T.J. give an exaggerated sigh. "Everyone who comes near her has the same reaction. No one is immune. No man, anyway." He casts a quick glance at Holly, who's scowling. "No matter what Holly wants to believe, Cay's not real. She isn't made of flesh and blood like we are. She was manufactured using artificial substances and fluids. She's a very expensive item created for use by very wealthy men. She's a toy."

Ash gives him a look. "Can we please stop talking about her?"

"All right, all right!" T.J. holds up his hands in surrender. "Just wanted you to know before things got any worse."

"Well, they're already bad enough." Ash stands. He feels embarrassed and foolish. "If there are any more surprises, maybe you could tell me about them in advance."

He slinks out of the room, not knowing where he is going and not caring. He just needs to get away. He's never encountered a pleasure synth before—never even been convinced the stories about them are real. But there isn't much room for doubt now. He still can't believe he was so completely besotted with her. Still is besotted, if he allows himself to admit it. He looks at her and he wants to be with her. He wants to be as close as he can get.

Sitting alone on a bench at the far end of Bay 5, where Starfire waits to be claimed, he slowly calms down. As he does, the feelings she generated in him begin to fade. He wonders suddenly what she is doing here. What need does the mysterious Shoe have for a pleasure synth?

The obvious answer is not one he cares to dwell on.

T.J. appears a few minutes later and puts him to work polishing a racer scheduled for delivery by week's end. This one is a sleek crimson Borlon-Essex Flash model Ash recognizes from pictures T.J. showed him the day before. Even though it is fresh off an assembly line he still hasn't seen, there are smears and smudges here and there, and the cleaning takes several hours of meticulous work. But it keeps him occupied, and that is what he needs. Even so, he looks up from his efforts every so often and casually surveys the bays farther down for any sign of Cay Dumont, half hoping she will appear.

She does not.

At one point while cleaning the Flash, Ash sees T.J. backing Starfire out of the last bay and onto the composite drive fronting Street Freaks. He looks out to see who has come to claim her. No one is there. He watches T.J. exit the vehicle and come back inside. Still no one appears. After a while, he goes back to work.

The next time he looks up, Starfire is gone.

T.J. comes over to stand next to him, watching him work. "I think we might make a Street Freak out of you yet," he says.

Ash shakes his head. "No thanks. I'm happy just being a fish."

T.J. doesn't say anything, but he doesn't move away either. Ash finishes with the tires and rims and steps back to view his work. "Is she still here?"

T.J. doesn't need to ask who Ash means. "She went out about an hour ago. She has things to do."

"Why is she here in the first place if she's a pleasure synth?"

T.J. exhales sharply. When he speaks, there is an edge to his voice. "You just got here. You don't know all the rules yet. So I'm going to cut you some slack. But I'm also going to tell you something important. Only once, though, because you've supposedly got this amazing memory and you shouldn't need to be told anything twice. We do a lot of things here at Street Freaks that we don't talk about with anyone. 'Anyone' includes fish like you. Among those things is the answer to the question you just asked."

Ash looks at him. T.J. is looking right back. The expression on his face suggests he has no further interest in discussing the matter.

Ash turns back to the racer. "I like this model. How does she run on the Straightaway?"

T.J. hesitates, decides he deserves an answer, and launches into a comprehensive explanation about why the Flash is fast but not as fast as Starfire. Ash listens with half an ear. He is thinking about his father's death. He is thinking how his father must have believed he could protect himself. Drivers of race cars must think like that too. They must believe that if they do everything right, they can beat the odds and stay alive. But sometimes they don't do everything right. Sometimes they make mistakes. And sometimes there are intervening factors and unforeseen circumstances that disrupt even the best of efforts and the most carefully executed plans.

When that happens, you stand to lose everything.

Right in the middle of T.J.'s explanation about the Flash, Ash breaks down. It happens so fast that he is bent over with his face buried in his hands and his eyes squeezed shut before he knows it. He's lost everything that matters. Everything. His family, his home, his way of life, and his chances for the future he had always imagined for himself. What he has now is a temporary refuge from which he can be ejected at any moment, a group of strange kids who are struggling with their own uncertain lives and secrets they won't talk about, and a dwindling supply of ProLx, which he needs to replenish soon if he is to stay alive.

He has let his emotions get the better of him, and he hates it. He should be stronger than this. But he understands so little of what is happening. He puts it on his father, blames him for all of it. His cold, distant, never-there-for-him father, obsessed with his job and his research. Killed because of it, likely. Dead because his obsession overrode his common sense. Why didn't he give a little thought to Ash? Why did he allow all this to happen?

When T.J. finally reaches down in a gesture of sympathy, Ash shoves him away. "Get off me!" he snaps.

"Okay, okay." T.J. backs off. "I just wanted to make sure you were all right."

"I'm fine. This happens now and then. A condition of . . ." He can't finish what he is about to say. The lie is so apparent it is ludicrous. He pulls himself together and gets to his feet.

"Got an idea," T.J. says at once. "We need a break. Let's take the Flick out for a spin. You can drive."

Ash straightens, staring at him. "What?"

"Hey, don't make me rethink this. I'm making a one-time offer. You want it or not?"

Ash nods at once. "Let's go."

They drop everything and head for the exit door leading onto the back lot. Jenny watches them leave without comment. Holly glances over and then turns away. Ash wonders how much they saw. For him, it's already old news. He's shelved it with all the other discarded, useless pieces of his life. His father's dead. He isn't. You got to keep moving forward or you stall out.

T.J. unlocks the Flick and directs Ash into the driver's seat. "You think you know what to do?" he asks.

Ash looks at the dashboard controls and nods. "I watched you drive her. I remember all of it."

"Okay, but be careful. Ask, if you're not sure."

Ash powers up the Flick, revs her engine hard, eases off the thruster pedal, releases the brake, and steers her out of her parking slot toward the front gates. When they get close, the gates open automatically, the laser bars shut down, and the tire shredders retract. Ash drives to the edge of the Straightaway, gives the traffic a quick look . . .

And floors it.

The Flick explodes down the composite like a savage beast, its engine roaring with pleasure. Ash accelerates so quickly that T.J. is thrown against his seat back, and a gasp of surprise escapes his lips. But then he recovers and begins to yell encouragement.

"That's the way you do it, fish! Pump it up! Go faster! She wants to be driven!"

Ash complies, shifting gears smoothly, taking her up notch after notch. The cars they pass come and go in a blur of colors. Their speed is so great that they are past other traffic almost before they can be certain what it is. Ash is grinning, his adrenaline pumping, his excitement blocking away everything but the moment. He has the Flick going nearly as fast as T.J. did on their first ride. He wants to exceed this; he wants to go so fast he is flying.

But he remembers T.J.'s warning and slows instead, easing the Flick back until she is running even with the cars around her, then turning her onto a side street and slowing to a stop against a walkway curb. Wordlessly, he exchanges a look with T.J.

"Told you," he says.

"Yeah, you did," the other boy says with a grin. "Guess you really have done some driving."

Ash shrugs. "A little."

"More than a little. Where exactly?"

"Africa."

"What? There's nothing in Africa! Wait, you drove across the Masai Veldt? In what?"

"Stripped-down Cherokees."

"How did you get your hands on those?"

"Don't ask."

"You swiped them, didn't you? So when did all this happen? How long ago? How old were you?"

Ash smiles. "I was ten."

T.J. stares at him. "You were not. No one drives like that at ten."

"I did."

"Look at you. Still waters do run deep. You're something else, fish."

He tells Ash to take them back to Street Freaks but doesn't say how to do it. So Ash drives around a little longer, only testing his limits when he gets back on the Straightaway. T.J. doesn't say a word. He just lets Ash drive.

When they pull back through the gates and drive around to the back lot to park the Flick, T.J. looks over. "Maybe it would be best if we didn't say anything about you driving."

Ash nods. "Driving what?"

They walk through the back door to find that Jenny is waiting. "Saw you drive in. Looked like Ash was driving. But I must have been mistaken. You wouldn't allow that, would you, T.J.?"

She doesn't wait for an answer. Instead, she links her arm with Ash's. "You come with me. The Shoe is back, and he wants you in his office."

- 9 -

Jenny leads Ash into her office. Inside, the Shoe is waiting. Whatever Ash was expecting, it certainly isn't what he finds. It doesn't bring him to a full mouth-open, eyes-wide stop, but it does cause him to toss aside immediately all of the possibilities he has been considering.

The Shoe presents a stunning picture. He is tall and slight, not in the manner of scarecrows or streetlamps but certainly in the way of fashion models. His features are finely formed, everything just a little softer than sharp. He is handsome without being pretty, his hair white-blond and his eyes a brilliant blue. He is of indeterminate age, neither young nor old, and he exudes an aura of boundless energy. His presence is commanding, generated less perhaps by his looks than by the self-assuredness he projects as he rises from behind his desk to make a quick but unmistakable examination of his guest. Ash cannot help but feel he is being measured against a standard devised by the man facing him, and the results will determine the direction of the conversation they are about to have.

"Ashton Collins," the Shoe greets him, extending his hand. "Welcome to Street Freaks. Pleased to have you with us."

The way he says it suggests he is doing more than being

polite—he is being genuine. Ash takes his hand, finding his grip surprisingly strong.

"You've had quite a time of it," the Shoe observes, coming around the desk to place both hands on Ash's shoulders in a fatherly gesture. "I don't know that I would have been as composed and resourceful as you were in making your way here. It must have been frightening to have your house invaded and your bots destroyed. Hazmats. Ugly things created to perform ugly tasks. And then your father's death. Uglier still. But you are safe here, and we are going to do our very best to help you stay that way."

He gestures to one of the chairs facing the desk. "Why don't we sit? Jenny, give us a moment alone please."

As Jenny closes the door behind her, the Shoe returns to his chair. He sits carefully, straightening his jacket, a gesture that suggests a man who values his clothes and appearance. Ash understands why. The Shoe is wearing creased slacks and a matching jacket of soft blue silk over a pink shirt that must have cost an arm and a leg. He could have walked into any vidview fashion room and been entirely at home.

"Now, then, let's talk about your situation a bit," he suggests, as if asking permission.

There is a peculiar lilt to the way the Shoe speaks, an accent of sorts, but one Ash cannot place. His tone of voice is not particularly deep, but his enunciation and volume are such that it draws you in. He seems to be well practiced in personal communication—a man who can command with words as well as appearance.

He reaches into a drawer of his desk, pulls out a pack of Sparx, and offers one to the boy. The Shoe doesn't seem to think this odd, although Ash finds it a bit weird and shakes his head no.

"What I want you to do for me," the Shoe says, "is to repeat everything you told the others. Jenny's already given me an overview, but I would like to hear it now in your own words. Everything you remember. Just start anywhere."

So Ash does. He goes through yesterday's events in their

entirety, starting with the attack on his home and ending with his arrival at Street Freaks. He leaves nothing out, including the fact that he still doesn't know what he is going to do next.

"Did you know my father?" he asks hopefully, finishing up.

"As a matter of fact, yes." The Shoe cocks an eyebrow. "We've done a little business in the past. But let's leave the matter of my relationship with your father for now. Let's talk about what seems obvious to me about this whole business."

"You mean why my father was killed? You do think he was killed, don't you? You don't think it was suicide?"

The Shoe gives him a look. "Your father was killed because he did something either to reveal or sabotage whatever he was working on for BioGen. It's obvious. What we don't know and have to find out is exactly what he was engaged in doing. But we need to talk about you first. I made some brief inquires earlier after talking with Jenny. There is a concerted effort afoot to track you down. This is not confined to any one police agency; it is system-wide. That level of commitment is usually reserved for the worst sort of criminal. It makes me wonder what they want with you."

"It makes me wonder too."

"It should. Those responsible for your father's death have brought pressure to bear on not only the L.A. Preventatives but also ORACLE. Hence, Achilles Pod. That suggests your enemies are people with a lot of power and influence at their fingertips. It points to BioGen because they were the ones your father feared. But why bother with you? I suspect it is because these people think you know something or are in possession of something that might expose them."

Ash frowns. "But that's ridiculous. I don't know anything. My father never told me what he was doing. This whole business is as much a mystery to me as it is to everyone else."

"Are you sure? Think carefully before you answer. Was there something your father said about his work at BioGen you might have forgotten or overlooked?"

Ash thinks it over for a few minutes. "Nothing." Then he leans forward impulsively. "Why are you helping me? You barely know me. You don't owe me this sort of effort. Why don't you just send me away and be done with it?"

"Are these your insecurities talking? Or your suspicions?" The Shoe smiles. His eyes twinkle.

"I don't want to be difficult," Ash says. "I appreciate the offer of help. But I'm pretty paranoid just now. One moment, my life makes sense. Everything is going along just fine, moving along smoothly. The next, I'm being hunted across all of L.A." He pauses. "Can we just say that instead of insecurity or suspicion it's curiosity?"

The Shoe laughs, rocking in his chair. "Why not? You're entitled to an answer in either case. I'm helping you because I liked your father. He was a decent, well-intentioned man who revealed himself to me in ways I may one day explain to you. He certainly didn't deserve to be killed and have his death labeled a suicide. I could ignore that and send you away. But then I would be directly responsible for what happens afterward, and I don't think I care to live with that."

"I do have somewhere else I could go, if you want me to."

"Oh, do you? To your Uncle Cyrus, perhaps?"

This catches Ash off guard. "You know about him?"

"Of course. It's my job to know about such men. A hard man, Cyrus. A smart, calculating man. He's driven by a passion to reform criminal justice and perhaps societal behavior in the bargain. He has great ambitions, great plans for the whole of the Territories, and I am certain he is fully engaged in pursuing them. He is not likely to let your father's death go uninvestigated. He will come to the same conclusions you and I have, and he will seek out those responsible."

"Then I should go to him."

"No, you should *not* go to him. Not right away, at least. Not until we know more than we do now. At Street Freaks, there are only six of us that need to keep your secret. At ORACLE, there are thousands. No matter how well-meaning or protective your uncle Cyrus, the danger of harm finding its way into your circle of protection if you choose to go there is much greater than here."

Ash thinks about it. There is something to what the Shoe says. He feels safe at Street Freaks, something he can't be sure of if he chooses to move again. The other kids—excluding Cay Dumont— are doing everything they can to make him feel he belongs there. He has already decided that trying to find his way to his uncle would be something of a crapshoot.

"All right," he agrees. "I'll stay if it's okay with you."

"Then it's settled!" The Shoe rubs his hands together in satis- faction and stands. "I have some work to do if we're to find a way to improve your situation. Jenny is using her considerable com- puter skills to investigate BioGen. She's quite adept and will find out something. While she is doing that, I will make a few personal visits to people who might be able to help in other ways. I want you to stay put. Your disguise is adequate but not flawless. I don't want you leaving the Zone for any reason—or even this building, unless you are in the company of at least one of the other kids. They know how to take care of themselves in this part of the city, and you don't. So you pay attention to them and do what they say. No arguments, no objections."

He reaches across the desk, hand extended. Ash grips it firmly, feeling better now than he has since he arrived. A moment later Jenny reappears and takes him out again.

"Guess you're stuck with me for a while longer," he tells her.

She nods. She doesn't seem surprised. "The Shoe can be very persuasive. What did he say?"

"He said he was going to look into things while you worked the computer."

Jenny nods. "He'll go into the Metro. He has lots of contacts there."

Ash hears a door close and looks back to see the Shoe head- ing for the mysterious door under the stairs. "Is he leaving already?"

"He doesn't like to waste time," Jenny says. "Besides, he prefers that his meetings take place at night. Fewer people around that way. Tell you what. Let's go talk with the others. They've been whining about a visit to Checkered Flag. Maybe we should break down and go."

Ash has no idea what Checkered Flag is, but when Jenny mentions the name to the others, they all become very excited. Everyone but Woodrow, who immediately says, "I don't like that place. I'll just stay here, thanks."

"Naw, you can't do that!" T.J. exclaims. "This is a party! We're celebrating Ash coming to stay with us. You are staying, aren't you, Ash?" He looks at Jenny Cruz. "Isn't that the reason you suggested Checkered Flag? A celebration for Ash?"

She nods. "Come on, Woodrow. No one will bother you. We'll make sure. Please?"

The others echo her plea, and finally the boy gives a reluctant nod, eliciting cheers all around. "Now back to work until tonight," Jenny orders.

Everyone disperses but Ash, who goes over to Jenny. "What, exactly, is Checkered Flag?" he asks.

She gives him a smirk. "You'll find out."

Since the day is already well along, he doesn't have long to wait. At quitting time, the sun is a red ball on the western horizon, and the poisonous L.A. air that Ash no longer worries about—though God knows why he has become so cavalier about its reputed side effects—is causing the sky to color up like a kaleidoscope. While the rest of the group waits in front of the building, T.J. retrieves a six-passenger Barrier Ram to serve as their transport. The Ram is a thick-bodied, jagged-edged monster similar to the vehicle in which Ponce and his Razor Boys were riding when they stopped Ash during his search for Street Freaks—only, this one is in better shape. The engine roars and spits flames from its tailpipes, and there is a decidedly vintage look and a dangerous feel to it.

"Hang on!" T.J. advises as he revs the engine until Ash is fairly certain the Ram will shake itself apart.

They rumble through the open gates, which promptly close behind them, and turn down the Straightaway. The four with working legs sit in regular seats. Woodrow's boxy frame is situated in an open space by locks that secure him to the floor. He seems resigned to his fate, a glum look on his young face. But he manages a quick smile when Ash catches his eye, so Ash smiles back.

The sixth seat sits empty. If she were there, it would belong to Cay. But there's been no sign of her since breakfast.

They reach Heads & Tails quickly, and this time the activity that was missing when Ash walked by on his way to Street Freaks is considerable. There are vehicles everywhere, big and small, bizarre and stunningly beautiful, racers and monster machines, some parked at the curb, some cruising past. Dance music blares from inside the building, a wall of sound that mere bricks and timber cannot contain. Neon brightens the corners and eaves, meshing with the huge sign that flashes HEADS & TAILS in steady cadence. Girls lean out of windows framed in scarlet lights, waving and calling out to passersby. A few stand outside on balconies, offering a none-too-subtle preview of what's available inside.

Ash glances over, wondering if Cay is there, and then hates himself for doing so. When she sees him looking, Holly gives him a nudge. "Don't worry. We won't make you go in there. It's not our kind of place."

"Might be his kind, Holly," T.J. calls over his shoulder from the driver's seat. "What about it, Ash-from-the-Metro?" When Ash ignores him, T.J. laughs cheerfully. "Hey, you can be yourself at Street Freaks, whatever you are."

They continue on, leaving the wildness and partying behind, the sounds and the colors giving way to quieter spaces and less ostentatious views. The buildings they pass morph back into more familiar businesses and outlets, most of them darkened and closed. The chain-link fencing, razor wire, locked gates, and security cameras are a constant presence.

A few miles farther on, they reach another area of enhanced activity. Vehicles and bodies are massed on the Straightaway and on walkways fronting buildings that are brightly lit and open to the public. T.J. turns the Ram down a rampway that takes them into an underground garage. They park and walk to a bank of elevators. Doors open at a touch, and they ascend to the main floor.

On stepping out, Ash discovers everything he needs to know about Checkered Flag.

The nature of the business is immediately obvious. It is a giant gaming parlor loosely decorated in a racing motif with a jumble of racetrack trappings and memorabilia. Vintage gaming machines line the walls on three sides and fill most of the available floor space, their look and sound immediately identifying them as either relics restored or replicas meticulously copied, the designs and formats decades old. They burp and chime and ring and honk with joyous abandon, and crowds gather around each, credits in hand, waiting their turns. A serving bar for food and drink dominates the fourth wall. Eating spaces enclosed with brass railings have been set aside here and there on the main floor and higher up on a balcony overlooking the action.

Jars filled with Sparx sit on every table and all along the top of the bar, clearly being offered free of charge. Patrons help themselves to handfuls.

"This is our kind of place!" Holly announces happily, ignoring Jenny's eye roll.

Holly sets out in search of a table while the rest wait, and after a few minutes she signals them over to a four-top set back against a railing with extra space for Woodrow to squeeze in. From the disgruntled looks on the faces of a couple moving away, it appears that Holly might have evicted them. Waving goodbye cheerfully, T.J. goes off to order drinks.

"Ever play any of these games, Ash?" Jenny asks.

"On my vidview at home." He looks around in amazement. "I didn't think the real thing existed anymore."

"Down here, it does." Holly grins. "Some things were better before than they are now. Today's games are so sterile and predictable. I like the challenge of machines you can knock around a bit to improve your score. Want to try one?"

Ash follows her over to a pinball machine that looks brand new and is decorated with ancient-looking bots, a huge animalistic furball, some men and women with weapons that include gleaming swords, and the words STAR WARS emblazoned across everything. An audience crowds about a young boy who is hard at work racking up points with quick, experienced usage of spring flaps that catapult and slap at stainless-steel balls. Those gathered to watch step aside without a word when they see Holly. Perhaps her reputation precedes her. Perhaps they believe that discretion is the better part of valor.

When the boy who is playing the machine times out a few minutes later, Holly replaces him with Ash, moving him into position and feeding credits into the pay slot. The machine resets, and his turn begins. He is completely enthralled with the game, even though he is not very successful. He uses up his three balls in less than two minutes, and Holly has to feed the machine once more. This time he does better, well enough to earn a few cheers from those gathered around him. He loves the thrill of trying to master the technique and would have stayed there all night had Holly not dragged him away on seeing T.J. return with food and drink.

Back at the table, Ash munches on some sort of meat sandwich and drinks a beer. T.J. has provided everyone with the same meal except for Woodrow, who doesn't eat or drink because the human part of him is sustained by nutrient feeds that connect to his throat through his neck. He is coming out of his funk now, and he laughs and smiles with the rest of them as Holly mimics with exaggerated gestures Ash's attempts at pinball.

Not one of them is old enough to drink under the laws of the United Territories, but they down the beers anyway. No one bothers with ID; this is the Red Zone. Ash has sampled beer only once before, and he didn't much care for it. But tonight he loves it. Cold, fizzy, and smooth, it goes down easily, and soon he is feeling its exhilarating effects. Sound and color are magnified exponentially, and everything becomes increasingly funny.

"Better slow down, Ash," T.J. suggests. But he pays no attention, guzzling his beer and asking if he can have more. When Jenny Cruz nods, T.J. goes off without a word and returns with another round.

Ash is sitting in something of a daze by now as he studies the people around him. They are almost all young, and they are an odd mix. Aside from differences in sizes and shapes and colors, they are almost all hybrids. Many have parts made of metal or composites meant to replace or improve upon flesh and bone. A few seem to have added pieces of animal fur to themselves. Many are tricked out with tattoos and metal jewelry. One or two have no human parts at all and appear to be bots. Some wear tanks and machines attached to their bodies, similar to the one that washes Jenny's blood. One girl has no discernible features but instead has a face that is little more than eyes surrounded by bumps and indentations and that feeds her through a tube attached to the side of her neck.

Their dress is as varied as their looks. There are sheaths, of course, some of them with garish designs and flashing lights. There are pants and shirts artfully ripped out and patched. Boots are favored, but some of the girls are barefoot. One tall girl towers over everyone wearing foot-high platform shoes. There are long, sweeping dresses and coats, short-shorts and skimpy halter tops, cross straps that reveal muscular bodies and large breasts, and dozens of other fascinating permutations.

An unaltered bot comprised entirely of metal and composites, a rather tall and graceful piece of work, glides over to Woodrow, and after running his sensors over the boy, asks him what he is. Woodrow is cautious. He replies guardedly that he is neither all of one nor the other, but some of each. The two strike up a conversation about the nature of life.

Ash takes it all in, feeling unexpectedly cheerful. People passing by their table offer greetings, and Ash is quick to answer—even without knowing who anybody is or even if they are addressing him. He finishes off his second beer and requests a third. Jenny Cruz shrugs and says something about it being his night. Off goes T.J., and after a few short minutes, back he comes with another brew. Ash accepts the offering gratefully and grins without knowing exactly why.

Holly offers a toast. "To Ash, former fish and honorary member of Street Freaks!"

Ash drinks deeply. A short time later he is aware of the fact that he is facedown on the table. He tries to lift his head and fails. At that point Holly appears. She reaches down, lifts him out of his chair, and slings him over her shoulder.

"Time for bed," she announces.

He is carried out of the room in a haze. There are gaps of time after that, and then he finds himself back in the Ram, belted tightly into his seat.

"Someone had a little too much to drink," he hears T.J. declare, and wonders who he is talking about.

After that, everything is a blur until he is unceremoniously dumped in a bed. Sprawled beneath a blanket that hangs half on and half off him, he falls asleep.

- 10 -

Ash wakes early the next morning and rises immediately. He doesn't do this because he is eager for the new day to begin. Quite the opposite. His head is a pounding ball of pain, and he feels nauseous. He moves quickly out of the bedroom where T.J. lies sleeping peacefully and Woodrow sits parked in his corner, and hurries down the hall to the bathroom, where he empties the contents of his stomach into the toilet.

He sits down on the seat afterward, his face buried in his hands, trying to will the throbbing in his head to lessen. He hasn't drunk a lot of alcohol in his life and certainly never as much as he did last night. He thought he counted three beers, but it might have been more than that. A lot more.

After waiting a moment for the last of the nausea to pass, he rises, goes to the sink, and splashes cold water on his face. It helps a little but not much. A medical supplies unit is inset into the wall to one side, and he opens it. A dispenser of pain pills draws his attention, and he dumps two into his hand and swallows them with a long drink of water from the sink.

"Better," he says, but it's more a plea than an affirmation.

He stands at the mirror for long moments looking into the face of the stranger staring back. Who is he? Not Ash Collins. Not the boy who once was and will never be again. This is someone else entirely. Spiky brown hair sticking out in clumps, metal jewelry glinting from the edges of his ears and nose, pasty face damp and drawn. Finding himself still dressed in yesterday's clothes, he strips to the waist. His upper body is bruised and scratched from fleeing the home he no longer has and from the struggle he underwent to get to where he stands now.

Who is he, indeed?

He strips down the rest of the way and showers. He stands beneath the hot water for a long time, letting the heat penetrate to where the aches and pains throb. When he is done, he tries to tame his unruly hair and liberally applies healing salves to the wounds on his face and body. He doesn't hurry. He knows it is very early, well before sunrise. No one else will be up yet, so he can enjoy this time alone.

The truth is, he had a good time at Checkered Flag with his friends. *Friends.* He contemplates the word a second time. He dares to allow himself to use it. Holly Priest, Jenny Cruz, Tommy Jeffers, and Woodrow (no last name)—they have done so much to try to help him, and that's what defines friendship, isn't it? He's lucky his father sent him to Street Freaks, even if he still doesn't understand the odd choice. He imagines the Shoe could give him some idea, but he hasn't had the chance to ask since learning he would be allowed to stay.

Besides, as far as he can tell, the Shoe hasn't returned.

In any event, if he hadn't come here, it is hard to imagine where he would have ended up. Probably looking for his uncle Cyrus. But when he stops to think about it, he realizes he doesn't even know where his uncle's offices are located. He's never been there, never bothered to look them up. Somewhere in the Metro. Coming here probably saved him from falling into the hands of Achilles Pod.

He moves away from the mirror and puts his rumpled clothes back on. With a dry towel draped about his shoulders for additional warmth, he goes down to the kitchen to find something to eat, thinking he will stay there until sunrise. He glances at the clock and sees that it is four a.m. Entirely too early for him to be up, but it is what it is.

He turns on the large vidview that hangs on the wall and watches the News Reader. The conflict in the Dixie Confederacy continues to dominate the reportage. Demonstrations have turned violent in many places, angry crowds clashing with the Confederacy Authorities. In the latest incident, two were killed and dozens injured. Buildings were set afire and vehicles smashed. The cities of Atlanta and Charleston are under martial law and lockdown.

He waits for mention of himself, but when it comes, it is brief and over almost before it begins. He reaches to turn off the vidview, and all of a sudden the great man himself appears, his uncle Cyrus Collins, commander in chief of the Calzonia arm of ORACLE. He stands before a bank of reporters and vidcams at a news conference, his face hard and set, all angles and planes, all purpose-driven intensity. He gestures as he speaks, and his movements emphasize how big he is and how suited to his office. Ash remembers his face, if not much about the man. One thing he does remember. He remembers how intimidating his uncle could be. He remembers how Cyrus towered over him, a mountain that defied climbing.

He is fumbling to turn up the sound when the news report shifts to something else, and Cyrus Collins is replaced by the image of a bridge spanning a river. Ash takes a moment to gather his composure. He is unnerved by his uncle's unexpected appearance. He feels overwhelmed and strangely helpless, as if even his uncle's mere presence on a News Reader diminishes him in some way.

Exhaling sharply, he switches off the viewer.

He is eating a sandwich when he hears a car door slam. He gets up, walks out of the kitchen and through the empty bays to the front of the building, and looks out. A Flash 5000—a sleek, two-passenger sports car—sits idling at the curb. Someone stands next to it, bending down to the passenger window and speaking to the driver. Then Cay Dumont steps back as the Flash drives off. She moves over to the gates, triggers a release, and walks through.

Ash has the presence of mind to back away from the window and return to the kitchen. He knows he should leave, go back upstairs, crawl into his bed, and close his eyes. But he will not back away from her like that, no matter how uncomfortable the thought of another confrontation makes him.

So he sits and waits, his pulse racing.

Moments later, she appears at the door and looks in. "A little early for you to be up and about, isn't it?" she says.

He blushes, and without stopping to think about it, he says, "Early for me, late for you."

He regrets it immediately, realizing how it sounds. But Cay only shrugs. "I'm used to it. Do you always get up at four in the morning?"

He shakes his head, trying to regain his composure, which has disappeared to some far-flung place. "I couldn't sleep."

She comes over and sits down across from him. He wants to kiss her. He wants her to kiss him. It is an irrational impulse. He takes a bite of sandwich, breathing in its smell, trying to distract himself from looking at her. He fails completely in his efforts.

"Ash, isn't it?" she asks. He nods. "I was a little rough on you yesterday, Ash. I was in a bad space, and I took it out on you. I thought you were another of Holly's rescues, some street kid she'd saved."

"I was, sort of."

"I didn't know who you were. I didn't know about your father. I thought you were coming on to me."

"It's okay."

She gives him a smile, and his throat tightens. She is so

beautiful he can hardly stand it. He thinks he doesn't belong in the same room with her. Even in the same world.

"Yeah, well. I didn't need to talk to you like that."

He nods, his eyes shifting to his half-eaten meal. "Forget it."

They are quiet after that for a few moments. Ash avoids looking at her.

"The others probably told you about me," she says.

He hesitates and then nods. "A little."

She removes the remains of the sandwich from his plate and takes a bite. "This is good. You can make me a sandwich anytime."

"I could make you one now."

She takes another bite of his. "No, this will do."

He stares are her, watching her eat. "What?" she asks, when she sees him looking. "You want this one back?" She is holding out his half sandwich.

He shakes his head. "I was just wondering. About synthetics . . . eating."

She gives him a wry smile. "We do everything you do. That's how we're built—to be like you." She pauses. "We don't need to eat, but we like to. We have taste buds and everything." She shrugs. "Eating is a form of bonding."

He wonders about waste disposal, but he's not about to ask a question like that at this point.

"I didn't like what T.J. said about you," he offers abruptly.

"No? Why not?"

"T.J. said you're not real."

"I'm not." She brushes back loose strands of her blond hair. "I'm made of synthetic materials. Hence, the designation 'synth.'"

"But it suggests things that aren't necessarily so. Right there, that gesture you just made with your hair? That's how any girl would do it. How you speak and move—that all seems pretty real to me."

She stares at him. "Depends on how you define 'real.' I'm made of the very best materials, and my brain is fully programmed to tell me how I should act. My critical thinking abilities are on a par with any human girl's, and I am capable of learning to improve myself when it is needed." She shrugs. "But I'm still a synth."

"Doesn't change how I see you."

"It will. Give it time."

He shakes his head. "If you stop and think about it, being a synth is all that sets you apart. If you ignore the materials you're made of, you're just like everyone else. Why should anyone say you're not real?"

She takes another bite of his sandwich and chews thoughtfully, never taking her eyes off him. "With T.J., that's just how he is. Everyone else?" She shrugs. "Maybe it helps those who see me that way justify what they do to me. And helps those that don't participate but just watch it happen feel better about themselves."

He looks down, embarrassed for her, and then wonders suddenly why he should feel like that. She seems at peace with herself. "Don't you think that says more about them than it does about you?"

She smiles. "You're an interesting boy—sort of cute too, for someone so clueless." Her blue eyes find his. "Are you offering to be my advocate in the ongoing debate about who's real and who isn't? No one else has applied for the job. Do you want it?"

"Sure," he says at once.

She nods, smiles, and rises. "It's yours. But let me give you a piece of advice. Don't spend your time worrying about me. Worry about yourself. You don't know nearly enough about Street Freaks to start feeling comfortable. You can't begin to know everything that goes on around here."

She starts from the room, hesitates, and then comes back and stands next to him. He looks up at her, surprised. "I can see what you want, even if you don't think it shows," she says. "You don't need to be embarrassed about it." She bends close and kisses him lightly on the cheek.

He barely notices when she leaves the room, his attention focused on the lingering impression of her lips against his skin.

He sits there until the sun comes up. When the others appear, he is still thinking about her.

Time passes. Three days. Five. Ash sees Cay occasionally, passing through the building, coming from or going to wherever it is she disappears to when she's gone. Once, she gives him a wave. Once they speak briefly but only to ask each other how they are. He thinks of her constantly, worrying about what she is doing and how much danger she is in.

She never talks about any of it with him, and he can never bring himself to ask her.

When he is not thinking of Cay, he is thinking about the passage of time and the apparent failure of either Jenny Cruz or the Shoe to uncover any fresh information about his father's death. It is all he can do to stop himself from asking what's taking so long, but he knows better than to do that. It is enough that he is being provided with a safe haven and friendship. It is enough to know that at least someone is trying. Without them, he would be on his own. How much would he find out then?

He asks Jenny at one point whether she knows if his uncle Cyrus is doing anything through ORACLE to find out what happened to his brother.

"As a matter of fact, he is," she tells him. "He announced an investigation into the cause of his death. He also put out a plea to the general public for any information about you. Your picture is still showing up on vidviews and reader boards. I think he is genuinely worried about you. You might think about sending him a vidmail to let him know you are alive and well and not to worry."

He could do that, he thinks. Perhaps he should. His uncle has reason to worry about him, given that he disappeared out of his home and hasn't been heard from since. What if that's the reason for all those reader board alerts—the latest of which now contain a monetary reward for information on him? What if his uncle generated them simply because he is worried about Ash? He has always assumed it was BioGen. But maybe while BioGen initiated the confrontation with the Hazmats, the searches by Achilles Pod were due to his uncle's efforts to find him. What if he is looking at this backward?

The matter resolves itself in an unexpected way. By the end of his first week at Street Freaks, he finds his supply of ProLx nearly depleted. He knows he has to do something to replace it if he doesn't want to risk an infection. But the Shoe's instructions are explicit: he is not allowed to leave the premises without at least one member of his new family accompanying him. In order to leave, he will have to reveal to one of them the truth about his immune deficiency problem. But which of them will he tell?

The answer comes as a surprise.

He wakes early almost every morning now, unable to sleep more than six hours even on the best of nights, restless and troubled by the continuing uncertainty of his situation. On the last day of that first week when he comes downstairs to the kitchen, he finds Cay already there, drinking coffee.

He enters and sits next her. It is all he can do not to stare. The lavender sheath she is wearing reveals every curve of her body. She looks him up and down while he tries desperately to avoid doing the same to her. "How are you holding up?" she asks after a moment or two.

He swallows hard. "Not so bad."

"Nothing new on your father?"

He shakes his head no and then abruptly asks, "Would you be willing to help me with something?"

It is an impulsive act, one he has not considered. Asking her for help has always seemed out of the question. Yet, as if any such self-imposed hesitation has never existed, he asks her now.

She studies him. "Sure." No equivocation, no hesitation. "What is it you want?"

"I need to get out of here for a few hours," he answers. He cannot make his eyes meet hers. "I haven't told the others, but I have a condition that requires regular doses of a particular medication, and I'm running out. I need someone to take me to a pharmacy so I can resupply."

She studies him some more. When she shifts to face him directly, every part of her body seems to move beneath the sheath. "You don't have a drug problem, do you, Ash? That isn't something I want to get involved with."

"No!" He feels insulted. "I have an immune deficiency problem. I was diagnosed a couple of years ago. My father started me on ProLx. He said it was the only thing that could help. If I don't take it, my immune system collapses."

"ProLx," she repeats. "Don't think I've heard of it. Do you have a prescription?"

He shakes his head. He doesn't, of course. His father always supplied him with his medication. He has the container with the two pills that remain, but there's nothing written on the outside.

"You haven't told the Shoe about this, have you." She makes it a statement of fact, almost an accusation. "Or the others?"

He shakes his head again. "Nope."

"I suppose you have your reasons." She considers him. "We could visit a pharmacy and find out if it's in stock and maybe figure out a way to get hold of some." She thinks. "If you don't want to tell the others what you're really doing, you'll have to come up with a reason we're going off together somewhere."

That's when he remembers what Jenny Cruz suggested about contacting his uncle. He has been careful not to use his personal vidview at any point following his arrival at Street Freaks, but if he can find a public vidview, any message he sends can't be traced back.

"I can tell them I'm going to message Uncle Cyrus and let him know I'm safe. It was Jenny's suggestion in the first place."

She hesitates. "Cyrus Collins?"

He nods. "My uncle."

"So you said." She considers. "Maybe we should go outside the Zone."

Ash shakes his head. "The Shoe said I wasn't to leave the Zone under any circumstances."

She smirks. "Do you always do what you're told?"

He blushes. "Well, I just . . ."

"The Shoe doesn't have to know everything. Are you afraid of him?"

"No." And he isn't. He just doesn't want to lose his only protection. "Okay, we'll go outside the Zone."

She cocks an eyebrow. "But you're not really planning on contacting your uncle, are you? You're just using that as an excuse to get your medicine. Or am I missing something here?"

He doesn't know the answer to that question. The pretext of contacting his uncle serves as a reasonable excuse for going out to replace his ProLx, but now he's wondering if maybe he should send a message while he's got the chance.

She makes a dismissive gesture. "Let's tell Jenny we're going to contact your uncle, but leave it for another day and just go get your medicine." She sips at her coffee and makes a face. "Yuck. Who makes this stuff?" She looks at him. "Want some?"

They sit together in silence at the kitchen table. A few times, she glances at him but doesn't speak. He tries to come up with things to talk about and fails. He tries to find something to tell her that she would find amusing or insightful and discovers he can't. He is so inadequate to the challenge that even sitting there in silence is excruciating.

Eventually Jenny Cruz appears, her slender tiger sheath sliding out of the shadows, and Cay takes her aside. Whatever she says to the other girl, it is enough to gain the permission Ash is seeking, and by midmorning he and Cay are out the door, aboard the Flick, and driving down the Straightaway.

"I didn't know anyone but T.J. was allowed to drive this," he says to her once they are off the premises.

He looks at her sitting in the driver's seat, pixie blond haircut and startling blue eyes fixed on the road as she handles the powerful vehicle like it's second nature. He is feeling euphoric, as if he is on a date with the girl of his dreams—which he obviously isn't, but this is likely the closest he will ever come to it.

"He seemed very possessive of it when I rode with him," he adds.

"What's your point?" she asks, her lips curving in a seductive smile. "I don't have a car of my own, so I took his."

He hesitates. "So you took it without . . ."

"Ash," she interrupts. "Do you know why I was brought into the Street Freaks family?"

It is the question he was told never to ask, and now she is asking it of him. Rhetorically, perhaps, but still. He shakes his head in response. "I guess I don't."

"I'm not tweaked like the others. Unless you want to consider me one big tweak. I was engineered from the ground up to be how I am. I was created wholly from synthetics. I wasn't born normal and then rebuilt. Not like Holly, whose body was enhanced with titanium plates and moric flows and miniature computers. Not like T.J., whose embryo was implanted in a machine surrogate and then after birth given scads of steroids and chemical cocktails and put through rigorous physical training. Not like Jenny, who suffers from a disease that would have killed her if she hadn't been turned into a walking blood transfusion. And certainly not like Woodrow, who lost every part of himself from the neck down. I'm not like any of them, yet here I am, a member of Street Freaks. Why?"

"Because . . ." He stops, not wanting to say what springs to mind because to say it will cheapen her. "People are attracted to you and want to please you?"

She gives him a look. "Well, that's one way of putting it. And it's true. Most of the time I get what I want. A very useful asset if you know how to exploit it properly. Men in particular, but some women, too, will do anything to get close to me. I trigger urges they can't resist. I don't have to try as hard as other pleasure synths because I'm not like them. I'm an advanced model. I turned out differently than they did. I turned out to be much more than they ever expected me to be. As a result, I've found better ways to take advantage of what I am."

He isn't sure what to say—he isn't even sure he understands—so he doesn't say anything.

"There's something else you should know about being a Street Freak," she continues after a moment's pause. "We're all one thing, but we're another too. We're one thing on the surface and much more underneath. Someday, if you stick around long enough, I'll explain it to you. Or perhaps you'll figure it out on your own, a smart boy like you."

Twenty minutes outside the Zone, she cuts the Flick sharply into a side street, drives perhaps a hundred yards, and comes to a smooth stop in front of a single-story building constructed of stucco composite and decorative stone. Heavy windows reinforced with steel mesh coverings dominate the front wall. If this isn't enough to tell Ash they have arrived at their destination, he needs only glance up at the familiar mortar-and-pestle pharmacy symbol anchored to the stone front to be sure.

"Remember," Cay says. "You lost the prescription and all you have is the pill. Prescriptions don't count for a lot in the Zone, so you will probably get what you want without it, so long as you can pay. And make sure you get your pill back afterward. I've seen some sticky fingers in these places. If things get tense, we turn around and go back outside and drive off. That probably won't happen. Businesses in the Zone only care about your credits. Stay calm, no matter what. Ready?"

She says it all quickly, a last-minute flurry of instructions. Ash nods. They open the doors, climb out of the Flick, and walk into the pharmacy. The service counter for prescription drugs and medications is at the rear of the store. Ash notices advertisements for Sparx hanging overhead, large and flashy, with lots of starbursts and printed confetti. They walk back and stand waiting for someone to notice them. An armed guard sits off to one side, looking them over. Especially Cay.

The pharmacist appears, and right away things begin to get dicey. For one, the pharmacist is a standard-issue service bot, not a human. For another, it's dressed as a woman.

Ash is immediately unnerved. He is not prepared for this. He has trouble giving his speech about his medication and lack of a written prescription but somehow manages. When he is finished, he reluctantly hands over his pill and steps back.

The bot doesn't even look at the pill. Instead, it says in a decidedly mechanical singsong voice, **I have no internal record of ProLx. I will need to check my computer files for information.**

The bot wheels away and disappears into a maze of shelves crammed with drugs and medical supplies. Ash exchanges a brief glance with Cay, who gives a small shrug. Off to the side, the armed guard continues to watch them.

When the bot returns, it says, **I have no computer record of ProLx. Please provide the name of the manufacturing company.**

Ash shakes his head. "I don't know. You don't have any record of it at all?" When the bot just stares at him, he adds, "Well, give me back my pill."

All drugs not registered in our system must be confiscated. Drug Enforcement Code, section 2122, paragraph 1: *In the event any drug or medication lacks a recognizable reference in Calzonian databases or in-store data systems, representatives of L.A. drug enforcement shall be notified. All unregistered drugs and medications shall be seized and held.*

Ash stares. He feels Cay's hand touch his arm lightly. "He

needs that pill to combat an immune deficiency condition," she tells the bot. "He only has two left. You have one of them. If you keep it, you are putting his health at risk."

All drugs not in our system must be confiscated. . . . The bot repeats the whole disclaimer once more. Ash watches his chances slip away.

"But his life is in danger," Cay continues. "Are you not programmed to save lives whenever they are threatened, under any circumstances? Isn't that a pharmacist's mandate?"

"Hey, what are you doing?" the guard asks, starting to rise from his chair and come toward them.

"Sit down!" Cay snaps in a tone of voice Ash has not heard her use before.

But the guard doesn't sit. Instead, he keeps coming. He is a big, beefy guy, much larger than the slender girl he approaches. But Cay simply turns to greet him, her small, lithe form gliding smoothly as she does so, her dazzling smile in place. She reaches out with one hand as if to embrace him, touches him gently on the back of his neck and drops him like a stone.

"You have an injured man," Cay tells the bot. "You must help him."

I have no authorization, the bot says.

"Prime Directive 32, threat to human life imminent. No authorization needed. Now help him, bot!"

The bot does so, coming out from behind the counter to assist, but not before setting down the pill on the counter. Ash waits a moment and then swiftly snatches it up and pockets it once more.

"Let's go," Cay says.

They move quickly for the front door, leaving the bot to deal with the unconscious guard. Ash glances back and finds the machine just standing there, looking down at the unconscious man. It does not appear to know what to do.

Cameras will have captured what's happened, he thinks suddenly. They will be identified.

"Bot pharmacists." Cay spits out the words. "The companies have so much trouble with drug robberies and theft in the Zone they can't get anyone else to work the counters. That one's good enough at its job of filling and delivering prescriptions in its database, but out of its comfort zone when it comes to anything else. It will call for help."

"The security cameras . . ." Ash begins.

". . . aren't working." She waves a dismissive hand. "Taken out a while back and replaced with dummies."

"You can tell that?" Ash says.

She grins at him, says nothing.

Out on the walkway, they hurry to the Flick and climb inside. Cay powers up the vehicle, and in seconds they are swinging back onto the Straightaway.

Ash leans back in his padded seat, breathing deeply. "That didn't go so well," he says.

"No, it didn't. We'll need to try something else."

He looks over. "What did you do to that guard? You barely touched him."

"I told you. I'm not like other pleasure synths. I am an advanced prototype, and those who made me gave me every advantage over the humans I was built to service." She sees him cringe but ignores it. "There is a certain amount of danger involved in what I do, so I was given tiny amounts of a very strong drug that secretes through the nails of two fingers when pressure is applied. If I am threatened, I just scratch the itch. Consciousness returns after twenty or thirty minutes, but by then I am gone."

"You knew how to override the programming of that bot too, didn't you? All that stuff about standing down."

She just smiles and looks straight ahead.

They don't speak again after that. Cay drives and Ash stares out the window at the buildings they pass. He tries not to think about all the bad things she must come up against every day while performing the services she was created to fulfill. He is marginally grateful to discover she has some source of protection against harm, but mostly he wishes she didn't need it.

Life seems much more real, he thinks, when you become friends with those who live it differently than you do.

They follow the Straightaway to within a mile of Street Freaks before she pulls over and turns to him.

"You're going to have to give me that pill," she says.

He gives her a questioning look. "I am?"

"ProLx doesn't exist in pharmaceutical establishments. That means we have to find a substitute. To do that, I have to have the pill analyzed." She pauses, seeing the look in his eyes. "It's the only way."

Reluctantly, he reaches into his pocket, retrieves the pill, and hands it over.

She tucks it in her pocket and drives on. But as they come within view of Street Freaks, Ash realizes something is happening. Armored assault vehicles sit at the curb. Black-clad police are visible everywhere on the grounds inside the fence and in the work bays as well.

In spite of the exemption order, Achilles Pod has breached the gates.

- 11 -

Cay slams on the brakes, her voice a hiss of dismay. "How did *this* happen?"

Without waiting for Ash to offer an answer, she wheels the Flick into a swift U-turn and heads back the way they came, thrusters powering them with a sudden burst of acceleration.

"What are you doing?" Ash exclaims, his eyes wide in disbelief. "We have to help them!"

She doesn't bother to look at him. "We are helping them. We're getting away before we get caught up in whatever trouble they're in. By staying free, maybe we can do something useful later."

They are already so far down the Straightaway he can no longer see the black-clads or their vehicles. Everything they've left behind has vanished that quickly. He glances at the speedometer. They are going well over a hundred miles an hour.

He glances over and guesses she might have done something like this once or twice before. He takes a deep breath and exhales, calming himself. "Where will we go?"

"Somewhere safe. Safer than Street Freaks, anyway."

She seems totally unruffled, and he marvels at her composure. He feels immediately satisfied that wherever she is taking them, it is the right place. He watches her hands on the wheel, her rapid shifts from one gear to the next, and her control over the street machine, so steady and sure that it never wavers.

"Does T.J. know you can drive like this?" he asks.

She shakes her head. "You shouldn't tell him either. This isn't something he needs to know. He and the others have fully formed opinions about what I can and can't do. I don't want to give them reason to reconsider those opinions."

Yet you are telling me, he thinks, and he cannot help wondering why.

Almost before he knows it, they have driven right out of the Zone and are headed south through the Metro toward the ocean. She is taking back streets now, staying clear of the freeways with their elevated flight lanes and flying vehicles. He is relieved when she drops their speed in half and turns on the sensors that detect obstructions, both human and otherwise, that might interfere with the vehicle's progress. Most of the new models have such sensors, but he is surprised momentarily to find them on the Flick. Still, even if it's been modified into a street racer from a bygone era, there's no reason sensors couldn't have been added. The kids at Street Freaks would have had little trouble doing so.

He glances out the windows and notices the neighborhood they have entered. Huge mansions with iron gates and long driveways line the street. There are security system signs and cameras everywhere. In homes like these, there will be direct lines to security headquarters and local divisions of L.A. Preventatives. Any breach, and armed support will arrive within minutes. That's what people who live here pay for. Intruders with half a brain would know what to expect and stay away.

"What are we doing here?" he asks, wondering suddenly what she intends.

"For now, hiding out. Later, we'll make inquires and hopefully learn a few things." She points ahead. "That's our destination."

He looks and somehow manages to avoid gasping. The mansion sits on acres of manicured lawn surrounded by carefully trimmed hedges and iron fencing. There are flower beds everywhere, banks of them meticulously laid out in intricate patterns. A tiered gazebo sits off to one side and overlooks what seems to be a stream.

We can't be going here, he thinks.

But that is exactly where they are going. Cay steers the Flick, turning into the gated entrance and pulling even with an identi-pad. The pad is blank, but when she presses the flat of her hand against it and holds steady for about three seconds, the ten-foot tall gates swing open for her.

"Welcome, Cay Dumont," a mechanical voice intones from a speaker set into the stone gate supports.

She steers through the entry and up the drive, her speed now reduced to almost nothing. She smiles at the look on Ash's face as he stares from one side to the other, taking it all in. *Are those peacocks? Is that a lake? Look at that incredible tree, all crooked branches and peeling bark, an ancient thing.* He knows she can see it registering in his eyes, and it seems to give her deep satisfaction.

They do not go up to the front door. Instead, at a gravel cutoff, they drive around to the back of the mansion and down a hill into a vale in which a smaller, much less ostentatious cottage sits. The cottage is a single-story structure with window boxes, a shake roof, a veranda with a porch swing, and flowers encircling the foundation.

"You live here?" Ash asks.

"Sometimes," she answers vaguely, pulling up to the door and climbing out. From across the roof of the car, she says, "Want to come inside?"

She unlocks the door by pressing her palm on another identi-pad and leads him into the cottage. It is bright and cheerful inside, everything new and gleaming.

"Your new home," she says. "For tonight, at least."

"The owner gave you this?" he asks, gesturing at the cottage.

"Gave me the *use* of it," she corrects. "For when I need a

place to get away. He lives in the main house; he is very old and not in particularly good health. Which reminds me. I need to let him know I am in residence."

She takes a red shingle from where it sits just inside the door and hangs it outside where it can be seen from the mansion. "There we go. Now sit while I see what I can find out about the others."

She uses a portable vidview to try to make contact. She powers up the screen, presses keys on a touchpad, and waits. No one responds. She tries again. Nothing.

From there, she moves over to a much larger unit attached to the wall and tries again. Still no response.

"Can't use my private vidview," she mutters. "Too easy to trace." She looks at him. "I have to go out. I need you to wait here. You'll be safe enough. No one will bother you. But I want you to promise me you won't try to leave."

"Maybe I should go with you?"

"Maybe I should go alone. If they're looking for you, the less you expose yourself the better, disguise or no. Can I count on you to wait for me?"

Only forever, he thinks. "I'll wait."

She goes out the door and closes it behind her. Seconds later the Flick powers up and she drives off. He resists the urge to look out the window to watch her go. He is already far too caught up in his feelings for her; he needs to regain some perspective. Mostly, he needs to rein himself in, even if it's only by denying this one small urge.

He spends the time she is away mulling over an unpleasant truth. If anything bad happens to his friends at Street Freaks, it is his fault. Achilles Pod was looking for him the first time they tried to enter; there is little doubt in his mind they were still looking for him when they finally got in. It is fortunate he wasn't there to be found, or they would all be in a lot more trouble than they already are.

He tries to think if anything he left behind will reveal his presence, but he doesn't think so. He brought almost nothing with him save his backpack, and that was emptied and stored away days ago. Even if it is found, there is no reason for anyone to think it belongs to him.

None of this makes him feel any better about what has happened. It only emphasizes how dangerous his continuing presence is to his friends. Has someone told them he is staying at Street Freaks? Was he seen and identified at some point? One thing is certain: he needs to consider that it might not be possible for him to stay there any longer.

When Cay returns several hours later, she does not look happy. "Communications at Street Freaks are still down. Worse, a couple of assault machines are parked out front. I couldn't get inside without being seen. The gates are still open, but the bay doors are down and the building is closed. I didn't see any sign of the others. So I decided to stay away. Maybe I'll try again tomorrow."

She sits down next to him on the couch. "Something is very wrong here, Ash," she says. "That pill you gave me? ProLx? I had it tested while I was out. The testing agency told me it is definitely not designed to protect the immune system. There's nothing in it that would do so. They think it is intended for another purpose, but they have no idea what. They've never seen or heard of it before. They recommend you have some tests performed."

"What? No. No tests."

"If you don't agree to the tests, they won't give you any more of the pills. They have to know what the pills do or they are in violation of the law."

"No tests," he repeats.

"Why not? Are you hiding something?"

"No. It doesn't . . ." He breaks off. "It's just too risky. Someone might recognize me. They might report me."

"Stop right there." She gives him a long, searching look. "I know you've been through a lot. I understand you're frightened. I would be too. But take a moment to consider. You're safe for the moment. What happens tomorrow? Or the next day? What about your health? You've been taking this drug for years, and apparently it isn't what you thought. So is your immune system compromised or not? Is this pill doing something other than what you believe? Don't you have to try to find out?"

Her argument is reasonable, and he knows she is right about him. But something about the idea of being tested is troubling. He can't explain it, but he feels a deep-seated reluctance to allow himself to submit to a physical examination.

"I don't know what the problem is," he says finally.

She reaches over and touches his cheek. "You need to find out, Ash. You need to know the truth. The sooner, the better."

He has one pill left, one ProLx. After tomorrow, he will be rolling the dice. It would be better to know than to sit around wondering.

"Look, I have an idea," she says. "How about if we take DNA and blood samples and send them to a lab? See if that reveals anything about your immune deficiency diagnosis. I have a kit. You won't have to leave the house."

He thinks it over and then nods. "All right."

"That's more like it. Come with me."

She moves into the little kitchen, and Ash follows. Even watching her walk gives him such pleasure, the sway of her body, the soft curve of her back and hips. He hates himself for thinking of her like this when he knows that's exactly how every other man thinks of her. Besides, his attention should be focused on trying to figure out what he will do once his ProLx runs out. He can't quite bring himself to believe the pills do nothing and that his immune system has never been endangered. If it's true, it means his father has lied to him for years. It means perhaps he has lied about other things as well.

He catches up to her and puts a hand on her arm. She turns immediately. "Please don't touch me."

He takes his hand away. "I didn't mean anything."

She grimaces. "Understand something. I have a problem with being touched when I am not expecting it."

"But you can touch me without asking?"

"Does it bother you? Because it bothers me."

He shakes his head. "Forget it. I just wanted to ask you if I could stay here beyond tonight. A few days, even. You know, until things settle down."

She gives him a long, searching look. "This isn't something else, is it? I know how I attract men. I wouldn't want it to be about that."

"No," he says at once. "I mean, no, that isn't the reason. I'm not . . ." He trails off, trying to find the right words. "I just want to be somewhere I feel safe."

She hesitates and then nods. "You can stay." She touches his cheek, a quick brush. "Just don't cross any lines."

He knows what she means. "I won't."

She sits him down at the kitchen table and brings out a small metal and plastic container about the size of a shoebox. She opens it to reveal a faceplate with digital readouts and controls, and engages several buttons that bring a tiny screen on the top of the box to life. Then she hands him a cotton swab.

"This is gross, but do it anyway. Stick the tip in your nose and move it around against the membrane. Then hand it back to me."

He does as he is told, hands it back, and watches as she inserts the tip into an aperture in the box and swirls it around for perhaps ten seconds. When a green light appears on the screen, she takes the swab out and throws it in the trash. Then she extracts a small amount of blood from his arm using a syringe and deposits several drops on a slide. Again, she inserts the slide into a slot in the reader and waits for the green light to appear. When it does, she engages her vidview, calls up a setting, focuses on the screen, dispatches an image of the readings, and shuts everything down.

"All done," she says.

"You've done this before," Ash observes.

She shrugs. "Maybe."

It has been an entire day without a word from anyone. There has been no mention on public vidview of the Achilles Pod assault on Street Freaks. Cay searches the news streams for some small word or picture and finds nothing—as if it was all beneath notice.

They make dinner together, Cay telling Ash what to do as he slices bread and she chops vegetables and browns meat for a stew. When it is all put together, they sit on the couch while it cooks, talking about music and vidview entertainment. She is knowledgeable about both, and as they converse, he begins to see her more and more as a regular girl. She becomes open and approachable in a way she didn't seem before, laughing and smiling like any other teen, trading information with him as if they were old friends. It is the first time he has felt anything but awe for her, and he is warmed by the experience.

They share dinner after dark, sitting across from each other at the tiny kitchen table. She eats with small, dainty bites, and her posture is perfect. She pours him wine to drink with his meal, and while he has sampled wine before, it has never tasted this good. He tells her so.

"I don't usually drink. Or at least, I don't drink much. But when I do, I prefer wine." She pauses. "Have you ever had a girlfriend?"

He shakes his head. "I was homeschooled in the Metro. Before that, I traveled with my parents. Didn't leave much time for girlfriends."

"You've never even been on a date, have you?"

His face turns hot. "Nope."

"Not the worst thing in the world, you know."

He blushes. "Guess not."

"Tell me about your mother."

He shrugs. "I don't remember much. I was pretty young when she died. Eight years old. She caught a fever while we were traveling in the African Combine. She was gone almost before I had time to realize how bad it was. She was kind and funny." He looks up at her. "She liked to sing."

"But she was gone before your father diagnosed your immune deficiency?"

"I was twelve. It was in a doctor's report after a routine exam. You think he lied to me, don't you?"

"I think you have to accept the possibility. But if he did, maybe he had a good reason. Let's wait for the test results."

"I hate thinking about it."

She pours a little more wine into both their glasses. "*Don't worry about tomorrow when it's still today; let tomorrow wait its turn.*" She smiles. "I always liked that saying."

"How did you end up at Street Freaks?" he asks suddenly. "You never really said."

She hesitates. "Didn't I?" She shrugs. "I was on the streets, trying to make something of my life, not having much luck at it. The Shoe found me and brought me home to live with him. The one time in my life I got lucky."

"How did he find you? Or any of them? How did it happen?"

She looks as if she might answer, and then she shakes her head. "Someday, I'll tell you. But not tonight. The answer is complicated. Personal too. Why don't we finish dinner, and I'll teach you to play Nines."

They finish their food and drink and clear the table. Nines turns out to be a card game that involves calling out challenges and offering gambits. Ash catches on quickly and does well in playing, but he cannot beat Cay. She plays cards the way she moves—smooth and steady and composed.

When they have finished three rounds, she tells him she needs to get some rest. She leads him to the couch and uses sheets and blankets to make him a bed. Then she goes into her bedroom and shuts the door.

He sits on the couch afterward, thinking about how much he doesn't know. Not just about his immune system and ProLx but about almost everything. For the first time, he wishes he had spent more time in the larger world and matured in all the ways the other Street Freaks kids had. He wishes he could be as self-assured and capable as they are. He feels inexperienced and naive next to them. He feels woefully uninformed. He thinks that escaping his penthouse home and the fate that overtook the bots was nothing but sheer luck, and he wishes it were something more.

Mostly, he thinks about Cay Dumont. He is surprised by how attracted he is to her. No one has ever captivated him the way she does. Not so much because she is irresistibly beautiful as because she is smart and resourceful. After their rocky introduction, he would never have believed he would crave her company. Just thinking about her makes him smile. She makes him feel good about himself.

He rises impulsively and knocks softly on her door. He doesn't have a good reason for doing so; he just needs to see her once more before sleeping.

"Yes, Ash?"

"I just . . . I want to tell you . . ." He falters.

"Open the door. I can't hear you."

He turns the handle and cracks the door. Her bedroom is dark, but there is a light on in the bathroom. He sees her shadow move in the light.

"I just want you to know how much I appreciate your help. To have you as a friend. I feel close to you . . ."

"Go to bed, Ash," she says, not unkindly.

He starts to close the door and sees her pass before the bathroom mirror, and in its bright reflection her naked body is clearly revealed. Her skin shimmers with pale luminescence, each curve and softness an astonishment that leaves him breathless with longing. He stares at her, mesmerized, and in that instant she catches sight of him in the mirror. He flinches and turns away quickly, embarrassed and excited at the same time, the heat rising through his neck to his face.

When he glances up again, pulling the bedroom door softly into its frame, the bathroom door is closed.

- 12 -

At breakfast the following morning, they sit across from each other in silence. Neither chooses to comment on the closing moments of the previous night. Ash thinks he should say something—offer an apology, make a clever remark—but he does neither. He eats sparingly, stirring the cereal she gives him in slow circles with his spoon, seeing in its vague patterns the depth of his longing and the hopelessness it suggests. He feels trapped in a narrative that draws him to its words and images but leaves him forever unable to control its direction. His life is a mystery, and he worries he is not the one who will determine how it ends.

Cay has decided to confront him in her own particular fashion—not with words but with a visual demonstration. She is dressed in a skintight sheath of floral Lycron over which she has draped a scarlet shawl that alternately hides and reveals various parts of her body. She wears this ensemble artlessly, as if no thought were given to its choosing, a casual response to the demands of the day ahead. It is a deliberate reminder of last night's unfortunate encounter.

He has no idea why she is doing this.

"Is there any word from the others?" he asks finally, unable to stand the silence any longer.

"How do you like my sheath?" she asks, ignoring him.

"It's . . . it's fine," he stammers.

"Pretty much what you saw last night, isn't it?" Her voice is flat and hard. "Did you like seeing me naked?"

He swallows hard. "That was an accident. I didn't mean to stare . . ."

"But you did anyway, didn't you?" She pushes back her cereal bowl and leans forward, fixing him with her strange eyes. "We've covered this ground before, but maybe we need to cover it again. I know you are attracted to me. Every man is. That's what I was created for—to draw men to me, to be irresistible to them, to be their wildest, sweetest, most incredible dream. But I didn't choose this life for myself; it was chosen for me. I was made to be this way by others, by rich and powerful men who desired playthings that would do their every bidding and never complain of what they were asked."

She pauses, searching his face. "It might seem as if I am a normal girl, a teen just like you. That's what I look like, after all. A young, pretty girl. That's how you think of me. That's how you want me to be. But that's not what I am, and I never will be. We are not the same, you and I. You have to stop thinking of us that way. You've created this half-baked fantasy about how we might be together, maybe fall in love. You think we could share a life. We can't. Not ever. I am a synth. I'm not even a 'tweener. I'm not good enough for that crude designation because there are no parts of me that are flesh and blood. No human parts of any kind. Even the others have that much going for them."

"I know what you—" he starts to say.

"No, Ash, you don't know." She cuts him off before he can finish. "You don't know anything. All of us who are Street Freaks are cobbled together. We are pretenders. We pretend to be human. We think of ourselves that way, even knowing it is a lie. We try to be human, but we have serious limitations. Woodrow is a human head on a rolling computer. Jenny is a walking chemical factory.

Holly is metal and motors welded to flesh and bone and possessed of so much raw power she can break down walls. Tommy is a test-tube baby grown up to become a test-tube soldier. And you know what I am."

She leans closer, her look intense. "Pretenders, Ash. None of us will ever have children. We can't reproduce. We lack the necessary equipment. Even Tommy. We don't feel pain in the same way others do because our bodies and minds and emotions are different than those acquired biologically. If something breaks, it can be replaced. A bit of plastic or metal. A bit of tissue. A computer chip. A program feed. We are tweaked and tweaked and then tweaked some more."

She takes a deep breath and exhales softly. "I can never be like you. So you have to stop looking at me like maybe one day there could be something between us. There can't. For so many reasons I don't have time to list them all. You can be my friend, sure. I would like that. But if you need something more, a stronger commitment, a promise of love, then no. Of course, if you absolutely, positively have to sleep with me in order to satisfy your curiosity, then let's just do it right now and get it over with."

Ash feels himself shrink inside. He feels physically ill; a shiver rattles through him. "No, I don't want that," he manages. "Not like that. I want us to be friends. I'm sorry about last night. I didn't mean to stare. I just saw you and . . ."

She holds up her hand to stop him from continuing. "Apology accepted. Look, I like you. But I won't like you for long if I think you're only interested in what's below my neck. I don't want you to think of me that way. All right? Can you accept that? Do we have an understanding?"

He nods, barely aware of what he is doing.

She pushes back and rises. "Come on. We have things to do. While you were dressing, Jenny sent me a vidmail. Street Freaks is open for business again. The Shoe wants us back. Right away."

|||||||||||||||||||||||||||||||||||||||||||

They depart the cottage and drive toward Street Freaks in silence, Cay concentrating on the road, Ash lost in thoughts of what they will find once they arrive. The day is sunny and bright, typical for Calzonia at this time of year, an encouragement if you believe in good omens, which Ash does not. Maybe once, before his flight from his home, his father's death, and the discovery that parts of his whole life are a lie, but not now.

"Did she say what happened?" he asks finally, unable to restrain himself.

She shakes her head without looking at him, eyes directed straight ahead.

"Are they all right?"

A shrug this time. "You know everything I do," she says.

As they turn onto the Straightaway, Ash automatically begins looking for the familiar black assault vehicles. He knows they are there. If he searches the shadows and the hidden spots along building walls and overhangs, he will find them. He knows members of Achilles Pod are waiting. It is all he can do to keep from scooting down in his seat in an effort to hide himself. But Cay rides tall and unafraid, so he can do no less.

He glances over, trying to read her expression. She is right about him. He cannot look at her without thinking of what she would feel like pressed against him. He cannot seem to help himself. This isn't all that draws him to her. In the beginning, maybe that was true. When he saw her for the first time, she was so stunning to look at there was no space for anything else. But now he has a different perspective. He has spent time talking with her. He has listened to her thoughts on what it means to be tweaked and, more importantly, what it means to be a pleasure synth. He has benefited from her knowledge and her help. He has come to know her better as a person.

So while he still looks at her in jaw-dropping wonder and longs to hold her and feel her press against him until they are one person, his attraction now runs deeper. He finds himself smiling at the way she cocks an eyebrow at him. He waits for her to look his way, to reveal herself unexpectedly through words or gestures. He thinks that everything he does he should be doing with her, and he cannot bear to think that this might never happen.

He would like to believe she might change her mind about being friends but never anything more. That she is not like him and never will be. That there are barriers to prevent any of what he yearns for. That he should stop thinking of possibilities that can never be more than daydreams.

He knows he should do all this, but he doesn't think he can. He doesn't begin to know how.

As they approach Street Freaks, he sees the lot is empty of assault vehicles and black-clad police. Everything looks exactly as it did when they left to find ProLx at the pharmacy. The fences surrounding the compound are intact. The iron gates are in place. There is no apparent damage to the building. The grounds are empty and the bay doors to the workplace are closed, but nothing looks amiss. He exchanges a look with Cay that reflects their shared surprise.

The gates slide open as they drive up. Someone inside has been watching for them. Cay pulls the Flick around to the back and parks it in its usual slot. Together, they climb out and walk to the rear door. It opens as they reach it, and Holly is waiting. She beckons them inside.

"They planted listening devices, but we found them right away," she says, giving Cay a hug.

She smiles at Ash but does not attempt to hug him. *I'm still an outsider*, he thinks. *I'm still not one of them, even though I would like to be.*

"Not that they would have worked anyway," she adds as she closes and locks the door behind them. Now she does give Ash a hug, nearly breaking his back. "We installed disruptors in the walls and ceiling a while back that fragment anything their spy gear might try to record."

When he turns, trying to straighten out the kinks from Holly's hug, Jenny is there. He sees at once what has been done to her. She has been beaten, her face swollen and bruised.

She touches her face briefly. "The result of a childish dispensing of retribution from that black-clad I sent packing last week. Seems he's been carrying a grudge for being shown up by a 'tweener. Not to worry. I'll heal."

She seems unconcerned about her appearance, her voice steady and calm. Ash, on the other hand, is furious.

"Who are they?" he asks.

"Ostensibly, Achilles Pod. But, of course, someone had to dispatch them. And that someone probably got their orders from someone else much higher up in the U.T. Government. We don't know who yet. I'm looking into it."

Holly is seething. "If they hadn't been holding weapons on the rest of this, I would have done a little makeover work on that black-clad for what he did to Jenny. Scrawny little coward! I might get another chance at him, though. They'll find an excuse to come back again at some point. They won't be able to help themselves. But we'll be waiting. And we'll be better prepared when they do."

She looks eager, as if she hopes they come back in the next five minutes so she can break a few arms and legs and maybe some heads in the bargain. Jenny touches her arm in warning. "Remember what the Shoe said."

Holly grimaces as she repeats what was obviously the Shoe's warning. "*Don't make trouble. Don't invite retaliation. Just stick to doing business.*" She pauses. "If they let us."

"They can't stop what they don't know about," Jenny says enigmatically.

"They caught us by surprise," Holly explains to Ash. "We have that protection order against any sort of searches. You saw Jenny use it a few days ago. But this bunch came with a writ of negation."

"What were they looking for?" Cay wants to know.

Jenny and Holly exchange a glance. "We're not sure," Jenny said. "They just showed us the writ, demanded entry, moved us all outside, and searched the building from top to bottom. At least, the parts of it they could access. They didn't find the hidden parts, the ones that mattered. When they didn't find whatever it was they were looking for, they took it out on me."

"The Shoe wasn't here to stand up for us," Holly says. "We're a bunch of kids. So we never found out what was going on. No explanation was offered. They stayed all day, poking around, looking things over. They seemed to be waiting for something. Then, after it got dark, they moved outside. Stayed all night, keeping watch. Stayed until a couple of hours ago. We waited until we were sure they were gone to bring you back. We didn't dare risk trying to contact you while they were still inside the gates."

Jenny shrugs. "Sorry to leave you out there by yourselves with no explanation."

T.J. sticks his beachboy blond head around the corner, grinning. "Oh, I bet it wasn't too hard to take, was it, Ash? All night alone with Cay?"

Ash feels himself turning red. "It wasn't like that."

It's a lame response, and T.J. just rolls his eyes. "No, of course it wasn't. Not at all. Anyway, the Shoe wants to see you. And, Cay, if you ever take the Flick again without my permission, you can bend over and kiss your pretty butt goodbye."

He stomps away. Jenny gestures toward the Shoe's office. "The Shoe got back right after Achilles Pod left. You better go in, Ash. He's been waiting for you. I think he's got something to tell you."

He gives Cay a quick glance and does what Jenny tells him. T.J. is waiting just outside the office door, lounging against the wall. He opens the door for Ash and winks suggestively as the boy passes him. "Tell me all about it later," he whispers. "Every detail. Don't leave anything out."

The Shoe is sitting behind a desk, his eyes fixed on the computer screen in front of him. His hands fly across the virtual keyboard, moving fluidly, barely touching the smooth black surface of the interface. He glances up, then away.

"Sit down, Ash," he says.

Ash sits. There is a long silence as the Shoe continues to labor over whatever task he has set himself. Then, abruptly, he sits back in his chair, his hands folding on the desktop, fingers locking. He is resplendent in a silver sheath with royal-blue piping and a scarlet sash. He is immaculately dressed, perfectly groomed, and completely at ease. He is the picture of confidence.

"You've had quite a time of it."

"I'm fine." Ash attempts a casually dismissive gesture and doesn't quite pull it off. "Better than Jenny."

The Shoe shrugs. "She's trained to deal with these situations, even one as unexpected and dangerous as this was. Achilles Pod is not to be fooled with. They have an absolute pass from the authorities. If they decide to kill you, you're dead. They might have to explain themselves internally, but they will never have to answer to any court of law. In this case, they seemed more intent on finding something than eliminating anyone."

"Finding me, you think?" Just saying the words makes him uncomfortable. "That's why they were here, isn't it. They were searching for me?"

"Entirely possible. But I can't be sure. I haven't been able to get my hands on a copy of their orders or the writ of negation. I don't know who authorized them. Jenny asked to see a copy of the writ the squad leader was carrying, but the name of the issuer was blacked out."

"But this was because of me, no matter who authorized or signed anything." Ash has made up his mind to face the truth. "This hasn't happened before, has it? You were protected until I came. Now you have police coming at you from every direction. Achilles Pod doesn't do this sort of work. This isn't right."

The Shoe shrugs. "So much of our world isn't. But we've been threatened before and come out of it in one piece. I just need a little more time to get a handle on what's happening. There's a reason for all this, and I intend to find out what it is. Meanwhile, this is still your home and you are still welcome to stay with us. That's mostly what I wanted you to know."

Ash hesitates. "Thank you."

The Shoe brings out a Sparx, unwraps it, and pops it into his mouth. "Don't thank me. Thank them." He gestures vaguely toward the door. "Your new family. All of them stood up for you. Every one. They told me they wanted you to stay. Insisted on it. No one pushes us around, they told me. Someone is always trying to do just that because of what they are. Street freaks. 'Tweeners. Riffraff and castoffs trying to pass for humans. They've heard it all their lives. They've learned to live with it, but they don't like that it's happening to you."

Ash is surprised. He had thought they would blame him for the intrusion and insist he had to go. He is warmed by the fact that they want him to stay. "I'm grateful," he says.

The Shoe nods. "That said, we have to accept the fact that your presence at Street Freaks presents an ongoing risk for all of us. If Achilles Pod was looking specifically for you yesterday, they had to have good reason to think you were here. Someone had to have told them. The hunt to find you isn't going to go away. Your face is still showing up regularly on the vidviews. And some are bound to be tempted by the reward offer. The search to find you has not been called off. You are still in a lot of danger."

The Shoe leans back again in his chair. "I don't like saying this, but you might be better off going to your uncle. Cyrus Collins is a powerful man. He can probably do more to protect you than we can. I'm not saying you have to leave, but maybe you need to at least think about it."

Ash nods. He knows things might be on the verge of spiraling out of control. He does not want his friends to be hurt because of him. What happened to Jenny is bad enough. He does not want any more harm to come to them if he can prevent it.

"Where did you go with Cay yesterday?" the Shoe asks suddenly. "You didn't say."

There it is. The one question he didn't want to answer. He shrugs, trying to come up with something. "I wasn't feeling well. She offered to take me to her doctor."

The Shoe regards him silently. "She exceeded her authority," he says finally. "But it turns out to be a good thing she did, doesn't it? Because, otherwise, you would have been here and Achilles Pod might have found you."

"She was just trying to help," Ash offers, not wanting Cay to get into trouble.

The Shoe nods. "Try to exercise better judgment next time. Now go back out with the others. Find something to do."

The Shoe motions him out the door. He goes without looking back, suddenly uncomfortable for reasons he cannot explain. On the face of things, he should be happy. He is still part of the Street Freaks family, assured of a place where he will be safe. Or free to leave and go to his uncle, where he might be even safer. A good choice to have. But he is troubled anyway.

T.J. falls in beside him. "Tell me about you and Cay."

"Nothing to tell," Ash says quickly.

"Oh, come on. You stayed with her all night and nothing happened? She's a pleasure synth! You'd have to be deaf, dumb, and blind for nothing to have happened!"

"Well, nothing did. We talked. That's all."

"You talked." T.J. snorts derisively. "If so, you missed the opportunity of a lifetime. If I'd had the sort of chance you did, I would've done more than just talk!"

Ash doesn't know what to think. He glances over at T.J. He wants to ask the obvious but doesn't. "Will you just put me to work?" he says finally.

T.J. leads him out into the bays and turns him over to Woodrow, who is tinkering with engine computers set up on blocks. Chips and diodes and connectors are spread out everywhere.

Woodrow glances up. "Welcome home," the boy greets him. Then he sees the look on Ash's face. "What's wrong?"

There is no good answer to that question, and Ash doesn't try to provide one. He simply shrugs, waits for T.J. to walk away, and then turns to Woodrow and asks for something to do.

Woodrow obliges, and Ash works all morning cleaning and sorting parts mindlessly, which allows him to spend time thinking about his situation. Slowly, he arrives at a decision. The Shoe is right. It is not safe here. Holly said as much when she told him Achilles Pod would be back. Achilles Pod does not accept failure. If they were told he is here, they will not stop looking for him. They will wait awhile, but eventually they will return.

This reinforces his belief that by staying he puts the others in danger. Worse, by staying he is doing nothing to try to solve the mystery of his father's death and his own untenable predicament. It is as if he is abdicating any responsibility for either. He knows the others are doing the best they can to help him. But he is doing nothing to help himself. He has become a passive participant in his own life. He has placed his fate entirely in the hands of others, and he knows he cannot leave it at that. The Shoe and the other kids mean well, but they don't see things the way he does. They don't have to endure his growing sense of guilt and frustration.

Midday, he goes to T.J. and takes him aside. "I want you to do me a favor," he says to the other boy. "A big favor. It may get you in trouble. It might be dangerous. But it will help get things at Street Freaks back to the way they were."

"Well, I like the last part," T.J. says. "Tell me more."

So Ash does, providing his reasons for why he should not remain at Street Freaks, trying to make his explanation sound rational and smart. "What I want you to do, as soon as it's possible," he says, "is to take me to ORACLE and leave me with my uncle."

T.J. stares at him. "Didn't we drop that idea a while back? You can't be sure where you'll end up if your uncle decides not to take you in. Here, at least, you know where you stand."

"But staying here puts all of you in danger. It won't end until they find me. If I go to Uncle Cyrus, everyone will know I am under the protection of ORACLE. Who's going to risk messing around with me then?"

T.J. thinks about it. "I'd have to ask the Shoe first."

"No. We don't tell anyone. Besides, the Shoe already said I should consider doing this."

T.J. shakes his head. "Doesn't matter. He would skin me alive if I didn't say something to him first. What if something went wrong? I wouldn't be heartbroken to have you out of here, but I can't do it your way."

"Up to you. But my mind is made up. I have to go. If you won't help me, I'll go by myself."

T.J. laughs. "Sure, you will. You wouldn't get two blocks. You wouldn't get one!" He shakes his head. "Look, how about if we try something else. Call it a compromise."

"What sort of compromise?"

"You call your uncle on a public vidview. Let him know you're okay. See how you feel about leaving here after talking to him. Just don't tell him where you are, no matter what. Don't say a word about Street Freaks."

Ash considers it. Maybe T.J. is right. It might be better to contact his uncle first. If he's willing to take Ash in, he could send someone to get him. That would go a long way toward reassuring him that he would end up in the right situation.

Still, he hesitates. Leaving won't be easy, even if it is for the best. These kids are his friends. It will be especially difficult to leave Cay. But he knows that at some point he must let go. It seems to him that this is as good a time as any. If they no longer share a physical proximity, it will be easier.

"All right," he says. "But you don't tell anyone about this. I don't want them to know until after I'm gone."

"Less fuss, huh?" T.J. gives him a nod. "Okay. As soon as I see a chance, we'll slip out. I know where we can make the call. You just go back to work. Be patient. Hey, don't look so bent out of shape. This is the right thing to do. Maybe Cay will show up and surprise you with a goodbye kiss."

He starts to turn away, but Ash takes hold of his arm. "Is there anything between you and Cay?"

T.J. smirks. "Yeah, fish. A whole lot of space."

Then he pulls away and is gone.

- 13 -

Time passes slowly while Ash waits on T.J. But the other boy studiously avoids speaking to him. Ash worries T.J. has decided his offer to help is a mistake, and Ash would rather not be reminded of it. He lets the matter lie. He practices patience. What else can he do? Going off alone would be foolhardy; he has no idea where reliable means of transportation can be found within the Red Zone. Attempting to find a way to make the call to his uncle on his own is unnecessarily risky.

He considers giving up on T.J. and asking Cay to help, about abandoning his decision not to involve her further in his problems. But Cay leaves sometime during that first night and does not return. He waits for her to reappear early the following morning, but she doesn't. He wants to ask someone where she is, but that would reveal him in a way he is trying to avoid. His relationship with Cay is private, his bond with her a personal matter, and he wants it to keep it that way.

So he waits some more.

Finally, on the second day, T.J. comes up, puts his arm around him in a brotherly sort of way, and steers him over to where Jenny is overseeing work on a new street machine. He waits for her to look at him.

"Gonna take our guest with me to get the engine parts at Lonnergon's. Let him air out a bit." He slaps Ash on the back. "Not to worry. I'll keep him tucked away so he won't be exposed to the watchful eyes of the larger Calzonia population. Come on, Ash."

After allowing him time to retrieve his backpack, T.J. whisks him through the dining room and out the back door to where the Flick is parked. "That was easier than I thought," he remarks as they climb in and buckle up. "Jenny didn't say a word."

She hardly glanced at them. She didn't even look surprised. She has barely spoken to Ash since his return. She has said nothing about her efforts to find out anything more about his father and BioGen. He knows that it is possible she has found nothing helpful and wants to avoid telling him so. But he cannot help feeling she has distanced herself for a different reason.

T.J. pulls out of the Street Freaks compound and turns the Flick down the Straightaway. He jams the thruster levers forward, and the vehicle's big engine roars in response. The tires squeal and the vehicle leaps ahead, screaming down the open roadway, gaining speed. T.J. is uncharacteristically silent.

Ash closes his eyes and tries hard to breathe normally. He wishes he were behind the wheel.

They drive to the edge of the Red Zone, farther than Ash has ever been. It is not much different at the edge than it is at the center—at least along the Straightaway. They speed past shops and warehouses, food joints and clubs, pleasure houses and gambling palaces, until finally signs for the borders of the Red Zone appear. Moments later, T.J. slows just enough to perform a stomach-lurching turn into a parking garage situated next to a substem station.

As he parks the Flick and shuts her down, T.J. looks over. "We have to take the substem from here. I don't want to risk taking the Flick into the Metro. Remember, you don't look like the pictures they keep showing on the readers. There's no way anyone can know who you are. Just act normal. You're just another rider."

They climb out of the Flick and walk into the ground floor of sub-stem #80. T.J. glances at the schedule board, nods, and points. The #35 is due in five minutes. They walk over to a ticket machine and purchase passes, go down a flight of stairs to the boarding area, walk out onto the platform where the #35 will arrive, and stand with the other riders, staring up the tracks. Ash shoves his hands in his pockets, glancing down at his work clothes. In fact, he does look like everyone else—his clothes rumpled, hair messy, expression a bit pinched—someone in need of a cleanup and a few more credits in his pocket. He has studiously avoided scanning the reader boards, but he knows that if he bothered to do so, he would see himself staring back.

The commuter arrives, pulling in with a whishing sound as sensors signal, electronic brakes engage, and the passenger cars come to a smooth stop. Ash and T.J. crowd in with the other riders and stand in a cluster, dozens of bodies pressing up against one another. No one looks at anyone else, which gives Ash an unexpected sense of security. He is out in the open and surrounded by other people, but at the same time he is indistinguishable from them. He glances at T.J., who gives him a small nod of acknowledgment. He takes a deep breath, exhales, and tries to relax.

They are not two minutes into their ride when he notices a young girl looking at him. He instinctively looks away.

She has recognized him, he thinks.

She knows who he is.

He forces himself to look back, and she smiles at him. Red hair, white skin, dimples. Metal jewelry decorates one ear and an eyebrow. Tattoos cover one side of her neck, disappearing inside her too-tight sheath. She seems friendly. He forces himself to smile back. She doesn't recognize him after all. She is only flirting. She takes out a bag of Sparx, unwraps one, and sticks it in her mouth, winking at him. She points to her hair, short and spiky, and then to his, which is similar, and makes an approval sign. He nods, shrugs.

But when she starts to inch her way closer, T.J. notices. Without a word, he moves next to Ash, wraps his arms around him possessively, and turns him around so that their faces are inches apart.

"Pretend you like me," he says. "Hug me."

Ash embraces him, and the girl gets the message and turns away.

"Another potentially embarrassing romance nipped in the bud," T.J. announces, smirking as he releases him. "What is it with you and pleasure synths, fish? You need to recognize them when you see them. Didn't Cay teach you anything?"

T.J. is back to referring to him as "fish." Ash doesn't like it. "I thought we agreed you wouldn't call me that anymore."

T.J. shakes his head. "You're leaving us. That means you're back to being a member of the general population. Might as well get used to it. *Fish.*"

He seems almost gleeful, using that teasing tone of voice. They ride the rest of the way in silence, standing close without looking at each other. Ash occupies his time thinking about what he will say to his uncle when they connect. He works on making up an explanation. He cannot mention the Street Freaks crew or the Shoe. He will have to come up with a story about where he has been and what he has been doing that doesn't include them. It will not be easy.

For just a minute, he considers the possibility that this is a huge mistake and he should have stayed where he was.

The #35 slows to a stop. They are at Metro Central. The bulk of the passengers disembark, Ash and T.J. with them. Following the crowd, they walk down the platform and climb the stairs to the cavernous hub station where voices echo and reader boards dazzle with light and sound. News, advertising, substem connections, and scheduling information. United Territories alerts scroll. There he is, and he looks away at once. He doesn't need to study it, doesn't want to think about it for fear even that small act will somehow call attention to him.

They pass through the central hall and out onto the open streets where T.J. hands him a mask.

"Put this on. We have to look like everyone else while we're here."

He has already donned his own, so Ash does the same. "Don't look at anyone. Don't talk to anyone. Don't stop for anyone. Got it?"

Ash nods. They step outside the station. T.J. is right. Almost everyone around them is wearing breathing masks. Without one, they would draw attention.

"No one will give us a second look with crowds this size," T.J. says, his voice muffled by the mask. "We'll just blend in. Come on, the vidview we want isn't far."

They set out along the walkway, sticking close to each other. There are thousands of people, all pressing ahead with as much speed as they can manage. All are wearing breathing masks. No one in the Metro wants to be out in the open without one. Ash remembers his father quoting statistics about how dangerous the air in L.A. is. Worse elsewhere, he used to say. Unimaginable in much of Mongol-China, but with hundreds of millions of people crowded together over there, Ash imagines a few thousand deaths mean nothing.

Yet in the Red Zone, breathing masks are disdained. As if those who live there care nothing for their health. As if they are invulnerable to disease. As if the Zone is impervious to the ills of the larger city. True, the air is better there for whatever reason, and the inhabitants must have built up some sort of immunity over the decades. But still, he can't quite wrap his mind around the casual disregard everyone seems to have for the masks.

They walk for blocks. Ash asks why there isn't a substem closer to ORACLE than Metro Central, which causes T.J. to snort derisively. "Think about it, fish. If you were running the Calzonian regional government, would you want to put a substem right under your nose? Would you want all these stinking, disease-ridden, dumbass voters pouring out of their skanky trains into your backyard?"

Ash sees his point. The government is comprised of men and women who view themselves as elites. They claim to be one with the people, but he hasn't seen much in his short life that suggests they believe this is true. He has heard the politicians speak; they all sound the same. He has listened to his father talk about how many decisions have delayed rather than advanced projects that could make life better. He has seen what failure to regulate and protect natural resources has done to their world.

Once, something might have been done to better conserve crucial resources. Now, all that's left is management of what little remains. They are reduced to replicating what was lost, using synthetic imitations. Half the trees in greater L.A. are plastic. Flowers bloom and die in a day. Water is recycled through vast reclamation projects that span entire city blocks. Every effort smacks of desperation.

The brave new world of genetics has made a stab at improving life, but the results are mixed. The Street Freaks kids are examples of what has been tried and continues to be tried in an effort to conserve, manage, and reinforce the population. But not everyone believes this is the way to go. Not everyone likes the idea of salvaging damaged bodies, of remaking humans into hybrids, of creating 'tweeners. Not everyone believes that inventing various types of bots to provide services is natural. Many believe the makeup of the human species should not be tampered with.

Even though the world's population is not growing but declining due to multiple causes. Wars, pandemics, dwindling resources for food and water, poisons in the air, homicides—the direction things are heading seems irreversible.

Almost no one seems to think the world is a better place than it once was, himself included. Yet suspicions of artificial humans continue to persist.

It occurs to him suddenly that it has been two days since he has taken ProLx, and he is out in the open air with hundreds of people around him, exposing himself to all sorts of viruses and germs with no protection for his immune deficiency condition. It has been two days since Cay sent his DNA sample to the diagnostics lab, and he has heard nothing back.

Surreptitiously, he glances at the people walking past. Most don't even see him. No one looks at much of anyone. They pass each other as if they are alone, isolated from everyone else. He sees faces that look red and feverish. He sees faces that are pale and haggard. He sees the possibility of sickness everywhere. He tries not to breathe too deeply, tries to avoid breathing at all. He shouldn't be afraid, but he is. He has lived so long believing he is more susceptible to illness than other people that it is difficult to believe anything else. His father has told him it is the truth.

But what if his DNA sample reveals it is a lie?

What then?

Ahead, a huge steel and glass building rises out of the stone-block jungle of lesser buildings that surround it, a heroic structure among ordinary constructs. It is intimidating beyond anything Ash has ever seen. It is huge and brilliant, the light reflecting off its surfaces in diamond flashes, the facade a seemingly impenetrable barrier. Broad, sweeping stairs wrap the entire front of the building, emphasizing the girth and weight of the structure. A solitary elevator at one end of the front of the building provides access to a secondary entry for those who cannot manage the stairs, but its location and diminished size make clear that the handicapped must manage as best they can.

T.J. brings them to a halt a dozen yards from the bottom of the stairs. "ORACLE Central. Intimidating piece of construction, isn't it?"

Though there are walkways fronting the building, passersby avoid getting close, choosing to walk on the other side of the empty street. When robo-taxis land, they do so a block away. A closer look reveals that while ORACLE Central is beautiful, there is nothing welcoming about it. It is stark, cold, and forbidding. Watchmen, another arm of the multi-tentacle organization, their uniforms red with silver piping, guard the front steps as if their intent is to keep people out.

"What are we doing here?" Ash asks, suddenly worried.

T.J. shrugs. "Thought you ought to see it before making up your mind about what to say to your uncle. You just need to be sure before you decide if you want to go in there." He chuckles. "Relax. You're not committed to anything yet."

He leads the way across the broad avenue and down a block to a gaming parlor crowded with players hunched over computer screens and control consoles. T.J. takes him right past all of them, not stopping until they are at the rear of the establishment, where a cluster of public vidviews housed in booths line the wall.

"Use one of these," he says. "Remember what I said. No mention of Street Freaks. No talk of the Zone. Here, this is the vidview code you need—it accesses the main communications center. Start there. Wait!" He grabs Ash's arm. "Mute your vid image. Take it all the way down so you're just a shadow on their screen. No sense letting them see what you look like just yet."

Ash hesitates, looks at T.J. "Don't worry, fish," T.J. says in an effort to sound reassuring. "I'll be waiting right outside the door."

Ash steps into the booth and slides the door shut behind him. He powers up the vidview, inserts the necessary credits, and enters the code. At the last second, he remembers to lower the resolution on his vidview screen to almost nothing. T.J. is right. He doesn't want to give them a look at his altered appearance if this is a mistake.

Only a few seconds pass before an image flashes to life on the screen, and a pinch-faced, bookish man with a bored expression appears.

"ORACLE Central. How may I direct your call?"

"Cyrus Collins, please," Ash says.

The receptionist shakes his head. "Commander Collins doesn't accept direct calls without an appointment. I can put you in touch with his secretary if you care to leave a message."

"No. I want you to tell him it's his nephew, Ash."

The man's hesitates. "Ash Collins?"

The way the man speaks his name is troubling. There is a hint of surprise and eagerness. Both would be natural reactions. But there is something else. A tension, an edginess. Ash almost hangs up, but at the last second decides to give it another minute. "Yes," he says. "His nephew, Ash."

"One moment, please."

The screen goes dark. He waits for something more. Almost a minute passes before the man returns.

"He's in a meeting and can't be disturbed. They'll tell him as soon as he gets out. Is there a code line where he can reach you? Or a vidview contact?"

Ash hesitates. "No," he says. "I'll call another time."

And he switches off the vidview.

He stands looking at the blank screen and makes a decision. The call is just another way of putting things off. He shouldn't need an appointment to see his uncle. He shouldn't have to stop and consider if meeting him is all right. Not in light of his father's death and his own disappearance. He is equivocating again, treading water when he should be swimming.

Instead of standing around, he will do right now what he should have done in the first place.

T.J. raps on the glass of the vidview door and gives him a questioning look. Ash opens the door and walks out.

"They said my uncle is in a meeting. They seemed to recognize my name, but they put me off. I'm going over there, T.J. Walk right in and demand to see him."

T.J. gives him a look. "Makes me nervous, but this is your party."

Ash starts to walk past him, but T.J. grabs his shoulder. "Let's not be too hasty, fish. You go in, if you want, see what you can find out. But then you call me and tell me you're okay. Let me know how things are going. I'll come in and get you if you need me to."

"Just walk right in and rescue me?"

T.J. shrugs. "If it's necessary, sure. What, you don't think I can do it?"

He claps Ash on the back and shoves him toward the door.

- 14 -

Ash departs the gaming parlor and crosses the street to Central. The imposing steel and glass structure looms over him as he looks up at it, and that alone threatens to crush his fragile self-confidence. But he pushes ahead, beginning the climb to its front doors. The climb feels endless. He tries to take some measure of comfort from knowing that he feels physically okay with the required effort, even given the unpleasant possibilities of what is already an overexposure to the elements and other people. But as if to counter this momentary surge of fresh confidence, he finds the level of his fear rising along with his ascent. Everything about ORACLE suggests limitless power. Even the name, spelled out across the front entryway, intimidates. The letters flash in slow, steady cadence, their scarlet bursts a warning to beware.

He passes between the Watchmen bracketing the entryway, but neither gives him even a glance. He's not worth the bother, he thinks, and he goes inside.

Once there, he finds himself in an entry area filled with scanning machines through which everyone must pass. Standing atop a metal disc within a glass cylinder, Ash watches as a series of bands intended to reveal weapons circle about him, examining him for weapons and explosives, noting every detail of his body and clothing on a viewable screen. When the scan is finished, he is required to provide his vidview number for identification. Ash goes pale, but it is too late to turn back. Unable to do anything else, he activates his chip and lets them take a reading. To his surprise, they show no interest. This must be the last place they expect him to surface. At least he has the element of surprise.

When they are finished with him, he is directed to a pair of diffuse glass doors that open into the reception area. He now stands in a huge chamber with rows of polymer backbenches surrounding a reception desk. In cubicles off to one side, clerks and other functionaries are seated at desks. More black-and-scarlet Watchmen stand guard. Embedded ambient corelights blaze from walls and ceiling, casting their brilliant glow over everything. The polished steel and chromic surfaces glitter like diamond facets. A low buzz resonates, voices murmuring words too vague to identify.

Ash walks to the reception desk and confronts one of several men and women who look either bored or overtaxed. The man he chooses is small and nondescript, his skin as pale as chalk, his eyes lowered. He is not a bot, but he might as well be, given his level of awareness. He looks up and immediately looks down again dismissively.

It is not the man he talked to on the phone. But he could be a close relative.

"Name," the receptionist says in a perfunctory tone.

"I don't have an appointment," Ash replies.

The man doesn't look up. "Who do you want to see?"

"Cyrus Collins."

The man's head lifts now. "Commander Collins doesn't see anyone without an appointment. Do you want to make one?"

"No, I don't want to make one. I don't need an appointment. I'm his nephew, Ash. He's expecting me."

The man hesitates, uncertain. "I don't have anything here that authorizes me to . . ."

"Call him," Ash says quietly. "You'll be sorry if you don't. My uncle is expecting me."

Apparently, the receptionist is quicker to react to threats than requests. Although he gives Ash a doubtful look, he triggers a fixed-station vidview below counter level and speaks to whomever is on the other end. "Is Commander Collins available? No? How long? When he gets out, tell him a boy is waiting to see him. Claims to be his nephew. No, I'm not kidding. That's what he says." He looks up at Ash. "What's your name again?" Ash tells him. "Ash," he says into the vidview.

He signs off and looks up. "He's in a meeting just now and can't be disturbed. They'll tell him when he gets out. Go over there and wait for me to call you."

"No," Ash says at once. "You call whoever you spoke to and tell him that if he doesn't find a way to get my uncle out of his meeting right now, I am going to walk out of here."

The receptionist stares at him. "You can't tell me what to do. How do I even know you are who you claim to be?"

"You don't. But you'll be a lot happier in the long run if you just do what I say. Call back upstairs and tell them what I just said. Or better yet, don't. Just send me up, and I'll tell them myself."

"No one—and I mean no one—is allowed above this floor without permission. I can't give you that permission."

"So make the call." Ash leans on the counter. "Look, I took a big risk coming here. My uncle is going to want to see me, I can promise you. But I am quickly losing faith in that happening. If I can't get in to see him, I'm wasting my time. So you call up there and tell them to get him out of his meeting, and you do it right now!"

The level of his voice has risen, and some of the other receptionists are glancing over with looks of concern. Soon, there will be Watchmen coming to find out what is happening. Ash can feel his opportunity to get to his uncle slipping away.

The man he is threatening grins. It is not pleasant. "You know what?" he says. "I'll make that call. Anything to get rid of you."

He engages the vidview. "The commander's *nephew* says his time is valuable. He says the commander better see him right away if he wants to see him at all. He says you better get the commander out of his meeting. He's pretty insistent about leaving if he doesn't get his way." He listens, glances at Ash, and smiles unpleasantly as he ends the communication.

"You better hope you're right about this," he says. "Now be a good little boy and take a seat."

Ash has pushed things as far as he can without getting thrown out, so he turns, walks over to the rows of benches, and sits down. He has barely settled himself in place when the glass doors from the entryway open and a black-clad member of Achilles Pod walks through.

There is an immediate drop in the temperature. All noise stops. Everyone looks away from the man crossing the room. The man doesn't waste even the briefest glance at the benches. Those who sit upon them are beneath his notice. Ash shrinks into his seat, dipping his head so that he is looking at the floor. He will be seen, he thinks. He will be discovered and taken away before his uncle even knows he is there.

But the black-clad policeman goes past him without reacting, stopping at the reception desk. "Lieutenant Cray," he announces in a bold, clear voice. As if everyone needs to know. "To see Commander Collins."

Ash knows that voice. He has heard it before. Where? His memory kicks in, the memory that never forgets. At Street Freaks, the first time Achilles Pod tried to gain entry, when Jenny Cruz stood up to them with her writ of exception and sent them packing. He was the squad leader.

The coward who beat Jenny when he finally did get into Street Freaks because he didn't find what he was looking for.

The receptionist has made contact with whomever grants or denies admission to the offices of Cyrus Collins and looks up at Cray. "You can go right up, Lieutenant."

Cray moves off. Ash feels his anger surface anew. No delay in admitting Achilles Pod officers to see his uncle, it seems. Easier than if you're a relative. He almost gets up and leaves. Everything about this suddenly feels wrong. He has put himself out here on a wing and a prayer, and all of a sudden it feels like the dumbest decision he has ever made. He should abandon his efforts to see his uncle now and get the hell out of there.

But he doesn't. He sits and waits because this is his one chance to turn things around. Going back now will feel like another failure, and he doesn't think he can handle any more of those.

Even so, he has almost decided he has no choice but to leave when his uncle abruptly appears, striding across the room from the elevators, the great man come down to the level of the common people. He goes directly to the reception desk, speaks to the man Ash talked with earlier, looks around as the man points at Ash, and stares. Clearly he does not recognize his nephew. Belatedly Ash realizes it's not only because it has been so long since they've seen each other but also because he no longer looks even remotely like his old self.

He stands, giving his uncle a better look at him, and without further hesitation, Cyrus Collins comes over and grips his shoulders. It feels as if he is being seized rather than embraced.

"Where have you been?" his uncle snaps, not quite shaking Ash but coming close. "I've looked everywhere! What were you thinking, not coming here? I've been frantic with worry. Don't you know what's happened?"

Cyrus Collins is a big man, powerfully built and rough-faced, his stern expression and harsh voice unsettling. His head is shaved, and his face is all angles and planes. There is no hint of softness in him, no suggestion of weakness or vulnerability. He is the sort of man that if you were asked to guess his profession, you would immediately think soldier or criminal. At this moment in time, Ash sees something of both.

"I know what's happened," Ash manages, trying not to look

paralyzed. "That's why I've been hiding out, trying to decide what to do."

His uncle suddenly seems to realize he has overstepped himself and exhales sharply, some of the emotion draining from his eyes as he eases up on his grip.

"And you didn't think it was a good idea to come to me right then and there? You didn't think you would be safer with me than being . . . well, wherever you've been? Where were you, anyway?"

Ash doesn't want to tell him the truth. "On the streets, staying with people here and there, people who didn't know me. I got by the best I could. I was scared, you know."

"I can imagine you were. But you should have come to me! I could have helped!"

"Does this mean you won't help me now? That I lost my chance?" Ash throws it out in challenge.

Cyrus Collins looks furious all over again. "You're like an attack dog, aren't you? No, of course it doesn't mean that! What's wrong with you?" He pauses, a puzzled look on his face. "What's happened to you, anyway?" He lowers his voice to a whisper, conscious of people glancing over. "What's with all the piercings? I don't remember your father saying anything about that when last time we talked. When did this happen?"

Ash straightens, angry himself now. "After Hazmats raided our home and destroyed our bots and looked like they had every intention of killing me!"

"All right, settle down." His uncle releases his grip on the boy's shoulders and drapes his arm around them instead. "We've been sifting through the evidence they left behind. But we still don't know enough." He glances around at the crowded room. "Let's continue this conversation in private. Come upstairs with me."

Without waiting for a response, he steers Ash past the reception staff, all of whom look down at their vidviews as if they have never seen anything so fascinating in their lives. Still coupled, Ash and his uncle board one of the elevators on the far side of the room, neither speaking. The trip up is swift and silent, and Ash cannot help feeling he has chosen a path from which there is no turning back. All he can hope is that it leads to something good.

On the eighteenth floor, they exit into a broad reception area. This space is also lit by corelights and decorated in chrome, leather, and slate. Paintings of exotic places Ash has never seen hang from the walls. Polymer furniture offers seating. Lieutenant Cray of Achilles Pod glances up from the chair in which he is waiting, then down again. Without a word either to him or to the several office clerks or functionaries or whatever they are that sit at various desks around the room, his uncle guides Ash down a hallway and into a conference room.

"Sit there," he orders, pointing at a broad table with a dozen chairs situated around it.

Ash does, feeling diminished with every moment that passes but growing determined too. He doesn't know where things are going, but whatever else happens, he is going to get enough information to make up his mind about his uncle. If not, he can always get word to T.J. and tell him he needs help. Although when he thinks about it, he cannot imagine what T.J. could do for him deep inside the bowels of ORACLE.

His uncle is saying something into a speaker on a communications pad set into the wall, but Ash doesn't catch his words. Finished, his uncle walks over and sits down beside him.

"You've been through a lot," he says. "Most kids wouldn't last out there on their own without help. Someone must have taken a liking to you. Or was this someone you already knew?"

The same question, phrased a different way, asked a second time. Ash is immediately suspicious. "I just wandered around the Metro, looking for food and shelter. I had some credits in my pocket. I made them last."

"The word I got was that you were down in the Red Zone." His uncle tosses it off casually.

Ash pulls a face. "Why would I go there? Someone's mistaken."

"Records from your father's vidview, retrieved after his death, had a message sent to you right before he died. What did he tell you?"

Ash has already decided how he would handle this question. He shakes his head. "I never got that message. I was probably running by then. The Hazmats broke into my house and chased me. I turned off the vidview in case they were tracking me. I barely got out as it was."

"But later? You must have thought to retrieve your vidview messages at some point."

"There was no message from my father. Maybe he never completed it. Maybe it got damaged in transit. I don't know. Is this important?"

"Just curious. Something's not right. Are you telling me everything?"

Now Ash is mad. "Look, Uncle Cyrus, I didn't get any message. Why are we even talking about this? They're calling his death a suicide, and you and I both know that's not so. He was killed. What are you doing about it?"

He goes on the offensive to deflect further interrogation, which is what all these questions from his uncle feel like. Let the commander in chief of ORACLE answer a few.

His uncle leans back. "You're right, of course. Your father didn't kill himself. Someone pushed him. I'm looking into it, but that takes time. What might help is if your father made any notes that would reveal who might want him dead. He was an important man working on secret projects for BioGen. He might have made enemies."

"What sort of secret project?"

His uncle shakes his head. "I don't know that. I only know he was working on something he considered very important. I was hoping you could tell me. Or at least tell me where to find his notes. There don't seem to be any at BioGen."

Ash has no idea about any notes, and just at the moment he

isn't sure he would tell his uncle even if he did. This conversation has taken an unexpectedly wicked turn. He had come here hoping to find sanctuary but instead has run into something decidedly less welcoming.

He has had enough.

"I never saw any notes, and he never talked about the projects he was working on. BioGen was pretty strict about that sort of thing. My father wasn't the kind to break the rules. Why don't *you* know what he was working on? You're the head of ORACLE. Can't you make them tell you?"

"You have a misconception about what I can and can't do, Ash." A rueful chuckle. "I can't go breaking into private records and forcing public corporate officers into revealing company secrets. I can make them talk about the circumstances surrounding someone's death, but in this case they claim to know nothing at all about what happened. I could ask for a search order, but a Juris Mentis wouldn't give it to me without evidence. So I am reduced to trying to find out if they lied before tossing them in prison and beating them with rubber truncheons."

Ha-ha. Rubber truncheons. Uncle Cyrus is making an attempt at being humorous. Ash is irritated anew. "So no one saw this happen?"

"No one who wants to admit it."

"Did he ever say anything to you about being in danger? You're his brother."

Cyrus Collins shakes his head as if Ash just doesn't get it. "Oh, yes. We were brothers. But we were never close. You never saw much of me growing up, did you? Nor I of you. Your father and I thought differently about many things, and some of those things kept us apart. Which means he kept you away from me. I regretted this forced separation. But he was always more the dreamer and I the pragmatist, and sometimes the two don't mix so well." He pauses. "Which one are you, Ash?"

Ash thinks this is a dumb question. "I don't know. I guess I'm still trying to find out."

"Well, you *should* know by now. Everyone your age should. We live in complicated, challenging times, but we have the means to overcome those challenges and move into the next century with some assurance that we can manage our future in the correct manner. Your father was trying to do that, but he kept getting in his own way. He was a brilliant man, a genius without equal in the field of biogenetics. He had such dreams, but he was afraid of following through. His worldview was always so cautious, so constricted . . ."

He stops abruptly, apparently having gone further than he intended in his assessment of his brother.

Ash pretends not to notice. "Am I allowed to stay here or not?" he asked.

His uncle nods. "You can stay as long as you like. Certainly until we sort this matter out. My personal quarters are on the top floor of this building. There is plenty of room for you there. But you are not to leave the building without permission. I need to keep close watch on you while I try to find out who's behind your father's death."

Ash shakes his head, frustrated by the idea of being housebound. "How am I supposed to help if I'm stuck in here?"

"It's just for a while, and it's for your own good. Everything will be provided for you." He pauses. "I could even offer safe haven to any friends who might have helped you while you were on the streets. In case they are in danger too. I don't want anybody hurt."

He leans over and gives Ash a friendly squeeze on his shoulder. "Look, I have to go talk to that Achilles Pod soldier. But I won't be long. You just wait here for me. Remember, you're a guest. Anything you want, just ask for it."

He rises and departs the room. As he closes the door behind him, Ash hears it lock.

Guess he's really serious about keeping close watch on me, Ash thinks. *Can't get into much trouble if I can't get out.*

But getting out, and getting out now, is exactly what he intends to do.

- 15 -

One thing about being a teen, assuming you aren't brain dead: you pretty much always know when adults are making something up. Or just plain lying to you. Uncle Cyrus is doing one or the other right now, of that much Ash is certain. He might not know how much is truth and how much lie, but the extent of the duplicity isn't the issue. His uncle is entirely too eager to find out about Ash's friends. He must have brought the subject up at least three times. Even more to the point, his uncle knows more than he is saying. Ash can sense it in his sketchy explanation of what has happened to his brother. No one in the position of power Cyrus Collins holds can be that clueless.

Ash's mind is made up. Things are being kept from him, and that's enough to persuade him he has made a mistake. Stick around longer, and he will find out the hard way what those things are. He's not going to allow his uncle to lock him up, whether it's for his own good or not. Best to get out while he still can. Better out there on the streets than locked up in here, no matter how dangerous it might be.

Getting out of ORACLE Central might be a challenge, however. Even getting out of the conference room presents a problem.

He walks over to the door and tests the handle. Frozen. The

lock is a magnetic seal triggered by a laser beam that passes from the door to the frame when the door closes. To open the door, you have to turn off the beam and release the lock.

But there must be a way to release the lock from within the room as well. They wouldn't install a lock in a conference room that only worked from the outside. The trick is in discovering where it is.

Ash spent much of his youth studying how things worked, mostly out of curiosity, tracking the information down and using his memory to store the knowledge he gained. Locks are among the devices he has researched, a common enough undertaking among teens, and he knows something about this one. The trigger to the lock is usually installed as a part of another function. He goes over to the communications pad and studies it.

Nothing he sees suggests a path to what he is looking for. Five minutes have already elapsed. His uncle could be back at any moment. He needs a better, quicker answer to his problem.

As if in response, the lock releases and the door opens. One of the office staff enters carrying a tray of bottled water and glasses. He sets it on the table and turns to leave.

Ash is already on his feet and running after him. "Wait! Just a minute! My uncle . . ."

The man holds up his hands in warning, then pulls out a stinger, ready to defend himself. *Against the commander's valued guest?* Ash would laugh if he weren't so scared.

"Whoa, I'm not going to cause trouble," he says quickly. "I just wanted to know how long my uncle is going to be tied up."

"Until he's finished with whatever he's doing," the man says, backing away.

Ash catches up to him as he reaches the door. "But there's nothing to do in here! This isn't right!"

The man is opening the door and stepping through. Ash comes after him, leaning on the frame. "Hey, wait!"

But the man turns away, and the door closes behind him.

Ash gives it two minutes, just to be sure, and then he tries the handle. It opens easily. One thing about these laser locks. Get any sort of substance on the lens of the reader, and it stops registering the seal. A spitwad, say—like the one he slapped on the doorframe's lens.

He eases the door open a tiny fraction and looks out. There is no one in sight. A hallway runs from the reception area past his doorway and disappears from view. He looks over at the windows in the conference room and notes the release that allows for them to open several inches each. He hurries over, cranks one open as far as it will go—which isn't far—and uses his backpack as a wedge to hold it in place.

Nothing in it but his K-bar and the breathing mask T.J. gave him. Nothing he can't give up.

He returns to the door, cracks it slightly, and looks toward the reception area once more. All clear. He slips through the doorway, removing the spitwad from the reader lens as he does so, and closes the door behind him, listening as the locks snap into place.

The way back to the elevators that brought him up goes right past all those people in the reception area and seems a poor choice. So he goes the other way. At the end of the hall, he turns the corner cautiously. No one in sight, but there are sounds of sudden activity behind him. He continues on, going deeper into the warren of offices. The corridor makes another turn, and abruptly he encounters a service bot exiting a solitary service elevator. He is quick enough to block the door open as the bot continues on his way; he slips inside.

He presses the button for the main floor.

He has been extraordinarily lucky so far, and he is aware that he has to be even luckier to get out of the building without being stopped. He has to hope his uncle remains tied up elsewhere until he is clear. He triggers his vidview to read the time. Five minutes have lapsed since his escape.

He touches his vidview and connects to T.J.

A disgruntled face stares at him. "What? Bored already?"

"No. Scared. I'm coming back. I need to get out of here, T.J. Really fast. Things have gone way wrong."

He can hear panic in his voice. The other's expression changes instantly. "Okay, can you get clear of the building?"

Ash nods. "I think so."

"Do so. Get down the steps to the street. I'll meet you there."

Then Ash is down in the reception area and crossing the room toward the entry. He is almost there when he hears raised voices behind him. He feels the fear rocket through him in a sudden jolt, but he manages to keep his attention fixed on his plan of escape. Without looking around, he moves swiftly to the closest door and passes through. The Watchmen nearby are looking in the direction of the voices and ignore him. By the time he is outside and halfway down the steps leading up from the street, they have locked the entry doors and shut down all passage in or out. He hears footsteps, and someone shouting at him, but he doesn't slow, continuing toward the walkway, watching as people around him scatter in all directions.

He is off the steps and into the street when T.J. appears, coming toward him at a dead run. He glances around. Two Watchmen are chasing him, both yelling at the top of their lungs. Ash breaks into a run, heading for T.J. The other boy is down on one knee, a weapon pointed in his direction. Ash experiences a moment of supreme terror. Two sharp bursts sound, and his pursuers go down.

T.J. is back on his feet, motioning for him to hurry. Together they race for the gaming parlor and burst through the front doors. Ash forces down the urge to run faster as they charge through a maze of machines and players to the far end of the shop, afraid of what might happen if he were to stumble and fall. He risks a quick glance back to make sure no one is following, and then they are through the rear doors and into the alleyway beyond.

T.J. grabs him and pushes him up against the building wall.

"What's up, fish?" he snaps. "Things didn't work out with your uncle, huh?"

"You just killed two men, T.J.!"

T.J. smirks. "Not likely. ORACLE doesn't like it when you do that. Stun guns don't kill you, in any case. Now, what happened?"

Ash shakes his head. "Just a real strong sense of things not being right. Relatives who really care about you don't usually lock you in a room and tell you it's for your own good."

"All right, then." T.J. lowers his voice. "Apparently they know you've found a way out, so we better start running. Come on!"

They head toward Metro Central at a swift trot. Ash is eager to put as much distance as possible between himself and ORACLE. By now, his uncle will looking for him. Going back no longer seems like a good idea. Maybe he is jumping to conclusions, but maybe he's simply coming to terms with something he was unable to accept earlier.

The warning signs were there, after all; he just didn't look closely enough. His father spent almost no time at all with his brother. Even though Cyrus lives alone and has neither wife nor children, the two remained conspicuously absent from each other's lives. His father did not go to Cyrus about what was happening at BioGen, even after he felt threatened. It was not to his uncle and ORACLE that his father sent Ash but to the Red Zone and Street Freaks.

Ash has never really bothered to look closely at why this might be so. But he does now. His conclusion is inescapable. Everything suggests the very real possibility that Cyrus Collins is in some material way involved in everything that's happened. Achilles Pod might be a quasi-independent police unit, but it is still an arm of ORACLE. And Uncle Cyrus is Calzonia's ORACLE commander.

He is suddenly sick to his stomach as the realization takes hold. He is considering the possibility that his uncle might be behind his father's death; the destruction of Faulkner, Willis4, and Beattie; and his own forced flight from his home. His uncle might be responsible for every bad thing that has happened to him over the past two weeks.

A deep humming sound fills the air, and Ash looks up in response. Three muscular blue-and-red L.A. Preventative transports are clearing the flight lanes of other traffic as they surge past, lights flashing. They are passing directly overhead and flying toward . . .

"Metro Central," Ash whispers to himself.

All around him, people are slowing to gape at the transports, wondering what is happening. In moments, Ash knows, the transports will land and L.A. Preventatives will flood the vast Metro Central ticketing chamber and loading platforms, searching for him. If he continues on, he will almost certainly be caught and taken back to his uncle.

T.J. never hesitates. "This way."

Behind them, the crowds are scattering. Something else is happening, and Ash imagines he doesn't want to get involved in whatever it is. They run faster, moving away from the commotion and Metro Central both. Ash is fit enough, but he is soon breathing hard. He thinks he should have brought his mask with him, but he left it in his backpack. He thinks he should have brought his backpack, for that matter, but that's gone too—along with his K-Bar and what's left of his credits, which until now he had forgotten about completely.

They reach the end of the street and rush into the lobby of a posh Westron Heights Skyline, one of many in an elite hotel chain in Calzonia. T.J. slows them and accepts the greeting offered by the bot doorman and receptionists smiling cheerfully from behind the check-in desks. They continue on through the lobby to reach the backside of the building and a hallway that houses vidviews, reader boards, and information kiosks.

T.J. slows and turns to face him. "Deep breath. You're going to have to man up. You got the cojones for it?"

"What do you mean?"

"Just down the hall there's a transmat."

"No," Ash says at once. "Not a transmat."

T.J. makes a face. "This is a bad time for you to go timid on me, fish. No, I take that back. You're not a fish anymore. That's over. From now on, you're just Ash. Because it looks like you're not returning to the general population after all. You're coming back to stay with us."

"There has to be another way," Ash insists. "*Any* other way. Those things aren't safe."

"Oh, well, then, let's see. We could try a different Metro sub-stem. But they'll all be crawling with L.A. Preventatives. We could take a robo-taxi, but every last one will have been alerted and all the bot drivers programmed to deliver you to ORACLE's front doorstep. Now let's review. What's left? Oh, that's right. Nothing! Except a transmat, of course. A mode of transportation that, by the way, is essentially untraceable."

"We could walk."

"Twenty miles? Me, maybe. But not you. Besides, we'd be out in the open and exposed for entirely too long. Way too risky. You put yourself in this situation by insisting on coming here. Now you have to do what's required to get yourself out."

He says it calmly, but there is an edge to his voice. Ash hesitates, then takes a deep breath. "All right. The transmat it is."

"That's better. Nothing's safe, Ash. Not for 'tweeners and not for you. Everything's a risk. You just go with the best choice available."

They go down the hallway to a door marked TRANSMAT in bold letters. T.J. turns the handle and they step inside. The room is banked wall-to-wall with air intakes, nodes, and digital readouts that glow and blink. At the room's center stands the transmat cylinder, which looks exactly like the pictures he has seen. Ash stares at it fixedly, as if it by doing so he might somehow persuade it to reveal whether it is working properly.

T.J. goes over to the programming console, sets the controls for a destination, deposits the required credits, and after a final perusal of his efforts, steps back.

"Inside, Ash," he says.

A deep breath fails to steady him, but he opens the transmat door and steps inside. The door closes behind him.

He stands in the middle of the cylinder, trying hard not to panic. For a moment, he is not sure if he has to do something more. T.J. is motioning for him to look down. He does so and notices the raised pad off to his right with a large green nodule that reads ENGAGE. He stares at it a moment, glances at T.J., who nods, then closes his eyes, gives up any hope of a long life, and presses the bump.

There is a whine as the transmat powers up, and a tingling rises from his feet to the top of his head, a sort of electrical charge that leaves him shaking. Suddenly everything goes black. There is an instant in which he loses consciousness—or at least it seems that way—as all thought and recognition leaves him. When he comes back to himself, eyes still closed, the tingling is still flowing through him. Then it disappears, and his body goes still. He waits patiently for something to happen, but nothing does.

Unable to stand the suspense, he opens his eyes. He is still inside the cylinder. He is still in one piece. Nothing has happened. He looks through the flexglass for T.J., but the other boy is nowhere to be seen. Something is wrong.

Then he realizes that the room and the transmat both look slightly different. Nothing is wrong after all. In fact, everything is fine. He has been transported to his new destination. He is inside a different cylinder. He presses the nodule on the pad that opens the sliding door and steps out into a chamber similar to, but marginally changed from, the one he started out in.

Standing in place, he listens to the transmat door slide shut again and begins checking himself to see if everything is still present and accounted for. It is. Remarkably, he feels no ill effects from being disintegrated and put back together again. He feels a burst of euphoria. Sometimes technology really is a wonderful thing.

Seconds later, T.J. comes through, exiting the booth as if nothing has happened. "Come on."

When they leave the room, they are in the lobby of another Westron. Wordlessly, T.J. takes Ash by the arm and walks him out the lobby doors and into the fast fading sunlight of a day steadily marching toward dusk.

"Where are we?" Ash says, looking around in bewilderment. "I didn't know they had Westron Hotels in the Zone."

"They *don't* have Westron Hotels in the Zone!" T.J. looks at him as if he is an idiot. "They don't even have transmats in the Zone! Neither one would last out the day. Come on. We have some walking to do."

They head out from the Westron down a broad street that quickly goes from upscale to downtrodden. The well-kept buildings and streets change radically, and all at once they are passing signs that indicate the boundaries of the Red Zone. T.J. doesn't slow, entering the Zone with Ash on his heels. They continue walking until they sight the substem that garages the Flick.

"How was your transmat experience?" T.J. asks. "All your necessaries still intact?"

Ash nods. "Think so. Guess I overreacted. It wasn't so bad."

"You see? I'm usually right about stuff. It complements my perfect physical engineering. So, did your uncle ask you where you've been?"

"Right away. I didn't say a word about Street Freaks. I told him I'd been hiding out in the Metro, living on the streets."

"He believed you?"

"Don't know. He retrieved the records from my father's vidview. He knew the last message sent was to me. He wanted to know what it said. I told him I never got it, that I was too busy running for my life from the Hazmats."

"But he locked you in a room, right?"

"Yep."

"Then he knows you're lying."

"Well, he's lying too. After locking me in, he went off to talk to that Achilles Pod guy Jenny faced down at the gates. He also asked if my father might have told me something or kept notes on what he was working on. He was pumping me for information the whole time!"

T.J. shakes his head. "Never should have gone there."

There are no signs of a police presence, and before long they are driving up the Straightaway for home. Ash is at the wheel. T.J. has insisted. Ash doesn't question it. He just drives. But what he really wants is to go to bed.

When they arrive and enter the building, they find Jenny Cruz waiting, an expression of disgust on her face. "The Shoe's gone out again, and he won't be back before tomorrow. So you're both off the hook until then."

The way she says it tells Ash she knows where they've been and what they've been up to. T.J. merely shrugs. "Ash hasn't done anything wrong. Just what the Shoe told him to do."

"I'm sure that explanation will interest him," she replies, her words icy.

"I'm sorry about this," Ash says.

"Which is why you're asking us to take you back again? That is why you're here, isn't it?"

He hadn't really thought about it. He'd just followed T.J.'s lead. "I guess so."

She shook her head doubtfully. "Go into the dining room, Ash."

Ash does what he is told, finds Woodrow and Holly waiting, and sits down at the table across from them. He feels badly about what might happen to T.J. It will be his fault if the other boy gets in trouble. His own situation seems unimportant by comparison. He might get tossed out on his ear—probably will—but it would be terrible if something like that happened to T.J. Street Freaks isn't really Ash's home, but it is T.J.'s.

Jenny and T.J. sit down next to the others, all of them facing

Ash. It feels like a tribunal, four confronting one. Jenny looks at him and waits for him to look back. When he does, she leans forward. "Tell us what happened. Tell us everything. No holding back, no half-truths. Tell us all of it."

So he tells her. Why not? Either they're going to help him or they're not. He is almost beyond caring. He gives them the full story, everything about his meeting with Cyrus Collins and their exchange in the conference room, how he was locked in but escaped, how T.J. found him and saved him, and how they managed to get out of the Metro and come back to Street Freaks.

When he is finished, the others stare at him, and then abruptly Jenny Cruz says, "You're in a tough spot, Ash."

Ash says nothing. He doesn't know what to say. He shifts his gaze from one face to the next and waits.

"Why is your uncle so desperate to get his hands on you?" Jenny asks finally. "There must be a reason. He's going to an awful lot of trouble to hunt you down. If it isn't to help you, what's the point?"

Holly clears her throat. "You have this phenomenal memory. You sure you didn't see or hear something you're not supposed to know?"

Ash shakes his head and repeats what he has already told them several times. "My father never showed me anything about his work. He rarely even talked about it."

"But your uncle doesn't believe that, does he?"

Ash is suddenly overwhelmed by the immensity of what he is up against. The weight of his difficulties and his inability to figure out how to lift it from his shoulders presses down on him. "I don't know what else to tell you," he confesses, his voice rough and uneven.

He manages to keep from breaking down, but only barely and only because he would be embarrassed beyond words. He is at a point by now where he isn't sure he can trust anyone. Even these kids he thinks are his friends. But he has to take a chance on someone, so he cannot afford to give them further reason to cast him out—especially when he feels it is right on the verge of happening anyway.

He takes a deep breath. "Isn't there something I can say or do to persuade you to let me stay? Just until I find a way out of this mess? I really don't have anywhere else to go now. I'll do anything you ask."

He means it too. No one besides the Shoe and the kids at Street Freaks is likely to help him. He never dreamed he would find himself trapped in the Red Zone and begging to stay, but there it is.

"Things have changed, Ash," Jenny says quietly. "Some of which we can't talk about yet. I can tell you this much. Your father and the Shoe knew each other. The Shoe and your uncle know each other as well. Your father was the link between them, but the circumstances are murky. Your father was involved in a very complex and secretive bit of research at BioGen. So secret I couldn't find out anything about it. Perhaps the Shoe knows, but he isn't saying if he does."

"So that's why my father sent me here?" he interrupts.

"Not exactly. It was probably for another reason—one I'm not prepared to talk about. In any case, it is dangerous for you to stay. Your uncle likely suspects you were hiding out here all along. He will undoubtedly have Achilles Pod take another run at us at some point. If he finds you here when he does, we are all out of luck. The Shoe included. He knows you left. He was probably relieved you did, and he might not be so happy to find you back. The four of us have a different view, but it isn't our call. It's his. So we have several problems to address."

He looks at their solemn faces and grins in spite of himself. All four faces bear mixed expressions. T.J. looks decidedly eager. Holly seems entirely confident. Woodrow looks like he always does—stoic and questioning—but also hopeful about something Ash can't begin to guess. Jenny is just plain poker-faced.

She will be the one who decides, he realizes. He does not feel reassured.

"So the bad news is, you're thinking of helping me?" he asks, trying to leaven the mood.

"Don't get your hopes up," Jenny says at once. "Our idea of helping you might not necessarily square with yours. There is a fresh risk to all of us involved if we do so. One besides the threat of another visit from Achilles Pod."

"What, then?"

"I'm not sure we should tell you that."

"I'm not sure you should either."

They stare at each other wordlessly. Then Jenny seems to make up her mind.

"Some of what we do here is considerably more dangerous than you realize. We do things we haven't told you about yet. Things that if they were discovered would put all of us in prison— or even worse."

Ash stares. "What sort of things?"

"If I agree to explain, you will first have to promise that you will stay and help us—no matter what I ask of you, no matter what your personal feelings might be. You could be a tremendous asset to us; your ability to memorize quickly and comprehensively could prove invaluable. But you put us all at risk if we cannot trust you. Our work is too important to let you jeopardize it."

She pauses. "In exchange for your help, we will give you ours. We will shelter and protect you. We will keep you safe and do our best to find out what happened to your father. We will tell the Shoe you have to be allowed to stay. We took a vote. We like you and we want you with us. But you have to commit. Now."

Ash continues to stare. He doesn't know which way to jump, but if the consequences are as serious as Jenny Cruz suggests, he needs to be sure about his choice. He takes a moment to consider.

"So what you want me to do must be pretty dangerous."

Jenny nods. "If we are caught, it is likely we will be terminated. You understand by now how 'tweeners are looked at. The authorities would find it more convenient to be rid of us. Especially if Achilles Pod becomes involved."

He nods. "But you run that risk by hiding me too."

"Risks are part of life. Some are more worth taking than others. We've all had close calls. We all understand how quickly our lives can be snuffed out. We accept that for the same reasons you will—for a home and a sense of belonging. Now you have to make a choice. Stay and work with us, or walk away."

What Ash understands is that whatever he chooses to do, he will be placing himself in danger. Whichever way he jumps, he could be found and killed. But taking his chances at Street Freaks feels smarter than going out on his own. He takes instant stock of his situation—no home, no family, no credits, and no recognizable future. It occurs to him in that moment that he could end up like his father and that the only way to find out why this has happened is to agree to Jenny's offer.

"I'll stay," he says. "I'll work with you."

"Good for you, Ash." Jenny's smile is genuine. The other kids are smiling too. "Now listen up."

- 16 -

Jenny leans forward in her chair.

"This is what else we do a Street Freaks, Ash—the part you don't know about. We break into corporate offices, hack into computers, and generally mess around with whatever we find. Sometimes we remove funds and put them elsewhere. Sometimes we siphon off information. Sometimes we sabotage or delete select files within a network. Sometimes we go in and destroy everything we can. We operate anonymously. We choose our targets carefully. We don't take unnecessary risks. We don't do more than needs doing. "

She pauses. "Much of what we do can be done without ever leaving the office. Hacking can disrupt just as thoroughly, if not more, as a physical intrusion. And it is less risky. But frequently online security is very good while on-site protections are weak. And in many instances, we decide that to carry out the sort of sabotage we think is necessary, we have to go into the computers directly. We vet our targets very carefully before deciding which way to go.

Ash gives her a look. "So you're thieves," he says.

"Nope. Corporate saboteurs. Stealing is the least of our offenses. Breaking and entering, grand theft, felony property damage, and corporate espionage could be added on. The law is pretty clear. But many corporations are rapacious and greedy, and it would be a mistake to feel badly for them. The ones we go after are so corrupt they can't afford to report what's happened after we're finished with them because they don't want the authorities poking around in their business accounts."

T.J. smirks. "Besides, it's not like anyone gets hurt."

Jenny gives him a look. "T.J. thinks it's all fun and games. It isn't. I meant what I said before. If we get caught, things will be bad for all of us. So we spend a lot of time preparing. We have our assigned tasks, our special skills, and our jobs to do. We keep each other on track and focused. We do not take chances, and we never leave anyone behind."

Ash has not heard anything that persuades him this is a good idea.

"Of course, we make a lot of money," Jenny continues. "Corporate espionage is extremely lucrative. We could make a lot more if we gave in to temptation and diverted a larger amount of what we take to ourselves, but that sort of behavior has a tendency to catch up to you in the end. Besides, our goal is not to enrich ourselves; it is to punish those who do and to funnel their corporate gains back to the larger population of the U.T."

Ash is not so naive that he doesn't understand the predatory nature of many corporations or the way they make their money off the backs of the people of the U.T. Many are corrupt and engage in illegal practices, hiding behind size and obfuscation. Many deserve whatever they get. But it diminishes his friends to think of them as thieves, whatever their motives.

Still, he will have to learn to live with his discomfort if he wants their help. He must become one of them, and when he does, he will be as guilty as they are. That is the plan, of course. To tar him with the same brush.

"How do you keep all this from the Shoe?" he asks. "Doesn't he suspect anything?"

T.J. breaks into a raucous peal of laughter. "Oh, that's really funny! That wins the clueless prize!"

"Shut up, T.J.!" Jenny snaps. She shakes her head, looks back at Ash. "We don't keep anything from the Shoe. We don't have to. He runs the whole operation."

Ash sees it instantly. This is where all the money comes from to fund Street Freaks, while at the same time the business provides the perfect cover for the Shoe's more illicit activities. This is exactly why he is the ringleader. He knows everyone, moves easily among the rich and successful, does business with corporations and corporate officers, and . . .

He catches himself abruptly. He sees the rest of it now. "That's why you're all here, isn't it?" he says. "That's why he brought you to Street Freaks. To steal for him. He chooses the targets. He makes the plans, and you carry them out!"

Jenny nods. "That's why you're still here, Ash." There is an edge to her voice. "The Shoe thinks you might prove a valuable addition to our business. We think so too."

"Thanks for the vote of confidence." He throws it off without thinking.

"Don't belittle it, Ash!" Holly snaps angrily. "What we do gives us food and clothing and a place to call home. The Shoe took us off the streets and out of the labs and experimental hospitals and brought us here. He gave us a life! He keeps us safe. He protects us."

She says it with such passion that it causes Ash to back off immediately. Of course they would feel this way. Why shouldn't they? No one else wanted them. Only the Shoe. A little corporate espionage and theft isn't much of a price to pay for a decent life.

"So, is that what you were planning for me all along?" he asks. "To help you steal stuff?"

"Don't be stupid," Holly snaps. "I brought you here to help you find your father and to keep the Razor Boys from cutting you into little pieces."

"But when we heard you talk about your memory, we were all thinking that maybe you could help us if you decided to stay on," Jenny adds. "You told us yourself you have a photographic memory. There are times when hacking into computers and downloading files would reveal that an unauthorized entry had been made. Sometimes we don't want that to happen. Think how much easier it would make things if you can read the pages, memorize them, and then, once safely back at Street Freaks, reproduce them."

"Any problem with that?" T.J. leans forward, his eyes narrowed. "You as good as you claim, Ash? Or maybe just half as good? Any limitation on how much you can remember?"

Ash shakes his head. "I don't know. I've never tested myself. But once I study something, I can pretty much remember all of it afterward."

Maybe, he thinks, he can sabotage their efforts, and by doing so keep some measure of self-respect. But he abandons the idea almost immediately. Playing games like that could get him tossed back out on the street or worse. Besides, he wouldn't think much of himself if he did so. These kids are helping him, after all. They've taken him in. They've put themselves at risk for him. How ungrateful would he be to suddenly turn on them? He cannot afford to start casting aspersions and making judgments on the only people who have stood up for him.

How honest was his father in his dealings with BioGen anyway? He doesn't know the whole of it yet, but when the truth is revealed, he has a feeling it won't be as bright and shining as he once thought.

"Okay," he says. "I'll help you."

"That's all we ask," Jenny assures him. "But we'll need to find out how good you are. We'll do that tonight."

"Tonight?" he repeats in surprise.

"A plan is already in place. You're the final piece. We go into Narwhal Systems at midnight. This is a company that has been diverting profits to foreign banks for years while reporting diminished returns in falsified annual reports to its shareholders. They've very good at covering it all up; audits have revealed nothing. Tonight, all that changes. T.J., see that Ash gets a full briefing on how this works. Provide him with a blackout sheath and night lenses. I have work to do."

"Wait!" Ash isn't finished. "What about the Shoe?"

Jenny looks confused. "What about him?"

"Well, have you talked to him about this? About me? What if he doesn't like the idea of you asking me to join up?"

T.J. snickers. "Yeah, Jenny, what if he doesn't like it?"

Jenny's glare silences him. "Look, I know you have questions, but let's leave them for later. Don't worry about the Shoe. I'll handle him. If you prove yourself, he'll be happy enough to let you stay."

She gets up and leaves. As Ash watches her go, T.J. leans forward from the other side of the table, his familiar smirk in place. "Here's the thing. The Shoe is the owner of Street Freaks. He's our boss. But it's Jenny Cruz who really runs things."

After the others have followed Jenny out, T.J. begins his explanation of what will happen tonight. Ash will go with Jenny, Holly, and himself. Woodrow, because of his age and physical limitations, will stay behind. They will use a specially designed vehicle to reach Narwhal's main offices. T.J. will stand guard while Holly breaks into the computer room, Jenny will hack into the files and locate the approximately twelve pages of documents they need to access, and Ash will memorize all twelve. The content is comprised of words with a few simple drawings added. It is important they don't attempt to transfer or copy the information. Even photography doesn't work with the new flashback computer screens that just leave you with a whiteout image. These computers would reveal any effort to penetrate their security protocols, and this particular theft needs to be kept secret.

"We have been searching for a way around Narwhal's protections for some time, but we've had no success. Jenny wants to see if you can do what you claim. This will be a test to determine if you are ready for larger things. If you fail the test, you're probably out on your ear. If you succeed, maybe you have a future with us."

No beating around the bush, Ash thinks. Tonight will determine if he stays or goes. It puts pressure on him in still another way. He is already uncertain about whether this is something he can live with, but now matters have moved well beyond worrying about that.

His explanation finished, T.J. leads Ash from the dining room to the mysterious door that sits under the stairway, the one through which the others have disappeared several times. It is both surprising and somewhat anticlimactic when he discovers it opens into a closet filled with cleaning supplies.

"Just wait," T.J. says, glancing over his shoulder with a sly look.

The closet is ribbed with dozens of narrow strips of cedar paneling. T.J. chooses several to press against at various places in what appears to be a random sequence. As he does, a portion of the floor slides away to reveal a set of steps leading down into a lighted cellar. Because the stairs twist within a covered well, he cannot see what lies below. T.J. starts down, beckoning him to follow.

When they get to the bottom of the stairs, Ash stares in surprise. The cellar is a huge, cavernous chamber hollowed out beneath the Street Freaks compound and reinforced with steel supports. There are no windows. Corelights are embedded in the ceiling at regular intervals. Workbenches are scattered about, sets of tools hang from pegged supports off the walls, and piles of scrap metal and automobile parts are heaped everywhere. Various machines for fabricating dominate the room, huge beasts that have purposes Ash can only guess at. There is a single lift for hoisting vehicles, but it is recessed into the floor and nothing sits on it.

"This is what Achilles Pod would *really* like to find," T.J. says. "The only ways in or out of this room are through the supply closet we just used and by an underground tunnel that leads to an abandoned warehouse five hundred yards down the block. We own that too. We use the tunnel for the vehicles. Street Freaks is equipped with devices that conceal this room from the detectors the police use to uncover hidden spaces, so they can't register that there's anything down here but dirt."

"So this is the real reason why hiding me is so dangerous," Ash says. "Achilles Pod might find out what's down here if they keep searching for me. 'Cause they won't stop, will they?"

"We can live with it. They haven't found out anything yet. Besides, that's not the only reason keeping you here is dangerous. You can be a problem all on your own." T.J. points to the far end of the room. "Tell me what you see."

Ash looks where T.J. is pointing, past the Barrier Ram AV parked to one side, back into the farthest corner where, ringed by spotlights that illuminate it from all sides, is a vehicle the likes of which Ash has never seen. It is boxy and ribbed with metal plates that overlap one another like scales. They are flat black in color with no reflective qualities at all. In fact, as Ash takes a closer look, there is no part of the vehicle that does not seem to absorb the light. Metal, glass, tires, and composites—nothing reflects. It looks like an ATV with street machine aspirations. Even as cumbersome and ugly as it seems, it has a dangerous, predatory appearance.

Ash shakes his head. "What is that thing?"

T.J. gestures. "I'll show you."

He walks over to a bank of switches and snaps several off. Instantly, the spotlights at the far end of the chamber go dark and the vehicle disappears. Ash tries hard to pick it out, crouched back there in the darkness, but even knowing it is there, he cannot see a thing.

"That, my friend, is the Onyx," T.J. says, coming back over to join him. "It was designed and built at Street Freaks, and it is the only one of its kind. It is a stealth machine, intended to pass within twenty feet of the human eye without being seen. Admittedly, the technology for rendering it invisible came from another source. It was intended as concealment plating for U.T. assault vehicles, but we sort of borrowed it for our own uses. Spotlights need to be focused directly on it for anyone to notice it in the darkness. Otherwise, it can pass right by you and you won't even notice."

"But wouldn't streetlights . . ."

"Not bright enough," T.J. interrupts immediately. "Not unless you park right under one. Even then, it wouldn't be distinct. You need direct light, and lots of it, to get a close look at her. She's not much good in the daylight, but we do most of our work when everyone else is sleeping. We'll be taking her out tonight. Come over here."

He directs Ash to a set of double doors set into a wall. A row of black sheaths hangs inside. He rummages about for a minute and then pulls one out. "This should be about your size. Try it on."

Ash takes it and looks around for a place to change. "In there," T.J. says, gesturing. "Use the door that says 'men.'" He smirks.

Ash goes inside. A long wooden bench fronts a row of lockers. He sees T.J.'s name on one of them. He opens a second, finds it empty, and claims it. He strips and pulls on the black sheath. It fits him perfectly, its stretching abilities allowing it to mold to his body. It covers him from his ankles to his neck. There is a hood as well. He pulls it on, and nothing remains of his face, just patches of mesh fabric covering his eyes and mouth.

Barefoot, he walks back out. T.J. is waiting and hands him a pair of black Forms. Forms are high-end footwear, and like the sheath to his body, they mold perfectly to his feet. The soles are slightly thicker than the rest of the shoe but allow him to move easily and comfortably after he slips them on. He knows about these shoes. Forms are made of a synthetic developed by the company that manufactures them. They are incredibly resistant to damage of any kind. These are very, very expensive shoes.

"We always wear blackout sheaths and Forms on a job," T.J. says. "They're warm, comfortable, and make it difficult to spot us. We sort of disappear. Like the Onyx. Does everything fit?"

Ash nods, testing the flexibility of his outfit one more time.

"Then they're yours. Here, take these." He hands Ash a pair

of smoky-lensed goggles. "For night vision. Helps you see in the dark. You'll need them later. We still have several hours before we head out."

Ash changes back into his regular clothes, and they go upstairs again. The time passes quickly. Ash might have been tempted to dwell further on what he has learned about Street Freaks, but the other kids don't give him a chance. They rope him into playing a game where they wager exorbitant numbers of credits they apparently don't have and then spend most of their time ribbing one another about how inept they are at the game. It involves dice and a playing board with numbers, and Ash is in debt to all of them almost before the game begins. Their laughter is infectious, and soon he is laughing with them. He really is awful at this game, but he doesn't care. He feels a kinship to these kids, a welcome sense of being brought into the fold and made a part of their family. He knows he will be tested tonight. He knows they have not yet fully embraced him. But it doesn't feel that way, and that's good enough for him. It's what he needs right now. He doesn't want to think about his father and BioGen. He doesn't want to ponder an immune deficiency condition that might not be real. He doesn't want to worry about what he is going to do later or consider the consequences of what it will mean to his life.

He wants this stupid game and the laughter and the feeling of belonging. He wants to be one of them.

Even if he knows he is mostly just pretending.

When it is time to go, he is ready. Leaving Woodrow behind, the rest of them file into the closet and down the hidden stairs to the underground chamber. They separate into their assigned dressing rooms to change and emerge ten minutes later clothed in black. Even Jenny Cruz wears a blackout sheath ribbed with the familiar tubing and equipped with a built-in unit for washing her blood.

T.J. leads them over to the Onyx and triggers the wing doors open. The interior is snug and padded and seats six. T.J. assumes the driver's position, and Jenny sits next to him. Ash and Holly occupy the next row.

When T.J. turns on the engine, there is no sound. The engine is powered by solar cells. The boy pulls the Onyx out of the brilliant circle of light that illuminates its strange form and disappears into the shadows beyond. A bay door slides to one side, and they drive into a tunnel that winds ahead for a short distance to a ramp that climbs to a second sliding door. Once aboveground, they are inside the warehouse T.J. mentioned earlier, a cavernous building that is virtually empty of everything but debris and cast-off materials. T.J. triggers cameras that monitor the outside of the building, studies what lies beyond, and once satisfied, opens a door leading out.

They are at the rear of the building where those traveling the Straightaway will not notice them. T.J. pulls through a gate that opens onto a narrow alleyway. Though they cannot be easily seen in the absence of direct light, it is better to stay clear of the busier streets. Even at this hour of the night, there is always traffic.

Ash feels a tingle of anticipation. He is adrenaline charged and experiences the first stirrings of fear. They are about to break into a building and steal information. If they are caught, things will become more difficult than they already are. He will lose what little freedom he enjoys. His friends could lose more.

They arrive at Narwhal Systems, a huge gleaming edifice rising high above the surrounding buildings. The corporate logo with the letters *NS* speared through by a ribbed horn is visible over the arched entry. Lights blaze in offices throughout, a warning that the building is occupied and alarmed. T.J. drives around to the side of the building and uses a handheld remote to open a loading bay door that takes them beneath the building to a series of loading docks.

He pulls the Onyx into a shadowed corner and looks over at Ash. "Ready?"

Ash, Holly, and Jenny climb out of the vehicle quickly and move to a bank of elevators. T.J. remains in the Onyx. They climb into the elevator, and Holly uses a cyber-splitter—a tiny beam-directed projector she holds right up against the digital readout to bypass the inhibitors that prevent ordinary traffic from stopping on certain floors. The elevator goes straight to 22. No one speaks as they stare at the changing numbers on the digital overhead.

When they exit the elevator, they are standing in a dark hallway. They don the night lenses and move down the hall until they reach a door marked AUTHORIZED PERSONNEL ONLY. Again, Holly uses the splitter on the readout panel, and again, the inhibitors and locks are bypassed. They enter the room that houses the mainframe units to all the individual computers throughout the building. There are no lights in this room either, and Jenny leaves it that way as she moves over to a terminal and takes a seat. The night lenses allow for perfect vision. In minutes, she has powered up the service unit, hacked into the security system that protects the most valuable files, bypassed the lockouts, and found what she is looking for.

"Here you go," she whispers to Ash. "Read them through. Memorize everything."

She steps away, and he takes a seat and begins. He reads quickly, his mind absorbing words and structure, his eyes roving swiftly along sentences from paragraph to paragraph, organizing it as he goes. He gives himself over completely to his task, clearing his mind of everything but the memorization. His concentration is complete, and he finishes in just over ten minutes.

"Done," he announces, pushing back his chair and standing.

"Done?" Holly asks in disbelief.

Jenny gives a nod of approval. "Holly, take Ash back out to the elevators and wait for me there. I have to wipe the cameras and then shut everything down so there won't be any evidence we were here. It will only take me a few minutes."

Ash accompanies Holly out of the room, and they stand facing each other. "That was impressive," Holly tells him. "Can you really remember all that?"

"I think so," he says, forcing a disarming grin.

Holly shakes her head and says nothing else. Standing next to her, Ash is reminded of how big she is. Her sheath molds to her body. He can identify the parts of her that are composite metals. One arm and shoulder, the opposite leg, and sections of her torso. There is no sound of component pieces moving when she shifts. He wonders how it feels to have so much of your flesh and bone replaced with alloys.

A few minutes later, Jenny appears. "Let's go."

They retrace their steps, hurry over to the Onyx, climb in, and drive away. In less than two hours, they have returned to Street Freaks.

Jenny immediately pulls Ash aside.

"Keyboard or transfer orally everything you remember onto this," she instructs, handing him a sophisticated recorder pad. "Use my office. It will be quieter there, allowing you to concentrate better. I'll take a look when you're done."

Ash goes in, closes the door, sits at her desk, and begins to dictate into the recorder pad. It takes him no time at all. When he is done, he scrolls through his recording, satisfies himself that everything has been set down accurately, and walks out.

Jenny takes the recorder pad from him and goes into her office. Does she need his help with the language? Some of it was admittedly technical and completely beyond anything he understood. Maybe he ought to say something.

He decides against it. If she needs his help, she will ask.

He goes over to sit down with Holly and T.J. Woodrow wanders up to join them. "How did it go?"

"Good," Holly says at once. "You should have seen how fast Ash memorized those documents. Talk about speed-reading!"

"*Presumably* memorized those documents," T.J. corrects. "We have to wait and see how much he actually remembered."

Ash says nothing. The minutes pass slowly. Woodrow says the alarms went off twice in their absence, but the monitors did not reveal the presence of any intruders. When Ash asks, the boy tells him Cay hasn't returned either. T.J. rolls his eyes and lets his tongue hang out.

When Jenny emerges, she is smiling. "Very good work, Ash. You passed with flying colors. Your memory is an astounding asset. You got it right almost to the last word."

Ash starts to thank her and then hesitates. "How do you know I got it right?"

"Because I copied the actual documents after you left. This was a test, remember? I had to know for sure. I had to let you think it was for real. We could have simply copied those documents ourselves. But there will be times when that isn't the case, and now we know we can count on you instead."

Ash nods slowly, more irritated than pleased. He almost asks what would have happened if he had gotten it wrong. But he decides at the last minute that maybe he doesn't want to know.

- 17 -

Ash sleeps well that night, untroubled by dreams. When he wakes, he feels rested and content. He is a member of this odd family now, and even the fact that he was tested to make sure he belongs doesn't trouble him. He can understand why Jenny would find it necessary. If their situations were reversed, he would have done the same.

Perhaps, too, he sleeps well because nothing bad happened. His worries proved pointless. Not once were they threatened. They walked in, hacked into the computer files, and walked out again. Maybe what they did was illegal, but it doesn't feel like it. Perhaps his concerns are unfounded. Perhaps Jenny is right and he is helping to bring the worst of the big corporations down a notch or two.

He realizes he is rationalizing because he slept well and feels good and wants his new life to start here, but the specter of ORACLE and his uncle are still out there, and he cannot afford to pretend that the threat they present to him will go away.

He lies back in his bed for a time, listening to T.J. snore, thinking about his situation. It is almost a week now since he sent his DNA and blood samples to the lab for testing, and he still hasn't heard anything. It is days since he took his last ProLx, and nothing about his physical condition seems to have changed. He is suffering no troubling symptoms or experiencing any adverse reactions. It appears he does not need his medication.

But he wishes he could be sure. The fact that he hasn't heard anything definitive may have something to do with Cay's still being away, and she is the one the lab would contact. He reminds himself he must be patient. Today, this seems easy. There is no reason to stress out when he is feeling this good.

He rises, dresses quietly, and goes down to find some breakfast. As he leaves the room, he glances momentarily at Woodrow, parked in his customary corner, sound asleep. He looks like an exotic toy. Ash lets him be.

The sun has risen and the day has begun, but no one seems to be up and about. The bedrooms are quiet, and when he walks downstairs, the bays stand empty.

Then he sees it through the window glass. On the other side of the bay doors, parked close to the building, sits Starfire.

He walks over for a closer look, peers outside, and scans the parking area. There is no one in sight. He finds it hard to believe Starfire's owner would simply leave the racer sitting out like this. But maybe it is not as vulnerable as it seems. Perhaps it has its own protections. Perhaps someone at Street Freaks knows it is there.

What a beautiful machine, he thinks, wishing suddenly it was his, wishing he could drive it. Of late, T.J. has been letting him drive the Flick, riding with him, instructing him on the finer points of racing. He seems to enjoy doing so, and Ash is happy to have the other's advice. He revels in the power of the Flick, but is besotted by Starfire. One day, he tells himself, he will have such a car.

He turns away and goes into the dining room. Holly Priest is sitting alone at the table, eating cereal. "Morning, Ash," she greets him, her broad shoulders hunched, her black hair spiky and mussed.

"Morning," he answers.

He grabs some coffee and toast and goes over to join her. "Everyone else sleeping?"

"Seems so. Good job last night."

"Will I be tested some more or am I really in?"

She glances up, her strong features wrinkling with silent laughter. "You can stop worrying. Don't let last night be a problem. You're one of us now. You're a Street Freak."

"How does it happen?" Ash asks, suddenly curious. "I know how I got here, but how about the rest of you? How did you end up here?"

He has asked this before, but he has never been given an explanation.

Holly shrugs. "The Shoe found us. He doesn't talk about it, but that's what I was told. I was housed at an experimental hospital where they rebuilt me after the accident. They didn't like what I'd become after they finished remaking me. Too much attitude. They were going to terminate me. But someone called the Shoe. He saved my life. I won't ever forget that."

Ash understands how she feels. He feels the same—grateful and beholden. But he wonders why the Shoe, of all people, was summoned to Holly's bedside. He wonders who made the call. Was the Shoe summoned for the others too?

"Did you know Starfire is parked out front?" he asks her instead.

She nods. "She was brought in early this morning. We have to prep her for the Sprint."

"What's that?"

She gives him a look. "Jeez, Ash. Your education is pathetic. You've been spending entirely too much time on the wrong things. The Sprint is a race. Not just any race. *The* race. Held once a year on the Straightaway. Street machines go up against each other for the Red Zone Street Racing World Championship. Bragging rights and a million credits. Worldwide pay-for-view coverage—although mostly fans want to attend in person. Each race is one mile, one opponent, one shot. Lose, and you're out.

Win, and you get to keep racing until you're the only one left."

"A million credits?" He gives her a look.

She shrugs. "The bragging rights are more important. All the machines are built by businesses located in the Zone. That's a requirement of entry. Street Freaks is one of those businesses. Starfire is ours. We built her for this year's race; T.J. will drive her."

"T.J.?" Ash is unable to keep the doubt from his voice.

"He's good," Holly says. "Better than good, really. He's won this race twice already driving our machines. He makes good use of that hand-eye coordination his chemical stew provides. All that genetically enhanced ability to assess what needs doing in a split second. Since he won the last two, he's the favorite to win this one."

Jenny walks into the room, pours herself a cup of coffee, and sits next to Ash. "T.J. is as good as Holly says he is. But there are other good racers and machines too. Most of the Zone's clubs are involved. Including the Razor Boys. They help build racers for Lonnergon's. Not as flashy or as fast as ours, but good enough to compete."

"Don't tell me Ponce drives."

"Okay, we won't," Holly cuts in quickly. "'Cause he doesn't."

She gives Jenny a look that Ash doesn't miss.

"The importance of the Sprint goes way beyond the race itself," she continues. "It's the one day of the year when everyone pays attention to the Zone. Otherwise, we're just a place for misfits and castoffs and illicit pleasures. But for this one day, everyone can see we're something more. Everyone watches us. On private vidviews or by standing in person along the Straightaway."

"It's about recognition and pride," Jenny adds. "The whole Zone is a part of it, and it carries them past the reputation it has otherwise. It shows they are something more—something important. This Zone is a place for those who like things the way they once were better than how they are now. Those who live here want the freedom to be the way they want to be. They don't want a lot of rules and conditions determining the direction of their lives. You've seen the people who live here. Outcasts and outlaws. Discards. That's how other people—people who believe themselves normal—see us. But on this one day, they see us as something more."

"Sounds like a big deal," Ash says, sipping at his coffee, which has cooled by now. He follows professional racing, but that's not street racing, and you can watch it for free. "So a lot of outsiders come into the Zone on race day?"

"Over two million will line the Straightaway. Millions more will watch on vidview."

"Right outside our gates?" Ash is suddenly worried. "But we don't have to go out there, do we?"

"We watch the race from our roof. But meanwhile we have one assignment—prep Starfire."

Which is what happens after T.J. and Woodrow wake and breakfast is completed. They bring Starfire inside, close the bay doors, and begin a carefully orchestrated series of preparations. The big engine is tuned, the fluids are changed out, the tires are balanced anew, gauges are recalibrated for accuracy, and relays and circuits are checked for flaws. Starfire is placed on a lift to allow for a close examination of her undercarriage, then brought down again so Woodrow can oversee a series of tests on the computers that determine her responsiveness to her driver's commands. It all takes an enormous amount of time because everything must be gone through with extreme care. For the first time Ash can remember, Jenny does not retreat to her office to work on her computers but instead stays with the others to oversee their efforts. She relies on a checklist that is pages long and runs down each page item by item. Now and then she stops to ask them to check again.

This takes the entire day and well into the night and continues the following morning. Ash pitches in to help the others. Frequently his job is to fetch and carry. Sometimes he helps with the heavy lifting, although much of the time Holly is strong enough to handle things by herself. He buffs and polishes Starfire's gleaming body and interior workings, following up as the others finish the technical and mechanical work. Her overall appearance is already striking, but on race day she must be perfect.

During these two days, he sees no sign of either the Shoe or Cay. He would like to ask the others where they are and what they are doing, but he cannot bring himself to do so. He waits up all night for Cay on the first night, on a pretext of studying manuals on computer repairs, about which Woodrow has been teaching him. Mornings, he rises early on the chance she might have returned and is still up, drinking coffee in the kitchen. Once he sneaks into her sleeping room to see if there is any evidence of her having come and gone, but her bed is made and the area around it is undisturbed.

He misses her badly. Some of it is due to his memory of their time together when they hid out at her cottage. Some of it is the way his imagination continues to work when he thinks of her, creating scenarios that will allow them to be together, to share a life. He imagines all the barriers that prohibit synths and humans from being couples torn down and all the prejudices and fears overcome. It is all foolish and unlikely, and he knows it. It is pointless and, when all is said and done, it will likely prove heartbreaking.

Still, his thoughts are of her, and he does little to discourage them because they are the sweetest thoughts he knows.

On the afternoon of the third day, after Jenny has gone down the checklist twice, she announces they are finished. Starfire is as ready as she will ever be. She looks beautiful; she has been washed and polished until she gleams. T.J. assures them she will look even better when he crosses the finish line as winner of this year's Red Zone Championship.

"Let's go out this evening," Holly says suddenly, looking around at the others. "Let's go have some fun!"

"Yeah!" T.J. agrees. "Let's go down to Winners Circle and see how everyone else is doing. They'll all be there—drivers, crews, fans, reporters, skints, and scarfs."

"Skints and scarfs?" Ash asks.

"High rollers and freeloaders. Jeez, Ash. You really are ignorant." He turns to the others. "Come on! Let's go!"

Jenny Cruz is reluctant to agree. She would prefer they all stay right where they are, out of the way, avoiding any chance of something bad happening. But she has learned by now she is in the minority on this sort of thing. She understands that Holly and T.J., in particular, need to find a release for some of their excess energy. So she only shrugs and say it's fine so long as they remember how the Shoe will react if anything goes wrong.

Ash, too, is anxious to do something besides sit around waiting for race day. It will be fun to mingle with others from the Zone who are involved in this event. He has listened to his friends talk about the race for three days, and he is as excited as they are to witness it. His look has changed again, so he is less concerned about being discovered than he was a few days back. Holly and Jenny have given him another makeover. They have left his spiky hair intact but dyed it red. They have added a patch-on tattoo to his neck on the right side, a dragon coiled around a racing vehicle. They have changed out his facial hardware. He has let the beginnings of a beard show, a scruffy shadowing of his jawline that they have dyed to match his hair.

Overall, he is more buff than before. His work at Street Freaks and his active lifestyle have slimmed him down and tightened him up. He will never be as sculpted as T.J., but he is more fit than when he arrived.

He still thinks about that last day. About Faulkner, Willis4, and Beattie. About his father. The images still haunt him. His father calling him on the vidview with his warning to run. The deaths of his house bots. His flight into the Red Zone. He still wonders how much of what he believed about his old life was real. He knows his immune deficiency condition may never have existed.

He knows his father may have lied to him. To protect him or to deceive him—which is it? He can't stop wondering.

But the pain lessens with the passing of every day. Somehow it doesn't hurt so much anymore. The past is over and done. What lies ahead is what matters.

They leave Street Freaks in lockdown and pile into the boxy Barrier Ram that Ash saw in the underground work space the previous night. T.J. takes the AV around to the front and through the gates. Ash glances over his shoulder as they drive away, watching the gates close and lock. He hopes that this time when he returns, he won't find the compound flooded with members of Achilles Pod.

The drive is a short one. Winners Circle sits near the end of the Straightaway where the finish line is positioned for the races. Ash realizes he glimpsed it that first day when he rode out with T.J., but he didn't realize what he was looking at. The building is low, squat, and sprawling. It occupies several thousand square feet of space. The walls are stone block, and there appears to be a glass dome at the center of the flat roof, the glass opaque and nonreflective.

The sign over the entrance—an arch with lots of neon that reads WINNERS CIRCLE—flashes on and off in an intense red glare.

The parking lot is already full of vehicles, but T.J. ignores this, pulls up to the door, and lets his passengers off, trying to make things easier for Woodrow. Holly, without asking, climbs out first, reaches back inside, and removes the bot boy effortlessly. She sets him down on the walkway and rubs his head fondly.

"See you inside," T.J. calls to them just before he triggers the doors to close.

Ash glances over at Holly as the Ram roars off for parts unknown. "Think he's coming back?" he deadpans.

Holly smirks. "With T.J., you never know."

They enter the building and another world. The interior is essentially one huge room, a cavernous chamber lit by a combination of streaming neon and throbbing strobes. Reflectors fragment and scatter shards of both. The effect is dramatic. The air seems filled with bits and pieces of color, as if confetti had been thrown into it. The room is crowded and hot. People are everywhere, many of them clustered in a broad open area where they dance to music blasting from giant speakers with such force that the floor is shaking. Most of the many tables surrounding the dancers are occupied. Once again, containers of Sparx are all over the place, available to anyone who wants one.

The dome that from the outside was nonreflective is alive with color inside. Intricate patterns wash across its surface in stunning images that suggest rather than reveal. The images seem to float, drawn by lasers that lance out from apertures cut into the dome's wide base.

In the very back of the room, a bar runs the entire length of the wall. Its chrome and glass surfaces reflect a mixture of brilliant colors that permeate the spaces given over to dancing and table talk. Dozens of stools front the bar, most occupied by couples with their heads bent close.

Everywhere, there is activity.

Ash notices the diversity of those around him. He sees everything from expensive sheaths to common work coveralls stained with fluids and dirt. Some patrons have faces that are clean and fresh. Others look to have come directly from beneath the chassis of the vehicles they work on. Some are tattooed and pierced with pieces of metal jewelry. Others have allowed nothing to mark their skin.

More than a few are part human and part machine. Everything has a slightly surreal look.

Holly, as usual, takes the lead, heading for a table deep into the room, one that seats six but is occupied by a single person. As before at Checkered Flag, she intimidates through sheer size and presence, and the table's solitary occupant is quick to get up and leave. Beckoning the others over, she flags down a server and places a drinks order.

"Just once I wish she'd let us order our own," Jenny complains over the noise engulfing them.

Woodrow snorts. "Doesn't matter. You always order the same thing anyway."

Soon they are seated, Woodrow rolled up to the table's edge, Jenny hunched over uncomfortably in her usual dissatisfied fashion, Holly sprawled all over the place, and Ash sitting up straight and looking around eagerly. He's never been anywhere like this before. Winners Circle has a decidedly different look and feel from Checkered Flag. There is no gaming, only dancing. The noise from the sound system permeates his body, the vibrations causing his insides to tingle. The lights are overpowering. Their flashes and changes of color cause him to blink constantly. People are vague shapes in the gloom and shadows, drifting ghosts. Everything melts and reforms, shifts and resettles, always moving from place to place.

"Back when everyone had street machines, before there were elevated traffic lanes and robo-taxis, they used to have clubs like this everywhere," Holly says. "This is where you went in the old United States if you were our age. Now clubs like these are mostly banned outside the Red Zone. Those that aren't banned, like in the Metro, are closely regulated. You have to buy memberships and pay bribes. I wouldn't step foot in one of those pretentious dumps for all the yuan in China."

T.J. returns and takes a seat. "Found parking right away. Got the magic touch. Hey, where's my drink?"

It arrives with the others moments later. Jenny pays. Ash sips at the cold blue liquid and feels it burn all the way down his throat and into his stomach. It makes him gasp in surprise.

"Strong stuff," Jenny observes archly. He feels a flush creeping up his neck to his face.

Woodrow touches his arm. "Sip slowly. That's Strojen."

"Strojen?"

"What you're drinking. The alcohol content is very high. Be careful."

He finds himself grinning at the thought of being cautioned by a fourteen-year-old boy who doesn't drink anything. But he remembers the morning after his night at Checkered Flag when he could barely lift his head without pain. So he pays attention to Woodrow's warning anyway.

Dozens of people come by their table to offer greetings and best wishes on the upcoming race. They clasp hands with T.J., tell him to watch himself, joke about the dangers of speed, and make light of the whole business. Some are competitors, other drivers and mechanics working for other companies. Some are friends. Many are strangers. T.J. is flushed and happy.

"Hey, T.J.!" Holly shouts suddenly. She stands and begins to shimmy to the beat of the music. "Come on! Get up! Dance with me!"

T.J. hesitates, shrugs, and then rises. The pair moves out onto the dance floor, joining the wild mix of swaying bodies and thumping music. Soon, they can't be seen at all.

Ash takes another sip of Strojen before setting it aside. He takes a moment to look around some more. Sparx, of course, are everywhere. But they're like chewing gum these days; no one thinks anything about it. Mostly, people dance or talk. But back in the shadows, there are couples kissing and touching. Even farther back, money and small packets change hands. In one instance, he sees a shoving match break out. But everything is over and done with quickly. There are security guards everywhere, positioned to make certain nothing gets out of hand. This is the Red Zone, and if order needs to be restored, it will be handled from within the club. L.A. Preventatives avoid this section of the city. For them to show, something terrible would have to happen. The owners of Winners Circle do not intend to let anything go that far, so they use their own people. They are strict about good behavior. Cross the line, and you are out on the street and likely banned from a return appearance.

Woodrow explains all this, apparently thinking from the look on Ash's face he's worried about what he sees. But Ash isn't worried; he is merely curious. He is taking it in and committing it to memory. This is all new to him. It is fresh and exciting. He is hoping he will have a chance to come back, not only to Winners Circle but to Checkered Flag too. But he can't take anything for granted. It is difficult to predict what the Shoe will and will not allow. Especially once he finds out that Jenny has decided to let Ash in on their secret activities.

Seconds later, as if to shatter any illusions he might have about the way his night is going, Ponce and his Razor Boys surround the table.

"What have we here?" Ponce sneers, bending so close Ash can smell his breath. "A bunch of freaks? Frickin' throwaways?"

"Don't be so hard on yourself," Jenny deadpans.

"Just here to wish you luck in the race. Where's the wonder boy?"

Jenny shrugs. "What do you care? Shove off, Ponce."

"Hiding, is he? A frightened little T.J.? Afraid he might lose? To a girrrlllll?"

He draws the last word out in a deliberate taunt.

She gives him a look. "The only loser around here is you."

"Oh, aren't you clever, Jenny Juice Box." He reaches down, grabs her head in both huge hands, and fastens his fingers around one of the tubes that connect to the ports in her neck. "Wonder what would happen if I yanked out your umbilical cord? How smart would that mouth of yours be then?"

Jenny is struggling to break free, her eyes wide with fear.

"Leave her alone!" Woodrow snaps suddenly. "Why do you always have to be so mean?"

Everyone turns. Woodrow is so small and helpless compared to Ponce that they all just stare at him in disbelief.

"What did you just say?" Ponce manages finally, his pierced

features tightening. His eyes are dilated, unfocused. His words are slurred.

"Don't hurt her," Woodrow answers.

Ponce releases Jenny and reaches over for Woodrow, placing both hands about the boy's head and tightening his grip. "How about I hurt you instead?"

"Do it, Ponce! Hurt him!" The boy who danced on the hood of the street machine when Ponce was threatening Ash is dancing here too. His eyes are wild, his face flushed. "Do it!" he repeats, his mouth twisting eagerly. "I want to see him hurt!"

The girl called Penny-Bird steps forward. "Leave it, Ponce. This is pointless. Let's go."

But Ponce is not about to let anything go. "Shut up," he hisses at her. "You don't tell me what to do."

Woodrow is grimacing with pain. Ash stands suddenly and faces Ponce. He doesn't think about it; he just does it. "Why don't you stop picking on people smaller than you?"

He can't believe it when he says this, but the words are out of his mouth before he can stop them. It is a challenge the other boy will answer, but he doesn't care. He hates Ponce and his big mouth and cruel behavior.

Ponce looks at him without recognition. Lights from the overhead lamps reflect off the metal plate embedded in his head. "Who are you?"

Penny-Bird grabs him by the arm. "Come on, Ponce. That's enough. We're wasting time. Let's . . ."

Without bothering to look, Ponce backhands her so hard she flies into the other Razor Boys like a rag doll and collapses in a heap. Ponce ignores her. "I asked you a question," he says to Ash, letting go of Woodrow and taking a threatening step toward his new target.

Ash braces himself. *One good punch*, he thinks. *That might be enough.* If he lives long enough to land it, of course. "You like hitting girls, do you?" He shifts his weight, moving away from the table.

"I'll like hitting you a whole lot more, you frickin' . . ."

He charges Ash without warning, fists swinging. But Ash sideslips the worst of the blows and uses his attacker's weight against him to throw him to the floor. Ponce lies stunned.

But only for an instant, and then he is back on his feet.

"I'm gonna' do things to you that will change your life!" he hisses.

Abruptly, Holly Priest appears, tossing Razor Boys aside like cardboard cutouts. She seizes Ponce by his shoulders and whips him around.

"You coward!" she screams in his face.

Ponce is big and strong and mean looking, but he shrinks to nothing in the face of Holly's wrath. He tries to break free, but she snatches him off his feet with what seems no effort at all and throws him a dozen feet. He lands atop a table that buckles and collapses, scattering the occupants in all directions.

Holly is not finished. She goes after Ponce at once, pulls him to his feet, and shakes him so hard Ash fears his neck will snap.

"I warned you," she hisses at him.

"Frickin' slag!" he screams.

He tries to fight back, but she slaps aside his feeble attempts. T.J. appears, rushes over, and grabs her, trying to pull her away, but she is beyond reason. She puts a hand—the one that is formed of metal coated with synthetic skin—about Ponce's neck and begins to squeeze.

"Stop it, Holly!" T.J. screams in her ear, throwing himself on top of her and yanking violently at her arms.

Then security guards flood in from all sides, knocking every-one out of the way, bearing T.J. and Holly to the floor on top of Ponce, a tangle of arms and legs and bodies. Weighted saps rise and fall, and Ash hears the sickening sound of leather striking flesh. The guards peel them off one another, haul them to the front of the building, and throw them through the door.

The other Razor Boys have Penny-Bird back on her feet. She

is bleeding from her nose and mouth where Ponce struck her but seems all right otherwise. She gives Ash an indecipherable look as her companions lead her away.

Jenny Cruz shakes her head, a look of disgust on her face. "Well, that was entertaining. I can't wait to see what happens when the Shoe hears about it."

"Maybe he won't find out," Ash says hopefully.

"Sure, Ash. Maybe he won't. Maybe the sun won't rise tomorrow either." She gives him a scathing look. "Don't be stupid." She turns away, heading for the door. "Let's just go home."

- 18 -

They ride back to Street Freaks in silence, barely looking at one another. The discomfort and regret is so strong Ash can feel it against his skin, an itch that can't be scratched. Ash drives because T.J. claims to still be woozy from the fight, and Jenny doesn't object. The big Barrier Ram hums along the Straightaway, and Ash can tell it is taking everything Jenny has to keep her anger in check.

She loses it completely when they pull through the gates and park behind the building. "What were you thinking!" she shrieks at Holly. "Do you have any idea what you've done?"

Holly doesn't bother to answer. No answer she could give at this point would satisfy Jenny. Instead, she just looks away, ignoring the other. She is battered and bruised, her clothes are rumpled and torn, and there is blood on her face and arms. She is clearly in no mood to talk to anyone. This makes Jenny even more furious, however, and she stomps off without another word, enters the building well ahead of the rest of them, and slams the door behind her.

Ash and the others trudge after her, their shared if unspoken intentions by now to find their beds and climb into them. Maybe all this will be a little more manageable in the morning. But not if the Shoe hears of it. Not if he finds out what happened. He will keep them penned up for the rest of their lives. He might do even more than that to Ash, once he finds out that the others have told him so much about their covert activities. But he won't hide from what happens if the Shoe confronts him. He won't try to distance himself from the others.

This is his family now.

When he gets inside, T.J. is waiting. He is standing back in the shadows and only appears when the others have passed by.

"Ash," he says quietly. "I have a problem. You've got to help me."

Ash follows him into the supply room. T.J. presses the pad that triggers the lights and closes and locks the door. Then he turns and holds out his left hand. Several of his fingers are deeply discolored and twisted into positions that make Ash cringe. This is why T.J. didn't drive them home. He couldn't. Not with that kind of damage.

"I need you to set them," T.J. says. "Get them back into place. Then bind them up for me. I can't do it with only one hand."

Ash shakes his head. "I don't know if I can. I've never set dislocated fingers."

"Don't worry. I'll talk you through it. Besides, it's going to hurt me more than you, after all."

"Maybe one of the others would be better at . . ."

T.J. seizes him by the front of his sheath with his good hand and yanks him close. "Don't be stupid, Ash! I can't let the others know about this! What if one of them tells the Shoe? If he finds out, I won't be allowed to drive in the race! Look, I helped you when you needed it. Now you help me!"

"How are you going to keep this a secret? Maybe I can set your fingers, but one look at your hand will tell the Shoe all he needs to know!"

"You let me worry about that. Just don't go all wussy on me." T.J. looks around, walks over to the medical cabinet, and starts pulling things out. "I'll get you what you need."

In minutes he gathers up tape, gauze, splints, and antiseptic ointments. He places them all on the counter, then turns around and braces himself. "Get over here."

Ash does. There is nowhere to sit, so they are going to have to do this standing. T.J. holds out his damaged hand. "Start with the middle finger. The second knuckle is out of joint. Take hold of my wrist with one hand and the top part of my finger with the other and pull firmly. Don't hesitate and don't stop halfway. Once you start, follow through. Don't be a fish. You're done with all that. You're one of us now. You're a certified Street Freak. Act like it."

Ash takes hold of T.J.'s wrist with his left hand. He can feel the tendons tighten beneath his grip. He fastens his right hand around the top part of T.J.'s damaged finger, hesitates, and looks at him.

"Don't waste time thinking about this," T.J. hisses at him. "Just go ahead and . . . *ughnnn*!"

Ash pulls hard, resetting the disjointed bones in one quick movement. "How does that feel?" he asks.

"You enjoyed doing that, didn't you?" T.J. exhales sharply. "Okay. Now do the third finger. Same thing. Twist it slightly to your left so it straightens out. Go on."

Ash does so, having a better feel now for what is needed, knowing how much strength to apply and how to do it quickly. In a matter of seconds, it is done. T.J. grimaces in pain as the adjustment is made. He is breathing hard, his jaw set, his brow furrowed.

Only the little finger remains. Ash examines it and shakes his head. "I think this is more than a dislocation."

"You think?" T.J. sneers. "It's at least a fracture. Pop it back into place and then splint it."

"Wouldn't hurt to splint them all for a few days." Ash takes a closer look at the damaged hand. "How did this happen, anyway?"

T.J. shrugs. "One of those security bozos might have hit me with a leather sap, or maybe I hit Ponce on his metal head. Or maybe Holly did it; she's got enough metal in her. I didn't see. I was buried in the pile. And forget about the splint. I've changed my mind. I can't drive if my finger is splinted."

"You're going to be in a lot of pain if you don't."

"Pain helps me focus. Now do it. Last one. Get it over with."

Ash straightens the crooked little finger. It seems to take forever. This adjustment seems to hurt worse than the others. T.J. makes almost no sound, but tears leak from his eyes.

When they are done, they go into the dining room and sit across the table from each other. "My genetic mix allows me to heal faster than most people," T.J. says, a touch of confidence creeping back into his voice. "I've broken fingers before. Dislocated my shoulder several times. No problem. One advantage of being a steroid-enhanced test-tube baby."

Ash nods at the damaged hand. "You're going to have to find a way to hide that from the others. It'll be obvious what's happened if they get a look."

"I'll wear racing gloves. The perfect camouflage. Flexible, ribbed with wire. I'll just say I'm getting into a racing mind-set. No one will think it's any stranger than anything else I do."

Ash isn't sure about that, but there is no point in arguing. T.J. has made up his mind, and he is not likely to change it. This race means a lot to him. In a way, it defines him. Winning this race is what he is known for. Ash is smart enough to understand T.J. doesn't want to lose that.

"I'm worn down," T.J. says after a moment. "But I'm wide awake too. Wired up. Want a shot?"

Ash nods agreeably, not understanding exactly what the other is talking about. T.J. gets up and goes over to a cabinet, opens the door, and brings out a bottle of amber liquid that he pours into two glasses. He carries the glasses back to the table and pushes one across to Ash. Then he lifts his own and holds it out in a sort of challenging gesture.

"To quick healing and fast cars. May they both be my friends forever."

Ash duplicates the gesture, and they clink glasses. Then they both down the liquid in one gulp, T.J. showing the way. As he swallows the contents of his glass, Ash thinks the top of his head is going to come off. He gasps for air and coughs hard. His eyes water, and he can feel his face flush bright red.

"What *is* that?"

T.J. is in stitches. "Whiskey. You never had it before? It's good for quick recuperation from injuries. At least, I like to think so. You don't need it like I do, but I thought you might want to share the experience."

Ash takes several deep breaths. "You could have warned me."

"What? And spoil the surprise?"

They sit companionably while T.J. talks about the upcoming race—which will take place in three days—postulating scenarios, sizing up the competition, and touting the attributes of Starfire. He dismisses his competition. He brushes off Ponce's threats. He is cheerful and demonstrative, the pain and discomfort of his injury lost in his enthusiasm. He refills both his glass and Ash's, downs the contents of his in one gulp, and gestures for Ash to do the same. Ash does, and this time the whiskey goes down easier, although he is beginning to feel fuzzy-headed.

"Can I ask you something?" he says after a few minutes.

T.J. smirks. "You can *ask* me anything. Whether I answer or not is another matter."

"That girl? Penny-Bird? The one who's with the Razor Boys? What's her relationship to Holly?"

"What makes you think there is one?"

"I just do. How Holly went off on Ponce? I don't think it was because of any of us. Not so much, anyway. I think it was because he hit Penny-Bird. So what does this girl mean to her?"

T.J. sighs. "She never said? I thought she would. She's been pretty open with you. But maybe the subject is too painful for her." He leans forward. "When Holly came to Street Freaks, right after Jenny and me, she had this huge chip on her shoulder. She kept to herself, hardly ever spoke. She was new to being who she was, still getting used to the idea that she wasn't just flesh and blood anymore, that now she was made of metal and synthetics too. She was angry with everyone, but especially her parents. I think probably that was the worst of it.

"Anyway, for months she pretty much kept to herself. She did what was asked of her, didn't complain, but stayed apart. She'd talk to you, but not with any real interest in what you had to say. It was weird for all of us. We did everything we could to try to bring her out of her depression, to make her happy. Nothing worked. The Shoe said to let her be. She'll come around. Give her time. Give her space. Let her heal in her own way."

He sips at his whiskey. He is on his fourth glass now, and he has slowed his drinking to small tastes. If the injury to his hand still pains him, he doesn't show it.

"Then, all at once, things changed. She met Penny-Bird. Found her on the streets, brought her home, and took care of her. They were like sisters. Jenny and me, we thought the Shoe would throw Penny-Bird out the door. She wasn't one of us; she was more like Holly's pet. She wasn't tweaked, wasn't a 'tweener, wasn't any-thing but a stray. He left her alone, though. Said she was good for Holly, was helping her recover from the anger and depression. I got it. The Shoe needed Holly; she was the physical backbone of our group. She was so strong, so . . . well, so indestructible. He valued that."

Ash remembers something Holly said to Penny-Bird that first day he came into the Zone and she rescued him from the Razor Boys. She said, "Why don't you ditch these losers?" He didn't understand the connection at the time, but he does now. "So how did Penny-Bird end up with Ponce?"

"She and Holly had some sort of falling out. I never found out the details; Holly refuses to talk about it. Typical Holly. One day Penny-Bird was with her; the next she was gone. Just like that. We all asked Holly what happened, but she just shook her head and told us to shut up. She was angry about it, but she was sad too. She was heartbroken."

T.J. pauses. "That last part. I've always been pretty sure it had something to do with how Holly sees herself. Think about it. She's a patchwork combination of organic and synthetic materials slapped together by doctors who claimed they were trying to save her life when all they were really doing was putting an end to it. She doesn't think there's much of anything left of what she was. She's more metal and plastic than flesh and blood. Half of her can't feel anything. There's no nerve endings, no blood vessels, no normal response functions to pain or pleasure. The woman part of her was destroyed by the surgery. Her childhood was over after the operations. In her mind, she was left a thing that no one could ever love or would even want. She can't have children of her own, can't make love, can't be normal in the ways most people can. She's immensely strong, and as a consequence, she can't ever forget that she can snap another person in two without half trying. She's a 'tweener, even in her own mind. She hates it. She hates what she's become. She doesn't think she's worth being cared about. I think all that got between her and Penny-Bird at some point, and that's why they had a falling out."

"So how did Penny end up with the Razor Boys? Why did Ponce even bother to take her in?"

T.J. drains the last of his whiskey and slams the glass down rather harder then necessary. "To hurt Holly. Ponce hates her. Hates that she's so much stronger than he is. Hates that she doesn't feel attracted to him. Ponce is like that. More insecure than Holly. Penny-Bird knows that. She was always impetuous, always trying to assert her independence. That's what she did here. She bolted from Holly straight for Ponce and persuaded him to take her in and make her *his* pet. Trying to get back at Holly that way."

Ash can see it clearly enough. Holly thinking she deserves what happened to her, that she has brought it on herself. This is her punishment for driving Penny-Bird away. This is her penance.

She accepts it as something she must learn to live with. This is how the rest of her life will go. Thinking it will never be different for someone like her.

"Yet she couldn't stand to see Ponce hit her," he says quietly.

T.J. shrugs, gets to his feet. "Course not. She loves Penny-Bird. Always will." He yawns and stretches his arms above his head. "I've had it. We can talk about this later. I'm going to bed."

He weaves his way out of the room, looking more than slightly bedraggled, his movements leaden and slow. Ash sits where he is and watches until the doorway is empty, and then remains sitting, staring at what's left of his whiskey. He doesn't want it, but he drinks it anyway. He has just finished when Jenny Cruz walks in wearing a bathrobe over her filter-ribbed sheath.

"Why are you still up, Ash?" she asks, taking note of the glass and the bottle on the counter. "Are you drinking?"

"Just a little," he says. "T.J. and I were talking about Holly. I asked him about her relationship with Penny-Bird. He was explaining it to me. Telling me how after they split up, the Razor Boys took Penny-Bird in to hurt Holly."

"As if T.J. would know anything about it," Jenny mutters, sitting down next to him. "Besides, it was more than that. He tell you about what else she does for them?"

Ash stared. "I guess not."

"Remember Ponce saying T.J. was worried about being beat by a girl? That girl would be Penny-Bird. She drives for Lonnergon's. She'll be facing him in the Sprint. And she's good. Maybe as good as T.J."

He thinks about it a moment. "But she can't be more than, what—fifteen or sixteen?"

Jenny shrugs. "Age doesn't mean a whole lot down here. All that matters is how good you are at something." She gives him a long look. "How are you holding up, anyway? You've had a lot to deal with."

"I'm fine."

"That so? You think you might get used to being one of us? A Street Freak?"

He smiles. "I like it here. Even with all the excitement."

"It's good that you do. Your old life is gone."

"I know."

"This is probably where you're going to have to stay. Maybe for a long time. Maybe forever."

He doesn't say anything for a moment, staring at her. "Where is this leading?" he asks finally.

She gives him a smile. "I'm going to tell you a few things I've known all along but have kept to myself. I would have said something before, but there were good reasons not to. You have to accept this without an explanation because I'm not giving you one. Part of it has to do with my not being entirely sure about you. Part of it has to do with a promise I made. But you need to know a little bit."

He doesn't know what is coming, but he can tell it isn't good. Still, she wouldn't be confiding in him if it weren't important.

She fingers the ports at the back of her neck as if to scratch an itch. "First of all, I knew your father. I know I said I didn't, but at the time I felt the lie was necessary. I knew him pretty well, as a matter of fact. Well enough that he confided some things to me, things he was keeping from you."

She pauses, glances past him to the open door, and then rises and walks over to close it. When she comes back, she sits where she was before but pushes her chair backward, as if to distance herself from what is coming.

"What I'm going to tell you, the others don't know. Your father sent you here for a reason, Ash. He thought this was where you would be safest. He told you he believed he was in danger because of his work at BioGen, and I think he was right. He was involved in high-level security experiments he told me were so controversial that if they were made public, it would have ruined the company and brought the U.T. Government down on their heads. But that wasn't what he was really afraid of. He was also doing some things BioGen didn't know about. I think someone at the company found out. I think that's what got him killed."

Ash stares. "I don't understand. What was he doing?"

"BioGen was using kids in experiments to learn how to remake or regrow damaged body parts. They would take them off the streets and out of homes where they weren't wanted and dissect them. All of us, the kids here at Street Freaks and lots more, were part of those experiments. Most of their efforts enjoyed some measure of success. We were among those considered failures, remakes that for one reason or another the company decided to terminate. Your father rescued us and brought us here. The Shoe took us in. He found a place for us. I think something about this threatened BioGen's work and that's why he was killed."

"The Shoe got all of you from my *father*?"

"I was the first."

Ash shakes his head. "So my father knew BioGen was experimenting on kids? Letting them die if they didn't like the results? Helping to make it happen?"

Jenny makes a face. "He wasn't exactly like that. I don't think he was involved personally, only that he knew about it. I also know he was afraid. We talked about it. He said anything he did to change things would put not only him in danger but also you. I think he was warned. He was trying to do what little he could to balance the scales. He made a bargain with the Shoe; he was allowed to bring those of us he thought could be useful to Street Freaks. He brought us here to find a home, and the Shoe gave us one. Some he took elsewhere, probably out of the city. Same arrangement as with us, I would guess. Placed them where they were needed and wanted. With the Shoe, we had to agree to work for him in exchange for a home. It was an easy bargain to make."

"So my father soothed his conscience by saving a handful out of how many? Dozens? Hundreds?" Ash is stunned. "How could he do that? How could he think that was enough?"

"Don't be so quick to judge." Her voice is calm and measured. "You don't know what sort of pressure he was under. You don't know the circumstances. Your father was a good man. He didn't like what was happening. He hated these experiments. He wanted them to stop. But he couldn't find a way. He knew he would probably only get one chance, and if he tried and failed, maybe no one else would ever try again. And even if he exposed it, what if no one was upset enough to do anything? We're castoffs, Ash. Damaged goods. Disposables. No one would miss us. Most probably don't even know we exist. We have no real value. It isn't like it's a sure thing that there would be a cry of outrage over what happens to a bunch of 'tweeners."

She shrugs. "Besides, on the surface of things, it could be argued that what the scientists at BioGen are doing is admirable. Think about it. They're trying to find ways to heal damaged kids so they can be put back into society and lead useful lives. It's hard to find fault with the concept. Where everything falls apart is that they're disposing of those who don't work out. These are kids, and they're killing them."

"Why are you telling me this, Jenny?" he asks. "You could have kept it a secret from me."

"Like your father did?" She shakes her head. "I should have told you sooner. But I wanted to be sure about you, and I thought there was time for that. Turns out, there wasn't. Achilles Pod never raided us before your father was killed and you showed up. We had virtual immunity with that writ of exemption. Now, suddenly, we're targets. Something is going on that none of us understands, and so far I haven't been able to find out what it is. Your father knew, but he didn't say. The Shoe says he doesn't know either, but I wonder. He doesn't tell me everything. He has his secrets, and he will do what needs doing to save his own skin."

Ash hesitates. "Maybe we should be doing the same thing. Maybe we should get out of here."

"And go where? We don't even know which way to run. We

have to figure out what's happening. I'll keep at it on the web. Maybe something will turn up. But in the meantime we have to hunker down for a bit."

"What about the race?"

"The race is unavoidable. There's nothing we can do about that. T.J. will have to drive Starfire. The Shoe is committed to it. After it's over, we can see."

He nods, feeling hot and cold at the same time, feeling sick. "I'm glad you told me about my father," he manages.

"I doubt it. Why would you be? But you have a right to know. Especially now that you're one of us."

"Something the Shoe still doesn't know about, does he?"

She shakes her head no. "I'll tell him when it becomes necessary. Probably when he returns and finds you still here. I'll have to tell him then."

"I shouldn't be here at all," he says.

"Don't start!" she snaps, a sudden edge to her voice. "Don't act like you don't have value, like you're something that deserves to be discarded. Are you your father's son or not? Because until just now, I thought so. Your father was a good person. He saved lives. He took risks. I look at you, and I see him. I hear him in your voice and recognize him in your expressions. You better accept who you are because maybe that's what's going to get you through this."

She sighs. "I took a chance on you, Ash. Don't let me down. Don't let any of us down. We're your family now, and you should respect that."

In fact, he does. The events of the past few days make him feel close to them. For a moment he considers telling her about his immune deficiency problem. But once again he doesn't. He isn't even sure what to say, now that it appears it might all have been a lie.

"One more thing," she says, getting to her feet. "Your uncle is involved in all this. I don't know how, but he is. He has to be. Your father specifically told me that he didn't want you near him. He kept you away deliberately. He sent you here so you wouldn't try to go to ORACLE. That's why I was so upset with T.J. for taking you into the Metro. But there's something else too. That writ of exemption we all relied on so heavily? It was issued by ORACLE and signed by its commander. That would be Cyrus Collins."

She paused. "So it would take his signature to contravene or withdraw the writ. There's no way around it. He is the one who sold us out." She gestures him toward the door. "You think on what that means. Now go to bed."

- 19 -

The following morning Jenny Cruz has Holly drive her back down to Winners Circle in the Flick. Once there, she orders Holly to apologize to the management of the club and to arrange for payment to repair or replace broken furniture and fixtures. When they return, neither one is saying much. Jenny collars the other members of the group and, with checklist in hand, has them go back over the pre-race preparations they have already covered twice before. Whether she does this because she intends it as a form of punishment for what happened the previous night or is just being careful, no one can say. Certainly no one is bold enough to ask, not even T.J., who appears wearing racing gloves.

By midday, when they sit down together for lunch, they have finished with the checklist and Jenny has pronounced Starfire fully prepped and in perfect shape for the Sprint. T.J. says nothing to Ash about his hand but does make a point of announcing to the assemblage that he expects to win the Red Zone Championship and has never felt more ready for anything in his life.

He follows this up with a covert wink that only Ash is meant to see.

When the meal is finished, Jenny hauls T.J. off to her office so he can walk her through the race, a preparation he undergoes each time he drives, Holly explains to Ash as they sit alone in the dining room after the others have left.

"He'll go through everything he intends to do, all the tactics he expects to employ, all the options he will have at his disposal should he need them. He has already written this down, so Jenny will see how thorough he has been and how ready he seems. If she thinks he needs encouragement, she will offer it. If he needs reining in, she will see to that too."

Ash lets her finish and then says, "How did it go at Winners Circle?"

A grimace and a shrug. "About the way you'd expect. Banned for six months, ordered to pay for all the damage—about three thousand credits—and warned not to do it again or I'm out on my ass for good. It's fair. I started it. I brought it on myself."

"What about Ponce?"

"Six months for him too."

"You think that's fair?"

"What's 'fair' got to do with anything?"

"He shouldn't have hit Penny-Bird. He's four times her size."

She gives him a sharp look. "You've been talking to T.J., haven't you? He told you about Penny and me."

Ash hesitates. "He told me a little."

"T.J. should keep his opinions to himself. He thinks he knows all about me, has me all figured out. He thinks he understands how it is with Penny and me, but he doesn't. He should worry about what's going to happen when he faces her in the Sprint, driver to driver." She points a finger at him. "And you should keep your nose out of it too. This isn't your business."

He holds up his hands defensively. "You're right. It isn't my business. But I was curious. I'm sorry about what's happened with you and Penny-Bird."

"Well, don't be. It's ancient history. Penny made her choice. She put herself in a position to allow Ponce to do what he did. She asked the Razor Boys to make her one of them. She asked to be taken in. Now she drives for Lonnergon's. So she doesn't matter to me anymore. She isn't my problem. She's yesterday's news."

By now she is practically in tears. Angry and red-faced, she gets up abruptly and stalks from the room. In the wake of her departure, he is quick to conclude that she doesn't for a minute believe even one of the claims she has just made.

Later that afternoon, the Shoe reappears. Dressed in silver-and-black sheathing with red piping, looking resplendent as always, he goes immediately to Starfire with Jenny in tow to examine the vehicle. He then questions her at length about its condition, the thoroughness of her checklist efforts, T.J.'s readiness, and a series of related subjects like weather reports and track conditions. Ash, standing nearby, hears most of it. The Shoe does not mention Winners Circle or last night's incident. He does not seem unhappy or disturbed. Rather, he seems almost unnaturally calm.

Then he walks over to Ash.

Here it comes, Ash thinks.

But while he is right to worry, he is wrong about what's coming.

"Are you excited about the race?" the Shoe asks, his smile open and disarming.

Ash nods warily. "I've only seen races on the vidviews. Never in person."

"You can't imagine what it feels like. You have to experience the Sprint to appreciate it. Millions of screaming people. Engines roaring like great beasts. The smell of exhaust smoke and engine oil and high-test fuels so volatile that if they ignite unexpectedly, they can blow a street machine to pieces—indescribable."

He pauses. "Of course, no one experiences it like T.J. does. A driver sees it like no one else can."

"I can imagine. I wish it were me."

The Shoe smiles. "Do you?"

Ash shrugs and nods. "Driving Starfire? Sure. Who wouldn't want to drive a car like that?"

"But could you do it?"

"What do you mean?" Ash is confused.

"Could you drive Starfire if you had to? Do you even know how?"

"Maybe. Why are you asking me this?"

"Because you're driving her in the race tomorrow."

Ash laughs, wondering what the joke is. "T.J. might have something to say about that."

"Not anymore he doesn't. He dislocated three fingers and broke a fourth at Winners Circle last night. You should know; you reset them for him." He pauses, cocking his head questioningly. "Did you think I wouldn't find out?"

Then he slaps Ash hard across the face, hard enough that it knocks the boy backward. Ash manages to keep his feet, but the force of the blow brings tears to his eyes.

The Shoe grabs a handful of shirt and pulls him close. "I don't like it when people lie to me, Ash. Especially people I am trying to help even when I don't have to. You've been a bad boy. In addition to last night's brawl, you went into the Metro to speak to your uncle without telling me. Didn't you?"

Ash is still in shock. The Shoe gives him a hard shake. "I can't hear you!"

"Yes!" he gasps, practically shouting it.

The Shoe releases him. "T.J. should know better. About taking you into the Metro. About his behavior last night. You should know better by now too. Sit."

He practically throws Ash onto a bench and then stands over him, looking down. Ash stares back, trying hard not to show fear. But this is a side of the Shoe he has never seen. He can be a scary, angry, threatening man. "You didn't have to do that," Ash says.

"Yes, I did." The Shoe's smile is not friendly. "T.J. can't drive in the Red Zone Championship with one good hand. He thinks he can, but he can't. So he's out. I need someone else. He suggested you. Guess he was impressed with what he saw when he let you drive the Flick. Says he's been teaching you and likes what he sees. Don't look so surprised. He told me all about it. He says you're good. Not as good as he is, but that's beside the point. I need a driver, and you're it!"

Ash shakes his head quickly. "No. I'm not. I'm not ready for something like that."

"Doesn't matter if you're ready or not. You're who's available. You have some experience from driving in Africa when you were a boy. T.J. says you can do it. So you're driving. You won't win, but at least you can make a decent attempt at it."

He leans close. "See, Ash, it's like this. Starfire's owner paid a lot to have her ready for this race and is depending on T.J. to drive. Excuses won't make him feel better if the car doesn't appear in the race. If he loses, he won't be all that upset. Races are lost every day. It happens. He doesn't even have to know it's not T.J. racing. So you're going to be my new T.J. You're going out there in his place to help me honor my agreement with the owner and never talk about this to anyone. Do you understand?"

Ash nods. He can see there is nothing to be gained by arguing. "But I don't know what to do. I have no experience with street racing. I've never driven a race like this. I'm not prepared."

The Shoe nods. "Doesn't matter. Jenny will help you with the preparations and T.J. will give you pointers on how to make Starfire go faster than her competition. Sharpen up that memory of yours and put it to use. Now get out of my sight."

Ash stumbles away, trying to get his head around what he's just been told. On the face of things, this arrangement is ludicrous. He's never driven Starfire. He has driven the Flick, sure. But that's not a bona fide racer. He has driven Cherokee stripdowns, but that was in Africa, and it was more joyriding than racing. How is he supposed to compete against these other drivers with as little training as he's had?

He hears raised voices and turns to see the Shoe and Jenny Cruz standing toe to toe and shouting angrily at each other. They are gesturing, and some of it is directed toward him. The Shoe has told Jenny, and she's probably telling him what Ash wanted to tell him—that he's insane.

But it is an argument she cannot win, and in the end she stomps away, coming over to where Ash stands with his hands in his pockets. "Come with me!" she snaps.

Inside her office, with the door closed, she faces him, flushed and clearly furious. "I didn't ask for any of this," he says quickly, trying to forestall what's coming. "I'm as unhappy about it as you are."

"I doubt it. This is the most ill-considered, foolishly dangerous decision I have ever heard." She throws herself down in her chair behind her desk and crosses her arms as if to demonstrate how much she hates what is happening.

"Why did T.J. tell him about me driving? Why did he even bring it up?"

She gives him a look. "Because he was pressured to suggest something? Because he believes maybe you can drive Starfire with no training? Because he's a pinhead? Take your choice."

"Where is he, anyway?"

"Hiding out where I can't yell at him for being so stupid, I imagine. Cowardly jerk!" She is steaming. "This whole idea is a recipe for disaster."

"What are we going to do?" Ash shuffles his feet. "The Shoe said you would help me."

"There is no help for you." She gives him a look. "But I will try to scrounge some up anyway."

She spends the next several hours walking him through the particulars of the race, starting with a description of how the race itself is run.

"It works like this," she tells him. "You race in heats, two cars in each pairing. The Sprint is a mile; it's a distance meant to test speed, power, and driving skill. There are tactics. You go fast, but you have to measure your acceleration, judge your tire grab on the road surface, your aerodynamic lift, lots of other things as well. In each race, you go head-to-head, the winner moving on to race again, the loser dropping out. You do this until only one car and driver remain. You try not to get killed in the process. If you win the championship, your future is assured. Not that this last part needs to concern you, because you won't win. You'll just be putting in your time and making a good show of it."

She goes over the functions of the car with him, pointing to each of the instruments and readouts and explaining what they will do. It helps that Starfire is so sophisticated that she practically drives herself. The decisions he will make have mostly to do with when to accelerate or slow down. That and keeping in his lane. He will have trouble enough just doing that, she assures him.

"Much of what wins these races depends on how smart you are about knowing when your competitor intends to make a move. The races are all very, very fast. Over in less a minute. Your instincts have to be set at a very high level. You have to antici-pate what the guy you are racing against is going to do and then make your move before he does. When will he try to get past you? When will he accelerate? Is he holding back or going flat out? Do you have enough time left to outwit him? Do you have too much?"

She pauses. "You also have to pay close attention to the other drivers. All of them are in Red Zone clubs, and they have no inter-est in watching T.J. celebrate another victory. They will be coming after you. You can't underestimate them."

Jenny puts him in a black box and lets him train on Starfire using sims. She gives him five different scenarios involving past Sprints. The visuals are more useful than the talks, and after completing the five multiple times, he finds himself growing comfortable with the idea of driving the racer. In the end, she tells him he will probably lose in the first race and not have to race again. But it won't matter; it will be chalked off to an upset and dismissed. So all he has to do is race clean. Stay in his lane. Don't get cute. Brake quickly after the finish line. Then get out of the car and move away. Don't talk to anyone. Remember he's playing a part. Don't let anyone know who he is.

"You can do that much, I expect. Pretend to be T.J. You're about the same height and build. In a racing suit, you'll look enough like him to pass." She throws up her hands. "Cat spit, but this is dumb!"

The remainder of the day passes quickly. Ash studies the instruments on Starfire's dash and listens patiently to Jenny repeat over and over how everything works. He ingests the information quickly, his retention ability so accomplished that after the second time through he can recite it all back to her verbatim. Eventually, she seems to realize this and leaves him alone.

T.J. does not appear.

More than once Ash thinks about the Shoe hitting him across the face—no warning, no holding back. It feels so out of character for the man he believed the Shoe to be that he can't come to terms with it. He can understand the Shoe being angry with him for disobeying. But did it really warrant a blow to the face? He wonders if his initial impressions of the Shoe might be wrong. Perhaps the Shoe is less kind and more ruthless than he had seemed. Perhaps his urbane and civilized behavior is a veneer, and a man of a different sort is hidden beneath.

Sunset approaches. Even after it grows dark, Ash still hears the sounds of construction taking place beyond the walls of their building. Workers are assembling viewing stands and rail barriers to contain the millions that will arrive on the morrow.

When he goes to the upstairs windows for a look, there are lights everywhere. They are fastened to portable generators and hung from poles and lines. The entire Straightaway is ablaze. Hordes of workers cluster along both sides of the racing strip, assembling viewing platforms. The structures are crude but serviceable. The more wealthy and influential of those who come to watch the race will be provided with a superior view of the action.

"Fat cats," T.J. says, coming up behind him so quietly Ash does not hear his approach. "Metro rich who can afford the exorbitant prices the Red Zone businesses will charge for the privilege of watching from an elevated position while comfortably seated. Everyone else will be confined behind the rail barriers and will have to stand to see anything. All day."

"Aren't the walkways public?" Ash says.

"What? Are you crazy? This is the Red Zone. Nothing's public where there's money to be made."

Ash shifts his gaze to the empty space in front of Street Freaks. The crowd-control barriers are in place, but no viewing stands are being assembled. "Why aren't you racing?"

T.J. slaps him on the back. "Because the Shoe said I wasn't. It's his reputation on the line, his responsibility."

"You should have insisted."

"Whoa! Now why didn't I think of that! I should have been firmer with him, huh?"

"This is stupid, me driving. It doesn't matter how much anyone explains things if I've never done it before."

"Too true. But the Shoe wants someone besides me, and you're the best choice he has." He cocks an eyebrow at Ash. "You are, whether you believe it or not. You have that great memory to call on. You have good instincts behind the wheel. I've seen you drive. You'll know what to do. You'll be fine."

Ash remembers Cay driving. She is actually better at it than he is. "Maybe he should ask Cay. She'd be a better choice than me. Either that or just forget the whole thing and drop out. Wait for next year."

T.J. smiles. "There's no way he would agree to either, Ash. Hey, after we eat, I'll give you a few final pointers."

Dinner is consumed around the dining room table. The Shoe cooks the meal himself before sitting down beside Jenny, surprising Ash once again. He's never seen the Shoe cook, let alone eat with them. The food is delicious, a large improvement over the slapped-together meals they usually prepare for themselves, but no one says so. Everyone is busy thinking about the Sprint.

When dinner is finished, the Shoe goes into his office and shuts the door, leaving the others to themselves. Holly tries to organize a board game and fails. Jenny suggests going over the strategy choices, but T.J. says it's his turn to spend time with Ash so he can help him get ready for the race. No one responds to that. They all know what has happened, but no one wants to talk about it. Even Holly is unusually quiet, although she does reassure Ash that he'll do just fine. Ash thanks her for saying so, even though he knows it is wishful thinking.

In the end they all decide to go up on the roof and watch the construction. By now the workers are hoisting into place huge flexible viewing screens that will allow tomorrow's audience to watch the race from any point along the track. The screens are twenty feet square, elevated and secured by wires attached to poles spaced all along the Straightaway. The ones on the Street Freaks side of the track obstruct their sight lines here and there, but not enough to prevent them from viewing most of what happens.

Ash takes it all in, fascinated. T.J. shares a glass of whiskey with all of them, handing one to Ash with an encouraging smile.

In the middle of things, his vidview lights up, the red dot appearing in front of his eyes. He switches on the air screen, and there is Cay.

"Can you talk?" she asks.

He steps away from the half wall, moving toward the back of the roof, as far away from the others as he can get. "Go ahead."

"I got the results back from the lab. It took longer than I expected. Seems they made multiple attempts to be sure they weren't missing something. The DNA and blood samples reveal no evidence of an immune deficiency problem. Your tissue samples are perfectly normal. What they did find, however, is evidence of a strong suppressing agent. It's throughout your system, suggesting long-term usage."

"ProLx," he says, still not quite believing it. "What's being suppressed?"

"They can't be sure without further testing. You might want to think about going to a medical facility and having that done. Maybe soon. You might still be in real danger, even if your immune system isn't compromised."

He studies her calm face, and in her features he finds a measure of relief. "Thanks for letting me know. Where are you?"

"Elsewhere."

"Coming to the race? Everyone's here."

"I don't think so."

"I miss you."

She stares at him. "You have to stop this."

She switches off her vidview, and his screen goes blank. He stares into space. "Too late," he whispers.

A short while later, they all go off to bed. Everyone drifts away one by one until Ash is left alone. He stares down at the long black ribbon of the Straightaway and thinks about what lies ahead. He tries to visualize himself driving Starfire.

He cannot manage it.

He goes down to his bedroom and lies awake for what feels like hours. The twisting and turning sounds that come from the bed next to him suggest T.J. is having a similar problem. Woodrow's corner of the room is silent. The bot boy makes no sound at all. Ash listens for even the smallest whisper of movement until he falls asleep.

When he wakes the following morning, everything has changed.

- 20 -

At first, Ash has no idea what has happened.

For one thing, he is no longer in his bed. He is sitting upright in a chair. He has a pounding headache and a strange metallic taste in his mouth. When he opens his eyes, the light in front of him feels so blinding that he shuts them again immediately. Was that a vidview he was looking at? He peeks through slitted eyelids and catches a glimpse of his surroundings. He appears to be in a mostly empty room. There is a din coming from somewhere, loud and insistent. Voices, thousands of them, roaring as one. It takes him a moment to understand. It is the morning of the race, and the crowds of spectators are gathered. He should be out there, putting on his racing suit, getting ready to drive.

But when he tries to move, he discovers he is bound hand and foot to the chair with his mouth taped over. He can turn his head, but everything else is securely fastened in place. When he forces himself to open his eyes again, taking care not to do so too quickly, he is facing not a vidview but a large window of darkened glass, looking out on what appears to be about a gazillion people clustered on walkways and bleachers one story below.

Then he glances around and realizes the truth. He is inside Street Freaks in the upstairs viewing room, staring out one of the dark-screen windows. The sounds are coming from a com unit taped to the wall off to one side. T.J.! Where is T.J.? But he already knows.

He wants to drive Starfire in the race.

He wants me to watch him win it.

He wants to show me—to show everyone, especially the Shoe—that he can do this, smashed fingers or no.

Ash knows the whiskey he was given contained a drug, slow acting but effective. He thrashes wildly. He has to get free!

But the chair is bolted to the floor and will not move. He struggles a long time, but nothing helps. In desperation, he begins trying to bang his feet against the chair and the floor, hoping someone will hear him. But he can't even do that. He is so completely immobilized that he can do nothing but stare out the window.

He can see the entire length of the Straightaway. A seething mass of humanity stretches along both sides of the raceway for as far as the eye can see. There are thousands upon thousands of people. Spectators have come from everywhere to witness the day's event. Adults and children both press against the barriers and fill up virtually every square foot of walkway. They carry sitting pads and collapsible chairs. They have either walked from the Metro or ridden one of the substems. No antigrav transports ever come into the Red Zone. Air traffic, while cleared to pass through any part of what constitutes L.A. airspace, are not welcome here. Preventatives or Achilles Pod or much of anything else notwithstanding, a violation of this unwritten rule is not something the transports would challenge.

Already, a handful of street machines are on the racecourse, giving their drivers a final chance to feel the surface beneath their tires. This is important, Jenny has told him. While the competition always takes place on straight-line racecourses with no turns or banks, each one has its own peculiar synthetic surface. A feel for that surface is crucial—a sense of how a machine will respond to it—vital to victory over competitors.

Engines rev up with thunderous roars. Some spit fire and smoke from their exhausts. All sit balanced over the rear wheels. The racing machines are of different shapes and sizes, reflecting the efforts of their makers to produce power and reduce drag. A few things are similar. The rear tires are monstrous, some taller than the roofs of the machines themselves. These behemoths lift the back ends of the chassis so they are raked forward at a deep, narrow slant, the smaller front tires shouldering a lighter weight. The gleaming bodies are covered with advertisements, wild drawings, and slogans. Every color combination and look imaginable is visible along the length of the course.

The crowds are enthusiastic and loud. Music blares out of ramped-up speakers from the pleasure houses and gambling palaces. Impromptu dancing breaks out here and there, some of it taking place on the course itself. L.A. Preventatives roam the edges, maintaining a presence while trying not to get involved, staying clear of what are mostly expressions of excitement. There are too few of them and too many civilians to keep everyone in line. If there were surveillance cameras, it would be easier to monitor what was happening and to lower the response time of the authorities. But even for today's event, the Red Zone refuses to allow public vidcams to be installed.

Ash takes in everything. Despite his horror of what is about to happen, he can't look away.

Hundreds of small tableaux reveal themselves. Here, a family arranges blankets and a picnic on the walkway. There, an older couple sets up chairs directly in front of Street Freaks' gates, apparently unaware that Starfire will be passing through momentarily. Farther on, dancers cavort, dressed in wild colors and trailing long ribbons. Children run with careless abandon, towing rainbows of balloons behind them.

Everyone is laughing and shouting and having fun.

Ash is appalled. T.J. has lost his mind.

Then a collective gasp rises from the crowd assembled

immediately below. He looks down and notices those closest to Street Freaks are turning to look at something. Starfire appears, pulling out onto the surround leading to the gates. Sunlight glints off her flawless sapphire surface, which bears the name STREET FREAKS scrolled in silver on each door panel.

Has there ever been a more beautiful machine? The crowd doesn't think so. The applause and shouts of approval from those closest soon spreads until it becomes an avalanche of sound. The giant viewing screens flare with fresh intensity, and there is Starfire in gleaming color, bigger than life, bright with promise.

Starfire is coming!

Starfire is here!

The cries of adulation are like a tidal wave. It seems that they will never end.

Suddenly, T.J.'s voice comes out of a com unit Ash had not noticed before now, set off to one side of the viewing screen.

Hope you're enjoying the show, Ash. You have a ringside seat with a great view and inside information. Sorry I had to drug and bind you, but you understand. The Sprint is my race. It belongs to me. Not to you or anyone else. No matter what the Shoe thinks. So try to understand. Don't be angry. We can talk it over later, after I've won. Don't take it personally. This is something I had to do.

The com goes silent.

From there, things only get more maddening. None of Ash's friends comes to look for him, clearly thinking him sealed up in Starfire. Apparently no one notices T.J.'s absence, probably deciding he is off bemoaning the unfairness of it all. Ash continues trying to get free but makes no progress whatsoever.

A parade follows, a lengthy pageant consisting of race contenders and their machines, musical bands, and a variety of acrobatic performers traversing the length of the Straightaway. The bands play heart-stirring anthems and familiar United Territories marches. Some move in lockstep, some dance in wild free form. Along the edges of the course, vendors hawk racing gear and souvenirs for purchase. Balloons fly everywhere.

But it is the street machines that are the center of attention, their gleaming bodies and bold colors on full display for the enthusiastic crowds as they make their way along the course, engines roaring, exhausts spitting fire, drivers waving gloved hands within sealed cockpits. Everything else in the parade is sandwiched between as if to serve as buffers.

Applause is long and thunderous for each machine, but at no point is it louder than when Starfire drives past. The stunning sapphire racer has caught the crowd's imagination, and it responds in the time-honored fashion, engine revving to a monstrous howl. Starfire is the epitome of what a street racer should look like. It is the personification of dreams and imaginings. Those watching adopt her as their own; they make her their shining hope. Even before the races begin, they have anointed their champion.

The parade lasts just over an hour, and then it is time to race.

From the roof of Street Freaks, Holly and the others will be watching it all unfold. Ash can see most of it. What he can't see directly, he can view on the huge vidscreens. The racers draw lots for pairing. When the matches are made, the racers queue up behind the starting line in the order of their draw, numbers one and two positioned first, and so on. Each pair of machines will compete, but the ultimate winners will be determined by times, not by who wins a pairing. Only the fastest will move on to race again. Half the field will be eliminated in the first round. The other half will race again. The fastest of this second round will race a third time, and only two will advance from there to the championship.

There are twenty-four racers at the start. This is the maximum number allowed. Admission is determined by application submission and review. The process is under the control of a race committee consisting of government officials and Red Zone businessmen. The members of the committee consider the merits of each application, the history of the racers, testimonials and letters of recommendation, and perhaps soothsayers, for all anyone knows. Probably money changes hands. Probably a lot. It is the nature of the beast. The selection process is undoubtedly rigged in some fashion, but no one has ever been able to prove it. What matters is that choices made by the committee are final. There is no appeal.

On the other hand, the choices have always been validated by the strength of the entries once they take the track, and there has never been a winner who didn't get there by virtue of possessing superior strength, skill, and speed. When the racers are on the course going head-to-head for the victory, there is no place to hide. In full view of millions of people, you can't cheat your way to the championship. If either one of a pair strays from the lines of an assigned lane, it is eliminated automatically. The vehicles are not permitted to engage physically in any way.

The first two racers are rolling up to the starting line, and an announcer is calling out the names of the machines and drivers. The crowd noise is so deafening that it is virtually impossible to make out any of it. But when the introductions are complete and the racers are in place, a series of bright flashes light the raceway on either side, the top rail of the barriers glowing with a bluish light that pulses and throbs in a steady rhythm.

They've turned on a force field, Ash realizes. The racers are built very low to the ground, all riding well below the top rail of the barrier. While the racing machines are not allowed to have contact with each other and are required to race in a straight line, there is always the danger of one of them going into the crowd. The force field is designed to prevent this.

At the start line, the first pair of racers rev their engines, building power for stronger thrust, shaking with anticipation, anxious for release. The signal flag that will start the race is lifted high, a deep red that will hold the racers in check until it drops. The starter is a seasoned veteran, and he knows exactly the moment that both machines are primed and ready. The crowd is roaring in anticipation, yelling and screaming, handheld flags and banners flying. The racecourse lies empty and waiting.

The flag drops.

The racers explode from the line, hurtling down the mile course. The one on the right fishtails slightly, just enough to cause it to lose a marginal amount of ground on its competitor, a black-and-silver Chronos that has been chopped down and streamlined. The vehicles tear down the Straightaway, gaining speeds that are breathtaking. The race is over almost before it has begun, as the Chronos pulls ahead at the finish line to win by half a length. It all happens so fast. The machines are beasts; they exude brute force and power. Their speed over such a short distance is shocking.

When they have pulled up beyond the finish line and driven off the track to the holding pen, two more advance to the starting line. This pairing is much odder than the last. One machine is massive, dwarfing its competitor, rendering it a water bug beside a lizard. The lizard is swept back and smooth bodied save for a rear spoiler, and its smaller front wheels ride two feet out on either side from its rounded nose. The second machine is small and low slung, so much so it appears to rest right on the surface of the racetrack. The driver, who is visible on the giant screens when the camera pans in on his machine, lies almost horizontal to the track within his cockpit, feet forward and head raised just enough to allow for a clear view of what lies ahead. The position looks uncomfortable and awkward. The machine, even with its huge rear wheels, looks insignificant.

It isn't. Once the race begins, it streaks off the starting line and surges ahead of the bigger machine to finish more than a length ahead, the howls and clapping of the crowd chasing it well beyond the conclusion of the race and into the holding pen.

Starfire is up next.

An instant later, the door to the room bursts open and Holly is there. She hesitates momentarily, clearly confused. Then she rushes over, breaks Ash's bindings with her bare hands, removes the tape from his mouth, and sets him on his feet.

"Just when you thought things couldn't get any weirder," she hisses. "He's driving Starfire, isn't he?"

Ash nods, tests his balance. He takes a step and totters. Holly catches him quickly. "Slowly, Ash. Take your time. There's nothing to be done about it now."

"I never thought he would do something like this," Ash mutters, shaking the numbness out of his arms. "He drugged me!"

"The Shoe will have his head." She reaches for his arm and loops it over her shoulders. "Come on. We're going up with the others."

They depart the room and head up the stairs to the rooftop. Ash takes a deep breath of fresh air. "How did you find me?"

She snorts. "Dumb luck. I was looking for T.J. Thought he was off sulking when he shouldn't be. Tried everywhere before I got to you. Last resort, and what do I find? You. Still can't believe it. Although, in a way, I can. This race is what he lives for."

When they reach the roof, Jenny and Woodrow are peering down at the crowd. They turn at the same time and both wear looks of astonishment.

"Ash!" the bot boy gasps. "What are you doing here?"

Ash shakes his head but doesn't answer. Holly helps him over to join them, freeing his arm when he is safely in place so he can lean against the half wall. He is already starting to recover, the feeling returning to his limbs and his head clearing.

He sees Starfire right away, moving slowly into place at the starting line.

The volume of noise that emanates from the crowd reaches a new level. The roar is deafening, the sustained fury of it—because "fury" is exactly the right word, the sound ferocious and maddened—sufficient to cause the viewing stands to shake beneath those who occupy them. Ash has never heard anything like it. The decibel level increases as the competitors are announced and the growls of their machines rise briefly in response.

Starfire is paired against a vehicle very similar in look, a fiery-red racer that mirrors her sleek lines and contoured surfaces. Many in the crowd wonder if Starfire has met her match. The thunder of screaming voices, stamping feet, and clapping hands could be for either or both of the competitors. It is impossible to tell. But it continues unabated as the pair nudges up to the starting line, snarling and spitting fire, shaking like animals ready to run, ready to fight.

"Holly!" Woodrow exclaims, looking at her.

"Shut up, Woodrow," she snaps angrily.

Jenny leans over to Ash and says, "Lonnergon's entry."

He stares at her.

"Penny-Bird," she says.

When the flag drops, the machines are mirror images of each other. They fly down the Straightaway side by side, straining to gain speed, each struggling to get an edge over the other. Neither can manage it. T.J. is good, but Penny-Bird is his equal. Sapphire blue and blood red, the racers tear down the synthetic surface of the racecourse, engines screaming as loudly and wildly as the crowds pressed up against the walkway railings. Sunlight glints off their mirror-bright surfaces in starbursts.

The finish line approaches, coming up fast—too fast, too soon—both racers flying toward it, still locked in combat, neither one able to get ahead of the other . . .

Until they thunder beneath the checkered flag, swept to victory as one by the howls and shrieks of the crowd.

It is over, but no one knows who won. No announcement is made. The racers pull up and await a decision. Vidcams will have captured the moment when they crossed the finish line and will determine which, if either, has found the extra few seconds needed to claim the victory. Instruments will have measured speed and elapsed time electronically, and the data will be examined. The crowd noise fades to a dull murmur as everyone awaits the announcement. The decision takes long minutes, endless minutes.

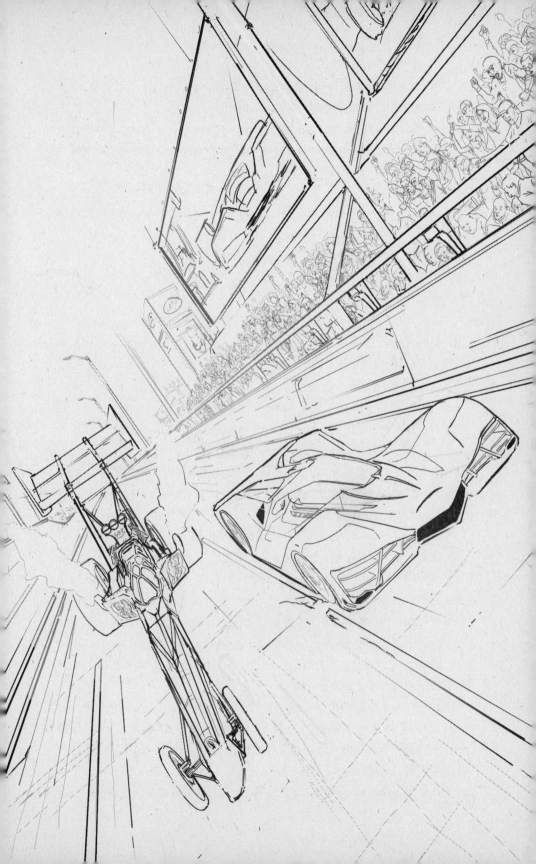

If Starfire has lost, Ash thinks, that will take T.J. out of the race and put an end to this whole charade.

A massive roar rises from the crowd. The huge viewing screens lining the Straightaway fill with not one but two names.

Starfire and the Lonnergon's entry.

It is a tie.

The roar of the crowd builds to a fresh crescendo that washes over the whole of the racetrack.

Ash feels his heart sink.

The outcomes of the rest of the races, although many are close and some sensational, feel anticlimactic. The crowd is excited each time, but its enthusiasm does not approach previous levels. When all the races are run, twelve winners are declared and will race against each other in pairs. The second round is scheduled to begin after a short intermission. Down along the racetrack, refreshments and souvenirs are sold by roving vendors while hearts are allowed to drop from throats and pulse rates are given an opportunity to settle.

The winners selected from the first round are matched in new pairings for the second race. Starfire's new adversary is the Chronos. They are positioned next to last. Time seems to drag endlessly as everyone waits for the competition to begin anew. But the second round goes much more quickly than the first, the winners in all of the rounds advancing easily. Even Starfire's battle against the Chronos is never in doubt, the blue-and-silver racer winning by almost two lengths.

Now only six remain. Among them are Starfire, the Lonnergon's entry, and the water bug. There is another intermission, this one longer than the first, ostensibly so that the drivers can ingest liquids and catch a few moments of rest, but it's actually to allow the audience to spend more of their hard-earned credits in the

Zone. Ash stares down helplessly from atop the Street Freaks building. He wishes he could speak to T.J. To tell him to stop now, to drop out. To tell him this is a mistake. His hand is a mess.

But he can do nothing, and all too soon, the third race is ready to start. This time only the two fastest will advance to the championship round.

Starfire is in the first pairing. She is matched against a long, needle-nosed emerald retro that harkens back to the machines from races that were held several hundred years ago in the old United States. These machines were called "dragsters," and they raced with their engines uncovered and much of their framework exposed. They were all engine and tires, odd-looking hunkered-down machines with big shoulders and raked bodies that narrowed sharply toward the front end. Starfire's competitor is one of those.

The start flag drops, and they fly off the line and tear down the Straightaway in a roaring surge that causes the dragster to veer into Starfire's gleaming body. There is contact, but it is minimal, and the dragster straightens out again almost instantly. But any contact is sufficient to disqualify the vehicle causing it, and when the race is finished—a race Starfire wins easily—the dragster is eliminated by rule.

The other machines race afterward, and now it becomes a question of whether Starfire's run was fast enough to put her in the final pairing. If the contact with the dragster slowed her sufficiently, she will be out of the running. There is a long delay as the officials examine the results. The crowd is restless, their muttering growing steadily louder, their dissatisfaction evident. Starfire didn't cause the contact, but that isn't the issue. What matters are the comparative times and whether Starfire is one of the fastest two.

When the announcement is finally made, a roar rises from the crowd. Starfire and Penny-Bird's crimson racer will race for the championship. Once again, both have finished the round with identical times.

The crowd loves it. Hundreds of thousands of voices shout

their approval, and the air vibrates with the sounds of their enthusiasm. The racers pull up to the starting line, revving their engines
in a guttural growl that with each fresh burst of barely restrained
power surpasses the roar of those watching. It feels as if the
ground is shaking; Street Freaks is vibrating all the way down to
its foundation. The air itself quivers with the volume of noise being
generated. The giant screens fill with images of the challengers,
the faces of the drivers within the cockpits and the machines
themselves as they ready for the start.

The anticipation builds, and time slows to a crawl. The starter
waits patiently, his red flag raised.

When it falls, it is as if the earth itself explodes. The machines
leap forward as one, engines roaring and oversized tires screaming as they seek purchase on the smooth synthetic surface of
the Straightaway. For the first few seconds, they remain locked
together, as if tethered by invisible bonds, keeping pace with one
another as they hurtle down the track.

Then Starfire begins to pull away from her competitor, a lead
measured by inches, then a foot. On the big screens, you can see
it. The cameras show clearly what the eye cannot.

Starfire has taken the lead. Ash can't believe it. T.J. is going
to win!

They are almost halfway down the track by now, but it seems
to have taken them forever to get there. Ash goes still, his eyes
glued to the track, watching the racers flit between gaps in the
giant viewing screens. On the screens, the gap between Starfire
and the crimson racer widens. And then, abruptly, it begins to
close. Penny-Bird is catching up.

They are past the halfway mark, the roaring of the engines
a booming thunder that engulfs the whole of the visible world.
Penny-Bird draws even with T.J. They are locked together once
more in a repeat of the first race, screaming toward the finish.

Then Ash sees it. A screen of smoke is coming off Starfire's
sleek body, wisps of it rising and evaporating in the heat of the

wash she creates with her passing. Something is wrong. Ash blinks against the sun's glare. Are those flames he sees? Those tiny blue flickers of light? Are his eyes deceiving him?

She's on fire, he realizes.

And in the next instant, *Get out, T.J.!*

But there is no getting out. Starfire is doing two hundred miles an hour and flying toward the finish line. Even if T.J. wanted to escape, there's not enough time. In the last three seconds before Starfire and her crimson opponent scream across the finish line, the checkered flag dropping in a series of sweeping figure eights, T.J. summons one final burst of power from his racer and pulls ahead.

But by now Starfire is engulfed in flames. Pinpricks of fire dance across her brilliant surface with wicked glee. She is still traveling at nearly two hundred miles an hour when the flames reach the fuel tank.

An instant later, she explodes in a pillar of fire.

Ash stands at the wall, staring down the Straightaway to where the smoke and ash plume skyward. There is a rent in the fabric of time, and he has fallen into it, blasted and emptied. He has quit breathing. He hears the sounds of horror and disbelief rising from the crowd. Thousands are surging toward the site of the explosion. They press against the barriers that form the force field, and eventually the railings give way to the pressure and the crowd pours into the street.

"I'm going down there!" Holly shouts.

Without waiting for a response, she disappears into the stairwell. How will she get there with so many people surging in the streets? Ash doesn't know. Maybe she will walk on air. Tears fill his eyes. Tommy Jeffers is gone. It isn't possible. His throat tightens. It was supposed to be him. *He* was supposed to be driving.

Behind him, Jenny Cruz is crying. Woodrow wheels up beside him and parks at his elbow. The bot boy says nothing, but a quick glance down reveals that his face is stricken.

A moment later, both Jenny and Woodrow are gone, and Ash is left alone. He stares down at the chaos on the Straightaway and smoke from the crash sight.

On the giant viewing screens, the vidcams are capturing reactions from those gathered in the viewing stands. Most are standing, their gazes locked on the debris from the explosion. A few are starting to leave.

The camera shifts to dignitaries and officials. A jolt of recognition shakes Ash as a familiar face comes into focus. Cyrus Collins. His shaved head, his robust muscular body, and his craggy face—his uncle radiates strength.

He also recognizes the girl clinging possessively to his arm, a girl so strikingly beautiful he cannot mistake her.

It is Cay Dumont.

A moment later, the vidcam shifts away.

- 21 -

Ash has quit breathing. He cannot speak. He listens to the sounds of horror and disbelief rising from below without hearing them. The crowd, which has milled about aimlessly since the explosion, finally begins to break up and move toward the substems or the boundaries of the Red Zone to make its way home again. The Sprint is finished, and they are anxious to escape the aftermath of a tragedy so terrible it will be replayed on vidviews for days to come. The big screens are already showing it over and over, sandwiched between interviews and commentaries and the usual suspicions and speculations of how it happened and what it means for the future of the annual Sprint competition. But in minutes, the race car's crash and the driver's death will become just another news story in an endless progression of news stories.

Ash stays where he is. The sadness he feels is deep and pervasive. But there is anger too. Anger at what happened, no matter the cause. Anger that he could do nothing but stand there and watch. Not that there was anything he could have done; there wasn't. But the feeling of powerlessness is maddening, even now. He wishes he could have done something to stop this from happening. He feels this might be his fault in some inexplicable way, another consequence of his coming to Street Freaks.

His anger shifts abruptly to Cay.

In his mind, he sees her arm linked to his uncle's. He sees her as an adornment, a bauble to flash. He imagines her as a plaything for his amusement. The pain he feels is enormous. Why is she with *him*? Why did she lie about coming to the Sprint?

He gives his emotions free rein for a long time, waiting until the worst of them have emptied out before going back downstairs to join the others.

There is no sign of the Shoe, but Holly has returned and is sitting with Jenny and Woodrow at the dining room table. He joins them, anxious to hear what she has to say. The cyborg girl drinks deeply from a bottle of soda, her smooth synthetic features hard and set.

"They aren't sure about the cause. Still investigating, they claim. But they're already calling it an accident. Something in Starfire malfunctioned, causing a fire. The flames spread to the fuel tank. End of story."

"Nothing malfunctioned," Woodrow snaps, his young face suddenly angry. "We checked everything. It was all working when Starfire rolled out of here. There were fire retardants installed everywhere. There were diffusers to smother flames. Automatic release valves. That wasn't what happened!"

His words are insistent and a bit defensive. Holly shrugs. "Maybe something ruptured when that dragster clipped Starfire on the track. T.J. got through that race, but it all caught up with him in the final." She shakes her head. "They just don't know. They might never know. There's hardly anything left that could help . . ."

She chokes on these last words. Ash and the others look away.

"Let's get back to work," Jenny says suddenly. "It might help take our minds off what's happened. The Shoe wants that Regal Flyer in Bay 3 ready by the end of the week, and it won't happen on its own. So let's get to it. Not you, Ash. You come with me."

She gets up and walks from the room, not bothering to look back. The others stare after her in disbelief and then slowly rise.

Ash follows Jenny into her office, where she is already seated behind her desk. "Close the door and sit down," she says without preamble.

Her face is grim, her voice clipped. Ash does as he is told. He has a feeling something is coming.

"It wasn't an accident," Jenny says when he is seated. "It was deliberate."

He stares at her. "How can you be sure?"

Jenny's eyes fix on him. "We know Starfire was in perfect condition when she left the garage. There was nothing wrong with her, nothing that should have malfunctioned. Preventatives against such failures are built into her components. Being clipped by that dragster might have damaged the body, but it would not have ignited the fuel tank or the feeds. The sideswipe happened nowhere near either."

She pauses. "So it's something else. By process of elimination, if it wasn't an accident, it was deliberate. If it wasn't a malfunction, it was sabotage."

"How is that possible?" he asks at once. "No one's been near her but us. You're not saying that one of us . . ."

"No, not one of us," Jenny snaps, her voice suddenly angry. "Someone else."

He stared at her. "My uncle."

"Let's go with that for a moment. Assume you're right. Let's assume he wanted the driver dead. How did he know who would be driving Starfire? It was only decided a day ago that it would be you and not T.J. So if the plan was to kill T.J., there had to be a reason for it. What would that reason be? Why would your uncle want T.J. dead?"

She pauses. "But if it wasn't T.J. he was after, it had to be you. How do you explain his decision to do it like this? Didn't that require him to go to an awful lot of trouble? He had to arrange for the car to be sabotaged, and he couldn't have done that before knowing you would be driving. Someone who knew—

which means one of us—had to have told him."

He thinks immediately of Cay and feels sick. But then he realizes Cay hasn't been back to Street Freaks since the decision was made, so how could she have known T.J. was out and Ash was taking his place?

"Here's something else to consider," she continues. "Your uncle has had more than one chance to see you dead, but in each instance it appears he wanted you brought to him alive, not killed. When he got his hands on you at ORACLE, he just locked you in a room and left you for later. If he wanted you dead, why didn't he kill you right away? Why wait until now and then try to make it look like an accident? Wouldn't it have been simpler just to make you disappear?"

"What if he didn't care which of us was driving?" Ash asks. "What if wants both of us out of the way?"

She gives him a look. "Think about that. Why would he destroy two million credits' worth of valuable property just to get rid of you? Again, there were simpler ways to get the job done."

"So that would mean he was targeting me specifically, since targeting T.J. doesn't make sense?"

She purses her lips. "Let's review what we know. Street Freaks took you in. We hid you from Achilles Pod and the L.A. Preventatives when they were hunting you. We kept you safe. Even after they got inside the compound using that negation order, bypassing our writ of exemption, they couldn't get their hands on you."

"What's your point?"

Jenny gives him a careful look. "BioGen, your uncle, the authorities, whoever—they still think you have information your father gave you. Information they don't want you to have. Information so toxic they can't afford to risk you keeping it. So they're hunting you, and somehow they've found out you're here."

He shakes his head. "I still don't get it. What does this have to do with what happened?"

Jenny shifts her gaze to her desktop, as if the explanation lies there. "You know I've been searching the computer for days, trying to find out something more about your father's death. Ever since Achilles Pod showed up with that negation order, I've been suspicious."

"You've found something out?" Ash asks.

"I've found a lot out, and it all points to your uncle. You already know his signature is on both the writ of exemption and the negation order. Now guess who shows up on BioGen's purchase manifests as its biggest client? ORACLE. Guess who sits on the board of directors of BioGen? Cyrus Collins."

Ash feels his blood turn cold.

She pauses, a finger lifting. "I'm not done. Guess who's listed on the territorial registration records as titleholder of Starfire? Who therefore must have arranged for delivery of Starfire to our doorstep several days ago? Who was the last person to have access to her before she ever got to us? Who might have had time to tamper with her?" Jenny leans back.

"All right." Ash feels his anger building. The conclusion is all too evident. "So it's my uncle who's responsible after all. But we're right back where we started. Why would he blow up his very expensive racing machine to kill either T.J. or me? That's what you're suggesting he did, isn't it?"

She shakes her head. "No, it isn't. Blowing up his racer to kill anyone makes no sense at all. Which is why I don't think he's the one responsible."

"Wait a minute." Ash holds up his hands to slow her down. "Didn't you just make a case for why he *did* do it? Haven't you just proven it?"

Jenny gives him a small smile. "What I've done is show you why everyone who knows enough to be suspicious is supposed to *think* that's what happened. I think someone is trying to shift the blame to your uncle."

"Well, who else would it . . .?" The blood drains from his face as realization sets in. "You think it was the Shoe?"

"Everything that happens at Street Freaks goes through the Shoe. You couldn't be here without him knowing. We couldn't have helped you once he knew you were here if he didn't approve. Cyrus Collins warned us by issuing that negation order to countermand our writ of exemption and sent in Achilles Pod to mess around with us. Didn't work. The Shoe let you stay anyway. But I think he's been playing a game of his own. A game with your uncle. A dangerous game. The Shoe is an opportunist; he always has been. He knew you were valuable to Cyrus. Maybe he told your uncle he should leave you where you were at Street Freaks and let him try to find out what your father told you. Maybe he did it to curry favor with a powerful benefactor, but maybe he extracted a promise of something more."

She shrugs. "I don't know. It doesn't matter. I do know that they've had an arrangement for a long time. Cyrus Collins uses us to get revenge on people who go up against him. Every so often, he uses us for his own purposes. He uses us to break into corporations he wants to damage or destroy—or simply to find information that will discredit specific corporate leaders. The Shoe and Street Freaks, in turn, get protection from interference in all their break-ins, legal and not, through our writ of exemption. The Shoe thinks none of us know this—and the others don't. But I found out a while back. Your father was the only one I told."

"My father knew? So maybe he was killed because of this . . ." Ash starts.

But Jenny is already shaking her head. "I don't think so. It was his death that triggered everything that's happened. I think it goes more like this: The Shoe is trapped in a situation largely of his own making. He let you settle in here and made you think he's your friend; he did so in large part to find out what you know so he can tell your uncle. But now it's looking like either there's nothing to find, or if there is, you're not going to open up about it. So he's left empty-handed and Cyrus is running out of patience. Thus the fraying of their relationship begins."

Ash frowns. "But how does killing T.J. do anything to help?"

"The Shoe wasn't trying to kill T.J. He was trying to kill you and make it look like an accident that had nothing to do with him. Who took T.J. out of the cockpit? Who put you in his place? If you were killed in a racing accident, it would be unfortunate, but it would also remove the problem of what to do about his failure to find anything out after promising he would. He saw his chance when T.J. damaged his fingers at Checkered Flag. Put you behind the wheel of Starfire in T.J.'s place. Rig the machine to explode—likely by remote signal. Cut his losses. Cyrus would lose interest in Street Freaks with you dead, and the Shoe would be in the clear. No one would ever know what he had done. Things could go back to normal."

She paused. "Except he didn't realize T.J. was so determined to drive that the broken fingers were not enough to keep him from doing so."

"He misjudged T.J.'s determination. But T.J. was going to take the blame either way. The Shoe would have told Cyrus it was T.J.s idea in the first place, his suggestion. Even though you refused it, T.J went behind your back and put Ash in Starfire anyway."

There is a long silence as Ash considers the unpleasant conclusion that the Shoe, whom he trusted to keep him safe, has betrayed him. On reflection, it doesn't seem as far-fetched as he might once have imagined.

"I guess he might be capable of something like that," he says.

"What? Of throwing you to the wolves? Blowing up your uncle's prized racer and you in the process? In a heartbeat, if he thought it would serve his own needs."

Ash stares at her. "But you don't know for sure. You can't. You're speculating that all this happened based mostly on your suspicion."

"Give me a better explanation than the one I've just given you."

Ash exhales sharply. He can't, of course. There isn't one. "So what do we do?"

She shrugs. "We'll confront him tonight when he returns. Get the answers we deserve. I just finished working this out. As you said, it's still a lot of speculation. I don't know for sure if I'm right."

But she is. She is exactly right. The more he lives with it, the more certain he becomes. Everything she has said makes perfect sense. Everything fits.

"This won't be pleasant." Jenny stands. "After all, the Shoe is going to have to make up his mind about what to do with you when he finds you're still alive. Maybe between us we can make him do the right thing."

They move out into the garage area and Bay 3, where Holly and Woodrow are working on the Regal Flyer, a retro machine with flames and pinstripes for decorations, a custom order they have been building for several months now. They work mostly without talking to each other, and then only when it is necessary to converse about what they were doing. No one mentions T.J. But Ash is certain no one has stopped thinking about him.

The afternoon passes into evening. It is late at night before the Shoe finally slips in through the back door. Holly has gone to bed and Woodrow is puttering around with computer parts in Bay 5. But Jenny and Ash are waiting to confront him, and they follow him into his office without waiting to be invited.

Ash does not miss the momentary expression of shock that crosses the Shoe's face when they lock eyes—but the look is gone almost as quickly as it appears.

"So T.J. ended up driving Starfire, after all," he says with a wry smile. He moves over to his desk and sits behind it. "That would explain the reason she made it all the way to the finals. However lucky or skillful you might be, Ash—no offense intended—you could never have managed it."

"Turns out I'm pretty lucky as it is," Ash responds, managing to keep his tone of voice steady.

"What is it you want?" he asks, seeing the looks on their faces. His clothes are rumpled and stained, and his face is haggard. "Speak up. I'm tired and I want to go to bed."

Jenny tells him, laying it all out clearly and concisely—everything from what she has learned to what she has surmised. To his credit, the Shoe doesn't try to cut her off or interrupt. He lets her get it all out before he speaks, and when he does, his voice is soft.

"That's one wild tale, Jenny," he says. "Really an amazing piece of creative thinking. But you know it isn't true."

They stare at each other. "Isn't it?" she asks finally. "You thought it would be Ash behind the wheel. You never considered that it might be T.J. You have something going with Cyrus Collins. An arrangement. He wanted to know what Brantlin might have told Ash, and you were trying to strike a bargain that would turn a profit for you. I know how your mind works. I've been here long enough to understand how you think."

"You don't understand anything."

"After Cyrus allowed Achilles Pod to breach the compound, you knew you had to get rid of Ash. Our corporate sabotage business was too lucrative to let him mess it up. So you rigged Starfire and put Ash behind the wheel. A major loss for Cyrus, but it didn't cost you a single credit and everyone thinks it was nothing more than an unfortunate accident. That's what you did, didn't you? Don't lie to me."

The Shoe starts to say something and then stops. He gives her a dark, threatening look. "You don't want to do this," he says quietly.

"I'm doing it."

He shakes his head. "The hell with it. You always were too smart for your own good. He shrugs, gives her a resigned look. "What difference does it make now. You've made up your mind. So, okay. You've gotten most of it right. What are you going to do about it?"

"What are *you* going to do?" she asks him back. "Isn't that the important question?"

He leans back in his chair. "Not really. I wish I didn't know half of what I do. I wish I'd done some things differently. Maybe then

T.J. wouldn't be toast. But I didn't and he is. It's too late to do anything about it now. There's nothing I can do to bring him back."

"You could tell someone what you know!" she snaps. "That won't bring T.J. back, but it would be a start to setting things right."

"I could tell someone what I *think* I know," he corrects her. "But I won't. What I'll do is keep my mouth shut. We don't have the muscle or the money to stand up to Cyrus Collins and BioGen. They'll eat us alive if we try. We're little fish swimming in a pool of sharks."

"So you're just going to go on ignoring what they're doing over at BioGen? They're killing kids with their experiments, just to make a larger profit. Cyrus is involved in all of it. He sits on their board of directors. He protects them from any sort of accountability. What about Ash's father? Do we just sit back and ignore what happened to him? Are we just supposed to forget all of it?"

The Shoe brushes her off with a gesture. "It would be better for you if you did. Do you think for one minute Cyrus Collins gives a rat's ass about a bunch of street kids? A few discards are part of research in every phase of scientific evolution that I can think of. I don't know what they're doing over at BioGen, and I don't think you know either. But I do know this. If Cyrus thinks for one minute we didn't get the message about sticking our noses in where they don't belong, the robo-sweepers will end up scrubbing us off the Red Zone pavement."

He looks over at Ash. "In an effort to try to set that part of things right, I'm going to do what I should have done in the first place. I'm giving you to your uncle."

"You can't!" Jenny snaps at once, incensed.

"Shut up, Jenny!" The Shoe continues to eye Ash. "You have become a huge liability. You've cost me uncountable credits and grief just by being here. Thanks to you, I'm saddled with some very powerful enemies. You've been nothing but trouble, and I want you gone."

Ash nods slowly. He guesses he would want that too if he were the Shoe. But it's the coward's way out, and he had hoped the Shoe would be better than this. He wants the owner of Street Freaks to honor his father's trust.

"You told my uncle I was hiding here, didn't you?" he says. "It was you."

The Shoe snorts. "He already knew. He learned about it from somewhere else, from someone on the streets. I tried to help you. I let you stay. Big mistake."

"You tried to use Ash to help yourself!" Jenny is practically screaming. "You tried to find out what he knew about his father's notes so you could give everything to Cyrus!"

"I think I told you to shut up once already, didn't I?"

Jenny starts to say something more, but the Shoe reaches out cat-quick, snatches the front of her ribbed sheath, and yanks her halfway across the desk.

"Don't say anything more, Jenny," he hisses. "You hear me? Don't. Not one word. Not about T.J., not about Ash, not about me." His smooth features are intense, dangerous. "You let Ash back in here after he left for ORACLE. You told him everything about our corporate espionage business. You made him a member of our family, and you didn't ask my permission about any of it. Who the hell do you think you are?"

He releases her, shoving her back across the desktop where she collapses in her chair, her face white. "You're just a 'tweener, Jenny. 'Tweeners are disposable. Don't you get it? Just because I saved you once doesn't mean I'll do it again!"

He pauses, his face dark. "So here's the deal. Listen closely, Jenny, because I'm only going to say this once. No more hacking into computer systems. No more poking around in the affairs of BioGen and ORACLE. All that's finished. You do nothing from here on out but what I tell you to do. That's not a suggestion. That's an order! If you can't follow it, get out!"

"What about T.J.?" Ash demands suddenly. "Because of you, he's dead. What about that?"

The Shoe wheels on Ash. "Better him than you, don't you think! You should be grateful it wasn't you!"

The truth solidifies for both Ash and Jenny at the same moment. The Shoe did rig Starfire to explode. He did intend to see Ash killed in what appeared to be a racing accident. T.J. was collateral damage, an unfortunate loss of a valuable employee but likely not much more.

A very long, uncomfortable moment of silence follows. Then the Shoe abruptly wheels away. "I'm done talking! Believe what you want!"

He leaves, slamming the door behind him. Ash and Jenny sit in stunned silence, staring after him. When Ash finally speaks, his voice is shaking. "You were right."

She nods, tight-lipped. She sits up and straightens her clothes. She brushes out a few of the wrinkles and looks out to where the Shoe has disappeared into his private quarters. "I never thought he would go this far. All that talk of being a family. All his promises to look after us. It never meant a thing."

"He's afraid."

"Very afraid. He should be. If your uncle knew what the Shoe tried to do to you, he would kill him."

"Only because he thinks I know something about my father's work. He thinks my father told me or gave me something. Not because he cares otherwise."

"Doesn't matter why."

Ash stands. "I'll leave right away. I'll go somewhere else. I don't want anything to happen to the rest of you. I'm already responsible for T.J."

She comes over and takes hold of his arms, facing him squarely. Her voice is steady and firm. "No, Ash. You aren't responsible. No one but the Shoe is responsible. He might think we can't do anything about your uncle, but he's wrong. We're not giving up."

"You can't afford to risk yourselves . . ."

"Ash, don't you see what he's doing? He's trying to rid himself of you. He needs to square things with Cyrus. Putting you inside Starfire didn't work. So now he'll get word to your uncle. Achilles Pod will come after you, and we'll never see you again!"

She releases him and moves to the door, peering out into the darkened bays. Even Woodrow has gone to bed. Ash can tell she is checking to be sure. She has a furtive, almost haunted look about her.

"What are you up to?" he asks.

She glances at him. "I didn't tell the Shoe everything. I didn't spend all my time on the computer searching for information about your father. I hacked into BioGen's security system—into the backup storage units where they store the locking codes to their files. They're encrypted, but I deciphered their keys and downloaded the results."

He stares. "Won't they know what you've done?"

"Not the way I work, they won't. Only problem we have is that the keys to the locking codes have to be entered directly into the mainframe units to get the information we need. It's an added layer of protection against hacking. I can't do it from an offsite computer."

"What are you saying?"

She gives him a look. "I'm saying if we want to find out what's really going on, we're going to have to break into BioGen."

- 22 -

That night, drifting in the gray world of transition between waking and sleeping, Ash dreams.

His dream comes and goes in small snippets between uneasy sleep and wakefulness, abandoning him when he verges on the latter and then returning when he sinks back into the former. There is a schizophrenic element to it that alternatively grips and releases him so that it feels as if he is living more than one life.

This duality is clearly revealed in the fragmented dreams he experiences.

In the first, he is sitting with his father in the kitchen of their sky tower home, eating breakfast and talking. His father is saying something important, but Ash isn't hearing the words. His mind is elsewhere. It is locked on a nameless inevitability so terrifying he cannot confront it directly, cannot make himself think about the details. Instead, he is frozen in place, pretending to listen while his father speaks, unable to understand him, his words a confused jumble.

A sense of impending disaster weighs heavily on him. Something is going to happen that will change his life forever.

In the next, he is in a medical facility of some sort. A hospital, perhaps. Or a research center. He comes down a hallway past any number of closed doors until he reaches a room where the door is open and enters. He appears to be alone, although he believes someone might have accompanied him. He waits patiently for an explanation. He sits on a chair molded of a synthetic material, the kind used for large gatherings in meeting halls. Once he sits, he cannot make himself move. He keeps looking around, sensing he is being watched but unable to find anyone. He is thirsty. He is sleepy.

He is afraid.

When a man finally enters the room, he is a vague presence and his features are unclear. He is dressed in white, and Ash presumes he is a doctor or at least a medical professional of one kind or another, but he is not entirely sure. The man does not speak. He stands over Ash and looks down at him. Perhaps he is deciding something. It is difficult to tell.

Abruptly, Ash is walking down another endless corridor of closed doors. This time there is definitely someone walking beside him. He recognizes the white medical coat, but without looking up at his companion's face, he cannot know who it is. And he cannot look. Will not look. He wants to, but his mind is telling him not to. Instead, he must concentrate on traversing this corridor to whatever waits at its end.

Because something is about to be done to him.

He will be changed in a way he does not fully understand.

Reassuring words are whispered in his ear, but they only frighten him more. A violation is about to take place. An intrusion will be made into his body, and no amount of reassurance can dispel how this makes him feel.

The scene shifts. He is in an operating room, lying on a medical table atop a cushioned, sheet-wrapped pad. His clothes are gone, and he wears a patient's white dressing gown. Bright lights beam down on him, blinding him, forcing him to squint. There are hands on him, probing. But his thoughts are scattered and unclear; he is sleepier than ever. He thinks he should not be, that it is dangerous to be sleepy, to be muddled about what is happening. Because something is being done to him, and he is not at all sure it is good.

More words are spoken, soft and comforting, but confusing too. The words linger momentarily, and then he slides into darkness, adrift on a raft of numbers and words and symbols. Where did they come from? They are long and complex, a tangle of equations and explanations, but he knows he needs to remember them. He thinks he has seen them before. They mean something to him, and he desperately wants to know what that something is.

He nearly wakes this time, the insistence of his determination to understand what is happening propelling him out of his sleep. But when he wavers, exhaustion pulls him back down, and he sleeps anew.

Still, he dreams. Bright lights continue to shine from overhead. He can hear the soft hum of machinery. The figure standing next to him braces against the table with his hands gripping the cushion and leans down. Soothing words are whispered, telling him it will be all right, everything will work out. He believes the man. The words and the voice convince him.

They should. They belong to his father.

A soft beeping wakes him. His father and the operating room fade, and the dream vanishes. He drifts in darkness, the beeping a slow and persistent presence.

When he is sufficiently awake to do so, he sits up in his bed drowsily, reorienting himself to where he is. The beeping, he realizes, is coming from his vidview. Since fleeing his home for Street Freaks, he has received only one communication—the one from Cay on the day of the Sprint about ProLx. Otherwise, nothing has come in or gone out. He has barely thought about his vidview in weeks.

He glances over at Woodrow, parked in his usual corner of the sleeping room. The beeping hasn't woken him. The room now belongs to just the two of them.

Because T.J. is never coming back.

As much to silence the beeping as to find out who is calling, he presses the node embedded behind his left ear and activates the message. A familiar face springs into view on the air screen directly in front of him.

Cay—and her expression is frantic.

GET OUT. ACHILLES POD IS COMING.

The screen goes blank. He is reminded instantly of his father's last message. For a moment, he doesn't move, remembering. Then he leaps from his bed, pulls on his clothes, nudges Woodrow awake, and charges down the hallway to the women's sleeping room. He is fully awake now and moving quickly. He flings open the door without knocking and rushes in. Jenny is sitting up in bed, reading from a screen. Holly wakes the moment the door opens, eyes fixing on him.

"We have to get out of here," he whispers, half afraid that whoever is coming might be close enough to hear. "Cay sent me a vidview. Achilles Pod is coming."

Jenny is already climbing out of bed. Her voice is calm, her words measured. "Go down and see if you can spot anyone outside. Holly, get Woodrow. Take him downstairs. Open the door to the underground and wait for us to join you."

They are all moving quickly now, not panicked yet but well on the way. Holly is pulling on a suit of body armor over her sleep clothes. Seconds later, she is on her way to fetch Woodrow from his bedroom. Ash follows her out the door, heading for the stairs leading down to the bays, intent on discovering how imminent the danger is.

He finds out quickly. He is halfway to the bottom of the stairs when he hears the horrendous crash that takes out the front gates. Through the front windows he sees a massive assault vehicle lumber into view. As Jenny stumbles down behind him, the AV shoves its way through the wreckage of the gates and rumbles toward the building. It is already at their front door by the time Holly catches up, bearing Woodrow in her arms. Terrified now, they hurry to reach the maintenance closet and the secret passage that leads to the underground. They are still a dozen feet away when escape hatches pop open on the AV to disgorge the black-clads of Achilles Pod.

Holly shoves Woodrow at Ash and pushes past him.

"We need more time!" she snaps over her shoulder.

She reaches a locked cabinet fastened to the wall and yanks the lock off with a single wrenching motion. Reaching inside, she brings out an assault weapon. It looks incredibly heavy, but she handles it with ease, releasing the safety, pulling back the charging lever, and swinging it about. Ash has no idea what it does, but as their attackers arrive at the entrance to the building bearing a portable battering ram, Holly faces them from across the room.

"Get out of here!" she hisses at him.

Jenny appears, and together they move toward the maintenance closet, their arms wrapped tightly around Woodrow, bearing his weight together. They are just inside the tiny room when the front door gives way. He shudders at the sound. It is the attack on his home all over again. These intruders are every bit as lethal and relentless as the Hazmats he faced when he fled the sky tower. Then, he believed he could find safety here. Now, he knows there is no safety to be found anywhere. Not for him. Not for any of them.

Carrying Woodrow, he and Jenny go through the trapdoor. At the bottom of the stairs, after setting the bot boy down, he thinks of Holly, facing their attackers alone, and runs back up the stairs to help her. He hears her weapon firing, a series of staccato grunts that end in sharp explosions. Smoke and gas fill the air with a choking, stomach-wrenching stench. He cannot see anything. A moment later, Holly is next to him, the weapon abandoned. She pulls him after her as she slams the maintenance closet door shut. Her face is flushed with excitement and streaked with smoky grit.

"Coming to help me, were you? With no weapon?" Her grin is fierce. "You're no fish, Ash Collins. Never were. Come on!"

Holly pushes him ahead of her down the stairs, closing the trapdoor and throwing the magnetic locks. Sweeping up Jenny and Woodrow, they hurry over to where the Barrier Ram is parked and scramble aboard.

"Drive, Ash," Jenny orders. "Stay calm."

She joins him in the front seat while Holly remains in the back cradling Woodrow in her arms like a baby. Ash powers up the Barrier Ram, its engine a nearly silent hum. No one attempts to break through the trapdoor. Ash feels his pulse begin to slow and his heart steady. It won't be so bad this time, he thinks. He won't have to fight to get free.

The heavy door leading out rolls up as Jenny triggers a release, and abruptly they are through the opening and barreling down the tunnel, the ceiling lights barely sufficient to show them the way. Behind them, the door closes. Ash increases their speed. He is unfamiliar with the Barrier Ram and sweeps too close to the walls. But only once does Jenny caution him, her voice soft and reassuring. Then they are climbing the ramp leading out of the tunnel and into the warehouse. They pull to a stop inside the sliding doors that front the Straightaway, and Holly sets Woodrow down and leaps out.

"Stay here," she orders. "Let me see what's happening."

She hurries over to a platform ladder and climbs high enough to be able to see out through the windows. She stands there a long time while the others wait.

"Cyrus must have found out I'm not dead," Ash whispers to Jenny. "Maybe he knows the truth."

She pauses. "Even so, this was awfully quick. I was sure they would wait a day or so before acting, even once they found out the truth. Makes me wonder what happened to change things."

Ash shakes his head. The databases available to the U.T. are vast and comprehensive. Not much escapes the dragnet that gathers up information on the citizens within its jurisdictional scope. Jenny, Holly, himself—even Woodrow—their files were lodged in there somewhere. Only a single recognizable thread is needed to unweave the whole tapestry of their identities.

"Their security system," Jenny says suddenly. "That's how. The computers must have detected my hack into BioGen's files and tracked it back to Street Freaks. And I thought I was being so careful. All they had to do was match us to the governmental database." She seems disgusted. "I went too far. I should have done a better job of covering my tracks."

"Maybe it wasn't you," Ash says quietly. "Maybe the Shoe decided to try to save himself by calling my uncle and telling him to come collect me," Ash says quietly.

Jenny nods. "There's that. Guess he's decided to disown us."

Holly is climbing down off the platform ladder and walking back to join them. "You can get out now," she says. "Achilles Pod seems to be done poking around. They're already climbing back into their AVs and driving off."

"Then we can go back?" Woodrow asks.

Holly shakes her head. "Not yet. They've sealed off the building. They might have left a few men behind. There's an assault vehicle sitting outside the gates. We'll have to wait them out. We need to be patient."

"Maybe Ash can contact Cay," Woodrow says.

"No," Jenny replies at once. "He can't risk a trace. Not if they know who we are, and by now I expect they do. We have to wait for her to contact him."

"If they don't find her first." Holly doesn't sound happy. "They'll be looking for her too."

"Maybe not. I'm not sure they even know about her. She was gone most of the time." Jenny looks troubled nevertheless. "Unless the Shoe gave them her name too."

"We can take turns standing watch," Holly says, ignoring her. "I'll go first. Everyone else stick close to the Barrier Ram. I want us prepared to get out of here in a hurry."

She goes back to her post, leaving the other three still sitting inside the vehicle. After a few minutes, Woodrow asks to be lifted down. Ash manages, but only barely, frustrated by his clumsiness as twice he nearly drops the boy.

"Don't worry," Woodrow says cheerfully after he is safely deposited on the warehouse floor. "Everyone but Holly has trouble moving me around. I make people clumsy."

Ash sits down next to him while Jenny remains in the vehicle, engaged in working on her computer, perhaps searching for better answers about what has happened. When Ash thinks to check on her a few minutes later, she looks up long enough to reassure him that things are fine. She is using a blind link that can't be traced back to start blogging about what BioGen might be doing with street kids. She chooses her sites carefully, and she covers her tracks. She can't take it too far because she isn't certain herself what BioGen's end game is supposed to be. But she can suggest that kids are dying, and that's more than enough to get a major online conversation going.

Ash sits back down beside Woodrow.

"Jenny's starting an online response to kids dying at BioGen," he says. "She thinks we need to trigger an awareness in the population now, just in case anything happens to us. Maybe someone in a position to do something will hear about it."

"People are afraid to do much when they would be putting themselves in danger. BioGen is a very powerful corporation."

"Well, at least we're doing something besides sitting around waiting."

"I wonder where we'll go once this is over," the bot boy says after a few minutes of silence. "We won't be able to stay here. Not if the authorities know we hacked into BioGen. They'll throw us out on the street. They'll take our home away. Or maybe even terminate us."

"That won't happen," Ash says at once.

"But we won't have the Shoe to protect us anymore. BioGen will see to that. He'll be on the streets with the rest of us."

"My uncle is the one we have to worry about." Ash looks down at his hands. He feels trapped. "It's like Holly says. He's the one behind everything that's happened. He's the one we have to deal with."

"He didn't turn out to be much of a relative, did he?" Woodrow deadpans.

Ash smiles. "Probably no worse than some others, if you knew the truth of things."

The boy is silent for a minute. "We might have to move to a different part of the Territories. Somewhere they don't look at 'tweeners in the same way people in most places do. Up north, they have programs for hybrids; they have schools and training facilities so we can be part of things. They don't think 'tweeners should be terminated up there. Maybe that's where we should go."

"Maybe," Ash replies.

But he isn't thinking about the future. He is thinking about the here and now. That may be all they have time for. How long will it take ORACLE to ferret them out? Can't be very long, given their current situation.

Time passes. Ash takes the second watch when Holly comes down from the platform. Daylight brightens their surroundings. He spends his time looking out at the Straightaway, watching the cars and the people passing by. He keeps a close eye on Street Freaks, but nothing changes. The ORACLE assault vehicle still bars the entrance, although there is no sign of Achilles Pod.

He waits patiently for a further message from Cay. But there isn't one. Morning passes into afternoon, and Ash begins to wonder if something has happened to her. His uncle, for instance. He remembers her clinging to him on the vidview. Almost possessively.

He is still thinking about it when Holly relieves him.

Hours later, shaking out her arms and rolling her shoulders, she comes down again, this time looking decidedly irritated. "We need food and water. We can do one of two things. Sneak back into Street Freaks through the tunnel or visit one of the food shops nearby. There's one less than a block away."

Jenny, awake now, says to Holly, "It's too dangerous to go back yet. We're better off trying a food shop. But who's going out there?"

Holly shrugs. "I guess I am."

"You're pretty recognizable," Jenny points out.

"Like you aren't. And we can't send Woodrow."

"I'll go," Ash says. "I'm the least recognizable. I won't stand out; no one will notice me."

"I don't know." Holly looks uncertain.

"He's right." Jenny fishes in her pocket and brings out a handful of credits. "Just go and come right back. No detours," she tells him, handing over the money. "Keep your eyes open."

He nods, and after first checking to make sure no one is watching, he slips out a side door. The sun beats down, its heat rising off the concrete and composite in waves as he makes his way across the surround to where a side gate opens through the fence. Easing through, he turns toward the food mart, which he can already see. Vehicles cruise the Straightaway ahead and pedestrians walk past, but no one gives him a second look.

At the corner, he crosses the street to his destination and goes inside. There is an old woman behind a counter ribbed with steel supports and enclosed by a protective screen of reinforced flexglass. Ash selects sandwiches and drinks from a counter display and pays. There is only one other person in the mart, a man who pays no attention to him. Ash leaves and goes back outside, taking a careful look around as he does.

Head down, he returns to the side street, walks up to the gate, and slips through. Taking one last peek over his shoulder, he hurries toward the door and suddenly has a feeling of being watched. He slows in response, his uneasiness pronounced. A casual look around reveals nothing out of the ordinary. He wonders if he should just keep walking, right past the building, right past the door, pretending at a different destination altogether. At least he wouldn't give the others away if someone really were watching.

But he decides against it. He decides he is letting his nerves get the better of him, and he shelves his doubts and continues on. He enters the building once more, sliding the heavy door shut behind him and bringing the sacks of food and drink over to the Barrier Ram. He is joking with his friends and unwrapping his purchases as the side door slides back with a crash and a handful of familiar figures burst in.

Razor Boys, and they are all armed.

"Well, well," Ponce says, pointing his Gronklin laser from one shocked face to the next. "Looks to me like we've trapped us some *freaks*!"

- 23 -

Ponce teases his captives a few moments longer, swinging the Gronklin from one to another, and then he settles it on Holly and fires. A frayed rope of white fire lances into Holly's flesh-and-blood leg, ripping it apart and sending her to the warehouse floor screaming in pain. The leg is left burned and torn, the white of her bones exposed, the red flesh raw and bleeding where it isn't cauterized.

Jenny starts to rush over, but Ponce turns his weapon on her. "No, no, Jenny Juice Box. Leave her be. I like hearing her scream like a little girl. Thinks she's so tough when she's got me on the floor. She don't look so tough now, does she?"

"You animal!" Jenny shouts at him.

Ponce roars with laughter. "Biggest damn animal in the jungle!" he crows. "Big enough to take down Street Freaks! You got a lot of people who don't like you, you know that? People willing to pay a whole lot of credits to anyone who hands you over. People who should have taken you out the first time I told them who you were hiding. But somehow they botched it. So now they need a pro who knows how to handle this kind of job. Oh, hey! That would be me!"

So it was Ponce who first reported him to ORACLE. Ash tamps down his rage. He doesn't dare move; if he does, Ponce will almost certainly shoot him. He takes a quick inventory. Five besides Ponce. Penny-Bird and four boys. They carry various types of weapons, none more dangerous than Ponce's Gronklin, but dangerous enough. Penny holds a short-barrel chopdown—the shotgun Holly referred to when she rescued him that first day he came into the Zone. An ancient weapon, but deadly. She stands off to one side, wincing at Holly's screams, looking decidedly unhappy.

Ponce is still talking, only now he's looking directly at Ash. "You must have done something really stupid to piss off ORACLE. Not that you don't do stupid things all the time anyway, just that you usually know enough to keep it in-house. But when they come into the Zone looking for you, it's clear you colored outside the lines. They put out the word. Offered a nice reward. Can't imagine anyone more deserving than us. So here we are, ready to collect."

"You don't know what's going on," Jenny says. "This is more than you . . ."

"Shut up! I don't need to hear it. You're dead meat no matter what you say. Where's the Shoe? Not sure if they want him, but if he's around I'll throw him into the mix with the rest of you. Why not?"

He saunters forward, the Gronklin shifting once more, a predator in search of a target. Holly has stopped screaming and lies curled up in a ball gripping her shattered leg, her eyes squeezed shut.

Ponce walks over and stares down at her. "Think you're so clever. We spotted your boy there out on the Straightaway from a block down, waited to see where he was going. He led us right to you. How stupid is that?"

He kicks her injured leg. She screams anew. "That's better. That's what I want to hear. I can't tell you how much I'm enjoying this, you cyborg bitch. I can't get enough of it." He pauses, studying her. "You know what? I don't think I'm quite done with you.

Wasn't anything said about what shape you had to be in when you got delivered to the black-clads. Alive, sure—but there's all different sorts of being alive, right? I wonder how you'd like losing an arm too? Maybe I can take off enough pieces that when they put you back together, you'll just be a bot with a head. Like your boxy little friend."

He gestures at Woodrow, who stares back in fear.

Ash knows he has to do something. He can't just stand there and let this happen, but he needs a weapon and there's nothing close at hand.

"Ponce, let's get this over with," Penny-Bird says suddenly. "Tie them up and give them to Achilles Pod. Forget the rest."

Ponce glances over at her. "Feeling all choked up about your old girlfriend. Think she might not be quite the same once I'm done with her? Don't tell me you still care?"

Penny-Bird goes white. "I don't like where this is going. You're making this personal. It's supposed to be about credits and influence, isn't it? Why are you making it about something else?"

"It's what I say it's about!" Ponce screams at her. "This ain't no fucking Speedway and you ain't driving! Think you're such hot stuff because you got Lonnergon's to put you behind the wheel? Well, you're nothing! Just another street slut! Shut your mouth and keep it shut!"

He turns back to Holly. "I think maybe taking off your arm would be a good place to start. This might hurt a little, so maybe you better grit your teeth, cyborg bitch."

He swings the Gronklin about so that it is pointed at her arm. Holly isn't looking. He levers a charge into the containment chamber, sights down its barrel.

Penny takes a step toward him. "Don't do this!" she shouts angrily. "Ponce, you hear me?"

"Not listening!" Ponce answers, laughing.

The barrel of the chopdown lifts. He grins.

"Ponce, look at me."

Penny-Bird doesn't scream it, doesn't shout it; she just says it as if she were asking when they might eat. But something in her voice causes the leader of the Razor Boys to turn. He sees she has her weapon pointed at him and starts to bring the Gronklin around. It's a big mistake and way too late. The shotgun discharges, and a dark rain of pellets hammers into him, blowing him backward like a rag doll.

Jenny screams. Everyone stares.

Ponce lies sprawled on the warehouse floor less than a dozen feet from Holly. His body is shredded, and his eyes are open and staring. For a moment, no one does anything but stare at what's left of Ponce. Then Penny-Bird swings the shotgun around so that it is pointing at the remaining Razor Boys.

They stare at her uncertainly. "You got one charge left in that chopdown, Penny," one says. "You can't get all of us."

"It's a shotgun, doofus!" she hisses at him. "I can get *parts* of all of you! I can mess you up good!" She pauses, glaring at the speaker. "Especially you, Torque. You'll be missing your head if you make one move I don't like."

"You can't do this," says another.

"Ask Ponce what I can do. Drop your weapons."

She gestures with the chopdown, and they toss their weapons aside hastily. Everyone stands very still, waiting to see what she intends to do.

She walks over to the scattered weapons and kicks them toward Ash. "Pick them up. Throw them in the back of whatever that thing is you're driving. Is that some sort of assault machine? Frickin' weird! You build it?"

There is a manic sound to her voice, and her Goth features are darkened further by the intensity that reflects on her face. She makes it look as if killing someone isn't new to her, as if she's done it before.

Ash picks up the weapons and throws them into the Onyx, glancing over his shoulder at Penny-Bird, who is watching him closely.

"You killed Ponce!" one of the club members wails suddenly. It's the boy who danced on the hood of the Razor Boys' street machine. "Why'd you do that?"

Tears run down his cheeks, but Penny-Bird ignores him. She acts as if he isn't there. Ash thinks she must have been a good match for Holly. Might be again, now that she's terminating her relationship with the Razor Boys. She crossed a line back there, made a choice. It seems to him she's doing what Holly asked her to do. She's coming home.

Jenny steps forward. "Holly needs a doctor, Penny. Right away."

The other girl nods. "Not any of the ones at Red Zone Medical. They'd give her up to the Preventatives. Do you know someone else?"

"I do," Jenny says. "It's not far. These people are skilled, and they don't ask questions. Holly will be safe with them."

Penny doesn't need to hear any more. She hands the chop-down to Jenny and turns to Ash. "Help me pick her up and put her in your machine. Be careful how you do it. Don't hurt her."

Together, they manhandle Holly off the warehouse floor and into the rear passenger seats of the Onyx. Holly is quiet now; Ash thinks she is unconscious—hopes it is only that and not something worse.

"You drive," Penny-Bird orders him, taking back the chop-down. "You seem to know your way around street machines." She walks over and picks up Ponce's Gronklin and levers in a charge, swings the barrel up and into a firing position. "You four," she says to the Razor Boys, who have been standing off to one side, keeping quiet. "Get out."

She keeps the Gronklin trained on them. "You say anything to anyone about what's happened here, and I'll come looking for you. You know I mean it. You keep quiet about this. You keep your mouths shut. You forget everything you've seen."

The Razor Boys trudge back through the side door, casting sour looks and muttered threats over their shoulders as they do.

A few furtive glances are directed at what's left of Ponce. No one says anything to Penny-Bird.

Once they are gone, she slams the side door and throws the locking bar, effectively sealing them out. "Dumbass jerks!"

Ash is already inside the Onyx when she climbs in the back with Holly. "Hey," she calls out the window to Jenny. "You and the bot, you're coming with us."

Jenny lifts Woodrow, then climbs in herself, buckling them both in place. Without waiting to be told to do so, Ash powers up the Onyx, triggers the opener to the big warehouse doors, and drives out onto the surround and from there out the back gates. In seconds, they are on the Straightaway.

Jenny provides directions, and Ash makes the drive as if he has been handling the Onyx all his life. He glances in the rearview mirror and sees Penny-Bird with Holly's head in her lap, her hand stroking the other girl's forehead, carefully moving aside loose strands of black hair. She's crying now, her face crumpled, her tough-girl attitude abandoned.

Ash glances over and looks quickly away. *She's only fifteen. Where did she find the courage to stand up to Ponce?* The threat to Holly must have given it to her. She might put up with a lot, but not this. The fact that she acted so impulsively, however, is telling. Holly and she are two of a kind.

When they arrive at their destination, Ash has to look twice to be certain Jenny hasn't made a mistake. They are in front of a large tumbledown residence of several floors, many windows, and lots of sheltering trees. It stands out in a landscape of few trees and smaller buildings. A sign out front reads PSYCHIC HEALING & SPIRITUAL COMFORT. The curtains that hang in all the windows have been pulled, and there is no sign of life. The surrounding neighborhood looks abandoned.

"Wait here," Jenny tells them.

She leaves the Onyx and goes inside the building. She is gone only a short time before returning with two very strong-looking nurses pushing a gurney. They reach in and lift Holly from the vehicle onto the gurney and wheel her into the building. Jenny and the others follow, although at the entrance, Woodrow announces he will wait outside.

"I don't like medical facilities very much," he mumbles.

The others enter and go down a hallway to a room with an examination table, where the nurses have placed Holly. The doctor who waits is young and scruffy and intense, his face bearded and marked by scarring. He begins examining Holly at once, cutting away her clothing to reveal the extent of her injuries. He appears unruffled by what he sees. Ash, on the other hand, is appalled. Holly is unconscious and breathing irregularly. Her leg is a mess of ravaged flesh and bone.

"The laser cauterized the wounds or she would have bled out on the spot," the doctor says. "I think maybe we can save the leg using a regeneration wrap. We can at least try."

He begins work with the nurses, prepping Holly for surgery. While Jenny stays with Holly, Ash and Penny-Bird are sent to another room to wait. They sit side by side without speaking. Ash checks his vidview log for communications he might have missed. Nothing.

"She'll be all right," he says finally.

Penny doesn't speak. She swings her legs like a child would; she's so small that her feet don't even touch the floor.

"That was brave, what you did back there," he adds after a few more minutes

"What's your name?" she asks.

"Ash Collins."

"Thought so. You've been all over the reader boards for weeks. You're the one she helped out on the Straightaway several weeks ago. The newbie. She saved your ignorant ass. But you don't look the same. They've done some work on you."

He nods. "Didn't like me the way I was."

"Yeah, that must be it." She takes a deep breath, exhales.

"I should have known this would happen a long time ago. When I first knew what Ponce was like. When I saw how much he hated Holly. Then maybe she wouldn't be here."

He doesn't respond, not sure what to say.

Her dark Goth features turn even gloomier. "She was always so stubborn."

"Is that why you left her?"

She gives him a look. "Oh, you know about that, do you?"

"T.J. told me. Before the accident."

"None of your business, really. Is it?"

"No, I guess not."

Penny-Bird sighs. "Well, what's the difference now?" She gives a brief shrug. "It's simple. She acted like I didn't know anything. She treated me like a child, even though I was every bit as tough as she was. She couldn't stop bossing me around, even when I told her to stop it. She kept trying to control me." She shrugs. "She wouldn't stop. That's why I left."

"She didn't understand, I guess."

"She understood. She just couldn't change." Penny's lips compress. "I suppose it didn't help, my being stubborn too. I thought by leaving I could make her sorry about how she was treating me. But it only made her dig in. She's so stupid proud. She couldn't admit she was wrong."

"She must have realized it once she saw how you could drive. That race with T.J. showed everyone how good you were."

"That race killed him."

He thinks to tell her she is wrong, but decides against it. She doesn't need to know about the Shoe.

She faces Ash squarely. "I was born and raised in the Zone. I lived on the streets for years until I met Holly. I know what it's like. I've learned to take care of myself. But Holly acts like I need to be protected. She doesn't understand that it's too late for that. All the bad stuff that could happen already has. Or if it hasn't, it will find me ready and waiting when it does."

Ash doesn't say anything. They sit together in silence until Jenny reappears. She enters the room and sits down across from them.

"They sedated her, gave her antibiotics and cleansers, cut away the flesh they couldn't save, and wrapped everything in a regenerative compress. If the synthetic tissue takes a liking to her body, it will stimulate her cells to grow back the muscle and flesh she lost. It will regenerate blood vessels and heal major arteries. The doctor says her bones are exceptionally resilient. But healing will take time and care. Someone will have to be with her until she's much stronger."

"I'll look after her," Penny-Bird says. "I'll take care of her."

Jenny nods. Her brown eyes have a calm, measured look to them. "Do you have a way to move her? Do you have someplace to take her?"

Penny nods at once. "I can find something. I was already planning to leave the Razor Boys when this happened. I was thinking my future would be a lot better if I just struck out on my own." She paused. "How long before she's ready?"

"Days. Weeks. Depends. They can't be sure. They want to wait until she's awake so they can see how she is responding."

"Can I go in and see her?" Penny-Bird's young face is stricken, but hopeful too.

"You can go in. But only for a few minutes. She's sleeping and won't be able to talk to you."

Penny-Bird rises and leaves the room. When she is gone, Jenny faces Ash. "We're going into hiding, all of us. Just until we can figure out what to do next. Cay is coming to get you."

He experiences mixed feelings on hearing her name. On the one hand, he is still angry about seeing her with Cyrus and wonders what he will say to her when they meet. On the other, he is relieved that nothing has happened to her. No one is safe, after all. Not even her. T.J. is dead, Holly is so badly damaged she might never walk again, and the Shoe hasn't been seen since yesterday. Street Freaks is locked down and under watch by Achilles

Pod. Their refuge has been compromised, and they can never, in all likelihood, go back again. The hunt for him continues, and he doesn't see it ending until he's caught. There is no way out of this mess. It feels as if everything is falling apart.

"You wait for her out front," Jenny says. "Tell Woodrow what's happened. And Ash?" She takes his arm. "Behave yourself. No random acts of heroism, no charging off to confront your uncle, no stupid decisions that might lead to disastrous consequences. You're a big boy. You can tell the difference between smart and stupid."

He nods, not much caring for her tone of voice, and leaves. He goes back down the hallway to the front entry and out to join Woodrow. He sits with the bot boy and tells him of Holly's condition and the treatment she is receiving. Woodrow looks relieved, his face losing some of the strain that has marked it since Holly was shot.

"She's very strong," he says. "Physically, but emotionally too. She will get better if she's kept safe."

Ash smiles. "I think Penny-Bird will see to that."

They sit together after that in companionable silence. They sit for a long time. He is thinking about going back inside to ask Jenny what might be keeping Cay when he hears the rumble of an engine reverberate in the afternoon silence. A moment later, a bulky all-purpose Bryson Utility rolls into view and comes to a stop in front of the building. He doesn't move. The tinted windows are so dark he cannot see who is inside. He would run, but he is beyond doing much of anything at this point.

Then the driver's window slides down. Cay leans out, grim-faced. "We don't have all day, Ash. Get over here!"

"Better do what she says," Woodrow whispers.

Ash reluctantly obeys.

- 24 -

Ash walks over to the passenger side of the Bryson and climbs in, slamming the door harder than is necessary.

"So where have you been while Street Freaks has been getting blown up?" he demands.

He says it with much more force than he intends. It sounds like an accusation rather than a question. His anger at seeing Cay with his uncle momentarily overrides his sense of relief that she is safe.

She gives him a look. "That's not a question you are allowed to ask me. You know that. I had things to do. I came as quick as I could."

"Not quick enough. Holly could have used you."

"There is nothing I could have done to help Holly. I was able to warn you about Achilles Pod. That was risky enough. What's this about, anyway?"

He exhales and looks down at his feet, realizing how he sounds. Accusatory, mean-spirited, and just plain enraged. He is ashamed of himself. "I'm sorry. I didn't mean . . . I was just . . . I was worried."

She keeps her eyes fixed on his face as he trails off. "Forget it. Tell me about Holly. How's her leg?"

He is eager to move on. "They treated her with a regenerative tissue wrap. Said they would keep her there until she was well enough to move around on her own. Penny-Bird is staying with her. You should have seen how she cradled Holly's head in her arms on the way here. She says she's going to look after Holly."

Cay nods. "They belong together, those two. Penny with Ponce and the Razor Boys was never right. It drove Holly crazy. Maybe this time they can manage to work things out."

"They're more than sisters, aren't they?"

She shrugs. "Why don't you ask them?"

"I don't think I should do that."

"Then why are you asking me?"

She engages the Bryson's heavy drive train, and the bulky machine eases into a long, sweeping turn.

"You know what your trouble is?" she says, pointing the Bryson back the way she had come. There is anger in her voice now. "You want to pigeonhole everyone. You like the idea of a world all nicely ordered and dependable. But that isn't how things are. People are messy and changeable. The world is fluid; the people who inhabit it are chameleons. You want to think of everyone as stable and identifiable, but they aren't."

"That's not so," he says. "I don't think that way."

"Yes, you do, whether you admit it or not. You need to pay better attention to how things work. People hide themselves in plain sight all the time. They show you what they want you to see, but they conceal the rest. Otherwise they would be so vulnerable they wouldn't be able to function."

"You seem to manage it all right."

"What does that mean?"

"Just that you don't seem to worry about hiding things. Oh, except from me, of course."

He loses it. Just like that, he lets his temper get away from him. But he stares at her defiantly nevertheless.

Cay keeps her eyes on the road, concentrating on her driving. She doesn't even glance at him. "What's going on here?

Does this have something to do with how you see me? Have you finally decided that I'm more pleasure synth than real girl?"

"No, of course not!"

"I think maybe you have. Let's lay a few cards on the table. What if I told you I've been with so many men I've lost count. How would you see me then? Pleasure synth or real girl?"

He stands on a precipice. A wrong answer here will banish him to the edges of her life for good.

"I'd see you the same way I've always seen you, right from the moment we met. Smart. Funny. Tough. Beautiful. The rest doesn't matter."

"Is that so? It matters to everyone else."

"I'm not everyone else."

"No, you're more deluded."

"Must be so! Otherwise, I wouldn't be in love with you!"

He just blurts it out, not really meaning to, but carried away by his dismay over what is happening.

She takes a long moment to reply. "Being in love with me is a waste of time, Ash. No one should be in love with me."

Her face so clearly reflects a mix of sadness and proud defiance that he is almost brought to tears.

"Why would you say that?" he asks. "Is it wrong for me to feel like this about you? When I look at you, I don't see a pleasure synth. I never have. I see a real girl just like any other girl, only better in every possible way. I don't care how many men you've been with. It doesn't matter. I only care about one thing. Finding out how I can be with you."

"You can't be with me," she says instantly. "Not ever."

His temper flares anew. "No? Why not? Because you're too busy with my uncle?"

The words are out before he can stop them. Or maybe he wants them out, even if he doesn't want to admit it. He feels defiant and strong as he speaks them. Speaking them is empowering.

She nods slowly. "So that's what this is all about." She makes it a statement of fact, a cold assessment of everything he's been dancing around. "You saw me with him."

"I saw you on the vidviews. Everyone saw you. Bigger than life, there you were—with my *uncle*! Even though you told me you weren't going to be at the Sprint. But I guess what you meant is you weren't going to be there with me."

He is so tangled up by his emotions, he almost breaks down. Too much has happened over too short a period of time, and he questions whether any of it has been good. It takes everything he has to hold himself together.

She still doesn't look at him. Her eyes are fixed on the roadway ahead. Her face is troubled, her posture rigid. "You have no idea, do you? No idea at all."

"No idea about what? What are you saying?"

She shakes her head. "Not now. We'll talk about it later."

He decides he better leave things where they are. But he is determined not to allow her to pretend the matter is settled. This conversation is far from over.

"Where are we going?" he asks, trying to keep his voice steady.

"Street Freaks."

"Street Freaks!" he exclaims. "But Achilles Pod has it in lockdown, and . . ."

"They've gone," she interrupts. "Back to wherever it is they go when they're not out finding fresh ways to terrify people. They've closed off the public entry, but the building is empty. I checked it out. Jenny needs us to retrieve her computer records and storage links before someone finds a way to download the information they contain. They are concealed and encrypted, but there's always the possibility the wrong person will find a way to hack in if given enough time. She can do some downloading and wiping off-site, but not all. So it's up to us."

Ash nods. It makes sense. Those records are valuable. They are also probably revealing. If he and the others are vacating

285

Street Freaks for good, Jenny will want to close up shop.

"What about the Shoe?"

Cay keeps her eyes on the road as she considers her answer. "He got back before me. He's still there."

"What if the black-clads make a return visit?"

"They won't."

There is an edge to her voice he doesn't understand. "How do you know they won't?"

She doesn't look at him. "They have no reason to." She pauses long enough to glance over. "Stop talking, Ash. We'll be in and out of there soon enough. Ask your questions then."

They reach the warehouse without incident and pull through the rear gates to park close to the back of the building. Cay triggers a control attached to the dash, and the doors slide open. They drive inside and slow down enough for Ash to see that Ponce's body has disappeared and the floor has been cleaned.

"Dumped him in an industrial waste disposal unit down the block and scrubbed the floors," she says, anticipating his question. "There's no evidence that anything ever happened here."

She drives on, triggering the ramp doors to the underground. They drive down the tunnel to its far end before pulling into the dimly lit recesses below the Street Freaks building. It looks exactly as it did when Ash fled Achilles Pod. There is no sign of entry. Nothing has been disturbed. Apparently, the black-clads did not discover the hidden trapdoor in the broom closet.

Cay brings the Bryson Utility to a stop. They climb out and walk over to the stairs leading up to the main floor. When they exit the broom closet, he sees that all of the computers and files have reappeared from beneath the floor of Jenny's office, everything activated, the machines humming away busily. Either a transfer or an erasure or both is in progress.

Cay gestures. "I had Jenny set the download in motion earlier by remote signal, transferring everything to a portable hard drive concealed in the cellar walls. Once the download is complete, we have to wipe what's left on the hard drives. Otherwise, we risk ORACLE finding out what we've done."

The way she says it tells him that Cay has made the decision to wrap up matters at Street Freaks, not Jenny. In some way, the pecking order among the kids has changed again, and now the least likely among them has taken charge.

Although, is she really all that unlikely a leader? This girl who not only can drive a street machine as well as T.J. could but also has the willingness to seduce the worst of her enemies in order to spy on them? She is a mixture of contradictions, and Ash is not sure he should assume anything.

"This way," she says, breaking into his thoughts. "The Shoe's out in the bays."

They leave the office and go out into the main floor of the garage. Sunlight pours through the windows of the bay doors in long, hazy streamers, brightening the room. Hand tools remain fastened in their assigned places along the back walls. All the lifts are down, and there are no machines present or evidence of work being done. The room looks empty and undisturbed.

It isn't.

Halfway down the length of the room, directly in the center of Bay 3, the Shoe hangs from a rope. Ash knows it's him without having to take a second look. The brightly colored, well-tailored blue and silver is immediately recognizable. His arms hang limply at his sides, the toes of his soft-soled boots point down. One end of the rope that suspends him is attached to an O-ring embedded in the ceiling. The other is looped about his throat. His head angles sharply to one side; the neck bones and cartilage have given way.

His face is indescribable. A death mask of pain and misery contorts his features. His end was clearly difficult, slow and agonizing, filled with suffering.

A chair lies beneath his feet, tipped on its side. It appears the Shoe stood upon it and, after putting the rope around his neck, kicked it away.

"That's how I found him when I arrived earlier," Cay says softly. She shakes her head. "Cyrus must have found out what the Shoe tried to do about you and didn't much like it."

Ash stares, unable to turn away. He feels Cay's hands grip his shoulders, and she turns him to face her. "Look at me. Ash, look at me. I don't want you going into shock. I need you."

He realizes his eyes are unfocused, staring at nothing. He meets her gaze. "Why would he kill himself?"

"He wouldn't. It's meant to look like he did. It ties everything up nicely for certain people. Despondent over the death of his driver, the crash of his prized car, and the collapse of his business, the Shoe kills himself. Too bad, but life goes on."

He nods, numbed by the casual dismissiveness the killing represents. "It doesn't seem right to leave him that way. Shouldn't we take him down?"

"If we do, we reveal that we've been here. It also opens up the question of how we got in. Better if people think we never came back at all. The Shoe is dead. It doesn't matter what becomes of him now."

She leans into him, the look in her eyes dark and dangerous. "The Shoe overreached himself. He played a game he was not suited for. He always did think himself smarter than anyone else. But your uncle knew what he was doing. I tried to warn him; I told him to back away. He just smiled and insisted everything would work out. And I think he really believed that. But after the deba-cle with Starfire, it was just a matter of time until Cyrus settled accounts—first with us, then with the Shoe. I told you before. Your uncle isn't anyone to play games with."

"How do you know all this?" Ash asks hesitantly.

She gives him a look. "How do you think?"

"But didn't my uncle know who you were?"

"He *thought* he knew who I was. He made some *assumptions* about who I was. Big difference. Don't ask me for an explanation just now. Maybe later." She backs away. "Come into the office with me. We'll wait there for the downloading to finish."

He does as she asks. There is a lot going on that he doesn't understand, but he knows he must be patient. He is horrified by what has happened but oddly resigned as well. They are all pawns in a much larger game, one that none of them fully understands. They are all at risk of ending up like the Shoe.

They sit in chairs across the desk from each other, listening to the computers work their magic, staring off into space.

"The Shoe was the only real parent I ever had," Cay says after a time. "He was kind to me. He took care of me. He did that when no one else would. Everyone else just wanted to use me. But he cared about me in all the ways that mattered." She paused. "He loved me. He never asked for anything from me. Not once."

"But you couldn't save him, could you?"

She shakes her head. "Didn't find out quickly enough to do anything about it. Found out Achilles Pod was coming for the rest of you, so I was able to do something to help you. But not him."

"You were with my uncle?"

She sighs. "Would you please stop asking questions when you already know the answers. Stop tiptoeing around, why don't you ask me what you really want to know."

But he can't do that. He is afraid of the answer. He knows hearing her give it will be too much for him to bear. He has to hope that what seems obvious isn't.

She is angry now, and he backs off from further questions about his uncle and her. He can barely stand to think about it, but he has to assume there is more to this than he knows. He has to believe in her if he wants to get through this.

The minutes crawl by. It is taking longer than expected to download the contents of the last computer. Cay wanders over to the front doors of the building and peers out at the Straightaway. Traffic is heavy, and night is coming on. There are no lights on inside the building; Cay has been careful to do nothing that would attract attention. Even the computer screens have been dimmed to black. As she stands at the door of the office, the hum and click of the computers providing a steady backdrop to her meditations, Ash watches her. He wonders again at the contradictions she represents. He wonders again about her life outside Street Freaks. She is a pleasure synth spending time with powerful men. She is mercurial and secretive, and she refuses to explain herself. She is older than the sum of her years; she is experienced and tough.

But sometimes, like now, she looks so young.

"No sign of Achilles Pod," she says as she walks back. She enters the office and checks the progress of the download. "Good. We're almost done."

Ash moves up beside her. "Too bad we can't get more of what we need out of BioGen. If they're behind all this, then that's where the answers probably are."

She shrugs without looking up. "Maybe not. Maybe they're someplace else."

Someplace else.

Her words fade, but as they do, they trigger a faint recollection. Images from his dreams abruptly recall themselves. As if a door into his mind has opened and a past he has forgotten is glimpsed, he hears a voice—his father's voice—speaking to him.

One day, you will need this information. So I am hiding it somewhere safe, someplace no one will think to look . . .

The words fragment, the sentence unfinished. Where is this coming from? A memory, suddenly recalled.

Someplace safe? Where?

He looks over at Cay, startled. "I had a dream last night. At least, I thought it was a dream. But now I think maybe it was a memory."

"A memory?"

"About something that was done to me. By my father."

She gives him a puzzled look. "Can you describe this memory?"

He tells her about the medical facility, the long hallway with the closed doors, the faceless medical man in white, the examination room, and the way he felt afterward as he was being guided back down the hallway. He repeats the words that were spoken to him, the ones he has just now remembered. Words that until now were hidden from him.

"It was my father, Cay. I'm certain of it."

Cay shakes her head. "I don't know, Ash. Your own father performed surgery on you? And you're just remembering this?"

"I know. But I have an idea. What if remembering now has something to do with my not taking ProLx? You said the lab tests on my DNA revealed traces of a suppressant in my blood. What if that was the purpose of the ProLx? What if it was intended to suppress my memories? And now, because I'm not taking it, it's not happening anymore."

She shakes her head. "But it would have to be a selective suppression, or *all* your memories would be gone. How could that be possible? No one makes a drug that does that."

"No one we know of. But what if my father did? He invented Sparx, didn't he? Why couldn't he have invented this? How big a jump is it to go from targeted mood enhancers to selective suppressants?"

He exhales sharply. "Sounds crazy, doesn't it? But I can't help thinking maybe it isn't. This dream—it wasn't like real dreams. You remember real dreams for a little bit, if at all, and then you forget them. But this dream, it's still there, clear and sharp. Like a memory would be if it were important. I think it really happened . . ."

He trails off, sudden flashes of other memories coming back in flurries and then in waves. "Wait a minute, I'm remembering something else . . . a lot of . . . words and images . . . just sort of exploded from nowhere . . ."

He buries his face in his hands, his palms pressing against his eyes. He is right on the edge of remembering everything, so close he feels as if he can almost touch it. He lifts his head and looks at her.

"He *told* me what he was going to do." He can hear the disbelief in his voice. Can hear the hesitation as he struggles to find the right words. "He said it would be necessary to suppress my memory of what he was telling me. Not wipe it clean—just hide it. Keep it from being discovered. Surgery would be necessary. Not a dangerous procedure, he said. Just a tweak."

He startles himself, realizing what he has just said and what it means about him. T.J.'s words come back to him. How was he tweaked? He wasn't, Ash had replied. But, in fact, he was. Just not in the same way as they were.

"Keep going!" Cay says eagerly. "Don't stop!"

"After the surgery, I would have to take medication to keep the memory from resurfacing. But if the medicine ran out . . . or if I quit taking the medicine . . . I would know . . ." His eyes widen. "I remember now! All of it! The medicine *would* run out, because he only gave me a little at a time, never more than a week's supply. He knew something might happen to him, and he wanted to be sure I would be able to do something about it." He felt a jolt of recognition at what this meant. "Cay, he used me as a storage bank! He manipulated my memory!"

Abruptly, he stops talking. More memories are resurfacing, pushing up from where they have been buried in his subconscious. They no longer wait for him to sleep. Suddenly, it is all coming back, the whole of what happened to him and why. The last effects of the ProLx are finally wearing off.

He looks at Cay, his face flushed hot with anger and shock.

"What is it, Ash?" she presses. "Tell me."

"My father made a recording of everything that was happening at BioGen and then hid the file."

"You're sure about this?" Now she is excited too.

"Very sure," he says, his memories sharpening even as he recalls them. He remembers everything!

He tells Cay, the words tumbling over themselves as he rushes to get them out.

His uncle *is* responsible for what's happened. His father said Cyrus Collins lost perspective and any semblance of meaningful judgment a long time ago, doing things no sane man should even think of doing, and needed to be stopped. Because if he weren't, the damage to the people of the United Territories would be irreparable. The hidden file would reveal this. It was too dangerous for Ash to know the particulars beforehand, but if his father failed to stop his brother or if something should happened to him, Ash's supply of ProLx would run out and his memory of everything would return. At that point, he was to make contact with someone high up in the U.T. Government and reveal where the hidden file could be found . . .

He chokes on the words, takes an unconscious step backward, and almost loses his balance. Cay grabs him.

"Hold on," she says, straightening him. "Take a deep breath. Where did your father hide this file?"

He stops again. The rest of it comes tantalizingly close and then clouds over. He tries to bring it back and fails. At that moment, the machines go quiet, the downloading of Jenny's files into the hidden portable drive complete.

He shakes his head. "I don't know. I can't remember the rest."

Cay jumps up immediately. She comes over to him, takes him by the shoulders, and pulls him out of his chair. "Not yet, you can't. But you will. We just have to find a way to help you. Come on, we're getting out of here."

- 25 -

Minutes later Ash is sitting next to Cay in the Bryson Utility as they drive out of the underground tunnel and head out onto the Straightaway.

Cay isn't talking. Not yet. They travel in silence, eyes directed at the road ahead. The silence looms between them like a wall. The Street Freaks building remains locked; they were careful to leave no indications that they were ever there. The Shoe still hangs from the rope in Bay 3. The computers in Jenny Cruz's office are emptied and scrubbed and returned to their place of concealment in the floor. Everything is back to the way it was. No sign of their presence remains. The portable storage drive is tucked inside Cay's purse. When they link up with Jenny again, they will give it to her.

Which will happen sometime tomorrow. Jenny called moments earlier, just before they were leaving Street Freaks. She and Woodrow are tucked away in a safe house somewhere in the north end of the Zone and will remain there until all four of them reconvene to figure out what to do about BioGen. Jenny has told Cay they need to get inside the building in order to access the main computers—the same thing she told Ash. Tomorrow they will meet to decide how to make that happen. And, more importantly, who will carry it out. Without the dexterity and strength of T.J. and Holly, the other four are severely handicapped. But it has to be done. There is nowhere else for them to turn, nowhere else to look for the information they need. It has to be somewhere in BioGen.

Until then, Jenny stresses, no one is to do anything. Cay gives her promise. Yet she is driving with a considerable degree of determination and intensity.

"You're bothered about something," Ash says finally. "What is it?"

"Jenny is too eager to break into BioGen without being sure it will help. I think the idea needs further discussion."

"So you don't think we should do it?"

"Not sure yet."

Ash pauses, thinking it over. "Where are we going?" he asks finally.

"My home," she says.

"Good. We can wait there and figure things out tomorrow."

"That's your plan, is it, Ash?" she says without looking over.

"It's not yours?"

Cay is silent a moment, and then she says. "No, it isn't."

They are almost to her cottage. The houses on the street are familiar by now, the landscaping recognizable even in the shadows beyond the open walkways. Overhead, moon and stars add their pale white light in a radiance that blankets the whole of the neighborhood and reflects like snow.

She glances over. "Let's clear the air about Cyrus. You seem to think my spending time with him is some sort of betrayal of you. You know how silly that sounds, don't you?"

"I do when you say it like that." He shifts in his seat so that he is facing her. "But I saw you hanging on his arm. After you told me you weren't going to the Sprint."

"Yes, well, I told you what I thought you needed to hear. I would have told you something different if I had thought you were capable of listening with a clear head."

"So seeing you with him was just me being delusional?"

"I was with him because I thought it was a good way to get information on what he intended to do about Street Freaks. It's what I do, after all. Jenny and the Shoe both knew about it; they were hoping I could learn something about your father and BioGen. Isn't that what you wanted too?"

"Not that way, I didn't."

"Oh, so now there is a right way and a wrong way? Listen to yourself! You sound like you're ten years old. If your concern is for my virtue, you're way too late. If your concern is for my safety, I am far more capable of looking after myself than you are. If your concern is that I might be selling you out, you and I are all done, right here and now. So if none of the above applies, ask yourself a question. Why would I agree to do it?"

He sees it now, and he is ashamed. "To help me."

"Ah, the light dawns!" She reaches over and pats his leg. "In spite of your foolish fixation on our future and your lack of worldly experience, I like being with you. At least, I like being with you when you're not mooning over me. I wanted to help you with your father. This was my chance to do so."

He nods. "All right, I jumped to conclusions without taking time to ask you what was happening. I'm embarrassed and I'm sorry."

"You have to understand. It's not what happens between your uncle and me, which means nothing. It's not the means I use or the measures I take. All that is programmed into me and no different than eating or drinking. Your uncle is a troll, but trolls are just trolls. I know how to deal with them."

She glances at him. "What matters is whether or not it was worth the time and effort. Did I get anything useful from expending both? Were they helpful in any way."

"Can we can skip the details?" he asks.

"Sure. Just so you understand. Now listen. We're only going to the cottage to get some equipment we'll need. Then we're going out again. To your old home at the sky tower."

He stares. "Why? What's the point of that?"

"If your father were going to hide something that would incriminate people who would hurt him if they found out, where would he do it?"

"BioGen?"

"No. BioGen is the enemy. Much too dangerous to hide a file in their computers when the information is all about them and can be traced back to him if found. Your father would have realized that. He wouldn't have risked it."

"So he hid the file in our home? But wouldn't they look there first?"

She nods. "But your father was a clever man. He created a misdirection of some sort to throw them off the track. Anyway, that's not the only reason we are going back. Your home is where everything began for you, where your father told you about the danger, where you were warned that you might have to run. Being back there now might help trigger other memories. You've remembered a lot, but you said it yourself—you haven't remembered everything. Being there might jog the rest loose."

"So you want to go back tonight? Without waiting on Jenny and Woodrow?"

"We don't need them for this. Besides, it would only lead to an argument with Jenny. You know she always wants to do things her way. Let's leave them out of it. This is on you and me."

"You don't know what might be necessary."

"I don't? What part don't I know? That we have to go back to your home and break into it? That your uncle will probably have it under guard? That we will likely have a fight on our hands? I don't know that?"

"Okay. But shouldn't someone know what we're doing? Shouldn't we at least tell Jenny and Woodrow what we're planning to do, even if we're not taking them along?"

"Oh, sure. We should just tell them. They won't mind. They'll understand." She smirks. "Even you don't believe that. Jenny will insist it's too dangerous. Like somehow it's safer for us to break into BioGen? No, we keep this to ourselves."

They have reached their destination. She pulls into the drive and slows until the gates swing open. Then she pulls the Bryson through and eases up the long drive and around the manor house to her cottage. The manor house is lit, but her cottage is dark.

She looks at him, waiting. "What?"

He shakes his head. "Even if I agree with you about keeping Jenny and Woodrow out of this, I don't agree that going back to my home and hoping that somehow my memory will return simply because of where I am is a good idea. Jeez, Cay, it's too dangerous."

"Well, jeez, Ash, do you have a better idea? By morning your uncle will come looking for us. How long do you think we can hide from him? He has all the resources of ORACLE at his disposal. He will hunt us down. That's how he is. I should know."

He stares at her. "You should know? What do you mean?"

"I mean I have some firsthand knowledge about his ability to track people down. I saw it happen. But I was lucky. I got out another way."

"What other way?" he says quietly.

She triggers a node on the dashboard computer, and the lights inside her home blink on. She sits where she is, not moving. For a moment she doesn't say anything.

Then she turns to face him. "Okay. I'm going to tell you all the stuff I've been holding back. It might help you get a grip on reality. Remember when I said all of us at Street Freaks were discards? That we were built or reconstructed to be a certain way but ended up as rejects? That we were meant to think and act exactly as humans do?"

She waits on him, so he nods. "I remember."

"Then you remember what I was built to do. I am a prototype— one so perfect it is virtually impossible to tell otherwise. The men who built me wanted me to have the emotional and intellectual responses of a real woman. A *human* woman. I was not to be an automaton. I was not to be bot-like in any way. I was to think and behave exactly as if I were human but to have one function and one function only. To please men like them. To be responsive and submissive to them in any way they directed."

She looks over, her perfect features suddenly sad beyond words. "But they overlooked something. Creating new life is unpredictable. Even when it's synthetic. Constructing me in specific ways is no guarantee I will turn out as planned. It isn't always possible to predict which responses will surface and take hold, even when what you build is so carefully designed and engineered."

He shakes his head. "What are you saying?"

"That I don't like doing what I was built to do. Not even a little bit. I was a prototype, but I turned out to be more real than expected. I was created to give pleasure to men. I was created to be their plaything. I was made desirable in order to attract them to me. I was not to question what was being done to me. I was simply to submit. But that isn't how I turned out. I developed feelings and a conscience. I discovered I didn't like being used that way. It made me feel like I was losing a piece of myself every time I let it happen."

She gives him a small smile. "So I stopped doing what they wanted, and just like that, I ceased to have a purpose. They didn't see any other possibility for me. I couldn't have children, couldn't procreate. What use was I? They looked at me exactly as they would a machine that no longer worked properly. They began to talk about terminating me." She pauses. "It was your father who rescued me."

The revelation shocks him. "My father?"

"From your uncle."

He hears the words, but he can't quite make sense of them.

"Your father was working at BioGen," she continues, not waiting on him. "He was lead scientist on their genetics engineering projects. I was one of those projects. After I was made, your uncle . . . appropriated me. I became his personal creature. I was still his when I began to demonstrate how unhappy I was.

I rebelled in ways that infuriated him. Deciding to terminate me was his immediate response. Easiest way to get rid of a problem."

She takes a deep breath, clearly uncomfortable with her subject. "Your father found out. We had become friends by then. He saw me differently than the others; he understood me. He could see what his brother was doing to me. So he bargained me away from his brother and brought me to the Shoe. I don't know what it cost him; he never told me and I never asked. Street Freaks became my new home. My refuge. The Shoe was like your father. He never asked anything of me, never expected any favors. Yes, he used me to gain information. Codes to security systems, security schedules at plants, locations of valuable designs and formulas—information like that. Anything Jenny couldn't find on a computer. I did it willingly. He saved my life; I wanted to do something for him."

"Like sleeping with strange men?" he snaps in frustration.

"Be careful. Don't say something you will regret."

"Is there anything I won't regret saying at this point?" He seethes with frustration and anger. "You should try listening to yourself! You tell me you hate it, but you do it anyway. You've even gone back to my uncle. How could you do that?"

She gives him a long, careful look. "We've already covered this ground, Ash."

Ash slouches in his seat, angry all over again. "There is a word for what he did to you."

"Nobody made me do anything once I got away from your uncle. Nobody used me again the way he did. I did what I chose to do once I was with the Shoe. That's what counts."

"Doesn't mean I have to like it."

She gives him a weary look. "You know what I am. You've known from the beginning. You can't keep pretending that I'm something else. And that's what you seem intent on trying to do. Even though I told you that thinking of me as some kind of fragile flower was a mistake."

"I'm entitled to think what I want."

"Not when you're being foolish. You think we might somehow have a life together—become a couple, maybe fall in love. Don't look at me that way. That's what you want. You want our relationship to mean something more than it does. It can't."

"But you've broken away from your old life! You don't have to go back to it!" He practically shouts it at her. "You have other choices—a world of choices. You can make any one of them. Then maybe things can change."

Cay shakes her head. "I'm a pleasure synth, and that's never going to change. I'm the leopard who cannot change her spots. I use that to my advantage. That's why I've been able to fool your uncle the last few days. He only sees me one way. You should be able to understand. You're grown up enough."

"I don't understand any of it," he insists stubbornly.

"Well, you better start understanding. Life will be a lot better for you once you do. Now get out of the car."

They walk to the cottage door. Cay taps in the code that unlocks the door and disarms the alarm. They go inside.

"Want something to eat?" she asks.

He mutters that he isn't hungry but then follows her into the kitchen where she begins fixing sandwiches anyway.

"You know what?" he says, watching her. "Forget what I just said. You're right. I have to get past how all this makes me feel. I have to learn how to accept things. None of it matters anyway. I don't care how other people see you. I don't care what you've done, or even why. It doesn't change how I feel about you. It never will."

She nods absently. "If you say so."

"So I'm not going to let you put yourself in danger for me."

She finishes making the sandwiches and motions for him to sit at her tiny kitchen table.

"Maybe you don't have anything to say about it."

"Maybe not. But that doesn't mean I can't say it anyway. One of us has to show some good judgment."

"You're pretty sure of yourself. You think you have this all figured out, don't you?"

He forces himself to stay calm. "No, I don't. I don't have anything figured out."

She takes a bite of her sandwich and regards him as she chews. "We don't have a choice, Ash. Neither of us. Especially now that we know what's at stake. We need to expose Cyrus before he catches up to us. Don't you see that?"

Ash closes his eyes in despair. "All I can see is how badly this is going to end."

"We have to take a chance. It's all we have left to work with." She brightens. "Hey, this is your dream come true. You and me get to go on a date. Think of it that way. Maybe you'll feel better."

"What if I say no?"

"Then say so now. Are you in or out?"

He looks away. "You already know the answer to that."

She gives him a smile. "You're right. I do."

She leans back, her sandwich finished. He is surprised to discover that he has eaten most of his as well.

"Why did we come here?" he asks. "To find nourishment?"

"Not really. But food is a good idea. We came to pick up a few things before breaking into your condo. Also I think we should wait until after midnight."

He remains unconvinced. "What if we can't break in? What if my memory doesn't come back? What if we can't find what we need? What if this is just another dead end?"

"As long as no one catches us, we're no worse off. But your father went to a lot of trouble to hide something important in your memory. Something that might help us bring down BioGen and stop what's happening to all those street kids. There's no reason to think we can't uncover it. We just have to keep trying."

Ash looks away, considering the risks. It doesn't take much thinking to realize how extreme they are. But it also doesn't take much to understand how few choices they have if they are to find a way out of this mess. The kids at Street Freaks have risked themselves for him time and time again. Now he has a chance to pay them back for all they have done.

Suddenly he wants to tell her something, to take a chance. He hesitates, unsure of how to say it.

"If we do this," he begins. "If we pull it off . . ."

He searches for the right words. Her eyes are fixed on him, and when he looks into them, he sees the possibilities that she keeps trying to deny.

"Go on," she says.

"Can we start over? Can we think about being more than friends? If that's what we still are? Can we just think about it?"

"You don't give up easily, do you?"

He shakes his head. "Not where you're concerned, I don't. I know you think I don't understand, that I'm naive and probably ought to grow up. But I think you're wrong."

She says nothing. She just looks at him. He cannot tell what she is thinking, but the intensity of her gaze is terrifying.

"I mean, the Shoe is dead and Street Freaks is gone, and we both have to start over somewhere. So maybe you could . . ."

"Change my spots? Even though I'm a leopard?"

"Yeah, I guess so. I know I'm not . . ."

"I could try," she says abruptly, interrupting him. She waits for his reaction, then nods. "I could try."

He smiles. "That's good enough for me."

When she goes into the bedroom to gather up the things she thinks they will need, he turns on the wall-mounted vidview. There is a show on about growing up in the Northwest Territories. What he sees makes it look attractive, but it fails to hold his attention. His thoughts are elsewhere. On what lies ahead, mostly. How they will get into his sky tower home, now guarded and locked. How Cay thinks she can trigger a return of his memory so that he will know where his father's file is hidden. How they will manage to retrieve it and escape before they are discovered.

What will become of them after this is over?

At some point a news bulletin scrolls across the screen about the troubles in the Dixie Confederacy. Mob action resulting in fires and property damage continues to disrupt the peace. Occupying public buildings and government offices is taking place everywhere. Secession demands surface anew. The list goes on. The attacks on government institutions are troubling. There is a suggestion that action on the part of the United Territories and ORACLE may be close at hand. Achilles Pod units are being readied to intervene.

Finally, Cay reappears, shuts off the vidview, and tells him to come into her bedroom. Strewn across her bed are sets of protective clothing, including blackout sheaths and Forms. Then she picks up a wasp sting—a small, compact handgun that fires knockout darts. Ash has read about them. Depending on the strength of the serum injected into the dart tips, you can either render a target unconscious or you can terminate it.

He looks at the tiny weapon and then questioningly at her. "Don't worry," she says. "You use it only if you have to protect yourself. Probably won't be necessary. Just don't shoot me by mistake."

She tosses him a blackout sheath and a pair of Forms and sends him back out into the living room to change while she does the same in the bedroom. When she emerges, she is clothed in black from head to foot, a sinuous panther ready to hunt. He is ready for her, his sheath and Forms molded to his body.

"I still don't remember where the file is hidden," he says.

"So let's go see what being back in your old home does for you."

"Yeah, okay. But how do we get into the building?"

She smiles and gives him a wink.

- 26 -

They drive the Bryson out of the Red Zone and into the Metro. Cay doesn't speak to him. She seems to have nothing to say. Ash understands this. He doesn't have anything to say either. There's nothing for it now but to follow through. They will gamble on her hunch about his memory. They will risk everything on going back to where it all began weeks earlier.

She doesn't ask him where to go or how to get there. She already seems to know, taking the streets he would have told her to take, turning at the corners where he would have told her to turn. He studies her profile. The blackout sheath covers her face and flattens her hair to her head, changing her look entirely. Her features seem hard and sculpted. On the surface, at least, she appears to be a different person.

They pull into a sky tower parking garage not far from his neighborhood and exit the Bryson. She retrieves a pair of heavy combat jackets from the rear of the vehicle and hands one to him.

Then she pulls back her sheath where it covers her head and shakes out her hair. She is herself again, strikingly beautiful and serene, all the hard edges gone. She looks at him. "What?"

"Nothing," he says quickly, pulling on his own jacket.

"We'll rent a jumper and fly to your home. Not to where you

live. To the jumper hive. You remember the code to your unit's garage? 82C, isn't it?"

He raises an eyebrow. "How do you know that?"

"I used the vidview in my bedroom to look it up. You can find out anything online, right?" She smirks. "So can you get us inside, once we're there?"

He nods. "If no one's changed the code."

"Why would anyone bother? Come on."

From there, they ascend by elevator to a jumper rental agency. As they near the service window, she tells him to let her handle things. She goes up to the window while he hangs back, but he can hear her talking to the agent. She is all cool and businesslike. She places her order for a jumper, provides credits to pay for it, allows him to scan her retinal chip, and they are off.

"You gave him your ID," he points out as they start down the rows of jumpers.

She glances over. "Are you afraid for me? Think maybe I don't know what I'm doing. I've had some practice at this, you know."

"I was just saying."

"He got what I wanted him to get. Someone else's ID. We synths are very versatile, you know. Not being creatures of flesh and blood, we are able to alter our identities. Another protective function against poor behavior in clients." She laughs softly. "Stop worrying."

They move over to the assigned jumper and climb in. Cay powers up the engine, and they roll to the hangar door and out onto the landing platform. Around them, the Metro is a dazzling array of lights and stars, bits and pieces of brightness shining everywhere they look, the refraction altered by the particle content of the poisonous L.A. air. So beautiful, Ash thinks, but so deadly.

They lift off smoothly, Cay working the controls as if she has been doing so all her life. And maybe she has. There is so much about herself she hasn't revealed. She points their little craft toward his sky tower home without asking for directions.

They rise into the upper traffic lanes, now all but deserted with midnight's passing, and level out. It feels to him as if he is moving through a black ocean. Lights flashing like bright fish sweep past, each set upon its own course. A sudden rush of uncertainty infuses him, and he wishes momentarily that everything were back to the way it used to be.

But that can never happen. There is only the future, and the future is an unknown.

They fly up to the building that houses his home, its black mass looming over them as they near, eighty-five stories of stone and steel and composites, its lighted windows beacons of watchfulness. They approach the hive, its reflective numbers clear from this height, and ease close so that Ash's side is pressed up against his unit's narrow apron. Ash knows what he is doing is extremely dangerous, but without a remote they cannot access his family storage area without entering his unit's code from outside. He releases the jumper door and climbs out, a chill wind whipping at his clothing as he presses himself against the building wall and carefully moves along the apron to the digital pad that will allow him to punch in his entry code. The unit door responds, sliding up to reveal a dark emptiness.

Ash steps aside, and Cay moves the jumper into its designated slot. Ash waits until she climbs out before closing the garage door behind them.

No words are spoken. Ash waits for directions. Cay moves over to the unit's interior door, spends a moment or two on the lock, and opens it. Hallway lights reveal an empty interior. On this floor, there are only hives and machines that clean the air pumped through the building. No residents live here.

With Ash leading the way, they walk to the elevators and summon one that will take them to Ash's floor.

Cay takes out her wasp sting. "Let me go first. You watch my back." She gestures at his weapon, tucked in his belt. "You better take that out and be ready."

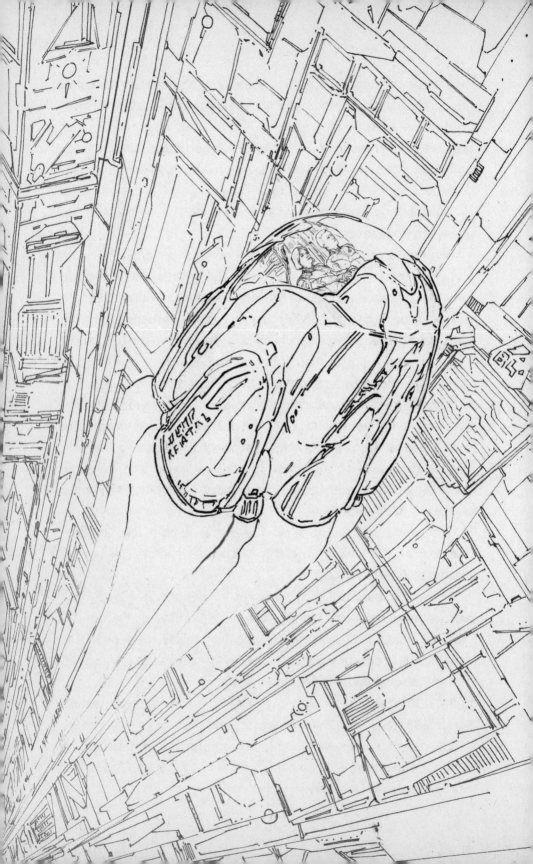

As the doors open, he feels a shiver. But when they step into the hallway, there is no one around. His home is farther along the corridor and around a corner, so they can't be sure yet who might be waiting. They move ahead slowly, listening for any sounds. There are none.

When they reach the corner, Cay motions for him to stop. With her back pressed against the wall, she sneaks a peek. She holds her position and then slides back again, turning to face him. Her voice drops to a whisper.

"No one in sight. But the unit is sealed with vid-alarms. We have to neutralize them before we can enter. Wait here."

She steps out into the hallway and looks more closely at the closed door. Everything is abnormally still, frozen in a kind of stasis that suggests to Ash anything might happen if he even breathes. He scans the hall behind him and then looks ahead again. Cay is moving toward the door, walking slowly, weapon raised. She gets to the door and stops. Ribs of wire crisscross the door, connected to the vid-alarms in a tightly spun spider web.

She backs away and returns to him. "Different plan," she murmurs and heads back down the hall, motioning for him to follow. At the first door they reach, she turns to him. "Who lives here?"

"The Kritzers," he whispers back. "They should still be in Europa."

"Anyone staying over while they're gone?"

"A nephew, sometimes."

"Does he know you?"

Ash thinks. "I don't think so. I can't remember."

"Seems to be an ongoing problem with you. Stay out of sight."

He backs away and plants himself flush against the wall. Cay knocks on the door, waits, and when no one answers, knocks again. She stands in plain view, smiling broadly at the peephole.

Long moments pass. Then Ash hears the locks release and the door crack open. "What is it?" a voice asks.

Cay goes into a long explanation about coming to see her

aunt, who doesn't appear to be home, and a seriously sprained ankle, which requires his help. A short exchange follows, and the door opens.

She is through the opening instantly, and by the time Ash catches up to her, the occupant—a young man—lies motionless on the floor. Wordlessly, Cay drags him all the way inside, and Ash follows her in and closes the door behind them.

"What does all this get us?" he asks, trailing Cay as she begins searching the unit.

"Didn't you say you escaped using a ledge that runs along the outside of the building?"

"Yeah. But you don't expect me to go back out there again, do you?"

"Afraid so. We need to get into your apartment if we're to find anything out. Don't weasel out on me now."

"You plan to get in through a window?" he asks.

"Can't go through the door."

"But the windows are alarmed too!"

"Is that what the management told you?"

"Everything in this building is alarmed!"

She looks at him with something approaching despair. "They don't alarm the windows of sky towers eighty-two stories up. Fact is they stop after the tenth floor. City codes don't require more than that. No builder alive spends credits on safety where it isn't required. Your windows might be locked, but they are definitely not alarmed. Trust me."

He isn't sure this is a matter of trust, but it is clear her mind is made up about how to break into his unit. He really doesn't want to go back out on that ledge, but he doesn't want to tell her he won't either. That doesn't leave too many choices.

She finishes making sure there is no one else in the unit, trusses up the Kritzer nephew, and then moves to the delivery port and steps outside, waiting for him to join her. The wind is just as strong up here as it was down at the hive level, and the temperature has dropped considerably. Already, Ash feels the beginnings of numbness in his fingers and feet.

Cay starts edging her way along the narrow ledge, using the handholds provided for cleaning and repairs to keep from falling. Ash follows, determined. *If she can do it, so can I. Just don't look down. Just keep moving.* It is a torturous journey, slow and uncertain, the wind trying to pry them loose from their handholds, the night cloaking everything but distant stars and tower lights. The roar of traffic rises up as if to taunt him, and the thought of dying is suddenly very real.

But at last they stand outside the laundry room window he used to escape the Hazmats that came for him that first day. Cay's hands work to gain a grip on the joint where the folding windows compress against the seal of the frame, and when she finally does, they open easily. Using her forearms for balance, she levers herself through the opening. Grappling for purchase, though his effort is much less agile, he manages to join her.

Once inside, they stand where they are and listen. There are no sounds or voices to be heard. The unit is silent. They exchange a knowing glance. It appears it is empty, but they cannot be certain.

Cay leads the way into the living quarters. Ash looks around in despair. Everything has been trashed. Even the cushions on the couches and chairs have been ripped apart. Carpet has been torn up and walls opened in huge gaps. The bots lie where they fell, silenced forever. There is barely enough of them left to use for salvage. Ash feels tears come to his eyes. Faulkner, Beattie, and Willis4. Seeing them discarded like this reinforces his anger.

He stops looking and directs his gaze at Cay. She nods and beckons. They go into the kitchen and sit across from each other at the little breakfast table.

"This is where your father told you about the file?" she whispers. "In your dream?"

"Close your eyes and try to recreate what happened. Think

about him, about his words, about anything he said or did. Don't try to force it. Just let it happen."

He does as she asks, hands folded on the table in front of him, eyes closed. He pictures his father's face, hears him speak the first few words of what will be a troubling, difficult admission, hears him give the beginnings of a warning that Ash will think unnecessary. His father speaks of personal danger that might spill over to include his son. He tries to explain what has happened and why. Words that make Ash feel as if perhaps he doesn't know his father at all. Words that sometimes make complete sentences and sometimes splinter in fragments, not all of which are intelligible.

He hears himself make a small sound of something between regret and dismay.

Hands fold over his. Cay's hands. Comforting, encouraging.

"Stay focused. Take deep breaths."

He breathes, relaxes, fades into the warmth and softness of her touch, imagines for a moment it might mean more than it does. Drifts. Images surface. Some are of his father speaking to him on that morning; some are of other things. His mother. Holly, facing down the Razor Boys. The Shoe, hanging from a rope. Suddenly, he sees T.J., smiling and carefree. The pain caused by his smile is too much to bear, and he pushes the image away.

"This isn't working," he says, his words rough-edged with what he is feeling.

"Just be patient. Just stay with it."

He does, but now things are beginning to repeat themselves, words his father has said more than once, comments and expressions that Ash has seen before. His memory is working hard, cataloging, organizing, sifting through everything. But there is a darkness keeping him from reaching the rest of what he knows is there—hidden and inviolate.

His hopes dwindle; his confidence fails.

He forces his thoughts again to his father sitting with him at this table, telling him of the danger they both face. It seems so long ago. He hears his father telling him he must run if he is told to. To Street Freaks. To safety.

Heart promise.

He'd almost forgotten. It was a ritual between them when he was little. His father would ask him to promise, binding his promise by placing his hand over his heart. So long ago. A lifetime, by now.

He hears his father asking for his pledge, for the binding of it by placing a hand over his heart.

His father insisting.

His fingers reaching up to touch his heart.

And without warning, rafts of numbers begin to recall themselves in an explosive flow.

They surface in fits and starts, in clusters that feel disjointed yet connected. They arise from wherever they've been hiding and begin to fit themselves together in ways that immediately feel familiar. His memory hums like a machine. The numbers flow. He recognizes these numbers and their significance.

He *knows* what they are.

He remembers.

His eyes open and he stares into Cay's. "What?" she asks at once.

"Locking codes," he says with an urgent hiss. "Given to me by my father. I just remembered!" He leaps to his feet and begins looking around hurriedly. "They must be codes to a computer file. It must be here! We have to find it!"

They search the entire unit, but there are no computers to be found. They look long and hard; they look everywhere. But two hours pass and their efforts yield nothing.

Then he stops where he is and shakes his head. He's mistaken. He's gotten it wrong. *But how can that be? Think!* He goes back to the table and sits, trying to remember.

Words surface, another piece of his submerged memories.

Don't ask me. I can't tell you that.

His father speaking. His father saying he won't tell him the identity of the man behind what is happening. About his uncle. Too dangerous to do so.

But he did tell him. Ash remembers now. Somehow he has forgotten until now. A memory suppressed by ProLx? *Wait! Something else.* Another fresh memory reaches out to him. A small but crucial scrap. The computer he searches for. One in which the locking codes will find and open a file . . .

"Cay!" His urgent hiss brings her to him, and he pulls her close. "It's not here! It never was!"

"But didn't you just say the exact opposite?" she demands. "What are you talking about? So it's not in a computer?"

"No, no! The computer isn't here!" His excitement is so intense he can barely get the words out. "Remember what you said earlier about a misdirection? You were right. My father knew if my uncle found out about the file he would go looking for it. So he couldn't risk hiding it here or in BioGen because he knew those were the first places his brother would look. So he chose somewhere else."

They stare at each other in the near dark, breathing hard. She grips his shoulders, fingers tightening. "What place?"

"Just hear me out. You were right. Coming here, sitting at that table, and thinking about it really worked. My father giving me the locking codes and telling me he would suppress my memory of it. Of everything about what was happening except the warning. But when the warning came, I would remember again. When I remembered the codes, I assumed the computer where the file could be found was here, but I was mistaken."

"You're sure?"

"Afraid so."

"So where is it?"

For the first time since they arrived back at his home, he casts aside caution and speaks in his normal voice.

"ORACLE Central. Hidden somewhere inside of Blue Skye."

- 27 -

Blue Skye?" Jenny repeats incredulously, leaning forward the moment she hears Ash speak the words.

With Cay, he has arrived at the safe house where Jenny and Woodrow have been waiting since yesterday, expecting to have a discussion that would help them find a way to break into BioGen. Hard enough to make that happen, but still far easier than breaking into ORACLE. Ash's news has thrown everything into disarray.

Jenny still can't believe it. "Why in the world would your father use Blue Sky as a hiding place?"

Blue Skye is the nickname for the dedicated server that acts as a backup central storage unit for files dispatched from all of the ORACLE divisions in the U.T. It is accessible only by ORACLE and no one else.

"He probably thought it was the safest place to put it," Ash answers. "Hide it right under his brother's nose."

"He must have had a way to access it," Cay adds. "It wouldn't have been all that hard with the commander of ORACLE as his brother."

Jenny is barely listening. "But why not use BioGen's computers? He had easy access there to almost anything. *We* would have access to almost anything too, once we knew where your father had hidden it. Housing his material in Blue Skye—where Cyrus has control of everything—seems a risky choice."

"Maybe not," Woodrow interrupts. They all look at him. Woodrow hardly ever says anything. "Blue Skye is strictly regulated by the U.T. It's a compartmentalized and segregated system. No one person has all the locking codes. That's how Blue Skye was constructed. It was a precaution against a central hacking attempt. Only the person who opens each individual storage area can access it. Ash's father couldn't hide it in a safer place if he wanted to keep it out of his brother's hands."

"And out of our hands too." Jenny won't let go. "How are we supposed to find where it's hidden in a warren of millions of storage units? How are we supposed to get into ORACLE to access Blue Skye in the first place? Do you know how difficult that will be?"

"Not that difficult," Ash says. "My father gave me both the locking codes to the area where he hid everything and the security codes to ORACLE Central. We can walk right in, access the material, and walk right out."

He has told them about the operation his father performed on him and the beginning of his use of ProLx. He has come to terms with his father's deception—not yet enough to be forgiving of it but enough to accept that his father must have thought it was the best way to preserve what he knew. Ash still feels like a test subject, experimented on and tweaked in the way his friends once were, made to be something he was totally unaware of and left to figure it out for himself. He does not like it one bit. He understands for the first time how they must feel.

Cay had him wait until morning before having this meeting, giving him at least a few hours of sleep at her cottage. Ash was not sure he had slept at all, his newfound memories turning over in his mind, his emotions in turmoil. He was awake so early he was dressed before Cay appeared from her bedroom to see how he was doing. Breakfast had been a mostly silent affair, both of them too keyed up with expectations of what lay ahead.

Now it is midday, and they sit in the tiny living room of the safe house, trying to work their way through Ash's revelations and the prospects of what should be done because of them.

"So you can get us inside ORACLE and open the Blue Skye unit your father created." Jenny looks suddenly hopeful. "Even if it won't be as easy as you make it sound."

Knowing smiles are shared all around. They see the light at the end of the tunnel they have been wandering through for weeks, and they are newly confident.

"You really are a Street Freak now," Woodrow says to Ash. "You only thought you weren't."

Ash isn't sure he qualifies, but he smiles back anyway. Close enough to count, he decides.

"Not so fast." Jenny is on her feet. "Everyone sit tight until I can determine if there is a way to break into Blue Skye *without* having to get inside ORACLE Central. It will save us a lot of trouble if there is. If not, we have to come up with a new plan."

She gets up and leaves the other three where they are, disappearing into the back room that houses her personal computer. She is in there long enough that by late afternoon they wonder if she is ever coming out again. Cay leaves without saying where she is going. Nothing new there. They pass the time watching the wall-mounted vidview for news of Cyrus and Street Freaks but find nothing. Whatever Ash's uncle intends to do next, he is keeping it under wraps.

It is growing dark when Jenny finally emerges. Her expression is haggard and frustrated; she looks defeated. "Nothing," she says quietly. "I tried everything, but Blue Skye is a fortress. We have to access what we need at the source."

"So we have to get into ORACLE," Ash says.

Jenny nods. "But first I want to get my hands on floor plans and figure out where the Blue Skye mainframe is housed. That won't be easy. And I'm too tired to do anything more tonight. Go on home. I'll call when I have something."

Feeling weary and frustrated, Ash troops out the front door to wait for Cay and meets her coming up the walk. "Discussion over?" she asks him.

"Jenny wants to get a copy of the floor plans for ORACLE so she can pinpoint the location of Blue Sky."

She turns around without a word, and they climb into the Bryson. For a moment, they just sit there, staring out at the night. "Your uncle is searching for you," she says finally. "Jenny better not waste time."

He nods, not bothering to ask how she knows what his uncle is doing because he can already anticipate her response.

"I hope we're not making a mistake," he says instead.

"Why would we be?"

He shrugs. "What if all this is pointless? Maybe whatever's hidden in Blue Skye won't change anything."

She gives him a hard look. "You don't believe that. Your father was killed because of what he knew."

"But I'm risking the lives of everyone at Street Freaks by trying to find out."

Now she is really angry. "Everyone understands the risk, Ash, and no one wants to drop the matter. BioGen is experimenting on street kids and killing the ones on which the experiments don't work out in the way they intended. All of us at Street Freaks fit that description. So we have a personal interest in seeing this through. I don't know what we'll find when we retrieve your father's file. But your father thought it was worth something, so I think we can assume that whatever we find, it will have value."

They trade challenging looks, but Ash gives way first. "Okay. I still hate the idea of being the one who's the cause of everything we're about to do."

She smirks. "This isn't as much about you as you seem to think it is. You coming to Street Freaks just happened to be the catalyst. But we're all in agreement on what needs doing, in case you didn't notice. No one opted out." She reaches over and shoves him gently, Have a little faith in your friends, why don't you?"

He sighs. "Yeah, all right."

He smiles, and she smiles back. "Good for you. Now let's get back to the cottage. I don't know how long we'll have to wait on Jenny. She's thorough, but she's slow."

"So you could end up with me as a permanent houseguest?"

She glances over. "Can you cook?"

He shakes his head. "No."

"Well, you better learn if you plan to stay."

She leaves it hanging, triggers the ignition, and they drive off into the darkness.

Another night is spent at the cottage with Cay in her bedroom and Ash on the couch. He doesn't know about her, but his sleep is restless. He is more than a little afraid of what lies ahead. He remembers how it felt going into ORACLE the last time. And that was through the front door and not by breaking in. He remembers the black-clads and the Watchmen and the strong, hard features of his uncle.

He does not want to do this, but there is no avoiding it.

They rise shortly after dawn and sit down to breakfast together. No words pass between them until the meal is nearly finished.

"You have the codes memorized?" she asks suddenly. "You won't forget them?"

He nods.

"I want you to stay close to me and do what I tell you. No questions, no arguments. Can you agree to that?"

"I think so. Will it just be the two of us?"

She nods. "Unless Jenny insists on coming. I can't stop her if she does. But it's dangerous for her with those tanks and tubes. She's so vulnerable."

Unlike you, he thinks. *Or me. We're invincible.*

"Let me ask you something," he says. "All these street kids who were tweaked by BioGen—what happened to them? Besides yourselves, what about the others? Were they all killed because they didn't work out?"

She leans back in her chair, shakes her head. "It's more complicated than that. You have to understand. Some of us were created by BioGen scientists—like T.J. and me. Some, like Holly, Jenny, and Woodrow, were reassembled because their human bodies failed them in major ways. Others were tweaked simply to test out new ideas for improvements. Reinventing-the-wheel sorts of ideas. These were most of the street kids snatched up by BioGen and brought in to experiment on. They were test subjects for various tweaks the scientists had dreamed up for how we might improve the human race. Some were successful. Most weren't."

"What were they doing this for? If all they were trying to do was reinvent the wheel, what prompted it?

"Think of it this way. You can build the perfect anything, but you can't always predict exactly how it will perform. Especially when it has a brain and the capacity for critical thinking and independent thought built into it. To get a better human, you have to provide both. Otherwise, you have an automaton, and they didn't want that. Turns out none of us liked what had been done to us. None of us wanted to be what we were expected to be. So we became expendable."

"Like babies born to parents," Ash says. "Parents have hopes and expectations for their kids, but you never know if they will be realized. Parents do what they can to shape their kids' lives as they grow up, but they can easily turn out to be something else entirely."

"No solution to that problem. Doesn't matter if you are flesh and blood or synthetic. If you can think and feel and comprehend the larger world, you can analyze and come to your own conclusions about who and what you want to be. T.J. was strong and brave and capable, but he didn't want to be a soldier. Holly never got over what had been done to her by her parents. Jenny and

Woodrow didn't like how they were being used like machines."

"And you?" he presses.

"I didn't want to be someone's sex toy. And that was a real problem not only because that was what I was created to be but also because I turned out perfectly otherwise. I was the ideal play-thing for needy men. I just didn't think that was all I was meant to be. Your father agreed."

"They would have killed you otherwise? BioGen would have?"

"It was already in the works. Your father put a stop to it; he got me out and brought me to Street Freaks. He gave me a home and a sense of place in the world."

"How did he get you out? That must have been hard. Don't they know where you are? Couldn't they come and take you back?"

She pauses a long time before she nods. "Yes, to everything, Ash. Now let's leave it there, please. I don't want to talk about it anymore."

She rises, goes into her bedroom, and closes the door, effec-tively ending the possibility of further discussion. Ash sits and worries and broods, his mind working through endless possi-bilities of how his father had managed to save her, and then he shifts his thinking to what comes next. He quickly grows tired of the exercise, but he keeps on anyway. Better to do something than nothing.

The call from Jenny comes early in the afternoon. It surfaces on Cay's private vidview while she is cleaning up lunch dishes. The discussion is short and private; Cay moves away from Ash as she talks in quiet tones. When she is finished, she comes back over and sits beside him on the couch.

"Jenny has assembled a set of floor plans. Not from ORACLE. Those were classified and secured. She tracked them down using records stored in the files of the companies that did the plumbing and the electrical. It took awhile to hack in because those copies were secured as well, but she managed it. She was able to pin-point where Blue Skye is located."

"When are we going in?" He feels eager, energized. They have something to do at last.

"Tonight. But we're going over to be with Jenny and Woodrow now. Grab your blackout gear and the stun gun. We're leaving in thirty minutes. Remember what I told you earlier. Take your lead from me."

He is annoyed that she is being so insistent on him doing what she tells him, but he guesses she is trying to protect him. After all, if he goes down, the whole effort collapses. They all have a lot riding on him. It is daunting.

When they reach the safe house and enter an hour later, Ash is astonished find Holly Priest and Penny-Bird waiting for them.

"Hey, Ash," Holly greets him cheerfully. "You look all geared up and ready to go."

She sits on the sofa, her injured leg still wrapped in a regenerative bandage but now also protected by a steel-ribbed brace that allows for bending at the knee joint and not much else. She wears a blackout sheath and Forms, and she has strapped black armor about her torso. Various weapons are holstered at her waist.

Penny-Bird wears a blackout sheath as well and carries her chopdown. When Jenny appears, she is similarly dressed.

"No," Cay says at once, looking from one to the other. "You're not going, none of you."

"Not your call, Cay," Holly says calmly, giving her a shrug. "We started this together. That's the way we're going to end it."

"Your leg was shot to pieces!"

"Cyborgs heal faster than humans. Faster than synths too. You know that."

"You'll have trouble moving." Cay is not about to concede. "If we get trapped, you won't be able to keep up with the rest of us. You'll be caught and killed."

Jenny makes a dismissive gesture. "Save your breath. I already made every argument I could come up with, and she tossed them all aside. She intends to act as rearguard along with Penny. It will only be you and Ash and me going into the center that houses Blue Skye. She'll just have to wait for us to get back to her."

Cay looks at Penny-Bird. "What are you? Fifteen or something?"

"Oh, there's an age limit for this sort of thing?" The girl snorts derisively. "Didn't realize. You do know I raced in the Sprint, don't you? That should count for something in the experience area. I can take care of myself."

"And don't start on me," Jenny added quickly. "I need to be there to help with the computers that will give us access to Blue Skye. I can't do that from back here."

"I suppose Woodrow is going too?" Ash asks in despair.

"No, he stays here. We need someone to chart our course once we're inside ORACLE using the floor plans I scrounged up. Woodrow will be our offsite control. He'll have the plans open on a computer connected to me. I'll be wearing a tracking device that will tell him where in the building we are at any given moment."

"So he can direct us?"

"That would be the plan. But there are risks. If someone at ORACLE guesses at what we're doing and the signal is jammed, we'll be on our own. So why don't you make use of that fabulous memory of yours and take a look at the plans while you have the chance. Memorize them in case we need them later."

He does so, going into the back room and using Jenny's computer to scroll through the documents, memorizing one floor at a time, taking care to do so in order, making sure he understands where Blue Skye is located. It appears from Jenny's notes, which have been added to copies of the plans she purloined, that it is on the nineteenth floor in a large blank space left empty on the originals, but over which Jenny has written in large block letters BLUE SKYE.

She comes up behind him. "It's the only place in the building Blue Skye could be, the only space not accounted for. There are dozens of power sources configured in the plans, which suggests the need for multiple feeds. The computers that receive and transmit documents probably don't require much, but the storage units that house and collate and file all those documents require a lot. This has to be it."

He doesn't say anything. He relies on Jenny, who knows far more than he does about such things. Instead, he finishes his memorization and goes back out to sit with the others.

The wait for darkness is endless. Everyone is left to their own devices, and mostly they fiddle with vidviews and coms. They restrict their accessing to public outlets and stay clear of private channels. They eat dinner standing at the counter in the kitchen where a meal of sandwiches and drinks has been provided. Ash does not know by whom and does not ask. He just accepts it and is grateful.

Woodrow sidles up. "Are you all right?" he asks.

Ash grins. "Are you joking? I'm jumping out of my skin. I'm working hard at not falling apart, and we haven't even left."

"It's the waiting," the bot boy says. "It works on your nerves, leaves you imagining."

"Will you be okay back here by yourself?"

"I'll be taking care of you, so I won't have time to worry about me. But I have an escape plan if I need one."

"Because they might come for you?"

He makes a face. "It's possible. If they track my signal to you, they might follow it back to me."

All day Woodrow has been working on something in his workshop, bits and pieces of things scattered all over the place. Ash can't resist asking.

"What are you doing back there?"

The boy grins. "You'll see."

Ash lays a hand on Woodrow's computer housing. "You be careful after we leave. Cut us loose if you think you are in any danger."

"Sure," Woodrow says, but Ash doesn't believe for a minute that he means it.

The day drags into dusk, dusk into darkness, and everyone is restless. They have run out of things to occupy their time, Woodrow included, and sit around talking in low voices and staring off into space. Waiting, because there is nothing else left.

Until finally Jenny rises and says, "All right, that's long enough. Let's get this done."

- 28 -

They walk out into the deep shadows at the end of a drive at the back of the house and find the Onyx waiting for them. Holly has brought it over from where it was in storage after Street Freaks was closed down. They climb inside, Cay taking the driver's seat without asking. Jenny carries the boxy unit Woodrow was working on, a slightly larger version of a laptop computer but differently shaped. Whatever it is, she is careful to protect it.

Woodrow has been left behind, already seated at a powered-up computer to track their movements. All of them have com units, which will allow them to communicate with each other once inside ORACLE.

Cay powers up the Onyx and drives out into the closest residential street and toward the city. Ash leans back in his seat, his gaze directed at the buildings and lights as they come and go in the wake of their passing. Overhead, the sky is clear and a wash of stars is visible in spite of the city lights. Other vehicles pass them by, unaware of their presence. Cay has to drive carefully, easing away from all the eyes that cannot see them. They are invisible predators, hunters in search of an elusive prey. That is how Ash sees their group, and what he believes his father's hidden file has become.

The drive is over too quickly, and they are within several blocks of ORACLE Central when Cay abruptly pulls over. Powering down the Onyx, she says to Jenny, "All yours."

Jenny has unhooded Woodrow's mysterious device to reveal a map screen and any number of switch pads and digital read-outs. Ash leans forward and determines that the screen is show-ing the ORACLE building. But even as he watches, the image changes, and suddenly he is looking at the same building ribbed with lines. The lines pulse softly with a reddish light, snaking everywhere along the walls and floors and roof of the building through a series of tiny boxes.

"What is that?" he asks her.

She glances at him and smiles. "Woodrow's magic. He's built a computer that can pinpoint all of the cameras that ward ORACLE after dark. If anyone enters without wearing the right badge, an alarm will not only sound but the cameras will track the intruder right through the building. There is no getting out if you're spotted."

"So how does this help us?"

"Woodrow's device allows us to shut down any or all of the cameras once we enter the building. Floor by floor, hallway by hallway, room by room. We can pick and choose where we want to go and subvert whatever surveillance might detect and track us. We can open a clear path from our place of entry to Blue Skye and out again. All we have to worry about are the Watchmen."

Ash shakes his head in admiration. A fourteen-year-old boy able to build something like that in a single afternoon? He wouldn't have thought anyone capable of such a feat. It demonstrates clearly why the scientists who saved Woodrow's life so greatly valued him.

"Hush now," Jenny whispers. "I have to concentrate."

She accesses the floor plans and scrolls through them until she finds what she wants. Then, one by one, she turns off vari-ous cameras, pausing each time as she does so to make sure a pulsating line disappears. She takes her time but finishes quickly anyway. "Done. Take us to the private entry," she tells Cay.

Cay brings the Onyx alive and pulls back out onto the street. At the first intersection she turns to her left and works her way behind ORACLE to a windowless wall where huge steel panels sit flush within the composite. Jenny reaches into her jacket and pulls out a small device, presses a button, a beep sounds, and the panel closest lifts. Seconds later Cay is driving the Onyx down a ramp and into a small parking area.

They all get out, Jenny still carrying Woodrow's blackout device, Holly now shouldering a Gronklin and Penny-Bird her chopdown. Cay hauls out a modified Sparz 200 and hands it to Ash, quickly explaining how it works.

"Backup only," she says, "if things get rough. Don't use it otherwise. Only if your life is in danger and there's no other choice."

Ash notes she takes nothing for herself. She is armed only with the wasp sting.

"How did you manage to get us in here?" he whispers to Jenny as they walk to a set of concrete service stairs.

She shrugs. "I hacked into the signal code for the executive parking. That was the easy part. The rest of the building is a minefield. Let's hope those security codes your father made you memorize do the job."

She notices the look on his face. "Well, you asked me."

He regrets that he did. He hates the implications of knowing how much is riding on his shoulders. A twinge of fear rockets through him, but he pushes it away. No time for that now.

They ascend the stairs, Holly leading the way and setting the pace, the others following. The lighting is dim but serviceable. They walk on cat's paws, making no sound in the Forms. No one passes them. No sounds reach them. They feel alone in the near dark, in the silence of the building, in the discomfort of their thoughts.

The climb seems to take forever. Ash loses count of how many floors they pass on their way to Blue Skye. Using an elevator is out of the question. Whatever they do, they want to remain invisible.

Finally, they reach the right landing and the adjoining door that opens onto the nineteenth floor, where the plans Jenny hacked indicate Blue Skye is housed. They stop to rest a moment, and Jenny makes some adjustments with the blackout device to turn off the cameras that service the hallways and rooms on this level. She has already restored all those she had disabled earlier, not wanting to leave them dark long enough for someone to discover there is a problem.

Having determined that no ORACLE personnel are present on their floor before disabling the cameras, Jenny gives Ash a nod. "Your turn."

Ash moves over to the digital keypad that sits next to the door leading out of the stairwell and keys in the security code. To his relief, he hears the locks release. He opens the door for the others. The hallway lights are on, as the lights are kept on in most office and public buildings at night. He glances at Holly as she passes him. She is noticeably limping but has not complained once. She holds the Gronklin at the ready, its big barrel pointing ahead. Penny-Bird is right beside her, chopdown cradled in her slender arms.

The others file in after them, eyes searching everywhere, breathing strained. Jenny points them down a hallway, and they ease ahead.

At the end of the corridor, heavy metal doors are sealed to prevent entry. Red lights blink above the locks and to either side of the doorframe. A warning that entry is restricted. Once again, Ash steps up to the digital keypad and enters a code, this one dedicated to the room where Blue Skye can be found. He takes his time, touching each key firmly, hoping that his father is right, praying he hasn't made a mistake.

To his relief, the door opens. Amazing, Ash thinks, that it should be this easy.

Now they are inside the chamber, and it is immediately apparent that they are in the right place. Blue Skye is everywhere. Banks of storage units are lined up in endless ranks, allowing access between their uniform columns. Dozens more line the walls. Jenny looks around and then proceeds to the right, picking her way carefully, eyes drifting down to the device and then up again. Ash notices that Holly and Penny-Bird are no longer with them, remaining at the doors to act as a rearguard while the other three search out the information Ash believes Blue Skye hides.

It takes only minutes for Jenny to locate the computer that services the storage units—a desk-mounted device with a screen and keyboard set off to one side and locked within a steel cabinet. Ash releases these security locks as well, and Jenny quickly powers up the computer to access the storage units. Ash and Cay look over her shoulder, watching as she roams through tables of contents, files and indexes, apps and nibs, hunting.

Long minutes pass, and she backs away. "I can't find it. I don't know exactly what it is I am looking for and don't see anything that suggests the source of the file. I need something more, Ash. Your father must have used a key under which he hid the information. There are millions of keys in these units. What words or symbols would he have used that he knew you would recognize?"

Ash stares blankly at the information on the screen. A twinge of memory tells him he should know the answer, but he cannot seem to find it. Columns run up and down in a dizzying array of markings, most of it signifying nothing. He has the locking codes. Why isn't that enough? Why hadn't his father told him about a key that would access the right files? Or told him something he would know to look for?

But then he had, hadn't he? Ash experiences an epiphany. Hadn't his father told him after all? "Jenny," he says. "Enter 'heart promise.'"

She does so, and the columns and figures begin scrolling in parallel lines all across the screen, the computer searching for whatever Ash has summoned. They wait as the search goes on, everything on the screen moving so fast but the answer seemingly no closer.

Until there it is. Two words appear in the center of a heart.

HEART PROMISE.

"Use the locking codes, Ash," Jenny says quietly.

She gets up from her seat, and he takes her place. Using only his memory, he enters the twin codes. The heart blossoms like a flower in front of him, opening its petals, and the files within reveal themselves.

Ash looks at Jenny, and she motions for him to move. She sits once more. From her pocket she produces a tiny storage device and triggers a wireless relay. Instantly, the files begin to download through AirTrans, and an instantaneous wireless transmittal siphons off the material while leaving no trace of tampering. In moments, they have everything they need.

They look at one another and then at Cay. A special, secretive moment is shared. No words are necessary. Success after so much and so long; victory where once there seemed no possibility of it. Jenny tucks the device into her clothing, and they start back down the corridors that run between the storage banks, returning to where they came in.

They find Holly and Penny-Bird waiting. Jenny gives them a nod, and they both break into broad smiles. Ash is elated. What they have found could bring down his uncle and clear his father's name. All they need to do is get back down to the Onyx and out of the garage and go somewhere they can view the material in private.

Holly eases open the door to the Blue Skye chamber, checks up and down the hall, and they all file out and retrace their steps toward the stairs.

And then their luck runs out.

There were all sorts of possible ways this incursion could go wrong, and Ash had believed he knew everyone single one and was prepared for it. He had believed that he would be ready when the worst happened, but he finds out now how mistaken he was.

Just as they pass the elevator, the doors open, and they are face-to-face with a pair of Watchmen. There is a scramble of surprise and a levering of charges into weapons, but only Holly is quick enough. Two charges from the Gronklin blow the Watchmen back into the elevator and leave them in ruins.

Instantly, alarms sound. The elevator shuts down. The locks on the doors up and down the hallway click into place, one after the other like links on a chain closing them in. Lights go out and a suffocating darkness wraps about them.

"Night vision!" Jenny snaps.

They activate the lenses that allow them to see in total blackness, and in their earpieces they hear Jenny calling Woodrow. "We're in lockdown! Get us out of here!"

"Go to the stairs you took coming up," his voice instructs, the boy surprisingly calm and steady.

They move down the corridor to the door they came through earlier and find it locked. Holly fastens her hands on the handle and tears it off. In seconds they are through and descending the stairs as quickly as they can. But they are moving through a thick, almost total darkness, so they have to be cautious and not trip and fall.

"I'm trying to find you an open path," Woodrow says in their ears.

Silence then. They continue down. They can hear doors opening and closing below them. ORACLE is hunting them. They slow automatically. "Woodrow!" Jenny pleads.

"Get out of there. Next landing. Through the door and turn left. Hurry!"

Again, Holly breaks the lock off with a sharp twist of her titanium wrist. They rush into the corridor beyond and find themselves in a warren of offices. Everything is still dark; the alarms shrill relentlessly, punctuating their rushed movements and increasingly heavy breathing.

Ash feels his heart pounding. His fears wrap about him like sharp wire.

We're trapped! We can't get out!

"Stairs at the far end," Woodrow says. "Go down."

Ash is confused. How can Woodrow know where they are or what they are doing? Then he remembers the tracking device Jenny wears. He must be able to see it on his screen. But how does he know where the Watchmen are? Or is he just guessing?

"Everything's blocked off." Woodrow still sounds unruffled. "You can't reach the Onyx. You have to get off two landings down and exit into the main lobby. Go out the front doors. Find your way from there."

Find your way. Out in the open. A death sentence.

But no one says anything. They just do what Woodrow tells them, descending the stairs, exiting two landings down and charging out into the lobby.

The Watchmen are waiting.

Laser charges explode all around them as they rush to find cover in alcoves and behind pillars and furniture. Holly fronts them all, an easy target for their would-be captors. She is hit twice right away. Sparks fly as the projectiles find their target, but the body armor absorbs the blows. The Watchmen are using light weaponry, the sort they would normally carry making their rounds, and it isn't enough. Holly takes down five of them right away, and the heavy *ka-chug* of Penny-Bird's chopdown signals the fate of two more.

Jenny crouches low behind an information desk while Cay and Ash go the opposite way toward the front doors. Jenny has no weapons, and Cay has only the wasp sting. Ash realizes he has to do more than stay under cover. It is impossible to be sure how many Watchmen are out there, but he is sure there are too many. He is sure they have no chance.

Doesn't matter. He powers up the Sparz and attacks.

It is suicidal and done without thinking. It is a reaction that in a saner moment he would not have even considered. But they are trapped and must break the trap's jaws. Weaving and dodging, he reaches the main reception counter. He fires repeatedly at those seeking to bring him down, and two of them drop and lie motionless. Holly is hit again, and this time, she sinks to one knee, head lowered. Penny steps in front of her protectively, the chopdown firing blindly and repeatedly as fresh shells are chambered in and discharged.

Ash turns back to Cay, who looks at him in disbelief. He reads her thoughts from her expression. *What are you doing?* He motions for her to go to Jenny and run for the front door. Without hesitating, Cay does so. The huge reception chamber is filled with ash and debris, alive with the echoes of weapons being discharged. It is a madhouse. Ash looks right and left, sees an opening, and rushes to reach Holly and Penny. As Penny provides firing cover, Ash levers Holly to her feet—an immense effort—and they limp for the front doors. Cay is there, crouched down with Jenny, but the doors are locked. In response, Holly shrugs off Ash, brings up the Gronklin, and blows them open.

Amid constant firing and the shock of charges that fail to score direct hits but do result in glancing blows and sharp daggers of pain, the five stumble back out into the night.

All of the entry lights remain off, and they are momentarily shrouded in darkness. Cay takes them left toward the handicapped elevators to one side. They are screened by smoke and night, but all save Cay have been wounded. They reach the elevator unchallenged, and to their surprise, it responds when Ash punches the button for street level.

Behind them, but still inside the building, figures rush here and there in an effort to find a way outside to stop the intruders. The group can see evidence of hesitation and confusion through the broad windows. The doors through which they escaped are now partially blocked. No one comes outside.

The elevator arrives. The five fugitives enter and it begins to descend. Cay triggers the garage door opener that brought them inside and then fiddles with a second device. A remote? The word leaves Ash's lips and goes into the com unit, and Cay gives him a nod. They can't get to the Onyx, so the Onyx must get to them.

Suddenly Jenny falters. Ash moves quickly, propping her up. He did not see her struck by any of the weapons fired at them, so he is confused at first. Then he sees the loose end of the tubing that ties into one of the ports at the back of her neck, blood leaking in a steady stream. He ties it off as tightly as he can and hopes he isn't killing her.

The elevator stops at street level, and they stumble outside just as the Onyx swings into view. A knot of Watchmen has finally managed to push its way through the blocked doors and is rushing down the stairs to intercept them. Holly stands up and begins firing, Penny-Bird beside her. The other three limp toward the vehicle. Because it is waiting in darkness, it is virtually invisible to their attackers, who must wonder where they think they are going.

Holly's counterattack scatters the Watchmen, and for long moments, the exchange of fire does no damage to either side. But then Holly abandons her efforts, grabs Penny's arm, and pushes her in the direction of the Onyx. Another few discharges from the Gronklin, and she follows.

They are almost there when Holly is struck in the back by a massive laser charge that throws her to the pavement. Penny hovers over her, trying to pull her to her feet, failing. For the second time that night, Ash goes to her rescue. Leaving the Sparz behind, he flings himself through the passenger door and charges over. With something approaching superhuman effort, he drags Holly back to her feet, and the three of them hobble and lurch toward the safety of the vehicle. Cay is giving them cover fire with the Sparz, standing just outside the driver's door, leaning over the hood.

For a second, Ash is certain they are all dead. Laser charges explode all around him. The cacophony of weapon fire is deafening, and in the distance he can hear the sound of sirens. They seem to be coming from every direction. By now the lasers are targeting the nearly invisible Onyx as well as its occupants, but so far its armor is proving resistant to any real damage.

Ash's thoughts are scattered and vague, his concentration focused on reaching safety. He is struck several times while hauling Holly, glancing blows once more and none fatal. Even so, the accumulation of hits is beginning to tell. The end feels inevitable. Time has run out.

But then somehow they are all back inside the Onyx and Cay is wheeling the vehicle into in a U-turn and taking them back into the near darkness of side streets and byways, leaving ORACLE behind.

The ride back to the safe house is filled with silences punctuated by grunts and hisses of pain. Injuries are examined and assessed. Holly will need medical care, and Jenny has to be looked at in order to have her blood washer repaired. Cay decides to delay any effort to reach the safe house, and instead they drive both to the medical center where Holly was taken before. Penny-Bird provides directions, her young face grim, her eyes frightened. Holly is strong, but this is the second time in a week she has been badly hurt. Even her enhanced constitution can't survive everything.

They arrive at the center. The old house is dark, its lights confined to the porch area. It is very late, and everyone is in bed. But Cay runs to the front door and bangs on it until someone appears. Minutes later, stretchers and bearers appear, and Holly and Jenny are carted away.

Before that happens, Cay reaches into Jenny's clothing and removes the thumb drive and tucks it into her pocket. "Not taking any chances on losing this after what it took to get it," she says to Ash.

She tries to reach Woodrow, but there is no answer. She exchanges a look with Ash, but neither says what they are both thinking.

Leaving Penny-Bird at the medical center with Holly and Jenny, the two climb back into the Onyx and drive to the safe house. They need to be sure Woodrow is all right. There is no need to do anything more about the thumb drive. Tomorrow is soon enough to examine it and send it to where it will do the most damage to BioGen and Cyrus.

On reaching the safe house, they find the front door broken down and the interior destroyed. Everything has been torn apart and every room has been searched. There is no sign of Woodrow or any of his computers. They spend long minutes hunting for some indication of what has happened to the bot boy but find nothing. Further efforts to reach Woodrow by vidview fail.

"He said he had an escape plan if he was found," Ash offers quietly. But he is not sure he believes it. Especially when Cay does not respond.

They have no choice now but to bide their time and wait to hear from him. It does not feel safe to remain where they are, so they decide to go to Cay's cottage and rest up until morning.

The drive seems to take forever. By the time Cay pulls the Onyx through the gates of the mansion, they are exhausted. The darkness feels safer now, more comfortable and less threatening. They park the Onyx, climb out, and walk to the door. Looking over at Cay, Ash risks a smile. She flashes one in response, a rare gesture and a reassurance that this business might finally be over.

She punches in the entry code, and they walk through the darkened entryway.

Instantly, lights flash on everywhere.

Cyrus Collins sits in a chair facing them, holding a small silver handgun.

"Hello, nephew," he says.

Then he shoots Cay.

- 29 -

It happens so quickly that Ash has no time to react. He barely registers his uncle's presence before Cay collapses beside him. Too late he steps toward Cyrus, not even sure what he intends to do.

By then, his uncle's weapon is pointed at him. "Don't be foolish. I'll shoot you, if I have to."

He is big and imposing, almost twice Ash's size. He radiates power and confidence. He probably doesn't even need a weapon, should Ash choose to ignore him.

The boy looks down at Cay, frantic with worry. "Why did you do that?"

His uncle shrugs. "Maybe because she's a loose end that needs tying up. Maybe because it makes things easier if she's out of the way. What difference does it make? You'd better worry about yourself."

Ash gestures helplessly. "At least let me see how she is."

His uncle shakes his head. "I don't think so. You stay where you are. You shouldn't have run out on me at ORACLE. So much of what's happened could have been avoided if you'd just stayed put. All you had to do was stick around and listen to what I had to say. Running away was a big mistake."

"A mistake? You killed my father!"

"Is that what you think? That I killed your father? Your father killed himself!" The granite features tighten. "I was there when it happened. He brought me up to the roof to tell me something. Maybe even to throw me off, I don't know. But he lost his footing and fell. You can think whatever you want, but that's what happened. Your father's death was his own fault."

Ash is shaking with rage. "You're the one who should be dead!"

"We see things a bit differently, nephew. Your father was a dreamer. He couldn't function in the real world. He refused to understand that he could save people who were trying their level best to destroy themselves. He wouldn't listen to me. That doesn't make me the bad guy in all this. That doesn't make me the monster you think I am."

Ash glances down again at Cay. She lies motionless, sprawled out like a rag doll. There is no sign of life. He can't stand seeing her like this. His hands ball into fists. "I've had enough! You do what you have to!"

Without waiting for his uncle's response, he kneels down beside Cay, feeling for a pulse. When he finds one, he exhales sharply in relief. Then he checks her over. There is no evidence of a wound. His uncle used a stun gun. She is merely unconscious.

Ash looks up. "There was no reason for you to do that."

Cyrus Collins shakes his head. "Why should you care? You do know what she is, don't you? She's a manufactured product! She isn't even real! She's a damn toy!"

Ash remains on his knees, anger and unexpected shame washing through him. He can't help it. The words sting. "She isn't a toy!" he shouts.

His uncle shakes his head. "That's exactly what she is. Anyway, forget her. Listen to me. Your father gave you something. Or told you something. Or arranged for you to find something. Something, nephew, which has to do with his work at BioGen and belongs to me. You went after it tonight at ORACLE. Maybe you even found it. I want you to tell me what it is."

"I'm not telling you anything!" Ash spits at him.

His uncle studies him a moment. "Aren't you the brave little lad?" He steps forward, seizes Ash by the front of his blackout sheath, and thrusts him backward onto the sofa, the gun pointed at his midsection. "You think you know everything, don't you? Got it all figured out. Everything that's happened, all the bad stuff, it's my fault. That's what you've decided."

Ash says nothing, his mouth a tight line.

Cyrus steps close again, looming over him. Then he cuffs him—none too gently—on the side of his head. "What if you're wrong? You can't stand the idea, can you? But what if you are?" He cuffs him again, harder this time. "Won't talk to me about it? Maybe I should be the one doing the talking. Maybe I should tell you a few things that will change your mind."

Ash forces himself to ignore the pain of the blows. "Nothing you say is going to make any difference."

His uncle cocks an eyebrow. "Let's find out. All you have to do is sit there and listen for a few minutes. Just listen, nephew. You can do that much, can't you?"

Ash ignores the impulse to say something less agreeable. *Stall, just stall.* The words echo in his mind, hot and fierce. He gives his uncle a curt nod.

Cyrus remains standing as he speaks, his hands loose at his sides, his weapon tucked back in his belt. He is completely at ease.

"Everybody says we're better off now than we used to be. I think that's bullshit. As head of ORACLE, I see more of what's happening out there than most, and it's not good. Things are falling apart. The U.T. was supposed to be a solution to the fragmenting of the old US, but I don't see where it's worked out that way. There are secession movements afoot almost everywhere— clearly evident in the Dixie Confederacy, but there are rumblings in the Northeast and the Northwest too. Riots, looting, burning, and killing—disruptions of the old order. Madness in pursuit of obscure principles and imaginary improvements. This country is on the verge of splitting up again, just like it did two hundred years ago when it was the United States. We survived it the first time, reconfigured but still united. I'm not sure we can survive it happening again."

Ash has no idea where this is going, but it doesn't matter. His uncle wants to talk? So let him talk.

"Here's the takeaway from all this." His uncle is into it now, his face flushed and his voice impassioned. "An inherent dissatisfaction provides the root cause of this unrest. It's just not in our genetic makeup for us to be any other way. If there isn't something identifiably wrong, we manufacture it. History shows this has always been true. Angry about how your life is going? Find someone to blame. Think our problems are the fault of people of another race or religion? Shoot one or two. Don't think we're getting a fair shake from the government? Bring it down, any way you can. If all that dissatisfaction could be eliminated or at least better managed, it would reduce the acts of disobedience and aggression to almost nothing. The problem is, how do you make this happen? How do you persuade an entire population to forego destructive behavior and simply accept the world the way it is?"

He is looking away now, immersed in his story. It is a recitation he has given more than once before, Ash thinks, perhaps to his brother but certainly to himself.

His uncle moves a few steps closer to the couch where Ash sits, and looks down at him.

"Brantlin's work was in the field of biogenetics and gene manipulation. Recent experiments centered on ways to repair people who were so badly damaged physically there was no putting them back together. But he was looking for ways to better manage behavioral aberrations as well. He was looking at altering emotional and psychological conditions. Not his field, of course, but that sort of thing never stopped my brother. In the course of these experiments, he discovered a drug that could suppress violent and disruptive urges. He saw it as a management tool for the mental illnesses that plague so many. Psychotic behaviors and emotional imbalances. Alcoholism and drug addiction. Genetic flaws that ordinary forms of treatment would never be able to eradicate entirely and sometimes not even manage."

Ash listens in spite of his distaste for his uncle, becoming interested. For the moment, he has stopped searching for a way to escape.

"All well and good, as far as it went. But your father's thinking was too limited. I saw a better, more far-reaching use to his discovery. What if this drug were given to the entire population of the U.T.? Not just a select few but everyone. Dosage would be determined by the user; just take it until you were mellowed out. Remove the danger of overdose at the source of manufacture by testing and observation of different groups, the way we with do with all our drugs. Trial and error. Eventually, behavioral patterns throughout the whole of the U.T. would level off until everyone's aggressive tendencies were muted. A sort of broad-based attitude adjustment."

His uncle pauses. "The problem, of course, is how to persuade people that this is not only good but also necessary. For most, it would be seen as the exact opposite. But I understood the value of the idea's implementation. People everywhere would become calmer and less aggressive, their attitudes steadier and their dissatisfactions muted."

Ash tries to keep his jaw from dropping. His uncle is serious. He wants to drug the entire U.T. population in an effort to achieve some sort of utopian harmony.

But if Cyrus Collins senses his disapproval, he doesn't show it. "So how do you get people who don't agree with you to change their minds? How do you go about arranging for this mass infusion without creating a panic? Simple. You don't ask them. You don't wait on them to agree. You just go ahead and give them what they need, just like you would any medication. You do what's best for them because that's what good government does. The only problem is one of implementation. How do you make sure they take this medicine? Again, simple. You put it in something almost everyone already uses on a daily basis, something so much a part of their existing diet they don't think twice about consuming it. Something they've already learned to regulate. You put it in a substance they all crave—one they all enjoy."

"Sparx." Ash says it aloud before he can stop himself.

His uncle gives him a thumbs-up. "Sparx. Everybody's favorite mood enhancer. A staple all over the world, but particularly in the U.T. They sell themselves. Hell, they don't even have to do that! You can get them for free in stores and businesses and in every nightclub and pleasure house all over the U.T. People love them. Adding the formula wouldn't change their perception of what they were consuming. No change in the flavor or the look would be needed. Users would still feel good about themselves; they would just feel a little more at peace and less inclined toward aggressive behavior. Their enthusiasm for the product would help sell it to those who don't use it."

"You can explain it any way you want," Ash snaps, "but you're still manipulating people!"

"We manipulate people all the time, Ashton. Grow up." Cyrus Collins pauses, considering. "Think about the bots and synths we've created. They've become an integral part of our culture. We engineer them to be compliant. We structure them to serve us in a productive way. Why should we not expect humans to respond in the same way? Why should we not see to it that they do? Engineering genetics the way we do with composite materials—how much difference is there in manipulating humans? If the result is a responsible and satisfied society, aren't we justified?"

Ash is beside himself. *My father died for this nonsense? T.J. and the Shoe died for this?* His uncle is off his rocker. He only just manages to stop himself from letting the words escape his lips. Instead, he says, "My father didn't agree with you about any of this, did he?"

"Your father." His uncle says it as if he puts a bad taste in his mouth. "He thought people *should* be different. He thought it was wrong to try to make people conform. He thought genetics should be manipulated only to help those clearly suffering physical, emotional, or psychological damage. Otherwise, it was best to let nature determine behavior. He thought genetic control was dangerous and drugs should never be administered wholesale. Apparently, he forgot about penicillin. He forgot about inoculations. Your father was a dreamer of the worst sort. He was impractical. And obstructive!"

He leans forward. "Genetic manipulation is here to stay. Hybrids are a part of our lives. Bots and synths and all the others serve us in nearly every capacity. But people in general don't respond well to changes in the human condition. Those made of flesh and blood don't like the idea of people that are synthetic. They want things to go back to the way they were.

"But things never go back. They only go forward. Change is inevitable. Change is the one constant. Your father understood that much, at least. He kept pressing ahead, working with new cures and developing new hybrid life-forms. Now others will take up where he left off. Who knows where it will all end? One day soon, these new creations may even replace us! The possibility is there. So if we wish to preserve our species, we better take control of how our population develops, and that starts with building a strong, cohesive, like-minded human race that will act as a unified entity."

Ash is stunned. He knows it is wrong to force people to conform. No matter the reason, no matter the cause, conformity is always about getting people to do what you want them to do. Which inevitably means someone must tell them what to do. Clearly his father understood this much better than his brother. Cyrus, he thinks, probably never even tried to understand.

"But you experimented on kids!" he argues.

"Street trash, nephew. Discards and refuse. 'Tweeners. Kids who had no purpose in life. Kids with no homes and no hope.

Kids picked up off the streets as a public nuisance. Kids given to us by their parents because they were so damaged they were on the verge of dying. Every great scientific breakthrough requires sacrifice. It isn't any different here. BioGen needed live subjects for their experiments. We had to take the ones we could find. Or create, like synths and hybrids. Most of them reacted positively to what was done to them, and those we released. But there were failures, of course. Those failures needed to be understood if they were to prove of any real value. Why didn't the enhancements we made work on them? Why were some of them so resistant to what we were doing?"

"Like the kids at Street Freaks." Ash makes it a scathing indictment. "They resisted being what you wanted them to be."

"I would have terminated them all if your father hadn't begged me to save them. But your father was the genius behind everything we were doing. It would have been ungrateful to refuse him his pathetic little handful of salvaged ingrates. Besides, BioGen's experimentation with enhancements and reconstruction was pretty much over by then. We had a larger, more far-reaching goal. Brantlin had discovered his miracle drug, and we were already testing it on other street kids. And it was working."

Ash shook his head. "I can't believe I'm hearing this. You're trying to justify killing kids!"

Cyrus Collins shrugs. "We had to discover what had gone wrong. We had to know how to fix what wasn't working. It was unfortunate but necessary."

Ash is seething. "You can't justify what you did! Doesn't matter where these kids came from! My father was right not to agree to this!"

"Well, he might not have agreed with it, but he let it happen! Except for those precious few he saved to placate his conscience. I thought it might be enough to keep him quiet. I was wrong. Nothing would satisfy him. He just couldn't make himself see the larger picture. He couldn't accept the fact that the termination of a few lives would result in the salvation of many."

"You threatened him," Ash says. "That's why he couldn't do anything! You told him you would hurt me!"

His uncle's smile is cold. "Is that so? It's all about you, is it? All of it was an effort to protect you. What a noble fellow, your father. What a paragon of virtue. I don't suppose he happened to mention anything about his special relationship with Cay, did he?"

The question hangs in the air, dark and terrible. For an instant, Ash hesitates. "What are you talking about?"

"Maybe you don't know as much as you think you do. Maybe your father kept quiet about what was happening not because of you but because of her. Maybe what really mattered to him was the possibility of losing his own personal pleasure toy. Maybe what really mattered was my threat to take her away from him. Cay did tell you about the two of them, didn't she? You did know what she was to him?"

Ash stares. All the breath goes out of him. "Shut up."

His uncle shrugs carelessly. "He wasn't the man you seem to think he was. So don't hold him up to me as an example of righteous behavior."

"I don't believe you."

"Well, whether you believe me or not changes nothing. The fact remains—he took something from me that wasn't his to take. And since he's no longer with us, you have to be the one to give it back. I can't have anyone interfering with my plans at this point. I'm not going to let that happen."

Ash takes a deep breath. His thoughts roil, and he feels something drop away inside. His father and Cay. How much of it is true? He wants to believe that none of it is, but a small voice tells him maybe he should open his eyes a little wider.

"I don't have what you want," he manages, the words sounding hollow. "It doesn't matter about my father and Cay. I can't help you."

"The last call your father made on his vidview was to you. I checked the vidview records after he fell. He must have told you something. Don't pretend he didn't. Don't lie to me."

"Too bad you weren't able to keep my father alive so he could tell you himself!" Ash snaps, his temper slipping its tether completely. "Try telling the truth, *uncle*. You killed my father, didn't you? Just like you killed the Shoe. And who's responsible for T.J.? That's on you too! Why don't you just admit it! Or are you going to keep claiming all those deaths were necessary for the greater good?"

The words are out of his mouth before he can stop them. Cyrus Collins stares coldly. Ash knows immediately he has gone too far.

His uncle shakes his head slowly. "You just won't see reason, will you? Just like your father. I thought there was a chance with you—that you would be quicker to understand the situation. Guess not."

He makes a dismissive gesture. "I'm done wasting my time on you. It appears we are going to have to do this the hard way. What happened to your father is going to happen to you, nephew, if you don't pay close attention. He had his chance and botched it. Now you have yours. I don't have the top of a building to throw you off, but I do have other choices."

"You *did* kill him," Ash hisses back.

Cyrus Collins gives an indifferent shrug. "What matters is that his death was quick; yours won't be. So listen closely. This is what's going to happen. You're going to tell me everything your father told you. You're going to give me anything he gave you. You're going to do that right now. If you don't, I will start hurting you. I will break off parts of your body. The softer, less resistant ones first. Then the harder ones. And I will keep doing this until you will wish you were dead."

He pauses. Any hint of friendliness has vanished from his face. "Or maybe you would like me to start with your beloved pleasure synth while you watch. Shall I wake her? If you prefer, I can hurt her instead of you. I'll take my time with her. I'll do unspeakable things to her. I'll leave her with nothing you would ever want any part of."

Ash goes cold all the way through. Cyrus Collins is a hard

man, and this is not an idle threat. He will do what he says.

His uncle sighs and shakes his head. "I don't want this, but you're forcing it on me. And it won't end well for you, nephew. Torture of this sort does things to your mind. Things you cannot imagine. I've seen it happen. Somewhere along the way, you will beg me to let you tell whatever you know."

His uncle's voice is calm. He might be describing the weather or a lunch menu. It is taking everything Ash has to stand there and not bolt. *Get out, get out, get out*, his mind is screaming at him. His eyes skid from one corner of the room to the next, searching for an escape route. But he cannot find one.

"You make me lose my temper and say and do things I would rather not," Cyrus Collins says softly. "But what's done is done. It's your turn. Tell me something that will save your life. Do it quickly."

"All right!" Ash snaps. "Maybe I do know something. Why don't you stop threatening and let me help Cay. Maybe that will jog my memory."

He is talking fast, still trying to stall. He knows he can't say anything about the thumb drive Cay carries in her pocket. It would mean that everything he has gone through would have been for nothing.

Abruptly, he remembers the wasp sting tucked in his belt behind his back. He reaches back as if trying to push himself to his feet, still talking.

"Okay, maybe we could make a bargain. You let Cay and me go, and I give you . . .

But his uncle is on top of him instantly, yanking him off the couch. Still holding him with one hand, he hits Ash squarely in the nose with the other. Blinding pain floods the boy's face as his nose breaks. He sags away, both hands reaching up protectively, tears leaking from his eyes. His uncle continues to hold him firmly in place as he backhands him twice. Ash cries out, the sound loud and sharp, a ringing in his ears. The pain blossoms until he is in agony.

His uncle snatches the wasp sting from behind his back and

tosses it aside. Then he flings Ash backward onto the couch once more. Fresh pain flares behind his eyes as his head bounces off the backrest.

"Planned on using that toy on me, did you?" His uncle is breathing hard.

"If I got the chance!" Ash's words are angry, defiant. He spits blood.

Cyrus grins. "Chances come and go, nephew. That particular one is gone. I'm tired of this whole business. Tell me what you know. Better hurry. My patience is about used up."

The pain from Ash's broken nose is crushing. Blood is running down his throat. Whatever happens next will probably be even worse. But he knows he cannot give in.

His uncle drags him back to his feet. "You're not playing with amateurs, nephew. How do you think I found out about you and your little synth? I was already suspicious when she started cozying up to me after running off with your father. When I saw the two of you together, I knew what it meant. I'd had cameras installed at your old home after you fled it. I thought you might return at some point. I was waiting for it. But I guessed wrong about what you would do next. I never imagined you would break into ORACLE. You and those 'tweeners your father managed to talk me out of destroying. You shot the hell out of my security and violated Blue Skye. For you to go to that extent, there had to be something you wanted badly. What was it?"

He strikes the boy across the face again and gives him another shove onto the couch. Ash sprawls there, his head spinning, pain ratcheting through him. He can barely focus his thoughts.

Then, out of the corner of his eye, he sees Cay's fingers twitch. Her arm moves, then her head. She is waking up.

"You're right," he says. "We thought what we needed was at ORACLE, so we decided to break in. We were searching for information about what you were doing, but we never found it."

"Is that so?"

"And my father didn't tell me anything in that last vidview. Just for me to get out. He'd warned me two years ago. I thought he was nuts."

His uncle starts moving in a direction that will put Cay directly in his line of sight. Ash stands up quickly to distract him.

His uncle's weapon comes up at once. "Careful, nephew."

Ash stands his ground. "Why don't you admit it? You plan on killing me as soon as I tell you what you want to know. Why do you keep pretending you have anything else in mind? Why keep lying about it?"

Cyrus Collins takes a step closer, as if to better control the situation. His eyes stay locked on Ash. "I guess you'll never know, since you don't have anything to say."

Cay is fully awake now. She lies on the floor facing them, her eyes fixed on Cyrus Collins.

"Cyrus!" she shouts. "Don't!"

Cyrus turns and points his weapon at her. Ash immediately throws himself at his uncle—no hesitation, an instinctive response. He is half his uncle's size and unarmed, but all he can think about is Cay. He slams into what feels like a wall, pain exploding anew through his damaged nose and face. But his momentum is sufficient to knock his uncle off his feet as he fires his weapon. The charge misses Cay and strikes a wall. Ash goes down on top, his fists pummeling Cyrus Collins wildly.

For a moment or two, they are a tangle of arms and legs. Ash manages to get both hands on the stun gun, forcing the barrel away from him. But Cyrus is hitting him repeatedly, his fist hammering into the boy's already damaged face. The pain is excruciating; the blood from his wounds runs freely in scarlet rivulets. His vision is dotted with bright flashes. Somehow he hangs on. Skin rips from his knuckles and blood is everywhere. He catches a glimpse of Cay as she dives for the wasp sting his uncle cast aside earlier. She snatches it up while still on her knees and turns.

He hears her weapon discharge, a sort of loud snap followed

by a high-pitched whirring. Cyrus Collins jerks sharply, grunts, and drops his weapon. Cay's stun gun scrambles his motor nerves, but he manages to yank Ash in front of him to use as a shield. Cay tries to find an opening so she can fire again but cannot.

Then Cyrus throws Ash into her, momentarily tangling them up. Ash struggles to get free, but Cyrus is lurching toward them like a drunkard, roaring in rage and frustration. He reaches Cay and fastens his hands about her throat. She fights to free herself, but the hands tighten and she begins to gasp for air.

Ash scrabbles at the carpet in search of the wasp sting, and his hand closes on the metal grip. He seizes it, aims it at the back of his uncle's bullish neck, and fires. His uncle stiffens, grunts, and starts to rise.

Ash fires again, and this time Cyrus Collins goes limp, collapsing in a motionless heap.

Cay rises, gasping for air. She looks as if she is possessed, anger radiating off her face in a visible shimmer. She snatches the wasp sting from Ash, fumbles with it a moment, and then hobbles over to his uncle. She gives Cyrus a cursory glance, pulling him up and shoving him back down again. Apparently dissatisfied with what she sees, she presses the barrel of the wasp close to his head and fires twice more.

Then she limps back to Ash and helps him sit up. They stare at each other. There is a moment of shared relief, of understanding that goes beyond words. Ash glances away first. But Cay reaches out and touches his face, and he turns back again.

"Look at you," she says.

"No, thanks," he mumbles. His face is so badly swollen he is barely able to talk.

"You're a mess."

"I know."

"Could have been worse."

"Oh, really? How?"

"We could be dead."

He glances over at his uncle, sprawled motionless on the floor in front of them, a grim reminder. "We almost were."

She sits next to him, pressing close, looping one arm around his shoulders. He doesn't respond. A long moment passes as he continues to look away. How did things come to this?

Then she says, "Remember when we first met and I asked you if you wanted to be my advocate if anyone tried to say I wasn't a real girl?"

"Yeah." He shakes his head. "I remember I took the job."

"Yes, you did. I'm giving you a promotion. Personal bodyguard."

He laughs, coughing painfully as he does so. He looks at her in disbelief. "I'm pretty sure I'm not up to it."

She gives him a smile that cuts to his heart. "Oh, I don't know about that." She leans forward to kiss him gently on his cracked and swollen lips. "I'm pretty sure you are."

- 3[] -

Her kiss is a sun coming out from behind dark clouds to brighten his world, and when she looks in his eyes, Ash is so in love it hurts.

"Your nose needs to be set," she tells him. She helps him move over to the couch and sit back so he can brace himself. "Hold very still. This will just take a moment."

She places her palms carefully on both sides of his nose and tightens her grip gently. She is very close to him, her face inches from his. He can see every mark—every cut, bruise, and contusion—she has suffered. Then he gazes into her startling blue eyes and feels everything else slip away.

"Steady," she whispers.

Then, with a sudden movement, she jerks his nose back into place. Fresh pain rockets through him, and he squeezes his eyes tightly shut as his tears come anew.

"All done," she says.

"Easy for you to say."

She takes his hands in hers and pulls him to his feet. "We better make sure all this has been worth it. Let's find out if we have what we need to put an end to it."

He nods, and she leads him over to where her computer is

closed away within a locked cabinet and brings it out. Together, they power it up, insert the thumb drive, and wait for it to open. They work in silence. Ash glances over his shoulder to where Cyrus Collins lies motionless. Cay never bothers. It's as if she has decided he no longer exists. Her eyes remain fixed on the screen, her fingers on the keyboard. Within seconds the contents of the thumb drive appear on the screen. They glance again at each other's damaged faces, grinning broadly.

It is all there.

Charts showing the territories into which the doctored Sparx have been introduced.

A timetable for introducing Sparx into the rest of the United Territories.

Areas considered especially troublesome and which, it has been decided, require special attention.

Formulas of varying strengths to be used in fresh batches of Sparx according to the perceived need for behavioral control.

The names of everyone directly involved in development and production of Sparx to be used for this purpose.

The list is surprisingly small. It appears Cyrus kept his secret from all but a handful of men and women working under his direction, most of them connected with BioGen. Those whose work involves packaging, distribution, and sales appear to have remained blissfully unaware of what was going on. But those names don't matter. What matters is exposing Cyrus and those who were his close accomplices. That alone will put a stop to what is happening.

Cay scrolls down. There is more. Ash's father has provided a list of the street kids whose lives were terminated after failed experiments. In some cases, there is only a first name. In some, there is no name at all, only a gender designation. In each case, the nature of the experiment is listed.

The list is hundreds of names long.

She dispatches the information by vidview relay to Jenny.

Once Jenny has it, she will know what to do. Cay sends a second copy to a blind storage within the Street Freaks database as a precaution. Then she closes the thumb drive, extracts it from its slot, and hands it to Ash.

She takes his hands. "Come with me."

Ash pulls up. "Wait. What about my uncle?"

She gives him a funny look. "What about him?"

"Do we just leave him?"

"He'll keep."

"But what if he wakes up? What if he comes looking for us?"

"Well, he won't have to look very far."

She continues moving toward her bedroom door. Ash pulls up again. "We're staying here?"

"What are we supposed to do? You should see yourself. You need patching up and serious rest. I can help you with both." She sees his eyes wander back to his uncle's body. "Stop worrying. He won't be waking up anytime soon."

When he continues to hesitate, she throws up her hands. "Fine. Let's make sure."

She goes over to a drawer in the kitchen and pulls out a bundle of lock ties. She carries them over to Cyrus Collins, kneels down, and binds him at the ankles and wrists, snugging the two together with additional ties so that his legs are drawn up behind his back.

"Happy?" she asks, cocking her head in a way that suggests there is only one acceptable response.

This time when she takes his hands, Ash follows without comment. "You heard him talking about his plans?" he asks her.

"Most of it. Those stun weapons don't have quite the same effect on synths. Safety precaution. Come on, I want to get started on you."

"I just want to be sure he sounded as crazy to you as he did to me."

She doesn't answer, doesn't even look at him. She is all but dragging him. He picks up his pace in response. What does it matter about Cyrus Collins and his plans anyhow? Why worry about someone whose career will be over in twenty-four hours, who will end up in prison and probably lose everything? His uncle intended to kill him just as he killed his father. As he killed the Shoe and maybe others he doesn't even know about. Who cares now about a man foolishly seduced by his vision for a better world, a man who lacked the common sense needed to recognize its flaws?

"I'm pretty tired," he admits.

"Don't go to sleep just yet," she says quietly. "I need to work on patching you up first, and then you can sleep for as long as you need to."

"I can't believe it's over. It doesn't even *feel* like it's over."

She squeezes his hand. "It isn't over. Not quite."

He doesn't know what she means, and he doesn't care. Perhaps it is the weariness and pain. Perhaps he just needs rest.

He is barely conscious of walking through her bedroom door and hearing the locks slide into place.

"I'm going to take off your clothes now," she says. His eyes open at that. "Relax. I want to have a look at your injuries. I need to see how bad they are. You took a pretty good beating. You need me to bathe you and clean you up. Don't be shy. I've seen naked men before. I doubt you look all that much different than they did."

"Men like my father?" he says softly.

He shouldn't have said this. He knows he shouldn't. But it is eating at him. He has tried to dismiss it from his mind, but it won't go away. He cannot make himself look at her. So she takes his face in her hands and holds it steady in front of her.

"You have to decide the answer to that for yourself, Ash. No matter what I tell you, it still comes down to what you think. So make up your mind. I heard what he said. Was he telling you the truth about your father and me or not?"

She is looking directly into his eyes. What he finds there provides the answer he seeks. His doubt fades. "He was lying."

"Your father was a good and decent man," she whispers, drawing him close, touching her forehead to his. "He gave me back my life. He never asked for anything. Especially that." She pauses. "But you should know that if he had, I would have given it to him."

She has him sit on the edge of the bed as she removes his shoes and clothes. She does so slowly and carefully, aware of the pain he is in and the possible damage he has incurred.

"You have either bruised or fractured your ribs," she tells him. He looks down and is surprised to find his entire left side is a vivid purple. He is aware of it aching, but so much else hurts—his nose especially—that he hasn't noticed it.

She produces salves and rubs them over the injured areas. To his surprise, the pain lessens. She bandages his nose and the worst of the cuts on his face, closing the wounds. She uses more of the salves while doing so. She gives him a small white pill. Again, the pain lessens.

"Stand," she says, and she takes off the last of his clothing. "Wow, look at you. A real-life boy. Wait here."

She rummages through her closet and produces a soft robe that she slips over him. Then she sits him down again and goes into the bathroom. He can hear water running. He thinks of the night he caught a glimpse of her through the door, completely exposed, incredibly beautiful. His thoughts drift to other times and places when he was with her, all tinged with the memory of how she made him feel.

She returns, helps him to his feet, and takes him into the bathroom. The bathtub is a huge round shell recessed into the floor. Its tiles sparkle in pale, soft light; she has lowered the overheads to almost nothing. He can find his way easily enough to his bath but cannot see what lies within the shadows beyond.

"Had it installed myself," she says, motioning at the tub. "A bit of self-indulgence."

She helps him step down into the shell and settle into the bath waters. He sighs audibly at the feel of their warmth on his skin, even though parts of his battered body sting at their touch. But the stinging only lasts a moment, and then a soothing comfort eases the pain.

"Feels good," he says.

"I added oils and balms to your bath," she tells him. "The longer you soak, the more they will help with your healing. Lie back. The shell wall is curved to support you. Close your eyes."

He does so, grateful for the relief. She is right. The bath wall supports him. There is music playing, a soft melody he had missed hearing before. He relaxes, content. He wishes he could stay here forever.

He opens his eyes when he feels movement in the waters. Cay is stepping into the bath with him. She has taken off her clothes. She is completely naked, her body gleaming and flawless, the realization of a dream he had dared not even consider. He stares in shock.

"I'm going to wash you," she tells him, settling into the water next to him. "I'll be careful."

"You don't have to do this," he says.

"I want to. Let me."

Why does he try to dissuade her? He loves her. He wants this more than he has ever wanted anything. She is giving him a gift. She is giving him herself. His breath catches in his throat, and tears leak from his eyes as she begins to run a cloth over his arms and shoulders. It is not so much the pain of his injuries that makes him cry. It is something much more profound and at the same time primal.

"How does that feel?" she asks.

"Good."

"Only good?"

"No. Wonderful."

The cloth is travels slowly over his body, carrying with it the healing oils and balms, reaching the damaged areas—the bruises, cuts, and abrasions, the sources of pain and discomfort. He adjusts his position however she tells him to so she can reach him everywhere. She takes her time, moving in and out of his field of vision, smiling as she does, leaning down now and then to kiss his damaged face.

"I love baths," she says at one point, a wistful sigh infusing her admission.

He nods in blissful agreement. He still cannot believe this is happening. "I haven't had a bath in years. Not since I was a child. And never like this."

"You've been missing out."

"I should have met you sooner, I guess."

She smiles but says nothing.

They stay in the bath until the water begins to cool, and when they climb out Ash stands in place while Cay dries first him and then herself. She is cautious with the places where he is injured and quickly pulls back when she sees him wince.

When they are dry, she takes his hand and leads him to her bed. "Climb in," she says.

He can't help himself. "Why are you doing this?" he asks.

"Get into the bed, Mr. Clueless, and I'll explain it to you. Where did you come from, anyway?"

He works himself beneath the covers, never taking his eyes off her, drinking her in, wanting to remember her as he sees her now, never wanting to forget. When he is settled, she says, "I need to get you something that will help you sleep. Wait here."

She is gone only a short time, and when she returns she carries a small glass with a greenish-tinged liquid. At her beckoning, he drinks it down. He doesn't ask what it is, doesn't hesitate. He trusts her, believes in her, adores her. He would do anything for her.

When he is finished, she takes the glass from him, sets it aside, and joins him in bed, sliding beneath the covers, pressing up against him, letting him feel her warmth and softness. He gasps in spite of himself as her arms reach around his neck and hips to pull him close.

"I am doing this because of what you did for me," she says,

her face inches away from his own, the rest of her closer still. "You were willing to give your life for me. Can you understand what that means?"

He shakes his head doubtfully. "I didn't stop to think about it. I just did what anyone else would have done."

"You're wrong. No one else would have done what you did. Men tell me they love me. They tell me all the time. But it is a chemical reaction they are responding to. It is not emotional. It is not love. When they have time to step back from the experience and think about it, they find they do not love me. I am not real to them. I am a pleasure synth, created for their personal use. What they feel is only momentary. They could never love me, not for more than the time that it takes them to enjoy me physically. That is not so with you. I can tell the difference."

She kisses him gently on the lips, holding the kiss a long time. He feels something of her pass into him with that kiss, a kind of infusion. She moves away again without comment.

"When you first met me, I knew you were attracted. Afterward, when we talked? You were kind and you demanded nothing. You were shy, and that was sweet. But you were a boy, Ash, and I didn't think your attraction was anything more than a boy's response. Worse, it was a typical male response. I liked you; I was even sort of interested in you. Didn't matter. I still believed your interest in me did not go beyond the obvious.

"But out there," she motions toward the living room, "with your uncle threatening to kill both of us, you put yourself at risk for me. You attacked Cyrus to stop him from shooting me. You did this for a pleasure synth. None of those rich and powerful men who used me as their plaything would have done that. But you did. I cannot tell you how that made me feel. I can never explain it with words. Only like this."

She kisses him then, another kiss, this one a little firmer and more demanding. He does not have a lot of experience with girls and kissing, but he knows enough to respond. He sinks against her, falls into the feelings the kiss generates. He gives himself over to the feelings and stirrings and passion.

Even as he does so, he feels a deep drowsiness seeping through him, a sort of creeping lethargy that infuses his limbs and body. He is having trouble focusing on what is happening. Cay is taking the lead, doing what she wants, and he cannot seem to act independently of her.

"Do you like this?" she asks.

"Yes."

Her hands move. "And this?"

"Yes."

"Would you like me to continue?"

"Please."

She touches him everywhere. She strokes and pets and soothes him. He is drifting by now.

"I love you, Ash Collins," she says at one point. "I want you to remember that."

"I will," he mumbles, lost in another kiss. "I love you too."

Then everything tumbles and spins, and what is happening feels wonderful but the particulars are difficult to grasp. He floats rather than lies in the bed. He catches glimpses of her blond hair and her startling blue eyes. Parts of her body swirl and fade. She whispers things to him, but he is not sure what these things are. He whispers back to her, but his words are lost in the haze that enfolds him. He cannot make himself think; his responses are inarticulate and somehow separate from his thoughts. He seems to be break-ing apart, separating out—his body, his senses, his words, and his thoughts—all of them fragmenting, all of them flying off into space.

At some point, everything falls away and he is gone entirely.

When he wakes, he is alone. He lies in Cay's bed in the cottage shadows, lethargic and sleepy-eyed, waiting for his head to clear and his body to strengthen. Daylight streams through the curtained windows. The night is gone. He looks around.

"Cay?" he calls.

No response.

He makes himself leave the comfort of the bed, his legs shaky as he walks from room to room, searching for her. She is nowhere to be found. Nor is there any sign of his uncle. His body has disappeared and the cottage has been straightened up. He looks out front. The Onyx is gone as well. He decides she must have driven out for food. He goes into the bathroom to examine himself, makes a face at what he sees, and steps into the shower.

As he stands beneath the cascading water, he tries to remember what happened last night. The early parts are clear enough. Everything up to when they were in bed together and she was kissing him. What happened after that? He wants to think he knows, but he can't be sure. He searches his memory for hints, for some little piece of reassurance that he is not mistaken. But everything is a jumble and the answers won't come.

He is dressed and sitting at the tiny kitchen table when he turns on the big vidview and news of Cyrus Collins floods the airwaves. He listens intently as the newscaster reports the details on his uncle's planned infusion of behavioral chemicals into Sparx in an effort to control the U.T.'s general population. Comments from experts and ordinary people alike regarding experiments performed on street kids are replayed. BioGen, implicated in these efforts, has been shut down pending further investigation. A number of alleged coconspirators have been arrested. Sparx are being pulled from the market, and people are being urged not to consume any more of them but to dispose of what they have stockpiled at designated sites.

Then the newscaster says something unexpected:

To recap briefly: The full extent of the involvement of Cyrus Collins and BioGen in an unauthorized dissemination of chemically altered Sparx remains to be determined. Much of this uncertainly is due to the mysterious death of Commander Collins during the night. The commander's body was discovered early this morning, following receipt of an anonymous tip, behind a well-known pleasure palace in the Red Zone. The cause of his death has not been released. Vidcams that might have recorded the events leading to his demise were not functioning. According to authorities, the investigation is ongoing.

Ash sits back. His uncle is dead? How did this happen? He stares into space. His uncle was alive when Cay trussed him up. Wasn't he?

He remembers Cay's lack of interest in the possibility of his uncle waking up. He sees her again in his mind, walking up to Cyrus after he was down and shooting him twice in the head. Making sure. A wasp sting carries a massive charge. At full strength, a single blast can kill a man easily. Two would certainly do the job.

Almost without thinking, he turns on his personal vidview and calls up his messages. Only one blinks bright red with the word "URGENT." He goes to it right away.

There is Cay.

She is projected on an air screen in front of him, but he realizes she is only an image from an earlier recording.

Then she is speaking.

I wish things could be different. I came close to believing it was possible. But last night I crossed a line. Your uncle would never have stopped coming after us. Giving him a chance to do so was unthinkable. Now we are safe from him. Look on the side table in the kitchen. You'll understand.

I spoke the truth when I said I loved you. I always will. Last night—that's what I wanted to give you.

Ash closes the vidview and walks over to the table. He missed it before, but now he sees the stun gun lying there. He picks it up and checks it over. Nothing.

Then he notices the charge setting is at maximum. He remembers her snatching the weapon away from him and going over to his uncle. He remembers her placing the barrel against his uncle's head. His mind spins, the words come unbidden.

She executed him.

He sits slowly, staring at nothing.

"Cay Dumont," he says softly.

Just to hear her name.

- 31 -

He remains at the cottage for the rest of the morning and into the early afternoon, unwilling to leave. In part, it is because he feels at home here. The memories of last night keep him tethered; the feelings they arouse when he walks the various rooms, always pausing by the shell bath and the bed, a comfort. In part, it is because he keeps hoping she will return—that she will change her mind or some quirk in her thinking will persuade her she has made a mistake in leaving him.

Somewhere deep in his heart, where truths cannot be denied, he knows such hope is false. But still he lingers.

By midafternoon, he admits there is no point in waiting longer. Resigned to the futility of staying, he walks out from the cottage to the road in front of the mansion and summons a robo-taxi. When it arrives, he orders the bot driver to take him to a nearby substem on the border of the Red Zone.

He will go to the only place he might find his absent friends: Street Freaks. He will swing by for a quick look. If there is a reason to stay, he will do so. Otherwise, he will have to come up with a new plan. He cannot imagine what it will be.

On the way, Ash flips on the backseat vidcam and listens to the latest news. It is all about Cyrus Collins and his links to

BioGen. His father's death is mentioned. By now, it is also about ORACLE and the role it might have played in what is being referred to as an unbelievable abuse of discretion and authority. He listens absently, his mind elsewhere. It quickly becomes clear there is nothing new to be learned, so he switches it off and rides the rest of the way in silence.

Once arrived at the substem, Ash goes underground to take the train. From there, he walks. An hour later, he stands in front of his destination.

He is in luck. The police tape blocking access through the gates is gone. There are no signs of Achilles Pod or any other police presence. It is early evening by now, and there are lights on inside the building. He walks up to the call box and triggers the digital pad to announce his presence. He is relieved when Jenny answers and the gate opens.

Jenny Cruz rushes out to greet him, enfolding him in her warm embrace. "We were so worried about you!" she gasps. "Thank goodness you're all right!"

"Not entirely," he deadpans, seeing the look on her face as she takes in the damage to his.

Inside the building, Woodrow is there to welcome him back too. The minute he sees the bot boy, a huge wave of relief washes over Ash. "What happened to you last night?" he demands. "One moment you were there on the link and the next you were gone."

"A malfunction," the boy answers. "Someone threw up a scramble signal inside BioGen, and I lost contact with you. Everything went dead. I couldn't manage to reconnect."

"But when we went back, the safe house was torn apart and you were gone!"

"A speedy exit proved necessary when the black-clads showed up. I went down into the basement and out through a tunnel to the house next door. I told you, Ash—always have an exit plan. I just needed to move a little faster than usual." He grins. "I can do that, you know, when I have to."

"So my father's file got into the right hands?" Ash asks Jenny.

"Everything we wanted to happen is happening. Maybe you've heard some of it. BioGen is shut down and Sparx are being pulled from the market and distribution centers so they can be destroyed. The people your father named as accomplices to Cyrus are under arrest. The story is being replayed on every news feed. Your uncle's grandiose plans are over and done with."

"Better yet," Woodrow adds, "the U.T. is looking into what happened to those street kids BioGen was experimenting on. They're tracking down everyone who was involved, using the names your father provided, demanding a full accounting. It didn't take long to get it either. There were some scared enough to provide information on all of the others. Just in time to save a handful of kids that were still being held captive, waiting their turn. But there's an end to it now. It's over and done with."

"So here we are," Jenny interrupts. "After I sent the records you and Cay forwarded last night to all the news agencies and the U.T. president and senate, I made a few calls to a couple of Red Zone officials who are still friends. Asked them how things stood. They said it was all right to return, that the lockout orders had been rescinded. The whole business with your uncle last night changed everything. Woodrow and I came back a few hours ago. Everything was the way we left it. The Shoe was still hanging in Bay 3, so we got him down. Kind of gruesome, but we had to do it. We owed him that much."

She pauses. "We heard about your uncle. Found dead behind Heads & Tails, no cause given. What happened, Ash?"

He tells them the parts of the story he thinks they need to know. He does not tell them everything. He does not reveal to them what Cay did for him afterward, how she washed him and slept with him, how they made love. He does not wish to divulge any of this. It is a private memory—fuzzy though much of it remains. But it is his memory alone; it belongs to him. Revealing any part of it would feel like a violation.

He does not mention the note.

"We haven't heard from her," Woodrow says of Cay. "Not since yesterday."

"Where's Holly?" Ash asks, hoping to forestall any further questions about Cay.

"Still at the medical center," Jenny says. "I think maybe they decided if they kept her there she couldn't do any more damage to herself. She was pretty banged up. Her regeneration wrap was torn to shreds, and she had cracked ribs and deep contusions. If she hadn't been wearing body armor, she would be dead. They said she'll be all right, but it will take her time to heal."

"Penny-Bird is with her," Woodrow adds. "Probably making sure she follows doctors' orders and stays put. But it's good you're here. We were really worried."

"No need to worry about me," Ash says, shrugging.

But Jenny shakes her head. "I don't think that's entirely true. Your nose? The way you walk and hold yourself? Your uncle did a number on you. It's off to the medical center with you, and no arguments."

It turns out he has fractured ribs, broken fingers and nose, cuts and lacerations, and bruises of such variety and numbers that he looks like a walking Rorschach test. At the medical center they look him over carefully, wrap his ribs and attend to his wounds, and send him home with a warning not to follow Holly's example. No one asks him what happened.

On the way back, after the silence drags on for too long, Jenny says to him, "Cay will turn up, Ash. She always does."

He nods and smiles. He hopes she is right, but wonders.

In the days and weeks that follow, Ash manages to stay busy. He drifts through his waking hours in a kind of daze, busying himself with work, trying not to think too hard or too long about other things. Street Freaks reopens. Jenny is in charge now. The Shoe left her the business—building, inventory, tools, equipment, and accounts—in a will they knew nothing about until after he was gone. He left her the abandoned warehouse down the block as well.

"He must have done it when he was feeling more generous about me," Jenny observes archly.

But Ash sees the tears.

They are back to building street machines and racers but are out of the corporate espionage game. It is an easy decision to make. They struggle along at first with just the three of them, forced to accept only a minimal number of orders. They look for more help but do not find anyone possessing the skills they want.

Or maybe they just don't find the kinds of people they want.

Then one day, two months later, just before closing, Penny-Bird walks through the door. It is the first time they have seen or heard from her since that last day at the medical center. From Holly herself, they have heard nothing, even after her discharge. Penny looks different than the last time Ash saw her. The Goth clothing is gone and some of the metal has been removed from her face and body. She smiles—a surprise to both Ash and Woodrow, who are standing in Bay 3 to greet her when she enters.

She walks over without preamble and says, "Business seems good."

"Not bad," Ash answers, glancing past her for some sign of Holly.

Penny sees the disappointment reflected on his face and shakes her head. "She isn't with me, so you can stop looking. She's back at our place. She's still recovering, but she's getting stronger. Her leg is healing; the tissue is regenerating. The wrap comes off in about a week, so we'll know more then. She's walking, though she can't be up yet for more than a couple hours each day. She'll need a few weeks, maybe a month, before she's doing much of anything else."

"That's good to hear," Ash says. "Will you tell her we miss her and want her back?"

Jenny walks out of her office and stands behind Woodrow.

Penny-Bird gives her a look. "Is that right, Jenny? Do you want Holly back?"

Jenny Cruz nods. "Does she *want* to come back?"

Penny nods. "Of course she wants to come back. This is her home. But only if I can come with her. If you'll have us both. She'd never ask, so I'm asking for her."

"So she doesn't know you're here?"

A dismissive shrug. "You know Holly. She's stubborn. She wants to be here, but she wants to set the terms."

Jenny cocks an eyebrow. "Why wouldn't we want you both? You belong together—here, with us. But don't wait. Move back now. Give yourselves a chance to settle in while she's recovering."

The smile on Penny-Bird's fifteen-year-old face is a revelation.

So they return, and while Holly continues to heal, Penny-Bird goes to work with the others. After the first week, they decide they can manage until Holly is well enough to join them. The new arrangement works fine. Everyone is content.

Which is not the case everywhere. BioGen is now under direct government supervision. The entire hierarchy has been dismissed. Sparx are off the market completely. New regulations govern the dissemination of BioGen products. Experiments on street kids are over. Across the U.T., there is widespread distrust of the company. It will take a long time to win that trust back. If ever. The old days are history. The autonomy and power previously enjoyed by BioGen is a thing of the past.

ORACLE has a new director and a new management board to oversee its operations. Achilles Pod has been reduced to a handful of shock units that function only in national emergencies. Various territorial Preventatives have been given sole responsibility for the crimes that occur in their regions. The black-clads that once dominated local jurisdictions are no longer permitted to do so.

Strife and discontent still surface regularly across the Territories. Separatist movements continue to flourish, engaging in demonstrations against the establishment and making demands for change. Sometimes the authorities respond reasonably; sometimes they do not. The resolution to the problems of the United Territories remains elusive.

Life goes on.

At Street Freaks, Ash undergoes a gradual transformation. He distances himself from the past and embraces his new life. He is reassured by the love and friendship of his friends, especially once Holly returns. They are a family in all the right ways—bonded not by blood, perhaps, but certainly by choice. They have a shared history that binds them. They have a shared understanding of who and what they are. They are not like other kids. They never will be. Ash accepts this. He is one of them now.

Eventually, he stops agonizing over his father. He quits trying to parse the truth behind his involvement with BioGen and Sparx. It is unproductive and pointless. He eventually stops dreaming of the nightmarish confrontation with his uncle and the events that brought the last of what remained of his old life crashing down. He works hard to forget. Gradually, the bad memories fade. His life is different in a good and satisfying way. He is at peace.

Mostly.

But there are limits to everything.

He cannot forget Cay. He doesn't even try. It would be pointless. His memory that retains so much retains everything about her with an iron grip. She is so deeply ingrained in his consciousness it is as if she is an actual part of him. Even while gone from him physically, her presence lingers. He knows her expressions, her movements, her scent, and all the modulations of her voice. She is not a ghost to him. She is flesh and blood and warmth and softness. She is never a toy, never a synth, never anything other than real. She is a thatch of blond hair cut short and blue eyes a mile deep. She is silk and iron. She is a voice whispering in his ear, a hand resting on his shoulder. She is the promise of things he has never had.

She is always there.

But she does not come back, in spite of the fact that Jenny has assured him she will. Yet he never stops hoping. On the days he is free to do so, he goes searching for her. He knows it is probably futile, but he cannot help himself. He surfs the global vidnet. He searches for her through inquiries on net chatrooms and by physically going out into the Red Zone and following up on rumors. It all leads nowhere.

On most nights, when his day is done, he sits alone in the darkness on the Street Freaks rooftop and thinks of her. He tries to remember if she ever said anything about where she might go if she were to leave. Or where she might want to travel one day, if she had the chance. Or where living elsewhere might appeal to her. All without success.

When he isn't trying to find her, he spends his time reminiscing about her. He relives the moments they spent together. He breathes the night air and finds her present. He looks up at the stars and dreams of small pleasures and bright moments yet to come.

They are still together. His memories keep her close.

She is not gone from my life. She never will be gone. She is out there somewhere.

He says this to himself, over and over. He repeats it like a mantra. It feels hopeless, but at the same time it feels empowering. As if by saying it, believing it, and bonding with it he can make it come to pass. It would be too painful to admit he might be wrong. It would be crippling. She will come back to him. She must.

That is the reality of his life.

Until one day he can wait no longer. He packs a bag and tells the others he is leaving. He will search for Cay until it becomes clear that the search is pointless.

Jenny shakes her head in obvious dismay but says nothing.

"You won't be able to find her, Ash," Holly counsels, one hand clasping his shoulder as if she might not let him go.

He nods. "It doesn't matter. I have to try."

"What happened between you two? You've never said. But it was something."

"Something I can't talk about. Not yet. Not until I find her."

He gives her a small smile, and she releases her grip. He starts for the door.

"What if she doesn't *want* you to find her?" Holly calls out.

He turns back, and the look he gives her is painfully hopeful. "What if she does?"

Giving her a wave, Ash goes out into the larger world to discover who's right.

About the Author

Terry Brooks is the *New York Times* bestselling author of more than thirty-five books, including the Fall of Shannara novels *The Black Elfstone* and *The Skaar Invasion*; the Genesis of Shannara trilogy: *Armageddon's Children*, *The Elves of Cintra*, and *The Gypsy Morph*; *The Sword of Shannara*; the Voyage of the *Jerle Shannara* trilogy: *Ilse Witch*, *Antrax*, and *Morgawr*; the High Druid of Shannara trilogy: *Jarka Ruus*, *Tanequil*, and *Straken*; the nonfiction book *Sometimes the Magic Works: Lessons from a Writing Life*; and the novel based upon the screenplay and story by George Lucas, *Star Wars*®*: Episode I The Phantom Menace*™. His novels *Running with the Demon* and *A Knight of the Word* were selected by the *Rocky Mountain News* as two of the best science fiction/fantasy novels of the twentieth century. The author was a practicing attorney for many years but now writes full-time. He lives with his wife, Judine, in the Pacific Northwest.

Shannara.com
TerryBrooks.net
Facebook.com/AuthorTerryBrooks
Twitter: @OfficialBrooks
Instagram: @OfficialTerryBrooks